D1452597

Barbarians at the Gates

The Decline and Fall of the Galactic Empire

Book 1

Christopher G. Nuttall

Twilight Times Books
Kingsport Tennessee

Barbarians at the Gates

Paladin Timeless Books, an imprint of
Twilight Times Books
P O Box 3340
Kingsport TN 37664
http://twilighttimesbooks.com/

First Edition, November 2014

  Library of Congress Control Number: 2014955269

ISBN: 978-1-60619-318-1

Cover art by Malcolm McClinton

Printed in the United States of America.

To Barb, who turned this into a readable manuscript.

Chapter One

The Luna Academy is the sole source of officers for the Federation Navy. Every year, five thousand young men and women enter the academy; five years later, the survivors are allowed to start the long climb towards command. The rewards are great, but so is the pressure. It is no surprise that the Academy rarely graduates more than a thousand new officers every year.
-An Irreverent Guide to the Federation, 4000 A.D.

Luna Academy, Sol System, 4092

"Cadet Garibaldi," Professor Kratman said, walking through the desks until he was standing right in front of his chosen victim, "I wish you to consider something for the benefit of your fellows. What do the First Battle of Zion, the Battle of Spider Bite and the Battle of Athens all have in common?"

Roman Garibaldi fought hard to keep his expression under control. Professor Kratman wasn't known for suffering fools gladly and the obvious answer—all three battles had been fought in space—was almost certainly not the right one. But then, there might not be a right answer; Kratman was hardly above throwing an unanswerable question at the class. The professor—his face was badly scarred by radiation burns, leading to much speculation outside class—was waiting patiently. Disappointing him was not an option.

Roman considered it briefly, thinking hard. All three battles had been studied extensively during Second Year, right before the cadets had passed their first tests. The three battles were significant—two had marked the start of a war; the third had effectively ended one—but there were hundreds of other such significant battles in the Federation's two thousand year history. He ran his hand through his blond hair and smiled as the answer came to him.

"Sir," he said. "The three battles represent *conceptual* defeats."

"Oh?" Professor Kratman said, peering down at him. "And were the defeats imaginary, then? Were the dead bodies floating in space delusions of an oxygen-starved mind?"

Roman shook his head, ignoring the titters from his classmates. If nothing else, Professor Kratman taught cadets how to think on their feet.

"No, sir," he said. "The defeats represented a failure of imagination by the losing side. They thought they knew everything and allowed themselves to be surprised by the enemy."

"Interesting," Professor Kratman mused. He made a show of stroking his hairless chin. "And would you care to elaborate for the benefit of your fellow cadets?"

"Yes, sir," Roman agreed. It wasn't as if he had a choice. Besides, he was uncomfortably aware that he might just be giving the professor rope to hang him, as Kratman was also known for allowing cadets to trip themselves up in the hopes they would learn from the experience. "Prior to the First Battle of Zion, it was commonly believed that aliens would be peaceful, rather than being just as violent as humanity.

When the Zion Defense Force encountered alien starships emerging from a previously undiscovered Asimov Point in the Zion System, they allowed themselves to be suckered into a position that allowed the Snakes to obliterate the entire force with ease. The result of this failure was the occupation of Zion and the First Interstellar War, which served as the catalysts for binding the Federation together."

Of course, he thought as he took a deep breath, *the Inheritance Wars are still a sore subject in the Federation.*

"In the Battle of Spider Bite, the...ah, loyalist commander *knew* that all he was facing were converted freighters and a handful of local defense starships. He charged through the Asimov Point, leading a fleet of battlecruisers and battleships, only to run into an enemy armed with compressed antimatter, a substance that had never before been used in combat. The result was the total obliteration of the Federation force and the Inheritance Wars.

"In the Battle of Athens, the rebel commander *knew* the loyalist forces would have to come through one of the Asimov Points in the system and had drawn up his forces to contest the gateway, as military doctrine demanded after the discovery of the first Asimov Point. The rebels were taken completely by surprise when the loyalists, using the continuous displacement stardrive, bypassed the Asimov Point network and assaulted their positions from the rear. It was the decisive battle of the Inheritance Wars."

Roman braced himself. "In all three battles, one side was presented with something completely outside its context," he concluded. "They suffered from a failure of imagination."

"An interesting viewpoint," the Professor said. He looked around the room. "Would any of you care to comment?"

"I would, sir," Cadet Blake Raistlin said.

Roman rolled his eyes inwardly. Cadet Raistlin was from one of the wealthiest families on Old Earth, with ties that led all the way up to the Grand Senate, and when they'd first met, Raistlin had tried to put the RockRat in his place. He had been astonished to discover that Roman was not only able, but willing to fight back.

But Raistlin had gone on. "How could any of the commanders have predicted that they would be faced with a threat outside their ... accepted *context?*"

Professor Kratman, unlike some of the other academic staff, showed no inclinations to play favorites. "Would you care to elaborate, cadet?"

Raistlin shot Roman a mischievous look. "The defenders of Zion expected to face human enemies, not aliens," he said. "Compressed antimatter was only a theory, as was the continuous displacement drive. How could they have prepared to face a threat they didn't even know existed?"

"Interesting point," Professor Kratman mused. He turned and faced Raistlin. "Do you believe that the universe is *fair,* cadet?"

"No, sir," Raistlin said. It was one thing that had been drummed into their heads since they had entered Luna Academy. The universe was *not* fair. It simply didn't care about humans—or aliens. "But you cannot blame a commanding officer for doing everything by The Book and then being defeated by something outside of The Book."

"The Board of Inquiry might disagree with you," Kratman said dryly, referring to the inquiry held whenever a Federation starship was lost on active duty. "Let us consider the situation, just for a moment. Why did the defenders of Zion believe that aliens would be peaceful and friendly? Answer—the general belief at the time, encouraged by the discovery of Graveyard a few years prior to the First Interstellar War, was that a violent and aggressive race would not make it into space. Their logic was fundamentally flawed as *humanity*, a violent and aggressive race, had already made it into space. They thought of humans as being somehow...less than aliens. If we made it through the bottleneck and out into space, why couldn't another violent race? Reasoning from a single example, like Graveyard, produces dubious results, not least because Graveyard might have been the result of an interstellar war."

Roman shivered. A few years after the discovery of the network of Asimov Points—which allowed instant travel between star systems—human explorers had stumbled across a dead world, destroyed by nuclear war. The level of devastation had been so high that no one knew what the inhabitants had called themselves. Their records had been so badly damaged that no one would ever know what had taken place to cause the war, or why it had been fought to such a dark finish.

"The Battle of Spider Bite is also indicative of the dangers of stagnated thinking and unchallenged assumptions," Kratman continued. "The loyalist commander *knew* that the rebels didn't have the firepower to take on his entire fleet. It should have occurred to him that they would not have declared independence and started the war without being sure that they had something that could tip the balance in their favor. And they did—compressed antimatter. The resulting disaster could have been avoided, if only by holding a formation that was more than a premature victory parade.

"The Battle of Athens represents a third such example. After fighting the Inheritance Wars for so long, both sides were looking desperately for a silver bullet that would allow them to end the wars without further loss of life. The rebels were experimenting with automated missiles that would allow them to sweep the Asimov Point without risking ships and lives; it was not a great intellectual leap to wonder if the loyalists were doing the same. Indeed, the rebels had their own gravimetric research program that would have led to the stardrive if the Inheritance Wars hadn't been terminated before they could put it into production. In short, the rebels allowed themselves to be pinned against the Asimov Point by a force that had entered the system from an unsuspected direction, and were obliterated."

He grinned. "Let us consider another two battles, shall we? Cadet Raistlin: what do the pre-space Battle of Midway and the First Battle of Sapphire have in common?"

Roman had to smile as Raistlin blinked in shock. If the Inheritance Wars were still a sore subject, the far more recent Blue Star War was effectively forbidden territory. Cadets were rarely encouraged to study the war, even in the privacy of Luna

Academy, while relatively little material on the war had made it out into the civilian sphere. The bare facts, of course, couldn't be covered up, but the precise details? The Federation Navy had restricted the data and covered up the reports, if only to spare the embarrassment. He wondered, absently, how the well-connected Raistlin would answer.

"Sir," Raistlin said. He had clearly decided to plunge for honesty, rather than dissimulation. "Both battles—both defeats—were the result of massive overconfidence."

"A very good answer, cadet," Kratman said sardonically. "An answer that is perfectly accurate, yet devoid of any actual detail. Please, would you elaborate for your fellow cadets?"

"Yes, sir," Raistlin said. Somehow, he managed to regain his balance. "In the Battle of Midway, the Japanese had an overpowering advantage in almost every important category. They should have brushed their American opponents aside and taken Midway, smashing the remaining American carriers at the same time. Instead, their overall commander divided their force and the Americans caught four of their carriers and sank them. The result was the sudden cessation of the Japanese advance.

"The First Battle of Sapphire, likewise, should have been a Federation victory. The fleet sent to secure the blue giant had enough firepower to take on the entire enemy force and crush it, but the commanding officer chose to break his fleet into three smaller forces and launch a simultaneous assault through two Asimov Points, while the third crossed interstellar space. The result of this...ah, poorly devised plan was the destruction of two of the assault forces, because they couldn't actually provide mutual support in their advance."

"And why did that happen, cadet?"

"Because coordinating a battle across interstellar distances is impossible," Raistlin said. "The three assault forces couldn't communicate with one another, while their opponents could use the advantage of the interior position to reinforce their defending forces—effectively smashing the attacking forces one by one."

"In other words, the commanding officer tried to be clever," Kratman said. He smiled, a rather humorless expression. "Being too clever or too dumb can cost you victory, or worse."

The Professor walked back to the front of the room and smiled at the cadets, this time with a hint of warmth. "There is actually a second point that both battles have in common. Both have been studied by military strategists—the latter battle with rather less enthusiasm, I should add—and extensively wargamed. Would you like to guess at the results?"

He paused, but no one took the bait. After a long moment, he went on.

"The conclusion, in both battles, was that the side that lost should have won. Overconfidence led to disaster—or, as Admiral Vane put it during the First Interstellar War, war is a democracy. The enemy has a vote."

He paused. "You have a question, Cadet Goldsmith?"

"Yes, sir," Cadet Karen Goldsmith said, and nodded.

Roman listened with interest. She rarely spoke, but when she did, she was always worth listening to. Besides, with long red hair and a remarkable smile, she was easy on the eyes as well.

"As I understand it," Goldsmith said, "in both wars it was primarily a matter of production. The resources available to the Americans and to the Federation far outstripped those available to their enemies. Once the victors had mobilized for war, their victory was certain. If that is the case, why were the battles so important?"

"*If* that is the case, cadet?" Kratman asked dryly.

Goldsmith flushed, but said nothing. History, Military Strategy and Moral Philosophy was not a class to be unsure of one's grounds.

"In one sense, you are quite right," the Professor said. "The sheer weight of firepower and material available to the victors ensured that they would be victorious. In a different sense, you are wrong; firepower and material alone does not win wars. Wars are fought—and thought—by intelligent beings. You might as well ask why the losers chose to fight at all."

He smiled. "In war, there are far more factors than just the material and armament. Is one side really committed to the war? If not, will they fight to the finish or will they abandon the war when the cost in men and material grows too high? The Japanese calculated that the Americans lacked the will to continue the war to the bitter end—oh yes, they knew about the disparity in long-term power. But America's short-term weakness did not lead to long-term weakness or defeat, not least because the Japanese lacked the firepower to capture or destroy America's industry.

"In the Blue Star War, the shock of the defeat forced the Federation Navy to clean house, while the political leaders who got the Federation into the war found themselves purged or marginalized. The defeat provoked fury among the high and mighty, who put aside their political struggles to unite and see the war through to victory. You may wish to consider what might have happened if the Senate hadn't been so unified. The Blue Star War might have been abandoned and the Federation's prestige would have been severely dented."

Roman considered the scenario as the Professor summed up his final lecture, outlining its relevance to the cadets and the Federation Navy. The reason the Outsiders were pushing so hard along the Rim—where the Federation's writ barely ran and outlaws and pirates hid themselves from Federation justice—was that the Federation Navy wasn't showing the will to either protect the human population or hunt down the pirates and the aliens who were supporting them. He recalled, bitterly, how his parents had died. After that, he had thrown himself into his studies and eventually won a coveted scholarship to Luna Academy. And if he earned a First in the exams, he would be on the short list to command his own ship.

"I was on the *Matterhorn*," the Professor concluded.

Roman blinked in surprise. The *Matterhorn* was a legend, one of the most famous ships in the fleet. The superdreadnaught had led the assault force into Sapphire and right into the ambush that had shattered the attacking force. The *Matterhorn* had been the only starship to survive, her CO somehow managing to get his wounded and bleeding starship back through the Asimov Point, losing over two-thirds of his crew in the brief encounter. He found himself looking at Kratman with new respect. All of the Academy's staff were supposed to have combat experience, but real combat experience was rare in the Federation Navy. The Blue Star War, the last significant conflict, was over sixty years ago.

"It was a nightmare," Kratman said. "We flew right into a trap and were lucky to survive. Others—people I had known since I was a cadet—didn't survive. You all have survived five years of the Academy, but your experience of the real universe is limited. And yet, if you pass the final exams, you will be on the track to command and, eventually, the Admiralty. If you survive..."

ക്കൊ

By long tradition—Luna Academy had been founded in 2161—the cadets were granted a free period after every class. It hadn't taken long for Roman—and the other survivors of five years of brutal winnowing—to realize that falling for the temptations of Luna City was a good way to lose one's place in the Academy. The cadets, after their first year, were expected to discipline themselves. Very few wasted their time partying when they had to study.

Roman nodded to Raistlin as the class broke up, some heading for the library and others for the simulators, where they would study the battles the Professor had outlined. A handful, who had been ordered to undergo extra EVA training or additional duties, looked downcast. Raistlin nodded back—despite his origins, he wasn't actually stupid—and made a show of walking in the opposite direction. Picking fights outside class was another good way to lose one's place.

"So," Cadet Sultana Narayanan said, "how much trouble do you think the Professor is going to get into?"

Roman shrugged. "None, I suspect," he said. The Blue Star War might have been forbidden territory, but studying the war was vital, if only to avoid making the same mistakes again. "I think there are times when he says things just to see how we will react."

It made, he decided, a certain kind of sense. The cadets who bought the official line hook, line and sinker wouldn't be showing the mental agility needed to command starships in battle. Besides, they were—or they would be, once they graduated—Federation Navy officers. They *needed* to think for themselves.

"Or maybe he wanted to tell us something without saying it outright," he added. "Something we had to pick out for ourselves."

"Maybe," Sultana said. It was rare for her to talk to anyone outside classes, but in some ways they were both loners. Sultana had left her homeworld under a cloud and Roman was a RockRat, part of an asteroid-dwelling society that rarely interacted with the rest of humanity. "Do you think that...?"

At that moment, the emergency alarm went off. "ALL CADETS REPORT TO SAFE LOCKS," the intercom bellowed. "I SAY AGAIN, ALL CADETS REPORT TO SAFE LOCKS! THIS IS NOT A DRILL!"

Roman and Sultana exchanged glances—the emergency alarms were never sounded, outside scheduled drills—and then started to run. A Safe Lock was never far away.

Chapter Two

The Senate, as laid down in the Federation Constitution, is restricted to only one thousand members—not counting the Grand Senators, who hold their positions until resignation or death. It should not be surprising, therefore, that representing the entirety of the Federation becomes a problem, or that there is a growing disconnect between the Senate and those they represent.
-An Irreverent Guide to the Federation, 4000 A.D.

Senate Hall, Earth, Sol System, 4092

"The Senate Committee on Outsider Incursions is now called to order," the Speaker said. "As per the Senate Security Act of 3702, I declare the room sealed."

Vice Admiral Marius Drake nodded impatiently. It had been a year since he had been recalled to Earth for "consultations," and ten years since he had been assigned to the Rim and ordered to hunt down and destroy the Outsiders. But the mission had not been successful, as the Outsiders were good at hiding from the Federation Navy—they'd had plenty of practice—and the Senate hadn't given him either the authority or resources to provide escorts to protect merchant shipping.

But as bad as that was, it was nothing compared to the last year's worth of inactivity on Earth—a complete and utter waste of his time. At first, the Admiralty had refused to admit that there *was* a problem with the Outsiders. And then everything had got worse once the politicians had become involved.

Politics was at the root of everything, these days.

Marius straightened his dress uniform as the room slowly came to order. At ninety-one years of age, he still looked young and handsome, thanks to the longevity treatments made available to promising young Federation Navy officers. His short, dark hair contrasted oddly with the gold dress uniform, to say nothing of the cape some sadist had designed for the Federation's naval officers to wear. Marius had no idea who had designed the cape, or why, but the uniform made him feel ridiculous. At least he'd honestly earned the medals on his chest. Perhaps the Senators would look at the medals and realize that he knew what he was talking about, unlike their paid military experts. It was astonishing how experts always provided advice that led directly to whatever their clients wanted to do.

Of course, that kind of wishful thinking was what had started the Blue Star War in the first place.

The Senate Hall was massive, holding not only the Grand Chamber—where all one thousand Senators and the Grand Senators passed laws that affected the entire Federation—but also hundreds of secure rooms for more private meetings. The chamber the Committee had reserved for its own use was small by the standards of the Grand Chamber, but it was still remarkably luxurious. No expense had been spared, not in the computer systems, nor the paintings that hung on the wall, or even the obsequious servants offering coffee or tea on demand to the Senators.

Marius had been brought up to believe that using human labor was a sign of decadence. In an age where robots were common, human servants were there merely to illustrate how important their masters considered themselves to be.

He looked up at the Senators and winced inwardly. They didn't look happy. Grand Senator The Honorable Carlton Brockington, Leader of the Conservative Faction, had somehow secured the chair for his own party. He was older than Marius and he hadn't aged anything like as well, unless Brockington was for some reason deliberately displaying his age. Fashions, for everything from clothing to faces and bodily shape, changed so rapidly on Earth that Marius, who had spent most of his life in interstellar space, had no hope of following them.

Grand Senator Alison Wallisch, Leader of the Socialist Faction, sat next to him, her blue eyes flickering from person to person. Her improbably beautiful heart-shaped face, surrounded by a mass of blonde curls, concealed a devious mind and—like all Senators—a certain ruthlessness and willingness to throw a friend out of the airlock if the friend threatened her power. Four of the other Senators were non-factors, brought in to bolster the two main factions, but Senator Chang Li, Representative from Nova Athena, and Grand Senator Rupert McGillivray were different. Despite himself, Marius, who followed politics closely, couldn't understand why either of them were on this Committee. Chang Li was from the Outer Rim and had no effective power base to speak of. And as for McGillivray...

"Vice Admiral," Brockington said in a cold, accusatory tone. "You have failed to defeat the Outsiders and restore peace and prosperity to the Rim. And now you come before us and ask for extra resources. Why should we assign additional starships and manpower to your command?"

Marius kept his expression blank, drawing on years of experience since graduating from Luna Academy. "The level of forces assigned to my command, Your Excellency, is insufficient for the task at hand," he said as calmly as he could. "If you want results, you need to assign me additional ships."

The senators murmured audibly, possibly talking to their staff members via communications implant. Of course, using such implants in public was impolite, but who would dare tell that to the Senators? Everyone else pretended not to notice, but Marius would remember the slight.

"You have been assigned over three hundred starships," Brockington said after a long pause. "Why is that insufficient?"

"Your Excellency, my area of responsibility covers over five *thousand* light years and four hundred inhabited planetary systems," Marius said. "The odds against me managing to place a single unit in a star system that is about to be attacked by pirates are astronomical. I cannot provide reliable protection for merchant shipping, let alone hunt down the various pirate bases, which are utterly impossible to detect in such a vast area of space. Furthermore, I have been denied the authority to insist on convoys being formed and escorted. Governor Barany has flatly refused my requests to institute even a limited convoy system, which my advisors have estimated would cut our losses by over a third."

He thought rapidly. *Should he bring up the other matter? If ONI was right, Governor Barany was actually taking money from the pirates. And that couldn't be allowed.*

"Worse, there is evidence to suggest that there are at least three unknown alien races in the Beyond, races that are aware of our existence and are actually providing help and support to the pirates. They may well have absorbed human technology, in direct violation of Directive 001. When I brought this to the governor's attention, he refused to grant permission to launch survey missions, let alone punitive raids against the unknown aliens. Instead, he promised to send the question to the Senate. I received no response by the time I was recalled."

It took everything he had to keep the anger out of his voice, but he managed it.

"The pirates have graduated from pest to serious annoyance," he continued after a beat. "They started by raiding freighters; now, they're raiding entire *planets* and carting off vast numbers of humans to use as slaves. We captured a pirate ship three years ago that carried nothing but human females, who were apparently destined for prostitution or slavery. The settlers out there are paying the pirates to leave them alone, giving them money or women in exchange for peace."

Marius hoped the Senators understood just how wrong that was, but worse was yet to come.

"And that's not all, as those settlers who refuse to cooperate often *die*, Your Excellency. This is most likely why pirates have destroyed at least four colonies down to the last man, woman and child."

There was an uneasy pause, as several of the Senators busied themselves with their terminals rather than look at Marius or their fellows.

"How many do you believe died in the last ten years?" Senator Chang Li asked. "How many humans have died because we didn't protect them?"

Marius considered her for a long moment. Back when the Federation was formed, the older planets had insisted they be allowed to represent their daughter colonies in the Senate, something that had dovetailed nicely with the limit on how many Senators could be voted into office. In practice, it ensured that the out-worlds, the ones at most risk from the pirates, had no voice in government. Senator Chang Li was only the third colonist to serve as a Senator, and she was isolated. The Senators had become aristocrats in all but name.

"The Rim records are of limited value," Marius admitted. "However, the best estimate I can give you is that over seventy *million* humans have been killed by the pirates, or carted off to serve as slaves, or have scattered and are hiding from both us and the pirates. The situation is intolerable."

"It is we who decide what is intolerable," Grand Senator Alison Wallisch said. Her voice was very cold. "I have here, in my implant, a communication from the governor. He states that Vice Admiral Drake has been unwilling to cooperate with the governor or local governments." She smiled thinly. "Perhaps you would care to explain why you showed so little respect for properly constituted authority, admiral?"

This time, it was harder to hide the rage.

"With all due respect, Senator, I discovered very quickly that sharing my operational plans with the governor meant that they were shared with the pirates," Marius told her. "I told the governor about a planned ambush; the pirates somehow avoided it. I told him that I planned a raid on a pirate base; the base was empty when I got there and rigged to blow with antimatter. I told him to keep the information in confidence and not to share it with anyone, not even his wife, yet somehow the information got out."

"Governor Barany is a man of the highest reputation," Alison said. "How dare you accuse him of...supplying information to the pirates?"

"The evidence is in his bank accounts," Marius said, throwing his last card onto the table. "He has a whole series of payments with no discernible source and..."

"Impossible," Alison said. She turned to her fellow Senators. "The admiral is attempting to excuse his own failures by blaming the governor! I move that we consider this in closed session."

There was a brief moment of silent communication. "I disagree," Chang Li said. Her almond eyes sought out Marius. "We need to send more starships into the sector to protect the population."

"At a colossal cost," one of the Conservative Senators pointed out. "Deploying an entire fleet into the Rim would strain our logistics quite badly and—"

"There are human lives at stake," Marius snapped, unable to control himself any longer. "Right now, *billions* of human lives are at risk of being kidnapped, killed, or simply wiped from existence. And here you are, worrying about cost!"

There was a long pause.

"I think, admiral, that you had better withdraw," Brockington said. "We will inform you of our decision in due course."

−−

"The governor is one of her men, of course."

Marius didn't turn as the Grand Senator came up behind him. Instead, he stared out of the massive window, looking down towards the towers of Federation City. Centuries ago, the city had been built to serve as a home for the Federation's Government, back after the First Interstellar War had taught the human race the value of unity. Now, it was just like any other city on Earth: massive towers, teeming slums and a monstrous overpopulation problem. The punishment for any crime, these days, was deportation, yet it was never enough to keep pace with the growing population. Sooner or later, the teeming mass of humanity was going to rise up and drag the entire planet down into a nightmare.

"You spoke truth to power," Grand Senator Rupert McGillivray said dryly. "What makes you think that that will go unpunished?"

Marius turned. McGillivray was old, perhaps the oldest man in the Federation. His white hair and short, white beard were an affectation—he could have altered it at will—but the slow motion of his walk and the way his body shook told the true story. Traditionally, a Grand Senator who reached such an age—his detractors claimed he was senile—should resign, but McGillivray had held onto his chair.

As the last of the Imperialist Faction—the faction that had provoked the Blue Star War—he was effectively impossible to dislodge.

"I like to think that the government would do the right thing," Marius said honestly. "Didn't they see the records from hijacked ships and ruined planets?"

"Of course they did," McGillivray said. "What makes you think they care? Everyone in the Senate is focused on keeping and expanding their power bases. Dead colonials along the Rim don't vote; wealthy citizens in the Core Worlds do so, frequently. Pleasing them is far more important than trying to stop the pirates."

He shrugged as he took one of the seats that allowed him to stare out over Federation City. The sun was setting in the distance.

"Admiral, no one of your high position can afford to be ignorant of politics," McGillivray said. "I know; you reached your position through merit and you deserve it, but merit alone isn't enough these days. There's a total deadlock in the Senate and no one is going to go out on a limb and suggest that sending a few hundred additional units out to the Rim might be a good idea, even with a clear and present threat to the entire Federation."

Marius nodded dismally. "But they're playing fast and loose with the security of the entire *Federation*," he repeated with emphasis. "How long is it going to be before we face an even greater threat?"

McGillivray smiled. "Are the new aliens a danger to the Federation?"

"I don't know," Marius admitted. "The Senate banned us from sending survey missions out to their space; hell, we know very little about them. The real danger is that they will get organized as a unit if we give them time, perhaps allying with the pirates and rebels. They have to know, by now, what life as an alien in the Federation is like."

The thought was a bitter one. The First Interstellar War had left a legacy of xenophobia running through the Federation. No alien race could be permitted to threaten humanity ever again. Aliens were second-class citizens even on their own home-worlds, denied weapons or access to spaceflight. They were banned from Earth and the Core Worlds, while the out-worlds often used aliens as a source of cheap labor. Marius had no more love for the aliens than the average human, yet even he was prepared to admit that no rational alien race would want to join the Federation.

Of course, the Blue Star War had made it clear what would happen to any race that *refused* to cooperate.

"True," McGillivray agreed after a pause. He leaned forward, assuming a lecturing pose. "The Conservatives want to keep things as they are, because they're effectively in charge of half the galaxy. They're allied with most of the big interstellar corporations because the corporations want to keep the laws and procedures they already have..."

"Keeping them on top," Marius put in.

"Precisely," McGillivray said. "The Socialists are trying to challenge this by distributing federal largesse to the population of the Core Worlds, the planets that can make or break Senators. In theory, they can effectively buy votes because they promise to keep the money flowing. In practice, what they're actually doing is damaging the tax base; the big corporations have the legal framework to escape taxation, or they're moving operations out to the out-worlds. So the Socialists raise taxes on smaller businesses and individuals, which makes their continued survival impossible, which means they're actually expanding the pool of needy people who need federal support to survive. Worse, because most of the Core Worlds are actually significant, raising taxes there is politically dangerous, so they start taxing the out-worlds, which causes massive resentment and a black market.

"Back when we had the Imperialist Faction, all three were balanced, but now..." He shook his head. "My family was there when the Constitution was first written," he said slowly. "And now I may live long enough to see the Federation tear itself apart."

Marius blinked. "Surely it's not that serious..."

"Oh, yes it is," McGillivray insisted. "You remember how reluctant they were to send ships to the Rim? They've been cutting the military to the bone in order to fund their pet projects; they've been cutting back on everything. The Survey Service has effectively been disbanded. The Asimov Point Monitoring Service has been placed on indefinite hold. They've even been skimping on ICN funding for the Rim and..."

Marius held up a hand, as etiquette demanded. A message had just downloaded into his implants. "They want me to head back to the Admiralty," he said flatly. He would have time to think about McGillivray's words on the way. "Thank you..."

"Thank *you*," McGillivray said. He winked. "It's astonishing how few people pay attention to me these days."

৪০৫৪

Admiralty House—the headquarters of the Federation Navy—was on the other side of the continent from Federation City. No one knew, now, why it had been built there, but it was tradition and, as such, could not be interfered with by mere mortals. Marius had his own theory; the Snakes, the first alien race humanity had encountered, had bombarded planetary defense centers with abandon, ignoring the danger to civilian populations. Building the HQ so far from the civilian population might just save civilian lives if the enemy took the high orbitals and chose to bombard the planet before invading.

The shuttle raced towards the city at several times the speed of sound. It was a sign of haste that the Admiralty had assigned his transport to the first available craft, rather than wait for an aircar. Someone in the Senate must have lit a fire under someone's ass. Marius didn't mind. The shuttle might be disarmed, but it felt more... natural than a luxury aircar. Sitting behind the pilot gave him time to rest. There was no point in trying to think, not after hearing from both the Senate and Grand Senator McGillivray. He'd find out what was waiting for him when he landed.

He looked up sharply as an alarm shrilled. It was the planetary defense alarm, an alarm that was never used, even in drills. The Solar System wasn't under attack—was it?

A moment later, the looming shape of Admiralty House—coming into view in the distance—vanished in a flash of blinding light.

Chapter Three

As the homeworld of humanity, Earth is the single most heavily defended world in recorded history. Only a madman would try to breach the defenses and claim Earth for his own—or so we are told. History is all about people doing the unexpected and, one day, Earth's defenses may be challenged from an unsuspected direction.
-An Irreverent Guide to the Federation, 4000 A.D.

Near-Earth Orbit, Sol System, 4092

Although he was on the command deck, Commander Jacob Fallon had been slacking off when the attack began. In theory, he was currently in command of Earth Defense Station Three. The truth was that command networks and override protocols linked all of the defense stations—and automated orbital weapons platforms—into a single, coherent whole. With Commodore Peking on Earth Defense Station One for a conference with Port Admiral Gordon, the commander of Earth's defense network and the Home Fleet, the crew of EDS3 had been relaxing. Nothing had threatened Earth since the First Interstellar War, centuries ago, and few members of the crew expected anything ever would.

Fallon came to his feet as alarms shrieked, dropping his small—and, technically, illegal—data terminal on the deck as the main display wall lit up with red icons. He'd never seen anything like it outside of drills, and even then the drills hadn't been too intense; after all, everyone *knew* that attackers could not reach Earth without fighting their way through half the Federation. There would be plenty of time to reconfigure defenses and reallocate resources to deal with any new threats.

Or so they had believed.

The main display zeroed in on a single, expanding red icon, flashing to yellow as it faded away. Where EDS1 had been, hanging over Earth like a protective shroud, there was nothing more than an expanding cloud of debris and superheated plasma. A second icon—confirming the detection of a nuclear detonation on Earth's surface—almost passed unnoticed.

Jacob was too astonished to speak, even as the alarms yammered and trained personnel struggled to respond to the completely unanticipated situation. What the hell was going on? All drills were scripted and announced in advance. It couldn't be a drill, but it couldn't be real...could it?

"Bring the station to red alert," he ordered his crew. *If that wasn't the most unnecessary order in the history of the Federation Navy,* he thought, considering the alert had automatically sounded. "Get me..."

He broke off as new red icons flared into existence. *Starfighters!* Someone had launched starfighters?

It seemed impossible, but someone *had*. They were attacking Earth's network of defensive installations. Jacob just stared, unable to speak or even think. The Earth Defense Stations were not only four times as massive as the largest superdreadnaughts or assault carriers, they carried far more missile launchers, starfighters, and armor, if only because they didn't need to fill their internal compartments with drive units and emergency supplies. Who would dare attack such massive formations?

"Launch our starfighters," he ordered, trying to sound as calm as he possibly could. He fell back on basic tactics, information he'd learned at the academy and then allowed to slip out of his head, because there was nothing else to do. The hostile starfighters had to be hunted down and destroyed before they caused more damage.

Except...where had they come from? No one could have slipped a fleet of assault carriers near Earth without being detected, even if their cloaking systems were superior to those of the Federation Navy. He couldn't even see who they should be engaging! And he didn't know who—or what—was in command. The entire datanet seemed to be stuttering...

౮ణ

Marius held on to his seat for dear life, struggling to comprehend what had just happened as the shuttle tumbled end-over-end. The internal compensations struggled to keep everyone alive as the shuttle was tossed through the air; it felt as if the hand of God had touched the shuttle.

There was no time for panic. Someone had nuked Navy HQ. There was no other explanation. An antimatter bomb, even an old-style antimatter device, would have wiped out the entire continent and he would be dead. The shuttle he was in would have been swatted like a bug.

He tried to access the emergency channels through his implant as the pilot finally managed to steady the craft, but there was no response. He had no way to tell if the blast was disrupting communications—although that should have been impossible, given the sheer level of redundancy built into Earth's network—or if someone was deliberately jamming communications.

The shuttle had stabilized, allowing him to look towards Navy HQ. Marius shuddered as an ominous mushroom cloud rose into the air, tinged with flickers of fire and shadow. No one had used a nuclear weapon on Earth's surface since the Age of Unrest. Only seven nukes had ever been used at all, even during the darkest days of the Third World War.

But then, by that point the winners had learned how to bombard targets from orbit and obliterate their enemies with nice clean kinetic strikes.

"We're alive," the pilot said in relief. "Sir..."

"The system is under attack," Marius said. "Hold your position while I try to find out who's in charge."

He linked his implant into the shuttle's communications nodes. Much to his relief, that allowed him to slip through the disruption and into the emergency network. It was already overloading because of calls from the surrounding area and would probably collapse. Linking into the military channels was harder—it needed his ID codes to gain access—and it seemed impossible to find a superior officer.

If Navy HQ had been hit, the enemy—whoever they were—had decapitated the Federation Navy. Home Fleet's commanding officers would be dead. He knew that, but he still held out hope that someone, anyone, might outrank him and be able to tell him what was going on.

The datanet should have linked him instantly to the senior surviving officer within range. Instead, it took minutes to sort through the conflicting tidal waves of data and finally locate the senior officer. Marius shivered again as he realized that the senior officer in the system—at least the senior officer plugged into the datanet—was a mere commander.

Dear God, how high had the casualties been? What had happened onboard EDS1 to slaughter the defenders of Earth?

"Sir, EDS1 is gone," the pilot said, answering his unspoken question. He'd been flicking through what remained of the flight control network. "The station has been completely destroyed."

Marius cursed. The attack was internal, then; there was no way to smuggle a nuke or an antimatter bomb onto a defense station without help. It had to have been an internal detonation. Nothing else, not even a bombardment with compressed antimatter, would have obliterated the station so quickly. He accessed the network again and swore, angrily. EDS2 had gone silent. The senior officer was still a mere commander.

"This is Vice Admiral Drake," he said as he linked into the communications network. "Here are my ID codes and command authority. I suggest that you verify them, then open a secure link."

There was a long pause.

"Admiral, I'm Commander Jacob Fallon, in command of EDS3," Commander Fallon said. He sounded as if he were on the verge of coming apart, either through shock or relief. No one had expected an attack on Earth, let alone what had to be an internal rebellion. "Thank God you're alive!"

Commander Fallon sounded relieved to discover that someone was senior to him and could therefore take charge. Marius accessed his implants, briefly skimming through Fallon's file. It was not a distinguished one.

"Just so," Marius growled. He would have to work with Fallon, no matter his limited experience. "We're still alive and I, for one, intend to stay that way. You have my command codes. Declare a Case Omega and run through the network, then let me know if there is anyone senior to me..."

"But sir," Fallon protested. "I don't have the authority to declare Case Omega."

"You're in command of a battlestation," Marius snapped. "You have the authority! Now, get in touch with the network and find out who's in charge."

He disconnected from the network and looked over at the pilot. "Set course for EDS3," he ordered. Fallon sounded as if he was on the verge of panic, which meant—if nothing else—Marius had to be on the scene to relieve him, if necessary. "Call up a flight of starfighters for escort and get them to fly top cover."

His implant buzzed as Fallon contacted him. "I ran a Case Omega, sir," he said. "You're the senior surviving officer within the Earth-Luna Sphere."

Marius nodded. The attack had clearly been carefully planned. Had they held off for another few minutes, he would have been in Navy HQ when it was destroyed. But if he'd maintained his original plans, he'd have been there at least ten minutes sooner. Which meant that if Senator McGillivray hadn't wanted to talk with him, Marius himself would already be dead.

The attackers, whoever they were, had planned to decapitate the defenses and they'd come alarmingly close to success. Their tactics showed a chilling level of ruthlessness. Breaking the taboo on using weapons of mass destruction on inhabited planets showed a single-minded determination to succeed, if only because of what the Federation would do to them if it won the war.

"Right," he said. "I am assuming command of the defenses of Earth. Give me a situation report, now."

"Sir, the datanet has been crippled," Fallon said. "I barely know anything..."

"Then give me what you have," Marius said patiently, checking the shuttle's ETA at the station. "What do you know about what's going on?"

"Ah...EDS1 has been destroyed, sir," Fallon said. "I have dispatched SAR gunboats and shuttles, but they don't hold out much hope of finding survivors. EDS2, EDS7 and EDS9 are non-responsive; they're intact, yet they're not linked into the command network and are refusing to respond to hails. I don't know their exact status. And there are dozens of enemy starfighters flying around, engaging the defenses."

Marius scowled. Starfighters needed a base—either a starship or a station—to operate. Their life support packs wouldn't last indefinitely, which meant that someone had to have launched them. But from where?

He glanced at the holographic near-orbit display as the shuttle rose out of the atmosphere and considered it. The starfighters could have come from the silent battlestations, yet if that was the case, there should be more of them. And then the treacherous commanders would have had to convince the fighter jocks to support them, too...no, it wasn't possible to form a conspiracy of that magnitude without Federation Intelligence or ONI getting wind of it beforehand.

He looked at the display again, and knew the answer.

"There are too many freighters in orbit—breaking orbit now," he said slowly. Converting freighters into makeshift carriers was an old trick. And now that the fighting had begun, hundreds of innocent civilian craft were breaking orbit and fleeing, unaware that some of their comrades were actually enemy starships. "Ten gets you twenty that at least one of them is working for the enemy..."

He frowned. "I want a general broadcast," he ordered. "All civilian ships within the Earth-Luna Sphere are to cancel their drives and prepare to be boarded. Any that refuse to stop will be fired upon and destroyed."

Fallon sounded shocked. "But, sir..."

Marius ignored the protest and drove onwards. "Have you re-established the command datanet yet?"

"No, sir," Fallon said. "The coordinating systems were mounted on EDS1, and were destroyed by the blast that took out the station."

And it never occurred to you to try to work around the problem? Marius thought, wondering what connections Fallon must have such that he had avoided being sent somewhere harmless, perhaps an asteroid mining station.

"I see," he said as coldly as he could. "Your station may not have been designed to serve as a command station, but the computers will be able to handle it for at least a few hours. And by then, we will either have won or lost the coming battle. Reboot the system and prepare for operations."

"Sir, the manual clearly states..."

"Fuck the manual," Marius swore at him. "This is war! Doing what the enemy expects us to do is a certain way to wind up dead, with the enemy laughing at us. Now, forget the manual and reboot the fucking system, right fucking now!"

"Sir, our escort has arrived," the pilot interrupted. "We should be on the station in ten minutes, unless we hit unexpected trouble."

Marius nodded absently, thinking hard. He'd warned the Senate about the dangers of largely unknown alien races, but he knew that no alien race could have launched such a devastating and precise attack. The level of access the unknown attackers had demonstrated they had internal help, which meant that whoever was behind the attack was trying for a coup, rather than destruction for the sake of destruction. Destroying Earth would have been easy—a single antimatter bomb would depopulate the planet—but anyone who wanted to replace the Federation with his own rule would need Earth's legitimacy.

And that suggested there had to be a second level to the plan. Destroying EDS1 and Navy HQ would cause confusion, but the disarray wouldn't last. Even if Marius hadn't stepped up to the plate, *someone* would have taken command sooner or later. There had to be an incoming enemy fleet heading towards Earth, having somehow been smuggled into the system. That, at least, was no longer impossible. The stardrive had seen to that.

"Ah, the network is up and running," Fallon said. He sounded relieved. Marius wondered how he would cope in a battle where multiple antimatter detonations would disrupt the network effortlessly. Coordinating a fleet in combat wasn't easy. "The three silent stations are continuing to refuse to respond."

Treachery or equipment malfunction? Marius thought. There was no way to know for sure.

"Link into Marine HQ at Camp Heinlein," he ordered. Unless the Marines had been hit as well, Major General Tobias Vaughn would still be alive. And Vaughn, who had once been the senior Marine on Marius's first command, was one of his closest friends. "Inform the Major General that I want armed Marines in the air and heading for the three stations. Once they board, they are to secure the stations and confirm their status, then prepare to start searching the civilian ships. If they meet with resistance, they are authorized to use deadly force."

"Yes, sir," Fallon said. At least he'd learned to take orders without objecting. "Ah, four bulk freighters are continuing to accelerate away from Earth, heading towards the Dead End."

Marius smiled, feeling the old excitement shimmering through his mind. The Sol System possessed two Asimov Points, but one of them—the Dead End—led only to a single useless star system, without even a handful of asteroids to arouse the interest of the RockRats. The Dead End was defended, of course, yet it was simply not as important as the Gateway, the second Asimov Point within the system. And there was no logical reason for anyone to want to go there, unless they had something illegal in mind. And *that*, to his mind, effectively confirmed their guilt. Converting a bulk freighter to a starfighter carrier was easy.

"Order the starfighters to intercept and move up gunboats in support," Marius ordered calmly. "If the bulk freighters refuse to surrender and hold position, the pilots are authorized to open fire. No further warnings."

Fallon clearly swallowed an objection. "Yes, sir," he replied. "I shall pass your orders on to the pilots."

Marius nodded. In five minutes, he would be aboard the station and ready to take command of defensive operations. But where was the enemy fleet? Their commander would have to strike a balance between secrecy and the need to strike hard before the defenders reorganized.

How close...?

೮೦೦೮

"We should do something," Raistlin protested. "We shouldn't stay here."

Roman couldn't disagree. For cadets, spending any time in the Safe Locks was a foretaste of hell. They were armored rooms, isolated from Luna Academy's life support system and, in theory, anyone inside could survive a disaster that took out the remainder of the academy. Now, with over seventy cadets from all five years crammed inside this one, tiny room, it felt claustrophobic.

"And what, pray tell, do you think you could do?" Proctor Amanda Wallace demanded. She was tall and, to the cadets, a force of nature. The proctors didn't teach, not formally; they supervised the cadets and, when necessary, provided discipline. "Do you think we could take *Emprise* and *Enigma* out into battle?"

Raistlin flushed red, while a handful of cadets tittered. *Emprise* and *Enigma* were the two old starships that had been assigned to the academy for training purposes, but they were *far* from state-of-the-art. Roman, and every other cadet, even those who had no intention of going into Engineering, had spent months crawling over the two ships, eventually flying them throughout the Solar System. They were in perfect working order, but hopelessly outdated. Any modern warship would scythe them down in seconds.

"There's nothing we can do," Amanda said. "We don't even know what is going on."

Roman blinked. His implant hadn't been able to access any information, but he'd assumed that was because he was just a cadet. But the proctors were clearly just as much in the dark.

"I suggest that you use your implants and study for your tests," Amanda continued. "I assure you that if you die you won't have to sit them."

Roman snorted at the bad joke and then caught Raistlin's eye, trying to let the man know Roman agreed with him. All hell was breaking loose out there, and yet here they were, stuck in the Safe Lock and unable to do anything, even run if necessary. Above them on the Luna surface, something was going on.

Cadets weren't trained to sit on their hands. So why was it that they hadn't been ordered to battle stations rather than the Safe Lock? Something wasn't right here.

He looked away, hoping to conceal his expression from Proctor Amanda. Feeling helpless wasn't pleasant, but what else could he do? In hopes of distracting himself, he called up the data for the tactical exam and started to run through it. It didn't work. His thoughts kept returning to the battle above, where the future of the Federation was being decided.

After all, why else would anyone attack Earth?

Chapter Four

The Federation grants vast authority to its commanding officers, if only because of the time delay in seeking and receiving orders from the Senate. If Case Omega is declared, the senior officer effectively becomes the federal government, with authority to issue orders to all branches of the services without regard for either tradition or formal procedure.
-An Irreverent Guide to the Federation, 4000 A.D.

Near-Earth Orbit, Sol System, 4092

The last time Marius Drake had set foot in an Earth-class battlestation had been ten years ago. In the interim, he'd forgotten just how depressing they were. It was obvious the former commander of the battlestation—now dead—had made an attempt to decorate the command center in a green and white style as opposed to the usual institutional gray, but it hadn't helped. It was still depressing, and worse, it contained a number of people who, if they were anything like the hapless Commander Fallon, were completely unready to defend Earth.

That had to change, and fast.

"No, I don't want a formal greeting party," Marius said in response to Fallon's question as he strode off the shuttle into the battlestation. If they weren't at war, Fallon would have had a point; now it was a waste of time. "Give me a status report, and right now!"

He glared up at the holographic near-orbit display as he took the command chair at the heart of the command center. The command center was massive, large enough to make it difficult for anyone to make himself heard from one end of the compartment to the other, and packed with consoles and officers. At least Fallon had managed to get the crew up and running, but no one seemed to know what they were doing. That did not bode well for Earth unless Marius was able to make them listen.

"The Marines are boarding the silent battlestations now," Fallon said. "They're reporting that their command software was contaminated by enemy computer viruses and that the stations are physically intact—and loyal."

Marius nodded, keeping his face under tight control. In person, Fallon wasn't remotely impressive; weak chin, weak eyes and a countenance that suggested sheer terror. He would have been handsome—*perhaps because he was the product of bioengineering*, the nasty part of Marius's mind suggested—if he had shown the moral character of the average dog. And like a dog, Fallon would undoubtedly have preferred to hide under the bed while others fought the battle for him.

He *had* managed to get through the report all right, but there was something still off about the man, something that suggested a simple inability to comprehend what was actually happening. He would have to shape up, Marius decided, and quickly, or else he would be relieved of command. No admiral could have a commander who didn't know what he was doing at the helm of the defense forces; if he'd been in this position earlier in his career, he would have made damn sure that *anyone* standing in the line of command knew what the hell they were supposed to do in an emergency.

"And the freighters?" Marius asked.

"The fighters are moving to intercept now," Fallon's operations officer confirmed. His nametag read CAFFERY. "The gunboats are moving up in pursuit. So far, there's been no response from the freighters, but the enemy starfighters are moving away into deep space."

"Right," Marius said, thinking hard. Were they heading towards cloaked carriers, or were they trying to mislead the defenders and planning to dog-leg around towards the bulk freighters once they were out of sensor range? If the latter, they were going to be disappointed. Earth's sensor network was second to none and the fighters would burn through their life support before they could escape its grasp. "And the StarCom?"

Fallon cleared his throat. "It was destroyed with EDS1," he said carefully. Marius concealed a smile with an effort. Fallon clearly thought his superior had forgotten that little detail. "We don't have any other link to Titan Base."

The Inheritance Wars had traumatized the Senate, what with the mutinies that had broken out on many Federation Navy starships, including the ships assigned to Home Fleet. The Senate had responded by forbidding the deployment of Federation Navy starships to the Earth-Luna Sphere—the area of space surrounding Earth and Luna—and insisted that Home Fleet be based at Titan Base, which had been Federation Navy territory since the Last King of Titan had led his people to the stars. It allowed Home Fleet to exercise without public oversight, but it also ensured that there was a time delay before reinforcements could arrive at Earth. And there would be even more of a time delay because the defenders would—in theory—be limited to radio waves or laser beams, both of which travelled at merely the speed of light.

But there was a way around that.

"Use Case Omega and get in touch with Federation Intelligence," Drake said. "You'll find a contact code in the database. They should have their own StarCom."

Fallon blinked. Marius understood his surprise. StarCom units cost upwards of twice the price of a new superdreadnaught, while they were limited in range and—once operational—alarmingly easy to target. The scientists kept promising they would find a way to reduce the price one day, but so far nothing had materialized. The fact that Federation Intelligence used StarCom units of their own was a closely-guarded secret. Marius had only found out about it because he'd needed to know.

He hoped that whoever had planned the attack on Earth *didn't* know, or his ace in the hole would be no such thing.

"But sir—" Fallon started.

"Trust me," Marius told him. "Oh, and don't take no for an answer. Once they admit they have it, tell them that I want to link to Titan Base and open contact with Home Fleet. I want them to prepare to move on my command."

He swung his chair around and tapped a control, resetting the display until it showed the entire Solar System. The grey sphere of the mass limit surrounding Sol, within which no stardrive could be used, shimmered into view, expanding out from the sun to a line just beyond Jupiter. The planets had their own mass limits, of course, yet Home Fleet could leave Titan Base and enter stardrive far quicker than if they had to depart from Earth. The planners had concluded it would speed up reaction times if there was an incident at any of the stars nearest Sol. Marius suspected they were being overly optimistic. The Blue Star War should have taught them the dangers of trying to coordinate operations over interstellar distances.

"Launch a shell of recon drones," he ordered without taking his eyes off the display. "I want a second shell launched ten minutes after the first shell, and then I want recon fighters moved up in random patrol patterns. Someone's out there, and I mean to find him before he finds us."

Marius stroked his chin. Someone a very long time ago—probably as far back as the Roman legions—had said that wars were ninety-nine percent boredom and one percent sheer terror. He'd reached the battlestation and the enemy starfighters had been beaten off, but now he had to wait and see what happened. Unless random terror was the objective, there had to be an enemy fleet out there, heading towards Earth. And if they were expecting Home Fleet to sit on the sidelines until the fighting was over, he might have a chance to give them a nasty surprise.

"Sir," Fallon announced, "Federation Intelligence has confirmed that they have a StarCom in the Earth-Luna Sphere. I don't think they're too happy with you."

"Fuck them," Marius said. This was no time for games. "Tell them to hold the unit at readiness once they send the first set of orders. We may not have time to power it up again..."

The display flashed a new icon, and then zeroed in on the escaping freighters. The icons representing intact ships had vanished, to be replaced by four expanding spheres of destruction. Marius swallowed a curse as the starfighters broke off, heading back to their parent fortresses, while gunboats closed in to investigate the remains of the freighters. The enemy, knowing they couldn't escape, had triggered the self-destruct systems—or someone, hiding under cloak, had sent a destruct command to their ships. There was no way to know for sure.

"The fighters didn't fire, sir," Fallon said. He sounded as if he was expecting to be blamed for bringing bad news. "The ships just blew up as soon as the fighters came within engagement range."

"We have a ruthless enemy," Marius agreed gravely. "Recall one half of the duty fighters"—he trusted the fighter controllers to issue the correct orders—"and give their pilots a chance to rest and rearm."

The enemy commander was *ruthless*, he noted in the privacy of his own thoughts. The enemy starfighters were doomed, unless they reached a cloaked carrier. He watched the shell of recon drones spreading outwards and asked himself again, *where* would *he put a force advancing on Earth? How would he position his ships for best advantage?*

He keyed his console and linked into the Marine channel.

"Toby, I need a report on the silent fortresses as soon as possible."

"They're crippled by chaos software," Vaughn said. His old friend sounded reassuringly competent, as always. "My engineers don't think there's anything fundamentally wrong with the hardware, but the main codes have to be purged and then rebooted—and if the chaos software remains in place, we'll have to strip out the cores and replace them."

"Purge the systems," Marius ordered tightly. They needed those fortresses. If the purge failed, they wouldn't be any worse off. "I'll assemble a scratch crew and have them sent over to replace the prior crewmen. Once the crew is aboard, you can start shipping the old crew down to Earth. We can't trust them, not until we find out who uploaded the chaos software in the first place."

"Understood," Vaughn replied. Marius knew that he would carry out his orders, or die trying. "Good luck, sir."

The connection broke. Marius leaned back in his command chair and made a show of looking up at the overhead bulkhead, trying to suggest a sense of unconcern about the whole situation.

"Have coffee and snack packs brought in for the duty staff," he ordered absently. They would have warning of the enemy's approach, unless the enemy's cloaking technology was far superior to the Federation's—and in that case, the war was lost anyway. "The remainder can get some sleep."

"Yes, sir," Fallon said. "Sir...shouldn't you get some rest, too?"

"Not at the moment," Marius said. It hadn't been *that* long since he'd served on the command deck of a battleship, hunting down pirates. And besides, he didn't know who he could trust to leave on watch. "It will all be over by the time I need rest."

He grinned while looking down at the communications display. It was surprising that there were only a handful of demands for information from the Senate, but procedures for dealing with such requests dated all the way back to the First Interstellar War—a time when a direct attack on the Solar System seemed alarmingly likely. The Senate would have to sit in a bunker under Federation City, waiting for news of victory or defeat, while the military fought its battle. His lips twisted into a droll sneer. The Senators were probably cowering, wondering which of their sins had returned to haunt them. After all, what *else* had the Inheritance Wars been about?

Time ticked by slowly as duty officers were replaced, given short breaks to rest and use the head. Others were assigned to emergency deployments and sent to the three damaged stations, two of which were back in the fight once their computers had been purged. Marius wasn't inclined to take chances, so he ordered additional security on the datanet—if the chaos software broke into the main computer network, the defense of Earth would fall apart—but he was too grateful for the additional firepower to be too paranoid. After the fighting was over, they'd have to pull the chips and go through the network with a fine-toothed comb. Someone with that level of access almost certainly had had the time to set up a few additional surprises for the defenders...

"*Contact,*" the sensor officer snapped. New red icons blinked into existence on the display. "Sir, I have multiple contacts, bearing...they're heading towards Earth!"

"Understood, son," Drake said with a smile. The sensor officer was so young that Marius wondered if he'd even begun to shave. "Give me a list of contacts, calmly if possible."

The sensor officer flushed darkly. "At least forty contacts, sir, some definitely superdreadnaught-sized," he said. "They're cloaked, so it is impossible to get a proper reading without launching additional probes..."

"And giving away that we've seen them," Marius concluded thoughtfully. He juggled the tactical situation in his head for a long moment. The enemy wasn't trying to be particularly subtle. He had aimed himself directly at Earth, with the clear intention of breaking through the remaining defenses and taking the planet. "Commander Fallon?"

"Yes, sir," Fallon said. He'd managed to get a bite to eat and some coffee before returning to the command center. Marius had thought about relieving him, but there was no one to take Fallon's place. It wasn't like serving out on the Rim, where Drake had been able to count on multiple trained and experienced officers to fill holes. The most experienced men in the system—apart from himself—were with Home Fleet. "They're here, sir."

"Yes," Marius said. "You are to contact Home Fleet and order them to follow this vector to Earth." He keyed his console, bringing up one of the contingency plans he'd considered while waiting for the enemy to show his face. It only required a slight adjustment to fit the actual situation, much to his relief. "They are to remain under cloak until they advance upon the enemy."

He studied the console for another long moment. "I also want Titan Base to prepare to launch a set of decoy drones heading on *this* course." The second course was a direct path to Earth, the kind of course a desperate or inexperienced commanding officer might attempt if he believed there was no other option. "They are to launch the drones at the exact time specified unless I countermand the orders personally. Do you understand?"

"Ah...yes, sir," Fallon said. "I just...why do you want the drones? They'll see them..."

Marius grinned at him. "Of course they will," he said. "They know that Home Fleet is somewhere within the system; they must know that, or else they're incompetents—and nothing they've done so far suggests that. And they think they've taken out the StarCom, which means we can't whistle up Home Fleet to reinforce the defenses..."

"But we *have* a StarCom," Fallon objected.

"Precisely," Marius said. "Without a StarCom, we will have to rely on lasers to warn Titan Base. Home Fleet—or, rather, the drones *posing* as Home Fleet—will make its appearance right where it would be if we truly were dependent on lasers or radio waves. And that will stop them looking for Home Fleet elsewhere..."

He leaned back in his command chair and smiled. "Send the signal, commander," he ordered. "And then we will see whose battle plan survives contact with the enemy."

The cluster of red icons representing the enemy starships moved closer, still trying to hide under cloak. Plotting and analysis specialists studied what returns could be gleaned from the recon drones, and concluded that the enemy fleet was actually larger than it had first appeared, with upwards of one hundred and fifty starships approaching Earth.

Marius ignored the whispered speculation in the background as to who was attacking Earth, but it was becoming an increasingly alarming mystery. Only the Federation Navy, by law, could possess superdreadnaughts, a measure instigated to prevent a system defense force from declaring independence and standing off the massed force of the Navy. That left only three possibilities: Outsiders, an unknown alien species...or a rebellious Federation Navy admiral.

He scowled. The Outsiders weren't organized, which suggested that they couldn't build superdreadnaughts, or crew them even if they did. An unknown alien race... that was possible, but they would have to be insane to attack Earth. The entire Federation would go berserk. The Brotherhood wouldn't need to drum up anti-alien hysteria after an attack on Earth, even one that had been beaten off by the Federation Navy. And how could aliens have obtained the sort of access required to take out EDS1 and Navy HQ? Along the Rim, the joke was that anything could be had on Earth for a large bribe, but somehow he doubted that anyone on Earth would sell out the entire planet, whatever the size of the bribe.

That left a rebellious admiral...

"They're decloaking," the sensor officer snapped. The red icons rapidly took on shape and form. Marius counted seventy-nine superdreadnaughts, nineteen carriers and one hundred and seventeen smaller ships, including one that persistently refused to be identified. The superdreadnaughts were all *Splendid*-class, which proved—beyond a doubt—that aliens were *not* involved. No alien race would have built an exact duplicate of a Federation Navy superdreadnaught. "Sir, I can't pull any IFF signals off them..."

"Unsurprising," Marius commented. Now they'd shed their cover, the enemy starships were picking up speed, boring directly towards Earth. "Hail them, Lieutenant Nicholls."

"Aye, sir," Lieutenant Nicholls said. There was a long pause. "They're not responding..."

On the display, new red icons—starfighters—began to appear.

"I think they just have," Marius said. If nothing else, the wait was over. "Commander Fallon?"

"Yes, sir?" Fallon leaned forward.

"Launch half of the ready starfighters to enhance the Combat Space Patrol," Marius ordered calmly. "Reload the other half of the ready starfighters for antishipping strikes and prepare to launch as a formation."

He studied the display again. "If they're smart, they'll come boring in and soak up the damage while getting to energy range. If not...well, it will say interesting things about their ultimate aims, won't it?"

"Admiral, we're picking up a signal from the enemy fleet," Lieutenant Nicholls said. "They're ordering us to surrender, or die."

"Melodramatic asshole," Marius said. He grinned as the blue starfighters moved out and into formation. "Send back: *Go to hell.*"

He keyed his console. "All units, you are authorized to fire at will. I say again, fire at will."

Chapter Five

Federation Naval doctrine is based around the use of overwhelming force. When the Federation goes to war, it brings the biggest stick of all to the party.
-An Irreverent Guide to the Federation, 4000 A.D.

Near-Earth Orbit, Sol System, 4092

Lieutenant Jack Peregrine braced himself as his FASF-45 Hawk starfighter rocketed towards the incoming enemy ships—and the wave of starfighters spreading out to intercept the incoming strike. Every fighter jock knew the mantra; blow through the defending pilots, put the missiles on the target, then turn to engage the CSP, covering the second strike as it was launched from the battlestations. His thumb came down on the firing key as his ship entered engagement range and his craft began to spit plasma fire towards the enemy starfighters. Without careful manoeuvring, at this range there was little chance of a hit, but the incoming blasts would make the enemy take evasive action and be unable to coordinate their countermeasures.

At least, that was what The Book said.

He smiled tightly. Of course, the enemy would probably have read the same handbook, and should know what he and the others in his squadron were trying to do. It would be interesting to see what they did in response.

"They're returning fire, skipper," he said, as new icons flashed into existence on his display. The enemy fighters weren't just evading, they were returning fire with enthusiasm. A lucky hit took out one of his comrades and another scorched a second starfighter, sending the craft tumbling out of control and the pilot bailing out of her vessel. If she was lucky, a SAR team would recover her after the battle ended; if she were unlucky, she would run out of life support and die far from home. "Here they come..."

A civilian would have seen a disorganized mob of pilots and wondered if the fighter jocks were drunk, mad, or both. Experienced military men knew better. Flying a predictable pattern was asking for disaster, especially considering the enemy had computers that worked just as well as his own, and could plot a craft's course with ease if it stayed predictable and safe. That was the way to have a plasma bolt or antifighter missile pick the starfighter off before the pilot even knew he was under attack.

The starfighters ducked and weaved as they passed through the enemy's swarm of fighters—the odds of an accidental collision were extremely low, although it had been known to happen—then the enemy swarm turned and gave chase. Jack grinned as the enemy fleet came into view, wondering if the enemy would screw up their Identify Friend or Foe beacons. Even with the most advanced technology and the best-trained pilots in the galaxy, it wasn't unknown for friendly point defense to accidentally engage friendly starfighters.

"Form up on me," he ordered as the strike commander designated targets. An enemy superdreadnaught blinked red in his display; that was his target. The other enemy ships would be ignored for now, although eventually they, too, would have to be dealt with. Jack knew they couldn't allow the enemy to keep their command datanets, which linked their point defense into a seemingly seamless whole. He noted absently that the enemy's point defense systems were putting out a staggering amount of firepower.

Of course, a single superdreadnaught possessed an awesome amount of firepower, while an entire fleet could render itself almost impregnable. But if he thought about that too long, he'd start worrying about his mission—and that would never do.

Jack gritted his teeth as his squadron zoomed into engagement range. None of the pilots, including himself, had seen action outside of simulations, and that lack of experience was going to get far too many of them killed. But he intended to be one of the survivors.

"Go!" he yelled.

The squadron rotated in place—a tricky maneuver at the best of times—and swooped down on its chosen target. The enemy ships retargeted their fire, sending thousands of plasma bolts and missiles flaring through space, picking off Jack's fellow pilots one by one. They only had to get lucky once, while the starfighter pilots had to get lucky every time. Sooner or later, Jack knew, luck ran out. The only question was if he would manage to get off his missiles before the enemy got him.

"Prepare to engage," he ordered his wingmates. "Fire on my command."

The enemy fire hadn't abated. Instead, it grew ever more savage. They knew—they had to know!—what he and the others were doing, all right.

It didn't take a genius to realize that some overpaid admiral had decided to start a civil war. Jack paid as little attention to politics as he could get away with, but it was clear to him that some of the admirals positioned along the frontiers had been effectively operating as independent warlords for a long time.

Besides, the superdreadnaught he was closing in on was clearly of Federation design.

The enemy superdreadnaught drew closer, its weapons spitting deadly fire towards Jack and his incoming fighters. It was a monstrous hulk and it seemed unbelievable that it could be brought down by a bunch of swarming gnats, but Jack knew better. Individually, the starfighters were harmless; collectively, they were lethal. The enemy superdreadnaught was putting everything it had into driving off Jack's fighters before it was too late.

"Fire," Jack ordered. The fighter shuddered as it unleashed both of its standard missiles. A moment later, his remaining fighters added their own missiles to the barrage. "Scatter and retire; I say again, scatter and retire!"

He smiled as he yanked the fighter through a tight turn and accelerated away from the enemy ship. The Federation's standard starfighter missiles carried a shield disruptor that allowed them to penetrate the enemy ship's shields and detonate against the unshielded hull. They seemed the perfect weapon, apart from the minor detail that they had to be launched at close range and most of their weight was drives, which meant they couldn't carry a heavy warhead. It was a shame that there had been no compressed antimatter on hand, but Federation Navy regulations were clear. Antimatter was not to be carried onboard starships and battlestations without an active state of war, as the risks far outweighed the benefits.

And earlier today, they'd been at peace. Or so everyone had thought, including Jack.

The enemy superdreadnaught flared with light as the missiles that made it through the barrage of point defense struck home. Explosions, each one devastating on a planetary surface, but almost unnoticeable against the vastness of space, billowed against her hull. For a moment, Jack allowed himself to wonder if the enemy ship would survive—superdreadnaughts were armored heavily to protect against just such an attack—before the superdreadnaught fell out of formation and exploded. The sheer fury of the explosion suggested that the ship had been carrying antimatter warheads, as well as the more conventional nuclear warheads.

Why would anyone fight for such people? Jack thought. *What does their stupid admiral over there think he's doing?*

His computers shrilled with alarm, too late. An enemy fighter had drawn a bead on him; it was too late to evade. Jack reached for the emergency cord, hoping against hope that somehow he'd be able to eject before the ship was hit…

Then three plasma bolts slammed into his starfighter. In the instant before his ship blew up, Jack wished the invading admiral and all those who followed him to oblivion.

And then, there was nothing but a ball of radioactive fire where Jack's ship had been.

ᛤᚼ

Marius watched as dispassionately as he could as his cadre of starfighters swarmed around the enemy fleet, which had settled into a position that allowed them to exchange missile fire with the defenses of Earth. He had the uneasy sense that the enemy commander had definitely expected Earth's defenses to be completely uncoordinated, for his tactics would have made perfect sense if he'd expected each battlestation to be thrown back on its own resources. As it was, he was giving the defenders of Earth time to reorganize and cripple his fleet.

And which of the admirals, he asked himself, *would rely more in sneak attacks than brute force?*

He turned to Fallon, who watched the display in disbelief. The commander was far too young to have seen service in the Blue Star War, but the scale of the engagement could hardly have come as a shock. After all, before the Federation had won the Inheritance Wars, many young men must've seen battles that had involved thousands of starships on both sides.

"As you will observe, commander," Marius said, "you can see certain patterns appearing in the data." He quirked an eyebrow, inviting Fallon to reply.

"Ah," the commander stammered, "you mean their reluctance to risk serious losses?"

"Precisely," Marius said. He had to smile. An orbital battlestation outgunned a superdreadnaught, but it was hardly as mobile, even with the orbital maneuvering drive units. Dodging incoming enemy fire wasn't an option. "They could have won by now if they'd flown into orbit and engaged us at close range, yet instead they're choosing to bombard us at extreme range. Why, I wonder?"

It wasn't a question, but Fallon tried to answer it anyway. "Because they're short on material?"

Marius shook his head. "They have to know that Home Fleet is around here somewhere, even if they think that Titan Base is still in blissful ignorance of events on Earth. The only way they're going to win against Home Fleet is by taking the high orbitals and forcing the Senate to surrender on pain of bombardment. So why aren't they trying to soak up the damage and punch through?"

He smiled as another enemy superdreadnaught was blown into flaming debris. The victorious starfighters broke off and headed back to the orbital fortresses for rearming before returning to the fray. And there was another interesting question; standard doctrine said that fighter platforms had to be obliterated to force the fighters to fall back, so why weren't the enemy ships trying to take out the fighter bases?

The answer seemed clear.

"They're wondering if they've been tricked," he said finally.

Fallon frowned in incomprehension.

"Think about it," Marius urged him. "Whoever they are, they've launched a series of sneak attacks on Earth that should have crippled our defenses. They came very close to crippling us, in fact, yet we're still fighting. Could it be that whoever is in charge over there is having second thoughts?"

Fallon voiced the obvious objection.

"Sir," he said slowly, "the Senate isn't likely to forgive this attack."

"No," Marius agreed. "But if the enemy thinks they've been tricked, they might be wondering where the Senate actually is, or what is really going on with Home Fleet... and then they might start thinking about contingency plans for what they need to do if they lose this battle."

He sat back in the command chair, thinking hard. The tactical section still hadn't been able to ID the superdreadnaughts, but Marius was mortally certain that he was facing a rogue Federation Navy admiral. And that meant...what? There were a dozen possible candidates for the rogue officer, all of whom were smart enough to know that he or she had crossed the Rubicon. Failure in the environs of Earth would mean certain death once the remainder of the Federation Navy, having mobilized their reserves, came for them. He frowned as another flight of enemy starfighters left their carriers and rocketed down towards the network of orbital battlestations surrounding Earth. The enemy commander had moved from launching a very bold stroke to playing it carefully, but Marius still had no idea who he was facing.

Who among the admirals would be so brazen on the one hand and so overcautious on the other?

Absently, he tapped the command display and checked on Home Fleet. It had been centuries since there had been more than minor piracy in the Sol System, but Home Fleet was responding about as well as could be expected. If Earth held out for another hour, perhaps less, the enemy would find themselves caught between a rock and a very hard place.

"They're retargeting their fire, sir," the tactical officer observed.

"Thank you," Marius said.

He nodded to himself. The enemy force had enough superdreadnaughts to produce mass fire against a number of different targets at once. The real mystery was why they had waited so long to do it. It suggested a certain inclination to conserve force and weaponry. After all, he reasoned, if they were caught by Home Fleet—having used up all their missiles in the Battle of Earth—the result would be disastrous.

For them, Marius thought. For *him*, it would be very satisfactory.

"They're focusing on this station," the tactical officer added unnecessarily.

"Move our automated platforms to provide additional coverage," Marius ordered calmly. A steady voice, he'd been told at the Academy, could prevent a commander's subordinates from panicking. Besides, it wasn't as if there was anywhere to run. They would either stop enough of the missiles to save EDS3, or die once the missiles knocked down the shields and blew through the heavily-armored hull. "Start updating EDS13 with our datanet coordination systems. Prepare them to take over from us if we lose the communications section."

"Aye, sir," the systems operator said.

"Enemy units opening fire," the tactical officer reported. All of the enemy superdreadnaughts were belching missiles, so many that Marius found himself wondering how they intended to control them all. Even a superdreadnaught only mounted so many fire control links, and they were firing more than any standard superdreadnaught could hope to coordinate at once. He understood a moment later when new emissions signatures appeared among the incoming swarm of missiles: gunboats, each one doubtless carrying fire control software, followed the missiles towards their targets.

"Order the CSP to take out the gunboats," Marius ordered, keeping his voice calm. "Redirect everything else to cover both us and the planet."

Inwardly, he was seething. The enemy commander hadn't just targeted his station; instead, the enemy commander ran a very dangerous risk of accidentally bombarding Earth in the process. Even without antimatter warheads, a single missile impacting on the surface at a significant percentage of the speed of light would do colossal damage. And, in a very real sense, the rogue admiral was holding the planet hostage.

Marius knew that taking out the gunboats meant more uncontrolled missiles flying through space, yet there was no other choice. He had to stop this rogue admiral, and stop him right now.

Space became a maelstrom of weapons' fire and destroyed missiles as the incoming attack came within range. All of the surviving battlestations launched counter-missiles, opening fire with massive primary beams, weapons designed to target enemy superdreadnaughts. Smaller point defense weapons were targeted on the missiles that broke through that line of defense, picking off hundreds more missiles before they had any chance of reaching their targets. Rail guns and pulsars added the final line of defense, detonating missiles just before they reached the station. At such ranges, the antimatter warheads were still dangerous, overloading the sensors and blinding the defenders.

And, inevitably, some got through.

"Brace for impact," the tactical officer shouted. His voice was automatically relayed through the entire station. "All hands, brace for impact..."

The entire station shuddered as four missiles slammed into the shields. Compressed antimatter was the most dangerous substance known to man. Huge explosions flared against the shields, burning out several shield generators and allowing the fires to rend the fortress's hull. Marius hung on for dear life as red icons flared on the display, warning of terrible damage. One red icon caught his eye—the containment systems had failed—and by all rights everyone on the station should be dead right now. Marius wasn't sure how they'd survived such a terrible hit, to be honest; if they'd been carrying antimatter warheads, the entire station would have been vaporized when the containment systems failed. Unlike a nuclear warhead, antimatter didn't need a complex triggering mechanism. Simply lowering the containment field sufficed.

"Report," he barked. Apart from the shockwave, there shouldn't be any damage to the station's armoured core. "How badly are we hurt?"

"Major damage to outer sections," the sensor officer reported. Blood streamed from a cut on his forehead. "We've lost most of our weapons, sir, but structural integrity is reasonably stable."

Marius glanced at the report flashing up in front of him and shook his head. "And the enemy?"

"Shifting their fire to EDS6," the tactical officer reported. "They must think we're dead."

"Or not worth bothering about," Marius said. Even if the enemy destroyed the station's weapons, her inner core would survive and would be worth rebuilding, even if they had to reconstruct the remainder of the station later. "Send a general signal to all stations. I want a focus barrage; every station in range is to launch a mass strike against the enemy. We have to show them that we're not dead yet."

He scowled as the system display flickered back into existence. The sensors were faithfully reporting the presence of Home Fleet's drones at the edge of the mass limit; the enemy, of course, would be tracking them already. If they were fooled, they'd either push their advantage against Earth, or break off the engagement. If not... they'd probably break off the engagement. Only a fool would accept battle against a superior force if there was an alternative.

And we have to keep them focused on us, he added, in the privacy of his own thoughts. *If they're focused on us, they're not thinking about other threats.*

"Sir, the enemy ships are adjusting their position," the sensor officer reported. Marius nodded. It was too soon to tell what they were doing, apart from altering their formation, perhaps to provide additional point defense from the undamaged smaller ships. Or perhaps...

"They're breaking off," the tactical officer said in disbelief. Marius ran through the tactical situation in his head and knew the truth. The enemy commander had seen Home Fleet approaching, despite the cloaking devices, and decided to cut and run before he found himself trapped against Earth. "Sir...?"

Fallon turned to look at him. "Admiral Drake, we could launch the starfighters, perhaps give chase..."

Marius considered as Home Fleet decloaked and went to maximum acceleration. The crews would be pushing their ships to the limit, but even so, it wouldn't suffice to catch the retreating enemy ships. The starfighters could slow the enemy ships down, perhaps cripple a few of them, yet even the fighter jocks couldn't maintain such a tempo for long. Besides, unless Home Fleet's carriers got into range, the fighters would wind up operating outside their effective range and end up running out of life support.

But it would drive the enemy away, and give them time. Which wasn't altogether a bad thing... still, he wanted to kill them now, while he still could. Perhaps there was still a way to do that?

"Launch one strike," he ordered. If they were lucky, they'd cripple a ship the Marines could seize, which would at least tell them who to blame. "Order Home Fleet to screen the departing force, but not to attempt to bring them to battle unless the situation changes."

He shook his head, dismissing the unspoken concerns. "Launch SAR gunboats and shuttles—call others from Earth or Luna if necessary—and start picking up stranded pilots," he ordered. "Shift the main defense command function to EDS12, then have the engineering teams start work on the fortress and..."

Marius broke off and laughed at their confused expressions. "All of this is mop-up work," he explained kindly. "Necessary, yes, and we will do it. But we also need to remember that we're alive, we intend to stay that way... and we beat back the enemy."

The crew of EDS3 still looked confused.

"We won," he said. Did they really not understand this? None of them had been tested in combat before, so perhaps they didn't. But they'd performed well, even Fallon, and Drake would say so in his report. "Enjoy it. We soundly kicked their arse!"

Chapter Six

As the old saying goes; Victory has a thousand fathers, but Defeat is an orphan.
-An Irreverent Guide to the Federation, 4000 A.D.

Earth-Luna Sphere, Sol System, 4092

"Now hear this," the intercom blared. "The emergency is now over; I say again, the emergency is now over. Luna Academy will stand down from alert status."

Roman looked up as the airlock clicked open, allowing them to leave the Safe Lock. For the first hour of the emergency—whatever it was—he'd tried to review his class notes, but afterwards he'd just tried to sleep. There came a time, always, when further cramming was not only useless, but actually harmful. The cadets didn't need to memorize information—not with the memory implants provided by Luna Academy—and cramming was a sign of panic.

A message flickered into his implant, and he read it, quickly. All fifth-year cadets were to report at once to the Assembly Hall. The polite wording of the message didn't quite disguise the fact that it was an order in all but name. No cadet with an inch of common sense would disregard the message, or choose to ignore it.

Besides, Roman could count the number of emergency drills—let alone emergencies—that had taken place at Luna Academy on the fingers of one hand. What could they want with him and the other cadets now? Could things have gone so badly that they were needed?

No, that couldn't be it. The proctors probably just wanted to debrief the cadets before they returned to their studies...no, there were no longer *any* studies. Professor Kratman's class had been the last prior to their exams.

He felt a familiar quiver in his chest as he contemplated the coming ordeal. Passing their exams would be difficult enough, but he'd sworn to himself that he would try for a First—a First, a perfect score on the exams and simulations that made up the final tests -- as it would set him on the path for rapid promotion. All Luna Academy graduates were commissioned as lieutenants once they graduated from the Academy, but there was no guarantee the Navy would send them anywhere exciting. A First would give him a certain degree of choice when it came to his initial posting.

Or would they be sent out into service—out to war—without taking the exams? The thought was attractive—and terrifying. What if they were going straight to war?

He was still mulling it over when he walked into the Assembly Hall. Years ago when he'd been a first-year cadet, he had spent hours here learning how to fit into the Navy. And, after he and Raistlin had gone at each other, they had both been disciplined in the Assembly Hall. It was astonishing how much humiliation could be crammed into simply having their misdeeds read in public, before being assigned to scrub toilets with toothbrushes. Now, the only time they saw the Assembly Hall was when they were mustered for inspection or when they listened to a guest lecturer. Some of the talks were interesting, touching on matters that were rarely covered at the Academy, while some were boring and tedious.

As he looked around, he realized that the hall hadn't been so crowded in years. Every fourth- and fifth-year cadet had been summoned. He caught sight of a few of his classmates and headed over to join them.

"Attention on deck!"

Roman stiffened automatically as the proctor called them to attention. A moment later, he caught sight of Commandant Leon Singh as the commander emerged from the side of the room and moved briskly to the stage. He had never seen the Commandant socially—cadets usually only saw the Commandant if they were about to be expelled from the Academy—and there were no shortages of rumors flying around about him, much less the small knife he wore at his belt. Singh apparently had special dispensation to wear the knife and turban along with his small, neatly-trimmed beard. Like most of the staff, Singh's file was closed to the prying eyes of students.

"At ease," the Commandant said flatly. His Federation Standard was neat and precise, but there was a hint of another accent behind his words. "For those of you who haven't figured it out"—his tone made it clear that he hoped that no cadet that stupid had survived the brutal winnowing of the Academy to date—"the Solar System was attacked. As yet, we do not know by whom, or why. We do know that *you*—the fifth-years, at least—will be graduating as soon as possible and will be going to war."

Roman swallowed. Death was a RockRat's constant companion, one that could strike at any moment. The fragile environments RockRats created in asteroids could be destroyed easily, through carelessness, while it was also easy for enemy ships to blow them apart. He'd known from his earliest days that a single mistake could kill him and his family, yet...he'd never truly faced the prospect of his own mortality. Now...he was going to war?

The prospect left him feeling unprepared, unready. It was tempting to believe that the war would be over before the exams were completed—providing they were even going to hold the exams at all, of course—and he officially graduated, but he knew that that was folly. Whatever had attacked the Federation, whoever they were, probably wasn't willing to give up that easily.

Suddenly, his worries over whether he would take a First or not seemed trivial.

"Barring unforeseen circumstances, exams will be held as planned, a week from today," the Commandant continued.

Roman and the other cadets remained silent, but he could tell that a few of them were excited, perhaps hoping they'd not have to sit exams after all. Luna Academy's exams were brutal.

"I suggest that you all familiarize yourself with the rules and regulations for the exams—don't just load them into your implant—and follow them to the letter," Commandant Singh continued. "Ignorance will not be considered an acceptable excuse. Those of you who *do* have acceptable excuses must have them on file for the Academy Committee in three days. I shouldn't have to tell you that failing to register any special excuse on time will result in it being disallowed."

His gaze swept over the assembled cadets. "These exams will determine your future as officers in the Federation Navy. The culmination of five years of work and study is about to begin. Are there any questions?"

A fourth-year Roman barely knew stuck up his hand. "Sir," he said, when the Commandant acknowledged him, "why are we holding the exams at all under these circumstances?"

A low rustle ran around the chamber, but the Commandant seemed unbothered by the question.

"You are too inexperienced to be called up at once, ideally," he said, simply. "Besides, we need to show that this attack will not force us to panic and change our schedules."

Roman wasn't sure he believed the answer, but he held his tongue.

"Good luck," the Commandant said. "You are free to approach your tutors should you require help, but don't waste their time. Dismissed!"

The cadets saluted and headed for the doors. Roman joined them, heading towards Professor Kratman's study. The professor *was* the only person he knew who'd fought a battle and survived. And he might know just what had actually happened during the battle over Earth...

੪୦ଔ

In Admiral Marius Drake's opinion, the Grand Senate Hall was nothing less than a testament to the wealth and power of the Federation. One thousand boxes, each holding a single Senator, were assembled in the massive room, allowing the President to see and recognize anyone who wanted to speak. The boxes were decorated with the red and gold of the Federation's emblem and the flags of the planets they represented, allowing each Senator to be instantly recognizable. The media, which was ensconced today in the Stranger's Gallery, far above the Senators, would be able to record everything. Only Earth and Luna could watch live as the Senators pontificated for the benefit of their voters, but no Senator could resist the thought of such a large audience.

Marius sighed. There was far too much work to be done in orbit, but the Grand Senate had insisted he attend the speech—and assigned him to a seat just underneath the President's box. It was a position of honor, he'd been told, and yet he would have preferred more time to rebuild Earth's tattered defenses. Who knew when the next attack would begin?

He stood as President David Yang entered to the strains of the Federation's anthem. The President, elected by Federation-wide popular vote, had almost no power, but he was the public face of the Federation. Yang—a tall, handsome man with short dark hair and faintly Oriental features—had been elected two years ago, and was midway through his current term. If Yang knew that he was nothing more than a figurehead, it wasn't apparent on his face. But as Marius knew full well, in times of crisis the Head of State had to appear to be in control. The reality of the situation was nowhere near as important, under the circumstances.

"Be seated," the President said, his words echoing around the chamber. The original designers had ensured that everyone could hear everything said inside the chamber. "A grave crisis is upon us."

There was a long pause.

"Less than a day ago, the planet Earth was attacked," Yang informed the Senators. "An atomic weapon was deployed on the surface of Earth, destroying Navy Headquarters and almost decapitating the system defense force. At the same time, a second weapon was used to destroy an orbital fortress, crippling our orbital defenses. After that, an enemy fleet entered the system; not from beyond the Rim, not from an alien species intent on overthrowing our rightful dominance of the galaxy, but from one of our own admirals!"

The crowd remained silent, which was puzzling. Normally, political speeches and press conferences were loud affairs, with questions being shouted from all directions. But now the room was silent.

Then the President leaned forward, his eyes glittering ominously.

"It is my sad duty to report to the Senate—and the Federation at large—that Admiral Justinian has risen in revolt against us," Yang continued. "Worse yet, his ships came within a hair's breadth of occupying Earth!"

This time, there was an outpouring of anger from the Senators and even from the media. Someone in the command room must have neutralized the sound barriers, allowing everyone to be heard. The thunderous response threatened to shake the room to its foundations.

Marius watched as Senators, both Conservative and Socialist, shouted their anger and rage. Admiral Justinian's allies were in grave danger. Glancing around the Senate Hall, he wondered how many of them were in the room, barely aware of the hammer that was about to fall. The smart ones would have boarded their private starships and fled.

But was it really Justinian?

The evidence suggested as much. Home Fleet, as Drake had expected, hadn't been able to run down the remainder of the enemy fleet, but they had scored a bit of success when the starfighters had caught an enemy cruiser by taking out its drive units. The Marines had stormed the ship—a freak hit had taken out the self-destruct—and managed to take some of the crew alive. Their interrogation hadn't been gentle, but it *had* been informative. And it had concluded that Admiral Justinian, Commanding Officer of the Seventh Fleet, was in open rebellion against the Federation.

That wasn't good news.

Admiral Justinian was known for being a careful tactician and strategist—and, of course, he'd had the sense to back off when it was clear he was losing. Marius had never met Justinian in person—their paths had never converged—but Justinian had a sound reputation throughout the Navy. And yet he'd risen up against the Federation, against the Grand Senate and the Federation Navy. Why?

I'll have to find out, Marius thought, darkly. He could imagine several reasons, from outright lust for power to a genuine belief that a military government was the only answer to the Federation's problems. And why were his subordinates following him? What had he promised them? The battle for hearts and minds had only just begun.

"We will not allow this rebellion to go unpunished," the President thundered, once the noise had dimmed to a dull roar. "We will assemble a fleet to hunt down and destroy the treacherous Justinian, along with anyone who knew of his treachery and supported him in it. We will hunt him down like a dog! His allies on Earth, the traitors who aided him to slip his weapons within the walls of our fortress, will be exposed and killed. We will not allow him to scare us into craven surrender."

Marius wondered just what the President was going on about. No one had yet mentioned surrender, or even compromising with Justinian, but Marius saw several problems with hunting Justinian down and destroying him. Considering Justinian had risked the attack on Earth in the first place, Seventh Fleet must be completely under his control, or he would never have dared mount the attack for fear of being knifed in the back. And that meant that the Federation Navy would have to break Seventh Fleet, which would require an enormous commitment of firepower...and they were assuming Justinian and his men were all they had to fight.

After all, who knew how many *other* admirals were thinking about rebellion? Perhaps Justinian had merely been the first to put theory into action.

"And yet, there is one who must be rewarded," the President said. A spotlight shone down from high overhead, drawing attention to Marius. "The man who took command during our gravest hour of need, who ensured the decisive defeat of the treacherous Justinian, must be recognized. For his services, Vice Admiral Drake is promoted to admiral"—there was an outburst of cheers—"and has been awarded the Federation Star. And, after he has been feted as he deserves, he will be a very important part of the mission to destroy Justinian once and for all!"

This time, the cheering went on and on. Marius held himself ramrod straight as the President left his box—as tradition demanded—and pinned the medal on Marius' dress tunic. The Federation Star was the highest award in the Federation Navy, and only the President—advised by the Naval Oversight Committee—could award it to a deserving recipient. The holder of the Federation Star was not only granted an additional pension from the Senate, but he had the right to claim a salute from anyone, regardless of rank, who encountered him while wearing the medal. It almost made up for the contempt he'd endured from the Grand Senate.

And besides, he told himself, with the Federation Star on his breast, who could deny him anything?

৪০৫৪

"And so I made the decision to hold back the remainder of Home Fleet," Drake concluded. Once the President's speech was over, and the Prime Minister, the Leader of the Opposition and the Leader of the Independent Movement had made their speeches, he'd been summoned to a smaller room, where he'd found himself facing the Naval Oversight Committee. The committee had briefly congratulated him on his victory, then demanded an immediate account of the entire battle from start to finish. "In my considered judgement, there was no point in attempting a chase."

"And that is precisely the point we wish to discuss," Senator Alison Wallisch said. Her nasal voice echoed unpleasantly in the smaller chamber. "It seems to us as if you chose to allow the treacherous bastard to escape."

Marius held onto his anger with an effort. If Alison had worked a day in her life—at least outside the political field, where everyone around her told her what she wanted to hear all the time—he would have been astonished. It had grown increasingly clear from both meetings that she didn't understand the realities of naval combat. Bringing the remains of the enemy force to battle would have been impossible, as long as the enemy commander chose to refuse to engage.

"The realities of interplanetary warfare made it impossible to intercept his fleet," he said evenly. There was no point in losing his temper. "Had I ordered Home Fleet to give pursuit, only the smaller units—the starfighters and the cruisers—could have caught up with the enemy."

"And you could have caught them," Senator Hammond pointed out.

"I would not have wished to *catch* them with smaller units, sir," Marius said. "The cruisers are designed for convoy escort duties or fast raids into enemy territory. They are not designed to face superdreadnaughts in open combat. Had I sent them against the superdreadnaughts, they would all have been destroyed, *without* delaying the enemy. The starfighters inflicted some damage, but the enemy force outran Home Fleet's carriers."

"This is not a productive line of questioning," McGillivray said. The Grand Senator winked at Marius before continuing. "The fact of the matter is that Vice Admiral— sorry, *Admiral*—Drake fought a battle for which he was unprepared, and turned a looming disaster into victory—a victory, I might add, that saved all of our lives. Or do you expect that Admiral Justinian would have spared us, once he took the high orbitals and forced Home Fleet to surrender?"

"I quite agree," Brockington said. The Leader of the Conservative Faction leaned forward. "Our current priority is defeating Justinian before his example leads others to rebel. A mighty force must be assembled to crush the viper in his den. Admiral, how do you advise we proceed?"

Marius frowned inwardly. Something was going on, something moving just beyond his awareness. The political waters were murky and there were sharks somewhere within the deeps. He pushed the lingering concern aside and concentrated on answering the question. Besides, under Case Omega, he was the senior surviving officer in the system.

"I have not yet had time to conduct more than a brief examination of the possibilities," he said. *That* was an exaggeration, for there had been no time to conduct *any* planning. He was making it up as he went along. "Admiral Justinian may be safely assumed to have the remainder of Seventh Fleet and the system defense forces in his sector. He may have allies from the other fleets, or links with Outsiders and rebel factions. Therefore, I believe that we should activate the Naval Reserve and use it to reinforce Home Fleet, which will allow us to dispatch a force superior to Seventh

Fleet and occupy his shipyards and industrial nodes. This may bring him to battle, if he is prepared to offer it."

It was basic military strategy, a mixture of generalities and very few specifics. Even so, he knew it should impress them, while the remainder of the planning could be done at Luna HQ. He'd already given orders for the back-up facilities—shut down for funding concerns—to be reactivated and staffed as soon as possible.

He looked up and wanted to scowl, but kept his expression carefully blank. It was obvious that the Senators were exchanging messages through their implants again.

"We thank you for your suggestions," Alison said slowly. "We will put them into effect as soon as possible. There is, however, another pressing concern. You usurped command under Case Omega."

Marius stared at her. That was a problem? "Senator, I..."

"Admiral Cuthbert Parkinson was the superior officer in the Sol System," Alison said with cold dispassion. Marius did a brief search through his implants. Admiral Parkinson's military career had been undistinguished, with nothing to explain his rapid promotion—nothing in the files, at least. And if he had been senior officer after Navy HQ was destroyed, why hadn't he identified himself? "You took his rightful command."

"Admiral Parkinson failed to identify himself to the command network," Marius said as calmly as he could. Reading between the lines, Parkinson's file fairly screamed *political appointee*. "I was unaware that he was alive. Time was short, and I had to take command as no one else appeared to be interested in doing so."

"And we forgive that transgression," Alison said. She smiled sweetly. "However, as senior officer, Admiral Parkinson will command the Retribution Force. You will serve as his subordinate."

"Yes, Senator," Marius said tightly. It took everything he had to keep his voice level. He couldn't resist a sardonic comment. "I understand and I will obey."

Chapter Seven

The fifth-year exams at Luna Academy are the toughest exams in the Federation.
They determine the future of the young officers who survive five years at the Academy.
Naturally, cheating is strongly discouraged and heavily punished on the rare occasions it
is detected. But the Federation Navy, it seems, has a use for a cheat who somehow man-
ages to circumvent the heavy security surrounding the Examination Hall.
-An Irreverent Guide to the Federation, 4000 A.D.

Luna Academy, Sol System, 4092

Roman couldn't help feeling nervous as he stepped into the Examination Hall.
Ten days had passed since the attack on Earth and slowly—very slowly—information had started to spread through the Academy at the speed of rumor. The cadets
knew, now, about Admiral Justinian and looked up his record, along with Admiral
Drake and the others involved in the conflict. And he'd tried to talk with Professor
Kratman, who had curiously been unavailable to him and every other cadet. All
they'd really been told was that they would be told everything about the war after
they completed their exams.

But few of the cadets really believed that would happen.

He sighed. If he could just take these exams and be done with them, maybe he'd
somehow be able to talk with Professor Kratman before he got shipped out. And
that might actually be much more valuable to him than taking these exams ... he
wondered, again, why they were even bothering with the exams?

Didn't the Federation know there was a war on?

The Examination Hall was separated from the remainder of Luna Academy by
nearly a mile of rock. It had been dug out as part of the early excavations that had
eventually become Luna Academy—like most complexes on Luna, the Academy was
mostly underground—and then sealed off by displaced rock. The only link between
the Examination Hall and the remainder of the Academy was a single tunnel, heavily
guarded and secured by the proctors. No one, they'd been warned, would be able
to take anything into the Examination Hall, while the Hall itself was sealed by all
manner of security devices known to man. Even if an enterprising cadet had found
a way to sneak an illicit communications device into the hall, he would have found
it useless. Rumor had it that anyone who *did* manage to cheat successfully would
be rewarded by an instant promotion, but the penalties for trying and failing were
harsh. Few attempted to beat the system.

"Remove all your clothing," the head proctor droned dully. "Understand; your person is your sole responsibility. The merest hint of anything suspicious will result in a
full and comprehensive search. The discovery of any cheating equipment will result
in immediate suspension."

Roman shrugged and started to disrobe, removing his cadet greys, followed by his
regulation-issue underwear. Privacy was never a big concern in a RockRat habitat;

besides, any reluctance he'd had about stripping in front of his classmates had been lost in the first two years at the Academy. No one paid undue attention to their fellows, no matter how attractive, as it was completely unprofessional.

Before he forgot, Roman added his terminal to the pile of clothing, which would be sealed away for later collection by the Academy staff. Of course, he still had his communications implant, but that would be useless inside the Examination Hall. It left him feeling oddly naked; on a RockRat habitat, a terminal meant safety, as it alerted the asteroid's emergency crews if something went badly wrong.

"When you are ready, pass through the security gates," the proctor continued. "Make certain that you have divested yourself of everything. You must not take anything into the Examination Hall."

Roman stood up, placed his small pile of clothing in the nearest locker and started to walk towards the gates. He made a final check of his implant, which had downloaded every file he thought might be relevant, before stepping through the gates. The memory implants could store everything a cadet might need to know, although they'd been warned more than once that having information in an implant wasn't the same as memorizing it, and it wouldn't necessarily help to have a chunk of information if one didn't actually comprehend what it meant. Besides, he had a private suspicion that he'd be tested on what information they chose to bring into the Examination Hall as well as their answers to the test questions.

The gate clicked as he stepped through, revealing nothing but a long, barren corridor. A cool breeze struck him in the face as he reached the proctor at the end of the passage.

"Here," the proctor said in a bored voice, handing him a small bundle of clothing, which would suffice for the Examination Hall. "After you've put this on, go to Room 101."

"Yes, sir," Roman said. "Thank you."

He donned the proffered clothing quickly, wincing at the fit—the pants were too tight and the top was nearly falling off. This must be another test in and of itself, as clothing this obnoxious surely must be yet another obstacle to overcome. Living in space could be uncomfortable at best, downright unpleasant at worst. He knew better than to think he'd get a large set of quarters all to himself for several years.

"Remember," the proctor said. "If you leave the examination room for any reason, you will not be permitted to return."

Roman nodded, wordlessly.

The briefing notes echoed through his head as he walked towards Room 101. The private—and very small—rooms were supposed to keep cadets from cheating, at least as a group. He'd been told that the small room he'd be assigned to would provide him with absolute silence and enough food and water to refresh himself, if necessary. But he still wasn't sure if the exams were strictly necessary. He really didn't know what to expect.

He braced himself as he reached Room 101 and pressed his palm against the scanner. The door clicked open and he stepped inside, taking in the familiar computer terminal—separate from the Academy datanet—and the small food processor in one corner. The room even had a working fresher. He took a deep breath, walked over to the terminal and sat down. The timer on the display counted down the seconds to when the exam would begin. It seemed deliberately designed to torment the eager young cadets.

Roman felt his heart begin to race and concentrated on calming himself, swallowing deeply. Some parts of the exam would be relatively simple—military law hadn't changed since the Inheritance Wars, although the interpretation was often arguable—and other parts would be complex, challenging him to think fast while under pressure, if these were anything like the exams he'd taken in previous years. He checked the timer again and stood up, fetching a glass of water from the food processor and placing it next to the terminal. The timer was nearly at zero.

"Attention," a dispassionate voice boomed. "The exam is about to begin. Take your places and prepare for the first section. Cadets who believe they require assistance are reminded that summoning assistance unnecessarily will count against them."

The terminal flashed once and the exam opened. He checked the first section and confirmed his name, ID code and class, and then opened up the exam proper. It was divided into sections, some with no specified time limit, others with a very limited period before the terminal locked down. There were no second chances with some of the sections, while he could go back to review others until the end of the exam.

Taking a deep breath, he opened the first section and plunged right in.

80C3

"I haven't seen you for a long time," Professor Kratman said. "I understand that you're quite the hero of the hour."

Marius nodded, holding up one hand in salute. Technically, he outranked an Academy Professor, but Kratman had been his commanding officer during the Blue Star War and it was impossible to break the old habit. Besides, he was a guest at Luna Academy; his decision to drop in had been made on the spur of the moment.

"It seems that the Senate doesn't understand that," Marius said. He'd tried to keep the bitterness out of his voice, but he couldn't do it. The Senate had him jumping through all sorts of obnoxious hoops, just because they could, and he'd had to hold his temper again and again and again. Even at nearly ninety years of age, his patience only held so much. "What do you think I did wrong?"

The Professor eyed him in surprise. "Why, nothing, admiral." He laughed wryly. "You need to step outside the Federation Navy every once in a while. This sort of behavior isn't at all surprising from the Senate. You haven't been paying attention to the local media, have you?"

"No," Marius said. In his experience, reporters were idiots, spies, or merely out to make a fast credit without caring about the consequences. He had never forgiven one particular news outlet along the Rim for reporting details about captured pirates that had made it impossible to bring them to trial. "Why should I care what they have to say?"

Kratman fixed him with an unrelenting stare. "You should know that war is birthed in politics," he said sharply. "Especially *this* war. Why don't you access the daily brief and check?"

Marius hesitated, and then complied, accessing his implant and using it to pull the latest round-up of news from Earth. There was, as always, a deluge of largely useless information, mainly revolving around what the most famous people in High Society were doing—or who they were screwing. He pushed that aside and concentrated on military news, searching for his name. There were over seven *thousand* hits in the previous twenty-four hours alone. It seemed as if the entire planet was talking about him.

The stories were nearly universally praiseworthy; they discussed his quick thinking, and his actions during the Battle of Earth. There were interviews with survivors of the battle, all of whom credited him with saving Earth, and live footage from the battle itself. The entire planet had seen a fortress explode in orbit and had known, for the first time in centuries, real physical danger. And he was the man who'd saved them.

"You're famous," Kratman said mildly. "Why do you think the Senate took fright?"

"I don't understand," Marius admitted. "Why did they take fright?"

"The Core Worlds are the only ones where public opinion must be taken seriously," Kratman reminded him gently. "Earth's population can make or break Senators—and don't they just know it! Why do you think they've never risked cutting the dole money handed out to the permanently unemployed, or the free food handed out to the starving, or the free access to the datanet and other public services? Earth's massive population of teeming sheep would *never* allow it. How many Senators would lose their seats, no matter how hard they tried to rig the elections?" He grinned.

"And you saved the entire planetary population," he added. "Now, you're their hero, the man who can do no wrong."

"Right," Marius said. He checked his appointments calendar with a frown. There had been literally thousands of requests for interviews, all of which had been refused by his staff. He'd simply never checked up on it before. "Why does that scare the Senate?"

"Think about it," the Professor said. "The Federation was designed to do the impossible—to provide interstellar government for the thousands of planets settled by humanity. The founding worlds were reluctant to create an overbearing political entity, so they attempted to hamstring the Federation by limiting the scope of its powers. But, as such entities tend to do, the Federation grew more powerful anyway, while the politicians became one great inbred family. The Inheritance Wars only enhanced that trend because the Federation won, and there seemed to be no reason to question the political situation."

"'If it ain't broke, don't fix it,'" Marius quoted.

"Precisely," Kratman agreed. He adopted a lecturing tone. "The problem is—and this affects all governing systems—that as the government grows more powerful, it tends to form an elite—a group of people whose sole concern is remaining in power.

Some of the elite genuinely believe in serving the population and work for their betterment, others are in it only for their own power, but all of them work to perpetrate the system. Each of the Senators, Marius, represents over a thousand worlds. If they want to get elected, they have to be part of the elite or be willing to join it. The ones who refuse to join rarely get elected.

"And the elites," Kratman continued pedantically, "because their hold on power is secure, end up becoming increasingly disconnected from the realities of life. They don't understand the basic laws of the universe, let alone the effect they have on others. They don't care that the out-worlds curse them as rapists who strip their worlds of natural resources and grind them under with oppressive taxes—after all, they're the *elite*. Why should they care?"

Marius sighed, seeing the truth of what the Professor was saying. But before he could get a word in edgewise, Kratman had gone on.

"While there were three factions in government, the whole structure held together remarkably well—astonishingly well," Kratman lectured. "But then the Blue Star War was launched, and the early offenses turned into stunning defeats. The Imperialist Faction lost power and collapsed into the morass of the elites. And yet the shock of that was mitigated, because the Imperialists were still part of the elite. The elite couldn't afford too much public humiliation because it would undermine their ability to remain in control."

Marius nodded.

"You know the problems with maintaining something the size of the Federation," the Professor added. "The Federation has to give vast latitude to its officers, or else they wouldn't be able to react in time to stop a small threat from turning into a large one. And yet, some of those officers see the inner corruption of the Federation and start considering declaring independence, or even attempting to make themselves Emperor. I'm honestly surprised that it's taken this long for one of the admirals to try to strike for the purple."

Marius winced. Admiral Justinian had wisely transferred most of his family to Harmony before he'd attempted to overthrow the Federation, but some of them—second- and third-cousins, mostly—had remained on Earth. The Senate had ordered them arrested, tried and sentenced to death, along with a handful of captured traitors who had aided Justinian in crippling Earth's defenses. Marius had forced himself to watch the executions—they had been broadcast live as a warning to any other would-be traitors—and then he had gone to the head and been savagely sick. He'd seen death before, as he'd ordered pirates thrown out of the airlock into the cold unforgiving vacuum of space, but the executions had been different. They had been nothing more than blood sport, or worse, the Senate lashing out at whoever was unlucky enough to catch its attention. Most of those second- and third-cousins hadn't even seen Admiral Justinian in years, and obviously had had no idea what Justinian was planning, but that hadn't saved their lives.

And when innocence was no defense, what good was the Federation for?

"And then, you saved their lives," Kratman said, breaking into Marius's train of thought.

Marius snorted. "Shouldn't they be happy with me?"

"Yes, of course, but much of the Senate has no grip on reality. You saved their lives, yes, but to most of them, it doesn't matter because you made yourself popular with the mob. Of *course* they're scared of you. They have to use you, but at the same time, they have to worry about what you might do..."

"I'm not about to make myself emperor," Marius protested.

"You're not one of the elite," Kratman countered. "That fact alone means they're probably going to be divided about what to do with you. They may attempt to marry you into the elite—there are quite a few eligible senatorial daughters on Earth—or they may set you up to fail. Your popularity with the mob makes the latter course dangerous, but given time...the mob will lose interest in you. And then you'd better watch your back."

Marius took a breath. The years fell away and he remembered the *Matterhorn*, the day they'd jumped through the Asimov Point and into Sapphire. He remembered how they'd been caught in an ambush at point-blank range, and how the super-dreadnaught had been crippled within the first few seconds of the ambush. And he remembered how then-Captain Kratman had somehow steered them back to the Asimov Point...they'd escaped the hellish slaughter, the *only* starship from the assault force to escape. They'd survived by sheer luck, and the determination of the starship's captain.

"You may wish to ask yourself another question," Kratman said. If he was aware of his former subordinate's thoughts, he gave no sign. "Who has promoted you to the media?"

"I don't know," Marius admitted. Earth's media was nominally free of control, but he knew that the Senate controlled many of the foremost media corporations. "Who...?"

"Good question," Kratman agreed. "I haven't the slightest idea. Someone seems to like you. Whoever it is, it's someone with very good connections in the Federation Navy. You may want to think about what you'll say when they come to you and ask for something in return."

"I didn't want to be a hero," Marius protested. "I just did what needed to be done."

"I know that, son," Kratman said with uncommon gentleness. "But most of the people on Earth don't know you as I do. They have to see it differently...and with all those piranhas among the Senators, you have to know that no one, not even the friendliest Senator, does anything for free."

Marius ruminated on this for a minute. "Thanks for talking with me. I'll keep all this in mind, I promise."

"Just watch your back, all right?" Kratman pleaded. "I've seen far too many of my old officers and men taken out by Justinian—and his allies—as it is."

80 03

Tired and emotionally drained, Roman Garibaldi staggered out of the Examination Hall hours after he'd entered. It felt as if he'd been in the room for years, as if his personal universe had shrunk down to the examination room and the terminal he'd used to answer the questions. All hope of a First had faded, to be replaced by the desperate hope that he might just have scraped a Third. A Fourth or below usually meant repeating the fifth-year at the Academy, though Roman wasn't sure if that still applied in wartime. He returned to his room, collapsed into bed and fell asleep.

Hours later, he awoke, ordered a small meal from the food processor, and then fell back asleep after eating it. He felt at loose ends; now that the exams had been completed, he had to wait until the proctors had completed reviewing their answers. All that mattered was passing the exams.

He tried to keep the thoughts of war from his mind, but he just couldn't. Would doing worse on his exams mean he'd be sent immediately to the front? Or would he be kept back as an incompetent?

The following morning, he was awakened at the usual time and ordered to report to the Assembly Hall. He wasn't the only one, as he noticed almost all of his fifth-year class had been summoned.

As he and the others poured into the compartment, he saw holographic test results hovering in front of his eyes. There were no Fourth or Fifth results, he noted at once; the unlucky cadets would probably be spared public humiliation. He scanned the Thirds and saw a couple of familiar names, but his was missing.

Bracing himself, he scanned the Seconds, yet his own name wasn't present. Thank goodness!

Taking a deep breath, he looked at the Firsts and saw, clearly, ROMAN GARIBALDI. He'd done it!

Friends shook his hand or hugged him, eager to share their congratulations, or demanding to know where he was going. He accessed his implants and searched for his orders. They were waiting for him in the network.

"*Enterprise*," he said in delight. The Federation Navy's latest flagship had been his first choice, although he'd known that even with a First, the odds weren't high. "I'm going to the *Enterprise!*"

"Congratulations," Cadet Sultana Narayanan said. Her accented voice was amused. "So am I."

Roman grabbed her and pulled her into a hug. At least he wouldn't be completely friendless when he arrived. Between them, he was sure they could learn the carrier's ways and fit right in. He barely heard the speech from the proctors, warning the non-First cadets that their orders were still being cut and that they'd be informed as soon as possible. He was going to the *Enterprise!*

"Come on," Raistlin said. All differences between them had faded, for Raistlin had made a First, too. "Let's party!"

Chapter Eight

The Federation Navy's standard doctrine for building and deploying carriers was developed during the First Interstellar War and refined over the following centuries. It should therefore be asked, loudly, why that doctrine was ignored when it came to building the Star Carrier designs.
-An Irreverent Guide to the Federation, 4000 A.D.

FNS *Enterprise,* Sol System, 4092

"We're coming up on her now," the pilot said in a bored tone, sounding as if he'd flown the mission hundreds of times before. "You may wish to come forward and watch as we approach."

Roman wondered how the pilot could be bored—wasn't the *Enterprise* the most famous ship in the Navy?—but accepted his invitation with alacrity, even though it was against regulations. There should have been a second pilot in the cockpit, but all kinds of safety rules were being violated in the desperate struggle to prepare the Retribution Force for its mission. He settled into the spare seat and watched as the carrier slowly came into view. He'd seen images, of course, long before the war when he'd prepared his request for assignment, but the image didn't even come close to the reality. A civilian might have regarded the huge carrier as ugly, yet Roman saw the *Enterprise* as beautiful, form melded with function in a way he found nearly impossible to describe.

Seen from their approach position, the carrier looked like a flattened cylinder, surrounded by launch and recovery tubes for her ten wings of starfighters. A pair of starfighters swooped down towards the shuttle, passing close enough for him to track them, before wagging their wings and flashing off into the great darkness. If the shuttle's IFF codes hadn't checked out, Roman was certain their welcome would be a great deal less friendly. The entire Solar System was still jumpy after the Battle of Earth.

The shuttle altered course, heading towards one of the rear landing decks; Roman gasped as he took in the mammoth drive units at the rear of the ship. Each of the drives—there were no less than *eight* placed around the massive cylinder—could provide a realspace velocity of 0.8C, even if the other drive units had been disabled. No other starship in the Federation Navy, even a superdreadnaught, could soak up so much damage and keep going. As the shuttle swept towards the landing deck, he saw the point defense blisters and missile tubes that gave the carrier her offensive and defensive punch. If necessary, *Enterprise* could go toe-to-toe with a superdreadnaught.

There had always been an *Enterprise* in the Federation Navy, even before there had been a Federation Navy. USS *Enterprise* had served as the flagship of the multinational task force that had stopped the Snakes at the Battle of Century, back during the First Interstellar War. She'd been lost the following year at the Second Battle of Ramadan, but by then she'd created a legend. FNS *Enterprise,* the first starship built specifically for the Federation Navy, had led the fleet that liberated Zion and gone on to serve in all of the remaining battles of the First Interstellar War. Since then, the name had been passed down the ages, even during the Inheritance Wars. The war that had threatened to tear the Federation asunder had seen the odd spectacle of ships called *Enterprise* fighting on both sides of the war. And there were those who believed that the First Battle of Sapphire would have gone the other way if the *last* carrier to bear the name had taken part in the fighting.

The shuttle passed through the force field around the carrier and set down on the landing deck. Roman didn't have to be told to grab his holdall; he did so and headed over to the hatch, ready to disembark just as soon as it hissed open. The carrier's internal atmosphere struck him the moment he stepped out of the shuttle with Sultana Narayanan hot on his heels. The *Enterprise* was clearly a ship that was frantically preparing for war. A handful of shuttles were scattered on the deck, while a pair of starfighters were being disassembled by the landing deck crew.

He felt the thrumming of the carrier's drives echoing through the deck as he hastened to the secondary hatch. They'd been warned not to remain on the landing deck for any longer than strictly necessary, and with all the activity he'd seen thus far, he could easily see why.

Once the airlock cycled, he saw an older woman wearing a commander's uniform waiting for him. His implant had been loaded with a complete crew manifest for *Enterprise*, but he would have recognized Commander Rosemary Duggan without it. She was a tall woman with short, dark hair and a grim, bulldog expression. She wore her uniform as if it were a weapon with which to beat her foes to death whenever her captain might command. As the XO of the *Enterprise*, she was God, as far as her subordinates were concerned.

"Lieutenant Garibaldi reporting for duty, commander," Roman said. Sultana echoed him a moment later. "Permission to come aboard?"

"Permission granted," Commander Duggan said. She had a sharp voice, biting off her words as if each cost her a credit. "Welcome aboard."

Roman saluted the flag, then the starship's crest of arms and finally the commander herself. Commander Duggan returned the salute slowly—he just knew that her eyes were crawling over them, looking for some flaw in their bearing—before nodding. He had the impression that they'd just passed a test of some kind.

"You both earned Firsts at the Academy, so I assume that you have the ability to follow orders," she said. "I want you to understand something. You do not have the experience that comes with your ranks, not yet. We will be working on giving you that experience as rapidly as possible, both in manning your stations and in working with the enlisted crew. You will be at the bottom of the totem pole until you convince me that you can handle the responsibility. Do you understand me?"

"Yes, commander," they said together.

"Good," Commander Duggan said. "*Enterprise* is the finest ship in Home Fleet, but we're being detached for the Retribution Force. That means I am going to work you to death over the next few weeks. We've had to assign half our enlisted men to other ships to make up for shortfalls in personnel, so we're drawing on newcomers from the Naval Reserve. The captain"—her tone sharpened—"understands that mistakes will happen in such an environment. But our tolerance of mistakes will fall sharply as we shake down and prepare for operations. By the time we depart the Solar System, we will have a working ship. And I will not hesitate to put you off the ship if you fail to measure up."

She smiled, a most unpleasant expression. "Do either of you want to leave the ship now and save me the trouble of filling out the paperwork to have you reassigned?"

"No, commander," Roman said.

"Oh, what a pity," Duggan said as soon as Sultana had echoed him. Her voice hardened. "Put your holdalls in your cabin, then report to me in Compartment 667-565 in ten minutes. Consider finding it your first test. Try not to be late." She turned and marched down the corridor, leaving them alone again.

Roman and Sultana exchanged a glance, and then both of them started trying to find Officer Country. It would have taken hours if he'd had to search, but a simple query from his implant to the ship's computer provided helpful directions.

Once they got there, Roman found out that despite the starship's colossal size, the cabin was small, barely large enough for both of them. It contained a small fresher and an even smaller food processor. He'd expected as much, though. Junior officers weren't given large cabins until they were promoted several grades...he shook his head. This wasn't how he'd expected to spend his first day on the *Enterprise*.

"So," he said, once he had carefully stowed his holdall under the bunk, "where should we find her?"

A quick check revealed that the compartment number Commander Duggan had given them was useless. It didn't match any real compartment number in the entire ship. Roman stared at it, feeling panic start to bubble up within his mind. How could he hope to rise to high rank if he couldn't solve a simple puzzle? It seemed impossible to link the number she'd given them to anywhere on the ship...

It was Sultana who figured out the answer. "Computer," she ordered, "locate Commander Duggan."

Roman had to laugh as the ship's computers helpfully provided the answer. Commander Duggan was waiting for them somewhere within the ship's interior. They followed the directions through a maze of passages and internal tubes—passing hundreds of workers from the nearby Baxter Shipyard—and finally reached a compartment deep within the starship's innards. Duggan looked up at them as they crawled out of the tube and smiled.

"You took your own, sweet time," she said. "How long did it take you to realize that the reference was bunk?"

"When we compared it to the ship's plans," Roman admitted. "The numbering system was completely different."

"A word to the wise," Duggan said. "The ship's *official* plans and the reality are somewhat different. The interior of the ship isn't detailed on any database outside the ship and Navy HQ. Why do you think that is, I wonder?"

Sultana crinkled her forehead, perhaps guessing. "To prevent spies from learning how to navigate through the ship?"

"Nothing so elaborate," Rosemary said. She looked totally at ease as she spoke, even though the noise of the drives was growing louder. "When they were building the ship, they discovered that some of the planned design was...imperfect. *Enterprise* was the first of her class, and there are always teething problems. In the end, they redesigned the affected sections and altered the interior to allow them to complete the ship."

She paused. "It may interest you to know that the original design, if it had been built as ordered, would have suffered a catastrophic internal failure if they had ever brought the drives up to full power. Many of the bulkheads would have collapsed."

Thank goodness for engineers, Roman thought. He leaned forward. "Commander ... why didn't they fix the problems right away?"

"*Enterprise* was the largest ship in the Federation Navy when she was built," Duggan said, sounding as if she was picking her words with great care. "Computer simulations only go so far when so many delicate compartments are involved. See what I mean about the importance of experience? An experienced engineer discovered the problem and reported it before they actually tried to install the internal systems. Now..."

Her expression turned savage, just for a second. "I have tasks for you," she said, her implant dumping files into their implants. "All you have to do is follow the instructions—*separately*—and then report back to me. Good luck."

Roman watched as Duggan scrambled up a ladder to an internal tube and wiggled through it, then he turned to look at Sultana, who looked as stunned as he felt. He opened the files Commander Duggan had sent to him and frowned. None of the tasks seemed complicated, which meant there was probably a sting in the tail for the unwary and inexperienced young officer. Some of the tasks promised to be boring—he had to check the filed FNRS-47 plans against the reality—and others made no sense at all, at least at first.

"I'll catch up with you later," he promised. "Good luck."

"You too," Sultana said.

Roman turned back to the internal tube. According to the plans loaded in his implant—the same plans he'd been warned couldn't be trusted—the first place he had to check was only two decks down from his current position.

Over the course of an hour, he realized what the commander was trying to teach him. He didn't know his way around the ship, not instinctively, and relying on his implants was asking for trouble. He got lost twice before he stopped listening to his implant and started to go by the markings on the bulkheads. Slowly, he realized just how the carrier's open areas went together. It wouldn't be long, he hoped, before he figured out the logic of the internal tubes as well.

The FNRS-47 files were particularly confusing. At the Academy, he'd been told that keeping up with the FNRS-47 files was important. Regulations clearly stated that there had to be an individual FNRS-47 form for each replaced component on the ship that accounted for its removal from stores, installation in the required unit and then removal and disposal once it had started to wear out. The Federation Navy designed components to be as durable as possible, but there was a strict pattern of replacement for every compartment in the starship, to the point where cadets had joked that ships were effectively rebuilt over the course of the year.

But in this case, it hadn't taken him long to realize that *Enterprise's* files were hopelessly out of date. Puzzled, he made a note of the discrepancies and went on to the next section.

The commander had ordered him to introduce himself to the fighter jocks, so he found his way down to Fighter Country and checked in with the CAG, the Controller Air Group. The CAG seemed underwhelmed to meet him, and only reluctantly organized a meet and greet. Roman was reminded, yet again, of his own inexperience. Many of the fighter pilots he met had fought in the Battle of Earth, and had been transferred to *Enterprise* only two or three days ago. The others had seen action out on the frontier. He could just tell, somehow, that they weren't too impressed with him. The Marines weren't much better, even though they seemed a hair friendlier.

"I trust we'll be seeing more of you," Major Shaklee said with a grin. The short, stocky Marine winked at him. "Young officers are encouraged to spend time in the gym, brushing up on their training with us. I'm sure you'll enjoy your time down there."

Roman felt like frowning, but he hoped the Marine hadn't realized it. RockRats kept themselves healthy, but they didn't go in for physical sports and rarely contributed athletes to the Federation Games. Luna Academy had insisted that all cadets learn to spar and encouraged them to develop skills in the martial arts, yet he'd never had the time to really work on it. The Marines, on the other hand, would ensure that he did more than the regulation workouts each day. And *encouraged* generally meant *ordered*.

He was thoughtful when he reported back to Officer Country and discovered that Sultana had completed her share of the tasks before him. It shouldn't have been a surprise—she had always had more patience for detail work than him—but it still rankled, somehow. It *was* surprising when Commander Duggan cut off their attempt to report to her and focused, instead, on something different.

"You did all the tasks," she said flatly. "Why did I give you those specific tasks?"

"You wanted us to get used to the ship," Sultana hazarded.

"Could be," Commander Duggan said absently. "What do you think, Lieutenant Garibaldi?"

Roman hesitated, and then took the plunge. "You wanted us to know the ship and its personnel," he said finally. "I don't just mean finding our way around, I meant actually knowing them..."

"Close enough," Commander Duggan agreed. "You have to learn to understand that the crew—all the separate crews that make up a carrier's personnel—are human. There are young officers who fail to realize that enlisted personnel are mortal, too." She shook her head. "You are expected to spend some of your off-duty hours—which will be few and far between for the first few weeks—socializing with your fellow officers. Marine and Navy alike."

She grinned, a completely different expression than her smile from before as it completely lit up her face. "And as for the forms?"

"There isn't time to fill them in," Sultana told the commander.

Roman lifted an eyebrow.

"I checked with the engineering officers," she told him. "They don't have time to do all the paperwork."

"And that is the second lesson," Commander Duggan added. "There are tasks on this ship that are genuinely important, and tasks that regulations *claim* are important. When we're in the middle of a desperate refit and working up period, we don't have time to worry about the paperwork, not with the level of redundancy built into the ship. We will catch up on all of that while we're in transit, by which time we should be functioning as an intact unit."

Her gaze softened. "You'll meet your fellow lieutenants in the Officer's Mess in"— she made a show of checking her wristcom—"forty minutes. I suggest that you each have a quick session in the fresher, and then study their files. After that, we can make some proper assignments for you. You'll both eventually end up in the tactical section—you're command track—but for the moment we need you elsewhere."

Roman nodded. "Commander, if I may ask, where are we going?"

"Nothing has been said officially," Commander Duggan said, "but I suspect from the scuttlebutt flying around the fleet that we're on our way to Harmony to make Admiral Justinian see reason. I just hope we get worked up by the time the hammer comes down on him. I'd hate to miss the show because we couldn't get there in time. And believe me, the captain will *really* hate it."

"Yes, commander," Roman said. It would be nice to believe that Admiral Justinian would surrender without further ado, but he'd seen the executions at the Academy of Justinian's distant relatives. They'd all been made to watch. Somehow, after seeing that, Roman was sure the admiral would refuse to surrender. "We won't let you down."

"See that you don't," Commander Duggan said. "*Enterprise* is the finest ship in the fleet, and we mean to keep it that way."

Chapter Nine

The problem with not having fought a major war for decades is that it is difficult to tell an experienced commanding officer from an inexperienced officer. The Federation Navy has thus developed an alarming habit of promoting officers for political rather than professional credentials.
-An Irreverent Guide to the Federation, 4000 A.D.

FNS *Enterprise*, Sol System, 4092

"Attention on deck!"

Marius stood with the other officers as Fleet Admiral Cuthbert Parkinson entered the *Enterprise's* briefing room. There had been no other choice for the flagship, not after *Enterprise* had been assigned to the Retribution Force, which worried Marius more than he cared to admit. The star carriers were, in some ways, a revolutionary design, but they had their weaknesses, weaknesses that would be as apparent to Admiral Justinian as they were to Marius Drake.

"Please be seated," Parkinson said once he had taken his place at the head of the table. "We have a great deal to cover, and very little time."

Fleet Admiral Parkinson was taller than Marius had expected from his file, although it was quite possible that he'd had his body altered to conform with the latest fashion. His short, dark hair topped a clear face and dark brown eyes, which contrasted oddly with the white dress uniform he wore. Marius hoped that he'd come directly from Earth and hadn't had time to change. An admiral who attended a meeting of his subordinates in full dress uniform wasn't a good sign.

Marius had asked Kratman about the Fleet Admiral, as his former CO had known Parkinson once. The Professor had told him that Parkinson was competent, nothing more. Parkinson could follow orders to the letter, but he didn't have the initiative to take advantage of opportunities as they arose. His career would have stalled out, barring political interference of course, if there had been any justice in the universe.

Marius had spent ten years along the Rim and had been insulated, to some degree, from the political storms of Earth. But because of what Kratman had told him, Marius had taken the time to carry out a thorough study of Earth's media while waiting for his new commander to take command of the Retribution Force. There seemed to be three separate story lines running through the media. One: Admiral Drake was the hero who saved Earth. Two: Admiral Drake had taken command illegally, preventing Admiral Parkinson from assuming his rightful place. Three: Admiral Drake's illegal decision to assume command had resulted in Admiral Justinian's force escaping certain destruction. The reports that upheld the third line had produced hundreds of pretty diagrams that bore no relationship to reality; all professed to prove that Justinian's fleet could have been intercepted and destroyed, if the *proper* man had been in command.

It wouldn't have impressed any halfway competent fleet officer, Marius knew. But civilians wouldn't know what to believe.

Kratman had been right. Again. Marius tried not to grind his teeth in despair.

Behind Parkinson, Captain Timothy Oriole followed him into the briefing room, even though *Enterprise* was his ship. At least Oriole was a known factor, a solidly competent man with a splendid record of courage and loyalty. The Federation Navy would hardly have given its flagship to an incompetent, even though Oriole had probably been bored floating in orbit around Titan Base. His dark skin showed no trace of awareness that he was the junior officer in the compartment, although as the admiral's flag captain—his tactical alter ego—he had more authority than was commonly realized. And besides, he had given up command of a cruiser squadron to command the *Enterprise*. There could be no questioning his capabilities, *or* his political contacts. He had the support of some very powerful people.

"It's good to see you all together for the first time," Parkinson said. His voice—and face—was stilted and formal. "I believe that we have set records in reactivating starships and personnel from the Naval Reserve in preparation for our departure to Harmony. I know that there have been some …issues—" he gave them all a droll smile, apparently begging for forgiveness, "—but we have managed to overcome them. We shall depart for Harmony within the week."

Marius kept his face expressionless with some help from his implants. Parkinson was understating the case, for the plans to reactivate and crew the starships stored in the Naval Reserve had floundered, and badly. Home Fleet had a shortage of experienced officers and men to serve as reactivation cadre, and they'd had to raid every command within ten Asimov Points of Earth for manpower. There were hundreds of thousands of crewmen who had never served together before being called to serve in the Retribution Fleet, and there had already been several nasty incidents. Marius was confident that all would all be resolved in time, but it would require a far longer outfitting and working up period than his superiors had accepted. As it was, they were going to have to continue their training exercises while in transit.

"I have been in close communication with the War Cabinet," Parkinson continued, "and we finally have our mission objectives. They are fairly simple in concept, and I am sure that we will have few problems carrying them out."

Marius's eyes narrowed. He'd thought that they already *had* their mission objectives: track down and destroy Admiral Justinian. He shared a glance with Major General Tobias Vaughn—at least the War Cabinet had confirmed him as the Marine CO for the Retribution Force—and realized that his friend was just as surprised. It wouldn't be the first time that orders had been changed alarmingly close to the departure date, yet it still was odd. The entire planet wanted the rogue's blood.

"First, we are to track down and capture—or kill—the treacherous Justinian," Parkinson said. "Second, we are to secure a number of vital points within the Harmony Sector and prepare to return Federation authority to the region. Third, we are to oversee a purge of Justinian's supporters and ensure that nothing like this can happen again. These matters will be overseen by the Pacification Units that have been attached to the Fleet Train, once Admiral Justinian's fleet has been forced to surrender or has been destroyed outright."

This time, Marius could tell that the more experienced officers in the room didn't like these orders by the set of their shoulders. Pacification Units had only one mission. They crushed all resistance to the Federation's will, regardless of who was doing the resisting, or why. Pacification Units had ground any spark of independence out of a hundred alien races and worse, had crushed human rebellion on a dozen worlds. Their deployment was a sign that the Senate wasn't interested in taking any prisoners. He shared another glance with Vaughn, sharing a single thought. The last time they'd encountered Pacification Units, it had been when their CO had vastly exceeded his orders and ended a rebellion by mass slaughter. It said something about the general attitude towards aliens that his actions had earned him a medal and a promotion, rather than a quick court martial and an even quicker firing squad.

"In order to accomplish our objectives, I have determined the most suitable route for us to take to reach Harmony," Parkinson continued.

He keyed a switch and a holographic star chart appeared over the table. Asimov Points were linked with beams of white light, showing the places where starships could hop from system to system instantaneously, while suspected enemy positions were marked in red. The information, Marius reminded himself, was over five months out of date.

"We will proceed from Earth through the Gateway and then up the Graveyard Chain," Parkinson droned on. "We'll hop across to Sparta from Violet Passion, and then proceed through the Archer's Chain until we reach Jefferson. We will secure the system, then proceed through the Harmony Asimov Point and secure Harmony. If Admiral Justinian wants to fight us, he will no doubt meet us there."

Marius kept his face inscrutable, but inwardly he was nodding in understanding. The Senate was clearly dictating instructions to their chosen commander, without regard for military logic. The proposed route took over a month longer than the least-time route to Harmony, but it had the advantage that valuable systems could be secured easily. The Jefferson System, in particular, was coveted by many interstellar corporations. The orders to "secure" the system could easily be turned into "occupy."

"Admiral," Captain Sanderson said, "it is well known that the Jefferson System is effectively impossible to defend. Why do you want us to attempt to secure it?"

"Those are our orders from the Senate," Parkinson said. His gaze swept the room. "I have been told—in strictest confidence—that Harmony will be stripped of its position as sector capital, and Jefferson will be promoted to take its place. Our orders are to ensure security on the ground so that the move can be accomplished with the minimum of fuss."

There was a long pause. Marius said nothing, considering his options.

"I do not expect anyone to attempt to resist us until we reach the Harmony System," Parkinson went on. "Therefore, I will be dividing the fleet into three components: the vanguard, the main body and the rearguard. The vanguard, under my command in *Enterprise*, will proceed ahead of the main body and show the flag to anyone even considering resistance. We will show them that we are not afraid to operate in their space, and that they can do nothing to stop us."

Marius frowned. The Fleet Admiral was not supposed to risk himself that way.

"The main body, under Admiral Drake, will serve as the muscle," Parkinson continued. "In the event they attempt to offer resistance prior to entering the Harmony System, we will reunite the vanguard and the main body and accept battle. Finally, the Fleet Train and a handful of cruiser squadrons will make up the rearguard, escorting our supplies and army divisions for operations against planetary targets. Are there any questions?"

There was a long uneasy pause. Marius finally decided to raise his concerns.

"Admiral," he said carefully, "I feel that splitting up the fleet risks having one of our sections defeated in detail and destroyed. I do not feel that Admiral Justinian will be standing on the defensive, not after some of his family and supporters were publicly executed. The Book gives him precisely no chance against our sheer weight of firepower, which means that he will be driven to be unconventional. We might jump into the next system to discover that we have flown right into a trap.

"Furthermore," he continued, before Parkinson could say a word, "the course you have suggested has a number of disadvantages. The enemy will be able to operate with the advantage of internal lines of communication and rotate forces to meet us at will, either outside Jefferson or within the Jefferson System proper. We are short on supplies and..."

"We will be drawing supplies from the fleet supply depots as we pass," Parkinson said sharply. "They are still in our hands."

"With all due respect," Marius said, "how do we *know* that they are still in our hands?"

He kept his expression blank, even though some of the junior officers now looked uneasy. There was—inevitably—a major time lag between sending a message from Earth and receiving it at the other side of the Federation, let alone receiving a reply. Even using the Asimov Point network and StarCom units—where they were emplaced—didn't allow a message to reach the Rim in less than six months. By now, Admiral Justinian's forces could have taken the two sectors closest to Harmony, and the Retribution Force wouldn't know a thing about it until they blundered into an ambush.

"They have confirmed that they are still loyal," Parkinson said shortly. He turned back to the star chart. "Addressing the issue of local governments, we will remove them..."

೪ಅಣ

"Perhaps you could spare me a few minutes," one of the younger officers said as the meeting broke up. "I believe that we need to talk."

Marius stared down at her in surprise. She wore the uniform of a Commodore, yet her white non-dress uniform showed no golden stars representing ships under her command. He hadn't paid attention to her at the meeting, but he studied her now, uneasily aware that she was studying him in return. She was short, with light brown skin and long dark hair that hung in a ponytail. A single red dot on her forehead marked her as coming from one of the orthodox Hindu worlds, even though the Federation Navy frowned upon displays of religious enthusiasm. He couldn't help but notice that she was remarkably pretty.

"Commodore Arunika," she said, as she held out a dark hand for him to shake. "Office of Naval Intelligence."

Marius nodded, bending over to kiss the air above her hand. The silver ring she wore on her finger caught his eye and he stared at it. He'd never seen one before, but there was no mistaking the silver band with the Star of David ingrained in the metal. Arunika led him through a pair of compartments and into a more private briefing room. He didn't protest at how she'd taken charge. The silver ring marked her as a member of the Brotherhood.

"You raised some important concerns, admiral," Arunika said as soon as the airlock had hissed closed and she'd carried out a brief check for bugs. "ONI has been crunching the numbers ever since we identified the person behind the attack on Earth. I'm afraid that our conclusions have been...ignored."

Marius's eyes narrowed. The Office of Naval Intelligence had been heavily politicized in the years before the Blue Star War. Eventually, they'd overstepped themselves and provided inaccurate and incomplete data to the Senate, data that the Imperialist Faction had used to argue its case for war. After the first defeats, the Senate had been looking for scapegoats, and ONI had found itself purged. The officers who had doctored the data—or simply refused to read what was clearly there—had been dismissed from the service, and ONI had been stripped of most of its responsibilities. Federation Intelligence, the civilian intelligence-gathering organization, had stepped up to fill the hole.

"I see," he said. Parkinson wouldn't have paid any attention to ONI without direct orders in triplicate from his political masters. "And what did you conclude?"

His implants reported that hers were requesting permission to transmit a file. He authorized it automatically and accepted the file, noting the level of security precautions buried in the document. If someone else had tried to accept it, the file would have destroyed itself and vanished.

"That's everything we have," Arunika said. "To summarize: Admiral Justinian has spent the last ten years—at least—preparing his rebellion. Most of the Federation Navy officers assigned to the sector served under him before, or are dangerously ambitious and intelligent. If that wasn't enough, the admiral has also been requesting an alarmingly large supply of spare parts from Earth—and setting up shipyards and industrial nodes in the sector. Depending on the assumptions we feed into our computers, Admiral Justinian may have a far larger fleet than we know, with a support network second only to the Federation Navy."

Marius frowned. "And if he had a larger fleet, why not use it against Earth?"

"We don't know," Arunika said. "It may interest you to know that two of three Federation Intelligence supervisors in the sector have met untimely ends. The first apparently went big game hunting on Ripley, and was killed by one of the more unpleasant creatures on the planet. The second was fond of patronizing the more... extreme whorehouses on Harmony and, eventually, he died in one of them. You don't want to know how. The third's reports showed no sign of concern but since the attack on Earth, he hasn't responded to attempts to contact him."

Marius saw the implications at once. "He's been turned," he said flatly.

"Almost certainly," Arunika agreed. "How confident are you that Admiral Parkinson can lead the Retribution Force to victory?"

Marius didn't bother to answer. Openly criticizing a senior officer was a severe breach of military etiquette, regardless of his personal feelings. There were times when it could be done legally, but not when talking to an ONI spook, even if she was pretty. And besides, she could probably read the answer in his face. He wasn't very confident at all.

"I suggest that you watch your back," she said seriously. "And if you need help, perhaps we can be of service."

She held up her hand, drawing his attention to the ring. "We are interested in you, admiral," she said. "Perhaps we can help one another."

"And what, precisely, is the Brotherhood's interest in this?" Marius scowled.

"The Brotherhood is interested in keeping the Federation stable and strong," Arunika said. Her eyes lit up with the light of the true fanatic. "If Justinian succeeds in overthrowing the government, or even in declaring independence and making it stick, the result is likely to be chaos. The Brotherhood does not approve of chaos."

"I wouldn't have thought that you would have approved of civil war, either," Marius countered. The Brotherhood...? The last thing he needed was another player with uncertain motives, particularly one with a long and secretive history. He wasn't blind to the implications of Arunika wearing the ring openly. It was a show of influence and power. "Why are you offering to help me?"

"Because we need to solve this problem as soon as possible," Arunika said. "There are other admirals who may be considering becoming warlords and attempting to seize power. If Justinian is crushed quickly, they may be deterred from attempting to plunge the Federation even further into a Civil War. We can do a great deal for you, admiral."

"Of course you can," Marius agreed. No two rumors about the Brotherhood agreed, but there was a general consensus that the Brotherhood was rich, powerful, and utterly ruthless in accomplishing its objectives. It had certainly made no secret of *those*. "But what do you want in exchange?"

Chapter Ten

The moment when a fleet departs is a moment of pomp and splendor. Many great speeches are made by political leaders. Behind them, however, is a hidden truth. Assembling a worthy fleet is growing harder and harder in these dark economic times.
-An Irreverent Guide to the Federation, 4000 A.D.

FNS *Enterprise/Magnificent*, Sol System, 4092

"I'm afraid the main bridge is out," Commander Duggan said calmly, "and we're all dead."

Roman grimaced. Today's simulation had started with the reserve tactical crew—including him—sitting and waiting for something to happen. In a real battle, he'd been told, it was unlikely that they'd have anything important to do, but the simulation was much more exciting. A freak hit on the ship's hull with a bomb-pumped laser had just taken out the bridge, and command and control functions had been transferred to the secondary bridge. His console had lit up with new icons, flaring towards the carrier...which was suddenly dependent on the secondary crew to spearhead her defense. No human mind could keep up with the speed of space combat—computers had to control the actual firing sequence—but human minds had to set the computers' priorities.

His hands flew over the console as his training asserted itself, even as part of his mind complained that the simulation wasn't particularly realistic. *Enterprise* was what the Federation Navy called a High Value Unit—wags complained that it really meant High Value *Target*—and she never operated alone. A small fleet of cruisers and destroyers escorted her everywhere, even when she went in for refit. The simulation, however, had *Enterprise* off all alone, surrounded by incoming enemy missiles. The engineering crew were already laboring to replace burned-out components and restore the lost shields, but until then a lucky missile could slip through one of the gaps in the shielding and impact against the hull.

The incoming missiles entered engagement range, but something was off.

He frowned as the data started to come through. The missiles were showing almost unbelievable behavior, things he'd never seen or expected to see in all of his training.

He checked and double-checked his data. No, what he'd seen was still there—the missiles were moving in random patterns that defied the best efforts of his fire control computers. It should have been impossible...no, it was theoretically possible to do it with missiles. But why would anyone want to bother, especially during the middle of a battle? The missiles risked burning out their drives and ending up drifting uselessly in space.

And then the first missiles that had been fired toward the *Enterprise* vanished.

He cursed as he realized why the missiles had acted in such an odd manner. *Enterprise's* point defense was currently firing in shotgun mode, pumping out so many plasma bolts into the right general area that some of them were bound to hit something. Yet the law of averages ensured that at least some of the missiles would get close enough to shift to terminal velocity and ram into the carrier.

Whoever had programmed this scenario was truly fiendish, he realized. Because if *any* of those missiles hit an unshielded section of the hull, most particularly with an antimatter warhead, the entire carrier would be blown to atoms, despite her armor and internal security systems.

Acting on instinct, he pulled out of the engagement—allowing the computers to handle it—and activated a sensor focus. There was no point in avoiding the use of active sensors, not when the enemy had clearly located the carrier and were doing their best to kill her. He swept the sensor focus across the incoming missiles and almost laughed out loud when he realized the trick. The smartass who'd designed the simulation had bent the laws of physics and allowed a set of enemy gunboats to accompany the incoming missiles, using their fire control links to allow much greater accuracy. The tactic wasn't particularly realistic—no gunboat could pull such maneuvers without overloading the compensators and smashing the pilot to jelly— but it was theoretically possible.

He keyed the console, overriding the previous targeting protocols, then activated the ship's huge broadsides. The primary beams induced instant fission once they hit their targets, although they were useless against a shielded starship because the shields had no matter to fission. But the gunboats were unprotected—and were rapidly exterminated.

Roman let out a sigh of relief. Their doom, moving at the speed of light, had struck them before there could be any warning of its arrival. Deprived of their command and control, the missiles returned to their original programming and streaked towards *Enterprise* on a least-time course. He was able to reprogram the computers just before the engagement was taken out of his hands. One by one, the computers picked off the missiles, leaving only two to slam into the shields. Nuclear fire blossomed out in the blackness of space, but the carrier was intact.

The screen flickered and brought up a new message. SIMULATION TERMINATED. Roman allowed himself a sigh of relief and stretched, feeling the sweat running down the back of his neck. It felt as if he'd been in the hot seat for hours, rather than—he queried his implants—seventeen minutes. But then, as he'd had hammered into his head at the Academy, a space battle rarely took very long unless the two sides were evenly matched. The weaker side would generally either break contact, or be destroyed.

"Not too shabby," Commander Duggan said as she emerged from the hatch. The simulation had said that she was on the main bridge, but it was nothing more than part of the scenario. In combat, the commander would be on the secondary bridge, ready to take over if the main bridge was taken out by the enemy. "You saved the ship."

"Thank you, commander," Roman said. He braced himself. They had been running simulations for days now, so heavily that he'd dreamed of them in his rack, and not all of them had been as successful. A handful had resulted in the entire ship being destroyed, or accidentally ramming an enemy ship. The senior lieutenants had joked about newly-minted lieutenants who had accidentally rammed entire *planets.*

"On the other hand, why didn't you allow the automated systems to take over sooner?" Commander Duggan asked. "You could have spent longer looking for the gunboats."

Roman considered his answer carefully. One thing he had learned was that neither the commander nor the captain had any patience for waffling. If there were several right answers, it was best to go for the one that made sense to him rather than the one he thought his superior officers wanted to hear. They were knocking him into shape and he understood why, even though part of him resented it.

"I wanted to ensure that they would continue to track the missiles, even if I was wrong," he said. "I didn't know for sure that it was gunboats doing the directing."

"Well, *something* had to be directing the missiles," the commander pointed out sardonically. "In your *copious* spare time, you might want to study the dynamics of missile control systems and how they operate in real life, as well as theory."

"Yes, commander," Roman said. He tried to think about when he could fit in time to study missile control systems, and drew a blank. Every minute of every day was crammed with tasks, from actually serving as assistant tactical officer to working on the vessel's interior, to spending time exercising with the Marines. And he'd been assured that he had an easy life! He wouldn't be getting much sleep, were it not for the fact that sleeping hours were mandatory.

"I see that you have a session with the Marines coming up," Duggan added. "I'm afraid that that has been cancelled. The captain wishes to hold a small dinner party for the new officers, and you're *invited*."

Roman nodded. No junior officer with a lick of sense would refuse an invitation to dine with the captain. He'd been told, back at the Academy, that some captains were very sociable with their crews—though always maintaining command distance—and that others hardly spoke to their subordinates when off duty. Captain Timothy Oriole seemed to fall somewhere in between. He'd spoken briefly to the newcomers when they'd first come onboard, but he'd left most of their training in Commander Duggan's hands. And perhaps that was for the best. Captains had absolute authority over their crews—and irritating his commanding officer could bring his career to a screeching halt.

"Thank you," Roman said.

"Hit the fresher and don your dress uniform," the commander ordered. "The party starts at 1700 precisely; try not to be late."

୫୦ ଓଃ

The superdreadnaught FNS *Magnificent* was one of the newest superdreadnaughts built for the Federation Navy. She was only five years old—Federation Navy personnel counted from the moment a ship first left the shipyard under her own power—and carried enough firepower to go toe-to-toe with anything smaller than a fortress. The ship had been refitted twice since her launch, but Marius Drake knew as well as anyone else with real experience that naval technology hadn't advanced since the

Inheritance Wars. There were a hundred small refinements made every year, yet there was nothing new or revolutionary in his flagship.

He stood in the Observation Blister and peered out into the darkness. The cold, unblinking stars shone back at him, mocking human pretensions to galactic rule. *You think you are so mighty,* they seemed to say. *But we will be here long after you and all your works have vanished from the universe.* It was easy to see why there were cults that worshipped the universe itself, believing it to be imbued with sentience, even though it apparently took little interest in human affairs.

Marius had never been particularly religious as an upbringing on Mars had left little room for religious introspection. Staring at the stars was as near as he got to any kind of overt belief. He'd seen people who prayed daily, to gods who might or might not exist, but he'd never been tempted to accept any of them himself. He believed in what he could see and feel; no god had ever spoken directly to him, unless the universe itself counted.

The hatch hissed open and his friend Vaughn stepped in, coming over to stand beside him. Marius didn't turn around, as he'd programmed the hatch to admit only Vaughn, once he'd personally swept the Observation Blister for surveillance devices. It seemed unlikely that anyone would bother bugging the entire ship, but he knew that the ship's computers covertly monitored internal conversation and occasionally flagged something for Security. This way, the computers would know where they were—their implants would see to that—but they wouldn't be able to listen in.

"You seem to have developed an attack of paranoia," Vaughn observed mildly.

Marius knew it was that very mildness that had caused many people to underestimate Vaughn. The Federation Marines were the Federation's shock troops, the most powerful and capable rapid reaction force in history: they boarded enemy starships, landed on enemy planets and were generally feared by the Federation's enemies. But Vaughn didn't seem like the type to do anything violent.

Before Marius could answer, Vaughn went on. "Do you honestly think anyone would dare to bug the second-in-command of the Retribution Fleet?"

"I don't know," Marius admitted. "Considering all that's happened so far..."

He started to outline everything that had happened since he'd learned that he wouldn't be commanding the Retribution Fleet, just so Vaughn could check his thinking. Despite his objections, Parkinson had split the fleet into three sections, just as Parkinson had said he'd do in the first place. Marius had even pointed out that this put Parkinson's life at risk, but Parkinson hadn't wanted to hear it.

But the stupidity didn't end there. A quick check had revealed that the Fleet Train had been joined by several luxury liners, which carried the new governors of Harmony Sector. The files had been sealed, but with the aid of a couple of intelligence officers, Marius had managed to work out a list of the potential candidates. They had all been men with very strong political connections.

None of them seemed to care that they were flying straight into a war zone.

"Honestly, Vaughn, what do you think of all this?" Marius asked. "Because this really doesn't look good, not from where I'm standing."

Vaughn considered it for a long moment. His thoughtful expression reminded Marius of when they'd first met, when he'd been the young commanding officer of a light cruiser and Vaughn had been the CO of the ship's Marine detachment. As the Marines reported only to the ship's captain—him—he and Vaughn had become fast friends, serving together as their careers advanced. When he'd been sent to the Rim to take command, there had been no other choice for Marine CO. He trusted Vaughn with his life.

"The Brotherhood's involvement is worrying," Vaughn said finally. "You never know who might be working for the Brotherhood, or reporting back to them. They've always been very well represented in the Navy, and nothing has ever managed to change that, so..."

He shrugged. "Watch your back, that's all I can think of right now. Though I wish I had better advice to give."

"Everyone seems to be telling me to watch my back," Marius said. He smiled, ruefully. "Perhaps I should wear body armor under my uniform, and sleep with a pistol under my pillow."

"Good idea," Vaughn agreed. "And make sure you carry a weapon at all times, not just in simulations."

Marius nodded reluctantly.

Centuries ago, the Snakes had attacked and occupied a handful of human worlds. They'd discovered that the inhabitants, once they'd gotten over their shock at being invaded by hostile aliens, were more than capable of fighting back against their alien overlords. By the time the nascent Federation Navy had retaken the occupied worlds, the Snakes had resorted to mass murder and genocide to eliminate the insurgents. Even then, they'd failed to make a clean sweep and thousands of humans had survived the bombings. The Federation Navy had rescued them and transported the survivors to a refugee camp on Terra Nova.

One of the resistance leaders had been a political genius as well as an unrivalled tactician. He'd convinced the remainder of the other groups to form the Brotherhood of Humanity, a society that would have only one objective—to ensure that no alien race could ever threaten humanity again. They'd begun life as a political pressure group, but they'd rapidly become one of the Federation's strongest supporters and proponents of a hard line towards aliens in the Federation. Rumor had it that two alien races that hadn't survived their encounter with humanity had been deliberately exterminated by the Brotherhood.

Even without committing genocide, the Brotherhood—now a secretive group with no visible chain of command—ensured that no alien ever became anything more than a second-class citizen in the Federation. No alien could ever be equal to a human, not in their eyes. It would be the first step towards human extermination.

And now the Brotherhood is interfering in my life, Marius thought sourly. What did they want?

Membership in the Brotherhood was hardly forbidden. The vast majority of the human population thoroughly supported the Brotherhood's stance on aliens and alien rights, or lack of them. Even so, the Brotherhood's members were generally encouraged to keep it a secret, adding to the society's mystique—and, he realized, making it easy to develop an exaggerated impression of their abilities. *In fact*, now that he thought about it, *had it been the Brotherhood that had encouraged Earth's media to turn him into a hero?*

"It seems to me that you have the choice between accepting their help or not," Vaughn said, breaking into Marius's train of thought. "And what might they be able to do for you?"

Marius shook his head. "Let's concentrate on surviving the next few months first, shall we?"

"All right," Vaughn said. "But you're going to be escorted by armed guards whenever you leave the ship. I don't think this fleet can afford to lose you."

Marius opened his mouth to argue, and then realized that Vaughn was right. Admiral Justinian's strike on Navy HQ had killed most of the Navy's high-ranking officers, at least the ones assigned to Earth. The officers stationed away from Earth seemed to have incurred the Senate's suspicion merely because they hadn't been on Earth or in the Core Worlds when the attack took place. And the remaining officers in the fleet, the Commodores who commanded the squadrons that had been assigned to the Retribution Force, were hopelessly junior to Parkinson.

"At least I convinced him to use recon drones first before we enter the Asimov Points closer to the Harmony Sector," he said bitterly, hoping Vaughn would understand. Recon drones that were capable of transiting through an Asimov Point were expensive, and the bean counters complained heavily whenever they were deployed. The Senate would not be amused when the Federation Navy presented them with a bill for a few hundred recon drones to replace the lost ones. "We might not be caught on the Asimov Point."

For a bare second, he was back on the *Matterhorn*, back when the superdreadnaught had flown right into a point-blank ambush. Admiral Parkinson wouldn't make *that* mistake, thankfully, but what was running through Admiral Justinian's head? It didn't take a tactical genius to deduce the Retribution Force's planned advance, not given the topography of the Asimov Points. Hell, Justinian could just keep his fleet in Jefferson and wait until his scouts revealed that the Retribution Fleet was advancing, and then move forward to meet the Senate's counterstroke.

"We both know that if your plan is going perfectly, you're about to lose," Vaughn pointed out. "I think you'd better be prepared to relieve Parkinson, if necessary."

Marius blinked at him. Vaughn was plain-spoken, but he was rarely that blunt.

"Think about it," Vaughn said. "Whatever criteria the Senate used to pick him, it wasn't tactical skill or imagination. He doesn't even have the imagination to make you do all the work and take all the credit. And I've met Justinian. He'll run rings around the poor political appointee and his noble benefactors."

He looked out at the unblinking stars. "I think you'd better be prepared for the worst," Vaughn added. "Someone has to be thinking about what could go wrong."

Chapter Eleven

Before the discovery of the continuous displacement stardrive, Asimov Points were the only way to travel between star systems. Even with the stardrive, Asimov Points are still quicker and more efficient. Having more than two Asimov Points in a system can ensure that the system has a bright economic future.

But if that hadn't been true of Sapphire, there might never have been a Blue Star War.
-An Irreverent Guide to the Federation, 4000 A.D.

FNS *Enterprise/Magnificent*, Sol System/In Transit, 4092

There was nothing to see as *Enterprise* approached the Asimov Point. There was no swirling wormhole of bright light and twisted colors, no sense they were approaching a gravitationally-distorted region of space. The stars seemed motionless, despite the fact that the carrier was travelling at one-tenth of the speed of light.

It was small wonder, Roman thought from a seat at the rear of the bridge, *that primitive space travelers had been so reluctant to believe in the Asimov Points. They wanted something more impressive than an invisible hole in space.*

He looked around, trying not to gawk like a civilian. *Enterprise* had no less than three command centers—the main bridge, the flag bridge and the secondary bridge—but the main bridge was impressive. The captain's chair—almost a throne—dominated the compartment, which was crammed with consoles and occupied by the best crew in the fleet. It was hard to imagine that they would ever meet their match.

"Now hear this," Commander Duggan said, her words echoing throughout the ship. "All hands prepare for transit. I say again, all hands prepare for transit."

Roman settled back into his seat and winked at Sultana. For once, neither of the two newcomers had anything to do onboard *Enterprise*. The captain, for reasons that hadn't been shared with his junior officers, had decreed that they could watch from the bridge as *Enterprise* went through the Asimov Point. Granted, doing so was nothing new for either of them, as they'd had to go through at least one Asimov Point to get to Luna Academy in the first place, but it *was* their first transit as commissioned officers.

"Humanity's gateway to the stars," Sultana said, so quietly that only Roman could hear.

Roman nodded. Back during the First Expansion Era, so long ago that far too much had faded into legend, a brilliant researcher into gravitational oddities—Irene Asimov—had theorised that wormhole links ran between objects with vast gravity fields, such as stars. Her research had allowed her to deduce that lines of gravitational force should have endpoints within the Solar System and, eventually, to pinpoint the Dead End. It had taken another year to develop the gravitational pulse generator that allowed a starship to transit through the Asimov Point, but once the first ship had made it through, there was no shortage of resources to pinpoint the Gateway. The

Dead End might have been a colossal disappointment, yet the Gateway had given humanity the stars.

"All stations report ready, sir," Commander Duggan said. She looked over at the captain. "We are ready for transit."

Roman looked up at the holographic display, shaking his head in awe. The Gateway was surrounded by enough fortresses to give anyone who tried to poke his nose into the Sol System a very bad day. During the First Interstellar War, every Asimov Point humanity had discovered was then heavily fortified—allowing them to be used as choke points to bleed the Snakes white—and the Federation had never relaxed its defense of Earth. Other Asimov Points in the Core Worlds might be unfortified—and barely charted Asimov Points along the Rim might not even be included in the Federation Navy's database—but Earth itself would be protected. The logic hadn't changed, even when the stardrive had opened inaccessible territories to human expansion. Asimov Points were still the quickest way to hop from star system to star system.

"Gateway Command confirms that we are clear to pass through the Gateway," the communications officer, Lieutenant Nicolas, injected. Nicolas had served on one of the fortresses defending Earth before she'd been transferred to *Enterprise* as part of the Retribution Force. Roman rather liked her, although their paths rarely crossed outside of the mess. "They're wishing us good luck."

The captain settled back in his command chair. "Take us into the Gateway," he ordered. "Spin up the transit drive and jump us out on my command."

"Aye, captain," the helmsman said. "We are within the Gateway."

On the display, *Enterprise* crawled past the armored fortresses and entered the sphere they guarded. It crossed Roman's mind—very briefly—that if the fortresses opened fire at effectively point-blank range, there would be nothing left of the massive carrier apart from free-floating atoms in space.

After all, they were currently in what amounted to a civil war. Who could you trust?

But, despite that thought, Roman still felt a thrill of anticipation as the captain issued the order.

"Jump."

There was a faint flicker of unease—gone almost as soon as he noticed it—and the displays flickered. And little else. But, despite the lack of drama, they had just hopped thirty light years in a split-second. The scientists swore blind that the transit wasn't *actually* instantaneous, but it took less than a picosecond, a time period that no human mind could measure. Roman was almost disappointed. Surely, his first jump as a commissioned officer should be more exciting.

But he knew he should feel fortunate. Only a handful of humans felt anything more than a brief shock when they passed through an Asimov Point, but those who did tended to do poorly in space. And if he'd wanted to stay in one place for the rest of his life, he would have stayed a RockRat.

"Jump complete," the helmsman said. "Moving to fleet position now, sir."

"Bring up the main drive and prepare to take us out," the captain ordered calmly. Roman sucked in his breath. *Enterprise* and the remainder of the Retribution Fleet had started their long crawl towards Harmony, a trip that would take more than a month. He looked forward to the journey, but he still felt a strange sense of foreboding. Who knew what was waiting for them out there?

"Madam Exec?" the captain asked, motioning toward Roman and Sultana.

Commander Duggan just shook her head, apparently understanding whatever it was the captain refused to say. "Come on, you two," she said to Roman and Sultana. "Those tactical simulations won't beat themselves, you know."

Roman nodded and stood up, taking one last look at the holographic display. The mighty carrier wasn't alone. Hundreds of starships followed, flickering through the Asimov Point and into formation. The massed power of the Retribution Force seemed unstoppable. And yet a chill ran down his spine.

"But if you think you're unstoppable," Kratman had said, years ago, "you won't look for your own weaknesses."

෪෬

Marius sat in the sealed observation blister, half-wishing he could see outside, even though he knew it would be unpleasant. Stardrive had many advantages, but it was dangerous to look out into space when it was activated. Instead, he looked down at his terminal, yet his thoughts kept wandering. It was hard to concentrate on anything.

For the first one thousand years of interstellar exploration, the human race had been forced to follow the Asimov Points if they wanted to cross interstellar distances in a reasonable amount of time. A star that possessed no Asimov Point—or no Asimov Point that linked into human-settled space—was unreachable, at least by Federation starships. Quite a few political renegades and RockRats had built STL colony ships and set out to found a colony somewhere well out of the Federation's reach. The discovery of the stardrive—allowing limited FTL travel without an Asimov Point—had placed some long-lost colonies back in contact with the Federation, or created new mysteries where colony ships had simply vanished into the darkness of space. Every space cadet knew the stories—the lost treasure ship of Titan, or the daughters of the King of the Stars—and dreamed about finding them somewhere in the interstellar void. Like most such myths, they were impossible to prove one way or the other.

No one was permitted to use the Observation Blister when the stardrive was activated, moving the fleet through an effectively endless series of tiny gravitational distortions. Marius, like most humans, could not have explained how the drive worked to save his life, but he did know that watching the effects on the starlight could cause sickness, perhaps even madness. Instead, he peered down at the latest report from the training exercises and thought dark thoughts about politically-appointed officers. He'd been given command of the massed firepower of seventy superdreadnaughts, which wasn't enough to deal with the potential problem.

Admiral Parkinson, to be fair, had agreed to continue with training exercises during the long flight to Harmony. During the first two weeks of transit, Marius had run every simulated drill in the book and several that had never been officially written down. He'd wanted to run some live-fire exercises as well, but Admiral Parkinson had vetoed the idea, citing concerns over cost and delays. But the results hadn't been encouraging.

The Retribution Force was shaping up, albeit slowly, yet it wasn't anything close to ready for combat. Given a few more months, he was confident that every unit would do its duty, but for the moment...he scowled and shook his head. He couldn't make soldiers out of a bunch of ill-trained reservists overnight. Especially considering that quite a few of the officers had been in the Naval Reserve because a superior officer had wanted to put them somewhere harmless.

It was easy to understand why. Some of them actually made Admiral Parkinson look competent.

He glanced down at the latest report and made a face. There was one advantage of dealing with Admiral Parkinson: the man didn't have the imagination to be dishonest, or even cook the files in his own favor. And Marius would have bet good money that he'd never heard of a Cover Your Ass code, allowing the files to be quietly reedited after the fact.

The Retribution Fleet had all the supplies it needed, locked up tight so some profiteering quartermaster couldn't make a profit by selling them on the black market, yet some of the commanders were jerking Marius's chain. The readiness reports on at least twenty superdreadnaughts would have been grounds for an immediate court martial during his first command. The commodore would have had the malefactors locked up and shipped home before they had known what hit them.

But Marius didn't have that option. As it was, he'd been forced to pull rank to reshuffle the commands so that each superdreadnaught squadron was led by competent officers.

A quick tap on his terminal brought up the star chart. There was no way to know how Admiral Justinian had placed his ships, but the further the fleet proceeded, the more likely it was that they would run into trouble. In two weeks, they would enter Jefferson and pass through the Harmony Asimov Point. If Justinian didn't show his hand before then, he would have to show it at Jefferson or fall back on the defensive.

He shook his head. Nothing he knew about the rogue admiral suggested he was a man who would be content to stay on the defensive.

There was no point in hoping that the fleet's progress was a secret. The Senate had loudly proclaimed the launch of the Retribution Fleet—they'd had no choice, considering the Battle of Earth, much less the executions—and pledged to bring Justinian to justice. Marius knew that a single commercial ship with military-grade sensors could have tracked them as they passed through the Gateway, then made a wide dog-leg around the fleet, passed through the *next* Asimov Point *ahead* of the fleet, and then raced home. It would be easy for Justinian to track the fleet and plan his ambush.

But why hadn't he attacked? In Justinian's place, Marius would have harried the Retribution Fleet and slowed it down until he was ready to crush it. Standard military doctrine stated that the attacker required a three-to-one advantage for certain victory. Sure, the Retribution Force was more than powerful enough to beat Seventh Fleet in a straight up fight, but then, Justinian would know that, too. He would have something unpleasant up his sleeve.

Marius shook his head and keyed another switch. If nothing else, he would do his duty unless relieved or killed in action.

"Personal to Admiral Parkinson," he said. "I have reviewed the latest exercise results. While I am happy to see that there has been considerable improvement, I feel that we need to concentrate on..."

め‍‍⊰

Roman's bottom hit the deck hard enough to sting, even through his protective "exercise suit." The suit provided very little protection, as he'd felt each one of the blows, and he was starting to wonder if that was deliberate. The Marines seemed to feel that it was their duty to knock the weak-kneed Navy officers into shape, and didn't mind bruising them along the way. Roman had heard from some of the other lieutenants that the Marines were working off their frustrations on the naval officers. It sounded plausible.

"You're getting better," Corporal Elf said. She made a show of wiping nonexistent sweat out of her eyes, then extended a hand to help him to his feet. "You almost had me."

"Right," Roman said. "I think with one more near-victory like that, I am ruined."

Elf giggled. No one would have taken her for a Marine if they'd met her out of uniform. She was short and slight, with short elfin hair and bright blue eyes. The first time they'd met, he'd made the mistake of underestimating her and she'd soundly kicked his ass around the training room. He hadn't ever been able to beat her yet in a straight fight, even at Circle. While he'd been training at Luna Academy, she'd been at Camp Heinlein on Earth and then Camp Paterson on Mars.

But then, all Marines were required to be deadly in both armed and unarmed combat.

Enterprise carried an entire Marine Regiment, one thousand men in all. Roman had given up asking why the Regiment's crest—a strange, alien creature that looked like a green pile of poop, with big eyes and two unrealistically huge plasma cannons—was tattooed on every Marine he'd met. Marine Regiments had their own traditions, and they were not for anyone else to know. On the other hand, the Marines were encouraged to work with the Navy crewmen as much as possible, even though one of their roles was internal police force if something got out of hand.

"You are definitely getting better," Elf confirmed, suddenly serious. "But you need a few more hours of practice."

She winked at him, which he didn't understand. Was she interested in him? He had no idea, but it wasn't the first time they'd met in the training room. So why did it keep coming up?

The thought was both exciting and terrifying. The Federation Navy forbade relationships between crewmen in the same chain of command, but winked at relationships outside such bounds. It was one reason why Marines and Navy crewmen tended to spend more time together than an outside observer might expect. The Marines labored under even stricter rules on fraternization amongst themselves, but seemed to have no real issues with Naval officers as almost all of them were outside their chains of command.

He shook his head and snorted as he headed for the showers. It was tempting to ask if she would like to spend time with him while they were both off-duty, but he didn't quite dare. What if he was wrong and she took offense?

Besides, he *knew* she was holding back in the training room. She could probably kick his ass with both hands tied behind her back.

Elf followed him into the showers, disrobed and stood under the hot water. Roman swallowed hard and looked away, soaping down as rapidly as possible. Elf seemed unaware of his near-panic, or perhaps she knew perfectly well. They made idle conversation about the mission as they showered, Elf bumping him gently from time to time. He couldn't tell if she was coming on to him, or merely playing with his mind.

"It reminds me of the engagement in the Ob'enn System," Elf commented as she dried herself. "We were surrounded by the rebels and cut off from any support—we *knew* that we were going to die. So the captain gets a squad of us up and tells us to act really dumb. We go out on patrol as if the enemy is millions of miles away and we're having a picnic. We make ourselves really obvious targets."

Roman frowned, keeping his eyes off her. "And they jumped you?"

"You'd think so," Elf agreed. "But no, they left us alone and even pulled back! Someone on the other side was too smart for his own good and decided that the reason we were prancing around like a pack of planetary militia was that we had really strong forces in reserve waiting to hit them when they attacked us. I couldn't believe it."

"I see," Roman said. He reached for his shipsuit and pulled it on, checking his internal chronometer as he dressed. He had twenty minutes before he was due to report for his next assignment, more training exercises. The pace hadn't slacked off, even though they were now only a few days away from the Jefferson System. "And you think that that's what Admiral Justinian has in mind?"

"I'm no expert on space warfare, but the principles are the same." Elf shrugged at him. "He's giving up territory to us without a fight. Why would he do that, but to gain time to prepare a counter-stroke?"

Roman thought about it from that angle. "It makes sense," he agreed. "Have you asked the major about it?" Roman had been astonished by how informal the Marines were, compared to the Federation Navy. There seemed to be very little awareness of rank among them.

"The major has tried to convince the captain," Elf said. "He says that the captain is convinced, but apparently the admiral is enjoying his victory march."

Roman flushed. Speaking disrespectfully of a superior officer was a military offense.

Elf nodded in understanding.

"Or," she added, "as our Regimental motto has it, sometimes you have fun, and sometimes the fun has you."

ॐCB

Five days later, Roman took his seat on the secondary bridge as the fleet came to a halt near the Jefferson Asimov Point. Nothing barred their way into Jefferson, not even a customs station. The thought made him smile. RockRats loathed customs officers, but no customs officer would try to halt the fleet to demand payment. The very thought was absurd.

"Now hear this," the captain's voice said throughout the ship. "Set condition one throughout the ship; I say again, set condition one throughout the ship. This is not a drill."

Roman braced himself. Jefferson was the last place Admiral Justinian could intercept the fleet, short of Harmony itself. It seemed impossible that he would allow them to occupy the system without a fight.

On his display, the first recon probes reached the Asimov Point…and vanished.

Chapter Twelve

The rewards of power in the Federation are vast, but the task of gaining it legally is not easy. Those who intend to aim for the highest positions are ruthless, devious and utterly determined to succeed.
-An Irreverent Guide to the Federation, 4000 A.D.

Jefferson System, 4092

Admiral Justinian still remembered the day when he had realized—for the first time—just how rotten and decayed the Federation had become. He'd been promoted to captain only six months before *Pinafore*—his first command—had been assigned to a rebellious system and ordered to keep the peace. It hadn't taken long for him to realize that there was little hope of preventing an insurgency that would either wreck the planet or force the Federation to land ground troops to suppress it. The local governor, the nominee of the interstellar corporation that had acquired the rights to develop and exploit the planet, treated the settlers worse than slaves. He'd casually broken some of the most sacred laws on the books and no one had bothered to do anything about it. The settlers had eventually been put down—in every sense of the word—by orbital bombardment.

Justinian had always been ambitious and watching the slow collapse of the Federation had turned his thoughts to how an intelligent and well-positioned person could take advantage of the chaos. He had seen the vast powers and responsibilities granted to Sector Commanders and, by the time he'd been promoted to commodore, he'd already been well on the way to building up a network of supporters and allies. The Senate was corrupt, the president was a non-entity and the Federation Navy was slowly coming apart at the seams. It had been easy to find supporters—and some backers who were prepared to forward money and political support. When he'd been appointed as Harmony's Sector Commander, it had been the perfect opportunity to turn his plans into reality.

If he'd had another five years, as he'd planned, his fleet would have had no difficulty in occupying Earth, convincing the Senate to surrender and overawing the other admirals. As it was, he'd received word that the Senate was on the verge of recalling him to Earth, convincing him that he'd better move now or abandon years of careful planning. The strike against Earth had been chancy—even though early reports suggested that the first stages of the operation had succeeded better than he'd had a right to expect—and, like all smart commanders, he'd had a contingency plan. The moment he'd heard that Admiral Parkinson was being put in command of the Retribution Force, he'd placed his own plans into operation. Sitting and waiting for the enemy to come to him was galling, especially as he'd been known as a commander who always took the offensive, but it would be worth it.

Otherwise, he would die with his fleet.

He smiled. In days of yore, emperors—and would-be emperors—had led their forces from the front. The Senate, of course, never left Earth. He knew who he preferred to be in command, the man who took the same risks as his crewmen. And he knew that his crews responded to that.

He'd had years to build up a whole secret source of manpower for his fleet and they were *his* loyalists. The Federation Navy had no idea just how badly it was outmatched. And if the new weapons worked as advertised...

"Admiral, the enemy is sending recon drones through the Asimov Point," Captain Caitlin Bowery reported. Tall, dark and strikingly pretty, Caitlin served as his Flag Captain. She had been his subordinate on his first command, and he had kept her with him as he had risen to admiral. His wife didn't like it, but if she wanted to be empress—and social queen on Earth—she would have to live with it. "They're ready to advance."

Justinian nodded. It would have been unwise to expect Parkinson to charge into the system without bothering to check it out first. Even he could see that the Asimov Point was the perfect spot for an ambush. The unimaginative clod would do what The Book ordered and probe the system first, and then—if there was an enemy fleet drawn up to meet him—bombard the Asimov Point with antimatter missiles until the enemy fleet was forced back from the maelstrom.

"Good," he said. Perversely, it would be some hours before the two fleets came to battle, even under the worst-case scenario. "Bring the fleet to condition two, but keep us under cloak. We don't want to risk discovery before it is too late for them to escape."

೮ාౡ

Roman's heart was beating so loudly as the *Enterprise* jumped into the Jefferson System that he was surprised no one else could hear it. He'd braced himself for the possibility of an enemy ambush, but nothing appeared to challenge their presence. He swallowed hard, cursing his dry throat, even as his mind mulled over the tactical situation. Doctrine said, quite clearly, that allowing an enemy unchallenged access into your system—and time to deploy and prepare for action—was equivalent to accepting eventual defeat.

"Launch ready fighters," the captain's voice ordered. "Prepare the remaining squadrons for immediate launch."

Roman did nothing. The command wasn't addressed to him and, in any case, he was locked out of the command systems unless something happened to the main bridge. He would be a helpless spectator in the coming battle.

Instead, he watched the system display.

The Jefferson System was unusual in several ways. It was a nexus of Asimov Points, with no less than nine Asimov Points orbiting the local star. That wasn't uncommon in and of itself, but as a general rule, the nexuses tended to orbit massive stars—like the blue giant Sapphire. Jefferson's primary, on the other hand, was a fairly common G2 star like Sol, with an inhabitable planet and several gas giants and asteroid belts for mining. The colonization rights had been snapped up by the Williamson Corporation, who had formed a development corporation and settled a colony on the inhabitable world. Oddly, the planet's settlers had paid off their debts fairly quickly and couldn't be legally sodomized by the Senate-supported interstellar corporations. With access to so many Asimov Points—and the legal right to collect tolls on interstellar shipping—the system had a bright future ahead of it. He scowled. It was easy to see why some Senators were salivating at the chance to place their own people in control of the system. Jefferson had played no part in the Inheritance Wars, but if the system was legally declared in rebellion against the Federation, all local authority could be disbanded and the planet placed into the hands of a Federation Governor. The locals would have no say in the eventual disposition of their system.

Enterprise slowly moved away from the Asimov Point, her escorts spread out around her. Even though everything seemed fine, Roman felt the tension level on the auxiliary bridge as it rose—apparently no one trusted what was going on, if he was any judge—and fought hard to stay calm. The unknown, the tutors had warned him, was more terrifying than any *known* threat, but he hadn't believed them until now. Somehow, staring at a display that showed absolutely nothing, apart from friendly units and the system's planetary bodies, really bothered him.

The enemy had to be out there somewhere. So where was he?

He thought briefly of Elf—felt a sudden stab of regret that he hadn't mustered the courage to ask her out—and then focused on his display. Behind *Enterprise* and the first part of the fleet, the heavy superdreadnaughts were flickering into the system, one by one. No one took chances with superdreadnaughts, as it took two years to build a superdreadnaught, even in the Jovian Yards, and it would take almost an hour to get them through into the system.

But where was the enemy?

ಬಂಠ

Marius was having similar thoughts as *Magnificent* emerged into the Jefferson System. His first inclination had been to assume that the enemy was lying doggo under a cloaking field, perhaps waiting for the superdreadnaughts to arrive before opening fire. If he'd been in command, he would have launched a squadron of light cruisers and destroyers into Jefferson first and had them survey the Asimov Point before he risked the flagship and her escorts. Admiral Parkinson, however, had refused to listen to him—and Marius had to admit that he might have been right.

Except...why would anyone abandon their best chance to give the Retribution Force a bloody nose?

He called up the system display and scowled. Every five minutes, a new superdreadnaught emerged through the Asimov Point and fell into formation. The Federation's position was growing stronger—even with *Enterprise* and her escorts already heading towards the Harmony Asimov Point—all the time, which was convenient, but suspicious. One thing he'd learned on his very first cruise under then-Captain Kratman had been that any plan that seemed to be working perfectly was just about to fail spectacularly. That was why the very emptiness of the space seemed to be mocking him.

Something was drastically wrong, and he needed to figure out why. Fast.

"Launch additional recon probes," he ordered. Admiral Parkinson hadn't ordered anything of the sort, but Marius didn't need to tell anyone that. What he was doing was in the best interests of the Retribution Force, and he knew it. He'd tell Admiral Parkinson that later, if they all lived through whatever was coming. "I want a shell of them around us at all times—in fact, replenish them at random intervals and have recon fighters move up to plug any holes in our coverage."

He sat back and scowled again as his tactical staff moved to obey. In a bad entertainment flick—one of the ones with steel-jawed heroes, awful dialogue and half-naked women—the enemy force would have slipped around the rear and gone onwards to wreak havoc deeper within the Federation. But the real universe didn't work like that. Admiral Justinian's force needed supplies and refits that only a fleet base could provide, which meant they couldn't simply abandon their base in hopes of punching through and taking Earth any time they pleased.

They *needed* to stop the Retribution Force, so where were they?

"Admiral, Admiral Parkinson is signalling you," the communications officer said.

"Put him through," Marius said tiredly. It was probably a complaint about how many recon drones he'd fired into the inky darkness of space. "And keep monitoring the drones."

No matter how he looked at it, the enemy's behavior made no sense.

Where were they?

ℝ℞

Everyone knew that StarCom units were expensive, therefore rare. Only a relative handful of Federation systems, even in the Core Worlds, had a couple of StarCom units; Jefferson, despite being a moderately wealthy planet, had never invested in them. There was no point. Perhaps, if it became possible to use the StarCom to signal across interstellar space, the economics would change, but until then everyone *knew* that there was no StarCom in Jefferson's space.

But everyone was wrong.

There was no *local* StarCom in the Jefferson System, but the Grand Senate's lackeys didn't know—couldn't know—that Admiral Justinian had stripped all nine StarCom units out of planetary systems in the Harmony Sector. Those units had been transferred to Jefferson in order to coordinate a trap. Now, the data FNS *Dandelion* collected was being transmitted to Admiral Justinian...and the ships waiting for the so-called Retribution Force were prepared to kick them all back to the Stone Age.

The crew of FNS *Dandelion* were as loyal to Admiral Justinian as anyone could wish, even though some of them believed that their current mission was bordering on suicidal. The small destroyer was lying in space, all of her systems stripped down to the bare minimum, monitoring the Asimov Point with passive sensors alone. The Federation Navy—the loyalist side, at least—wasn't trying to hide. *Enterprise* had blazed her IFF to the whole system, and it was hard to hide a superdreadnaught's emission signatures from ultra-sensitive passive sensors. Captain Muller was quietly pleased with his crew's performance; the entire crew was even speaking in whispers, as if the loyalists could hear them through the soundless depths of space.

"I think that all of the heavies are through," his sensor officer murmured. "The third component of their fleet seems to be hanging back."

"Wise of them," Captain Muller grunted. He turned to the communications officer, a newcomer to his ship. "You may begin transmitting at once."

There was no response from Admiral Justinian, but Muller and his crew hadn't expected one. They settled back to continue monitoring the Asimov Point, ensuring that the Federation Navy hadn't somehow pulled a fast one and slipped additional units into their Retribution Force.

Those Senatorial lackeys didn't know it yet, but they were walking right into a trap.

ꟸꟸ

It was a common problem with deep-space warfare—at least away from the Asimov Points—that it was generally very difficult to predict the enemy's movements accurately enough to lie in wait for him. The Battle of Athens had taught the Federation Navy that the age when enemy assaults had to be funnelled through Asimov Points were over. Admiral Justinian, however, had had an advantage; his enemy had settled on the most direct route through the Jefferson system. That might not even have been such a bad idea, were it not for the fact that the StarCom network gave Justinian a degree of tactical flexibility that his opponent lacked.

"They're coming on in, fat and happy," Caitlin said in disbelief. "Don't they even know to be careful?"

Justinian shrugged. He'd read Parkinson's file, but there was no way to know what was going through his opponent's mind. He might believe that the system genuinely was empty—it wasn't as if the locals were going to warn him, even without his orbital weapons platforms ensuring that the system remained compliant—or he might be preparing a deadly trap of his own. Or perhaps one of his more able subordinates, like Marius Drake, had talked him into something more subtle than his own preferred tactics. They certainly weren't trying to hide, after all; active sensors were sweeping the darkness, unaware that their targets were almost invisible except at very short range.

"Prepare to engage," Justinian ordered. "We will engage them at Point Cannae."

"Aye, sir," Caitlin said. She checked her console. "Time to engagement: seventeen minutes and counting."

ꟸꟸ

The live feed from all of the recon drones was being fed into *Magnificent's* flag bridge. It seemed as if there was nothing out there, an eerie darkness that sent chills down Marius's spine. It felt almost as if they were alone in space, without even the warm light of a G2 star nearby. *Enterprise* was picking up speed, nearly five light minutes ahead of *Magnificent* and the other superdreadnaughts, which also bothered Marius to no end. Any data his sensors picked up would be five minutes out of date, but there was nothing he could do about it. The long-promised StarCom system for real-time coordination was a dream.

"Admiral," the sensor officer said slowly. "I think I have something."

"Show me," Marius snapped. A blur appeared on the main display. "What is...?" Understanding clicked, too late. "Get me the flag," he ordered. Whatever he did, it would be five minutes before Admiral Parkinson picked up his warning. "Now!"

୫୦ଓଷ

Roman had been studying the tactical console when all hell broke loose.

"Incoming missiles," the tactical officer barked. Alarms rang out throughout the ship as a swarm of red icons appeared out of nowhere. It looked as if at least thirty superdreadnaughts had been lying in wait. "Again, I say, incoming missiles..."

"Bring point defense online," the captain snapped. His words echoed through the command network. "All hands brace for impact; I say again, all hands brace for impact."

The display updated rapidly as *Enterprise's* point defense engaged the incoming missiles. Roman, having nothing else to do, studied their pattern and frowned. Conventional tactics were to throw everything at the largest ships first, but only a handful of missiles were targeted on the *Enterprise*. The remaining missiles, over four hundred of them, were targeted on their escorts. It was almost as if the enemy intended to strip away *Enterprise's* protective cover, while leaving the star carrier intact.

But that was insane...wasn't it?

He stared down at his display, puzzled. Hundreds of missiles were dying, but the remainder were getting through to their targets. And some of the missiles looked... odd.

Why?

୫୦ଓଷ

Admiral Justinian's techs hadn't been able to make a new breakthrough in force field technology. What they *had* managed to do was combine two very old concepts—matter-antimatter power generation and shaped force fields—and install the result in the smartest missiles the human race had been able to devise. The problem with antimatter warheads was that it was impossible to shape the blast, ensuring that most of the energy was radiated out into space. But the combined missiles, ungainly though they were, were able to direct most of the blast into a single lance of unimaginable power. The force fields lasted little longer than a handful of seconds, but it was enough.

And, by combining the schematics of *Enterprise* with the homing missiles, they knew precisely where to aim.

୫୦ଓଷ

"Incoming! Brace for..."

Enterprise's very hull seemed to scream as deadly lances of energy speared deep into her vitals. Roman clung onto his console for dear life as the entire ship shuddered violently. The lighting flickered out for a second, just before a shockwave sent someone flying across the secondary bridge and into a bulkhead. The console flared with red light, warning that it was now *the* tactical console for the entire ship, and Roman was suddenly her tactical officer.

"She's dead," Sultana said in alarm. "Roman..."

Roman turned to see Commander Duggan. Her body was crumpled against the bulkhead, her head hanging at an unnatural angle. It didn't take a doctor to know that there was nothing that could be done for her, not now. He keyed the internal communications system, trying to contact sickbay anyway, but the entire system seemed to have crashed.

Roman stared up at the status display in alarm. Judging from the reports, whatever the hell they'd been hit with had penetrated the hull only ten meters above the secondary bridge. It took him a moment to realize why—and then he almost had a fit of the giggles. Commander Duggan had told him that the yard dogs, working on the ship, had lowered the secondary bridge down two decks.

It had saved their lives.

"Case Omega," the internal monitoring system announced. "Case Omega is now in effect."

He sobered quickly. Case Omega meant that the captain was dead...and the chain of command was broken. If the flag bridge had been hit, the admiral and his staff were probably dead as well. His duty was to report to whoever was senior, once the internal monitoring system determined who had both seniority and a pulse. They couldn't *all* be dead...

"Case Omega completed," the intercom announced. "Lieutenant Garibaldi is in command."

Roman stared at the console. He was *nineteenth* in the chain of command. He couldn't be in command. One of the senior lieutenants had to have survived, or the engineer or the major...but none of them was apparently in the chain of command.

"Captain," Sultana said formally.

Roman flinched. She was his junior by bare hours.

"We have more missiles incoming," she told him. "What are your orders?"

And the crushing weight of command fell on Roman's shoulders.

Chapter Thirteen

Fiction is full of examples of crippled starships somehow making it back home, but in reality it is rare for a cripple to escape. When a ship is crippled, but not destroyed, it generally means that the enemy intends to take her as a prize.
-An Irreverent Guide to the Federation, 4000 A.D.

Jefferson System, 4092

"Admiral Drake, we have multiple incoming contacts on attack vector," the sensor officer reported. Her well-trained voice revealed no panic. "Designating contact details now."

Only a few hours into the system and everything is going to hell, Marius thought bitterly. *But at least the penny has finally dropped. We finally know where Justinian is.*

"Show me," Marius ordered.

He swallowed a curse as the holographic display lit up with red icons. His first inclination was to dismiss what he was seeing, for it looked like something out of a first-year tactical planning assignment at the Academy. Entire *fleets* of superdreadnaughts and carriers were bearing down on his fleet, lighting up their drives in a manner that ensured they would be detected. It looked as if the entire Federation Navy had rallied to fight beside Admiral Justinian and his allies. His second, more coldly rational thought was that it was a trick. The sensors were picking up over *ten thousand* superdreadnaughts, an impossible figure. If Admiral Justinian had had such a force, he would have blown through Earth's defenses and Home Fleet, winning the war in a single blow.

"Designating group one as Bogey One," the sensor officer said, attempting to give shape and form to the oncoming threat. "Designating group two as Bogey Two..."

Marius nodded to himself as the display continued to sharpen. The sight before him suggested that Justinian was deploying decoys, using ECM to fool his long-range sensors into having flights of fancy. But the rogue admiral would know that Marius wouldn't be fooled—and he'd positioned his decoys so that the Retribution Force would have plenty of time to get over their panic, if Marius had been inclined to panic. Most of those ships weren't real, he knew; the only question was which ones were *genuine* starships. Picking the wrong course could lead to a close-range engagement against a superior force.

"Admiral, Bogey Four is launching starfighters and gunboats," the sensor officer reported. "The smaller craft will reach the Asimov Point in seven minutes—mark."

New red icons flared into life on the display. Bogey Four was *behind* the Asimov Point and piling on the acceleration, attempting to reach the Asimov Point before Marius and his fleet could double back and escape. It showed a degree of tactical coordination and flexibility that should have been impossible. All promising officers were taught to hold to the KISS Principle—Keep It Simple, Stupid—and Justinian, it seemed, had tried to launch as complicated a feint as possible.

Or they might transit the point themselves, Marius thought coldly. The third prong of the Retribution Force was still on the other side of the Asimov Point, awaiting orders to transit into the Jefferson System. They weren't escorted by anything larger than a battlecruiser, which meant that a single superdreadnaught squadron could slaughter the transports and commandeer the yachts before they could scatter and run. If the supplies were lost, the Retribution Force would be unable to reload its missile tubes once the engagement was over—assuming a victorious engagement. Admiral Justinian might just have pulled off the strangest victory in the history of space warfare.

"Communications, prepare a mass launch of courier drones," Marius ordered. A mass launch would fire upwards of a thousand courier drones towards the Asimov Point. The enemy wouldn't be able to intercept all of them, unless they'd manage to develop something completely new. But the enemy starfighters would be on the Asimov Point before the courier drones got there. He shook his head. It was the best warning he could give the remainder of the Retribution Force. "Stand by to record a message."

"Drones ready, sir," the communications officer said. "Standard emergency protocols engaged."

"Record," Marius ordered, keying his console. "Admiral Hawser, this is Admiral Drake. The Retribution Fleet has been ambushed; do not attempt to transit the Asimov Point into Jefferson. Cloak your ships and withdraw from the Asimov Point; I say again, cloak your ships and withdraw from the Asimov Point. If you do not hear from us in twelve hours, or if enemy ships start transiting the Asimov Point in force, declare yourself in command and head back to base—the long way around. I am attaching an up-to-date copy of our sensor logs with this message. Good luck."

He released the key. "Message saved, admiral," the communications officer said. "Permission to launch the drones?"

"Permission granted," Marius said. He turned to face the sensor officer as the first drones appeared on the display. "I want you to launch a second shell of sensor drones towards the advancing contacts. Ideally, I want to get drive field readings on the craft before they get into weapons range. And then launch a third shell of drones towards *Enterprise.* I need to know what happened to the admiral."

He settled back in his command chair and caught his breath. On the display, a cloud of blue icons flashed towards the Asimov Point, while smaller red icons moved to intercept them. Courier drones were the only way of communicating from system to system—and only then when the system possessed Asimov Points—and the enemy would have no difficulty in understanding what Marius was trying to do. If the third prong received no warning, they might be caught by surprise if— *when*—enemy superdreadnaughts came after them. He caught his breath as blue icons started to vanish, only to smile in relief as a handful of drones made it to the Asimov Point, flickered and vanished. The third prong would be warned, unless there was another enemy force lying in wait.

He shook his head, dismissing the thought. Unless Justinian had somehow developed the coveted interstellar FTL communicator, that would be a trick too far.

"Enemy starfighters are redeploying, sir," the sensor officer reported. "They may be falling back from the Asimov Point..."

"Or preparing to come after us," Marius finished. Starfighters were the most dangerous threat to starships, providing they operated in large numbers with suitable bases. The price they paid for being so fast and deadly was short legs. Unless there was a fleet of cloaked carriers floating nearby, it would be hours before Admiral Justinian could direct starfighters against his fleet. Gunboats, on the other hand, had much longer legs, but they were also easier targets. He ran through the possible outcomes in his mind and scowled. Admiral Justinian was very definitely calling the tune. Or maybe...

"Raise Captain Al-Barag," he ordered. "We will take the fleet into cloak for a few seconds and then start randomly cloaking and uncloaking our ships, When his ships are cloaked, he is to detach himself from the main body and split up his squadron. They are to attempt to get close to the incoming forces and determine which ones are more than just sensor ghosts."

"Aye, sir," the communications officer said. He paused. "We do know that Bogey Four includes some real carriers, sir."

"True," Marius agreed. No one had yet found a way of using ECM to create a false impression of starfighters in combat. "Let's see if we can find out how many of his ships are real, shall we?"

The seconds ticked away slowly as the enemy fleets continued their stately advance. It was maddening, in many ways; he could pick an enemy fleet at random—except Bogey Four—and advance on it, knowing that if it was nothing more than decoy drones and sensor ghosts he would punch right through and put himself beyond all possibility of interception. And yet, there was the unanswered question of what had happened to the *Enterprise*. *Magnificent* hadn't recorded a signal reporting the carrier's destruction, which suggested that the ship had merely been disabled—and Admiral Parkinson was definitely out of contact. The time delay alone would have made it impossible for him to exercise any kind of command, at least over Marius's force. And yet, if *Enterprise* and her escorts had been destroyed, Marius could have broken free of the trap, gambling that they wouldn't run into a *real* enemy force.

He reviewed ONI's data and scowled. How many superdreadnaughts did Admiral Justinian have under his banner? Officially, he shouldn't have had more than one hundred—not counting the losses he'd taken in the Battle of Earth—but if ONI was right and the admiral had spent nearly ten years preparing his rebellion, he'd had time to more than triple his fleet. And then, there was the question of what other forces might move to support Justinian. How many local defense forces had added their firepower to the admiral's fleet?

"Sir, Bogey Four is launching additional starfighters towards us," the sensor officer reported. "Interception in nine minutes—mark."

"Launch the ready starfighters," Marius ordered. The CSP would need to be reinforced, and quickly. Admiral Justinian was clearly intent on wearing Marius down as much as possible before he committed his superdreadnaughts to the battle, which was...interesting. If he was being sensitive to losses—starfighters were regarded as expendable, not an attitude that endeared senior officers to the fighter jocks—it suggested all kinds of interesting thoughts about how strong he actually happened to be. "Load the remaining starfighters with standard gun packages and prepare them for launch."

"Aye, sir," the CAG said, through the datanet. "I am launching fighters now."

Marius allowed himself a tight smile. Admiral Justinian had committed one tiny, but potentially fatal error. He had given Marius as much time as he could possibly want to prepare his starfighters, switch out antishipping packages and replace them with gun packages, and even give his fighter jocks some rest before they were launched into combat. Standard tactical doctrine called for the immediate launch of all starfighters as soon as danger threatened—an attitude shaped by the loss of FNS *Invincible* in the assault on Crichton during the Inheritance Wars, when her commander had decided to shelter his pilots inside the bays for as long as possible, only to lose his ship to an enemy battlecruiser at point-blank range.

Who knew—perhaps it wouldn't be Marius's force that was worn down after all.

"Bring up the point defense datanet and hold it at condition two," he ordered. They needed the datanet if they wanted to win this battle, as it linked the entire fleet into a single whole, coordinating point defense and making it far harder for starfighters to penetrate to engagement range. If it went down, Marius' fleet would suddenly become a ragtag handful of starships, each one thrown back on its own resources to defend itself against incoming starfighters. "Switch the controlling hub randomly and set up alternate command networks. I do not want to lose the network, even for a second."

"Aye, sir," the tactical officer said, nodding. Fighter jocks hated the datanet—datanet systems had killed more fighter jocks than any other invention, even antifighter missiles—and knocking the datanet down as fast as possible was standard tactical doctrine. "Condition one at engagement range?"

"Yes," Marius said, shortly. "Switch the datanet to condition one automatically as soon as they enter engagement range." He settled back in his command chair as the enemy starfighters closed in on his ships.

"Admiral," the sensor officer said, "we have a reading on *Enterprise*. She's adrift—very low power. There are no emissions from the hulk, not even her IFF. Bogey Seven is advancing on her position."

Marius was unwillingly impressed. There were plenty of stories about starships being disabled, rather than destroyed outright, but few of them had any basis in reality. Normally, inflicting enough damage on a starship to cripple it meant destroying it, either directly or when the target ship lost its antimatter containment fields and vaporized. But whatever had happened to the *Enterprise*, Admiral Justinian had managed to target his shots precisely, leaving behind a dead hulk. And that meant he intended to capture the fleet's flagship and use it to bolster his cause.

Not for the first time, Marius wondered just what had gone through Justinian's mind when he decided to rebel. Did he have an ambition to become emperor, or did he have another aim in mind? And if so, what was it?

"Get us as close to the *Enterprise* as you can," he ordered finally. "Stand by to engage the enemy."

He knew it would take ten minutes to reach weapons range of *Enterprise*, providing they were not impeded. On the other hand, Bogey Seven was clearly much weaker than the other enemy fleets, unless they were superdreadnaughts posing as battlecruisers and Marine Landing Craft.

He ran through the converging vectors in his head and frowned. Admiral Justinian had timed it just right. If they attempted to save *Enterprise*, they would be caught by four converging enemy fleets and forced to accept an engagement on very unfavorable terms—assuming that all the enemy ships were real, which they couldn't be.

It was an old adage in military history—even back in the days when navies meant ships floating on the ocean—that a stern chase was a long one. On the other hand, the starfighters launched by Bogey Four were capable of accelerating to their maximum speed almost instantly, in harsh contrast to the lumbering superdreadnaughts, and were rapidly gaining on his fleet.

He braced himself as the starfighters raced towards the blue sphere surrounding his craft on the display, the moment when they could be engaged by his point defense, wondering what particular tactics would be used by the enemy this time. Would they try to strip away his screening elements first, or would they ignore them and press in towards the superdreadnaughts? If Admiral Justinian anticipated a long battle, it would be the former; hell, that was what Marius would do, if the positions were reversed. Assuming that they couldn't return to the Asimov Point they'd used to enter the system, it would take hours before they could retreat through another Asimov Point or escape the mass limit and go to stardrive.

The CSP spread out to intercept the incoming starfighters. Standard doctrine stated that the best counter to one starfighter was another starfighter. Unlike some of the standard tactical doctrine, it wasn't something Marius had any real objections to, even though he was a big ship admiral. Keeping the lethal little starfighters and their shield-penetrating shipkiller missiles as far as possible from the battle wagons struck him as a very good idea. The CSP had only seconds to intervene before the enemy fighters blew through them—their escorting fighters peeling off to take on the CSP, forcing the invading pilots to worry about defending themselves—allowing hundreds of starfighters to flash through and fall upon the fleet like wolves upon a herd of sheep. Some of the CSP moved in pursuit, leaving Marius to whisper a silent prayer under his breath that their IFF systems wouldn't fail at a crucial moment. It was an unacknowledged reality that, far too often for comfort, the point defense networks had been known to engage friendly fighters.

"Point defense network switching to condition one," the tactical officer said. "Point defense engaging the enemy...now."

A single superdreadnaught mounted hundreds of point defense weapons. Seventy superdreadnaughts—and their escorting carriers, battlecruisers and destroyers—mounted enough point defense to make the cockiest of fighter jocks blanch. Now, with the datanet weaving the ships into a single entity, hundreds of starfighters were picked off one by one. No starfighter could survive a hit with a point defense weapon, although a lucky fighter jock might—*might*—manage to eject into space before his fighter disintegrated. Marius wondered grimly what would happen to his pilots if they were rescued by the enemy. The Inheritance Wars had seen a wide range of prisoner treatments—some had been treated well, others had been stranded on hellish worlds, if prisoners had been taken at all—but surely Admiral Justinian would be smart enough not to annoy the Senate any more than he already had.

And then, there was the Federation Navy's attitude to consider. Treating captured prisoners badly would fuel a desire for victory and revenge.

"They're targeting the carriers, sir," the tactical officer said. The sheer randomness of the enemy flight paths had defeated any attempt to analyse their targeting priorities, until it was too late. "*Illustrious* and *Shokaku* are primary targets; *Graf Zeppelin* may be a third..."

"Steer the CSP over to cover the carriers," Marius ordered calmly. The enemy targeting made perfect sense. Picking off the carriers would destroy his ability to mount a proper CSP, leaving his ships naked and vulnerable to repeated fighter strikes. "Refocus point defense; defending the carriers has absolute priority."

It was too late. The starfighters had already started to launch their missiles towards *Illustrious*, hammering the fleet carrier hard. For a long moment, Marius allowed himself to hope that the carrier would survive, seconds before it blew up into a ball of radioactive plasma.

Shokaku was luckier; one of her primary flight decks was wrecked, but the remainder of the ship survived intact. Her other flight decks would still be able to launch and recover fighters.

The remainder of the enemy starfighters pulled back, abandoning the attack and racing back towards Bogey Four. Marius knew they'd be back.

"Admiral," the sensor officer snapped. "Look at *Enterprise*!"

Marius stared.

"What the...?"

Chapter Fourteen

The following are not considered line officers under Case Omega: Engineers, Doctors, Intelligence Officers and Non-Commissioned Officers. They are not to be considered to be in the chain of command.
-Federation Navy Regulations, 3900 A.D.

Jefferson System, 4092

Back at Luna Academy, each cadet had to go through a test that dated all the way back to the early days of human expansion into space. Indeed, its origins were somewhat mythological. The cadet was given command of a simulated starship—with the consoles manned, often, by a real starship crew—and ordered to complete a particular mission. What the cadet wasn't told was that the simulation was rigged; no matter what the cadet did, the mission would lurch from disaster to disaster until the simulated starship was finally destroyed. Roman had, afterwards, asked the instructor why they were put through a test that had no victorious outcome. The instructor had replied that the test was intended to measure how they coped with stress, and how quickly they thought under combat conditions.

"Get me a full damage report," he ordered, duly aware that he was barking orders to the chief engineer, a man with more years of service than Roman had been alive. The temptation to just give up was overwhelming, yet who else was there to take over? Everyone who outranked him was dead or missing, presumed dead. The poor bastards who'd been on the bridge when spears of antimatter fury had burned through the shields and hull would have been vaporized. "How many sensors do we have left?"

Enterprise was tumbling through space, but thankfully the gravity had remained operational, Even so, he could feel it in his inner ear, a sense that something wasn't quite right. The carrier had not only been crippled, but punched out of formation and, without a clear idea of how badly damaged the ship actually was, he didn't know if he dared power up the drives. The emergency systems had powered down the drives as soon as the ship had been hit and there was no way to know if they were still operational. The internal sensor network had been badly damaged and was barely functioning.

"The external sensor network is largely intact," Sultana said. She sounded icily calm and in control, shaming him. RockRats were supposed to know, in their blood, how dangerous space could be and how only quick action—and no panic—could save lives. "We have incoming."

Roman stared down at the tactical console. He should have taken the command chair in the center of the compartment, but there was no replacement for the tactical position, at least until they managed to find another lieutenant. Most of the tactical section would have been killed in the attack. There were enemy starships approaching *Enterprise*; four battlecruisers and a host of smaller craft. The sensors finally identified them as Marine Landing Craft. The rebels intended to board *Enterprise*!

Over my dead body, Roman thought coldly. He'd admired and respected the captain and the XO. It would have been a betrayal of their memory to tamely surrender the carrier to Admiral Justinian and the rebels. Besides, they were coming in fat and happy, believing that *Enterprise* was completely crippled. And that, part of his mind insisted, offered an opportunity to strike back.

The damage report started to scroll up in front of him as the internal datanet came back online. It wasn't as bad as he had feared, even though it was still pretty bad. The main bridge and flag bridge—and surrounding compartments—were completely destroyed. The internal emergency system had sealed off the affected compartments before the atmosphere had been vented into space. One of the antimatter beams had gone through the port flight decks and effectively destroyed them, leaving the starfighter pilots stranded and unable to escape; another had destroyed one of the drive units. The remaining drive units—and shield generators—were intact, as were most of the weapons. *Enterprise*, given time, would be able to escape, yet it was doubtful that the rebels would give her time. It didn't take years of experience to know that the damaged carrier was going to maneuver like a wallowing pig.

He ran through the vectors in his mind and smiled. Admiral Justinian hadn't brought his superdreadnaughts close to *Enterprise*, either out of suspicion or because he wanted to point them at Admiral Drake instead. The battlecruisers would be in short range—almost point-black range—within minutes, but the Marine Landing Craft would dock with *Enterprise* before the battlecruisers were close enough to have no hope of evading his fire.

"Deploy the Marines," he ordered. "Put them in position to repel boarders."

He spared a single thought for Elf, and then turned back to his console. His plan was insane—he'd have been reprimanded sharply for proposing it at the Academy—but if the enemy just *knew* that *Enterprise* was crippled, they might not be too careful. On the other hand, if he opened fire too soon, the battlecruisers would stand off and pound *Enterprise* into a drifting hulk.

The enemy starfighters were engaging the remains of *Enterprise's* CSP, clearing the fighter jocks away before the Marines moved in. Some of the pilots ignored the enemy fighters and targeted the Marine craft, thinning the force before they had a chance to dock with the *Enterprise*. Roman winced as he saw the starfighters wink out, one by one, knowing that each icon represented a living human being. How many of them had he known personally before the fleet had entered the Jefferson System?

Somehow, he pushed the thought aside. There would be time to mourn the dead later.

"Keep the active sensors offline," he ordered as the enemy battlecruisers moved closer. A single active scan could tell him everything he wanted to know—at the cost of revealing *Enterprise's* true condition. He had no doubts about how they would react if they realized the truth. "Track the battlecruisers with passive sensors only, but keep uploading the targeting data to the missile tubes."

Enterprise's designers had sought to create a starship that was a cross between a carrier and a dreadnaught. Roman had been told by Commander Duggan that, like other ships that attempted to combine two separate roles, *Enterprise* managed to be mistress of neither. She couldn't stand up to a superdreadnaught—or even a battleship—nor could she launch and recover her fighters as rapidly as a fleet carrier.

On the other hand, at point blank range the battlecruisers wouldn't know what was coming their way until it was far too late.

"The enemy Marines are moving in to dock now," Sultana said dispassionately.

Roman turned to look at the internal display. The Marines—*his* Marines—had deployed themselves to repel boarders. The enemy was being predicable, heading for the holes they'd made in the hull. Roman wondered, suddenly, if Elf was thinking of him, perhaps cursing him for placing her in a death trap.

"Roman...ah, *sir*..." Sultana said.

"Spit it out," Roman ordered sharply.

"Two minutes until the battlecruisers are within point-blank range," Sultana said. "Can I suggest that we open fire on the remaining landing craft at the same time?"

"Make it so," Roman said. The thought was a good one, even though the boarders might try to disable the ship's weaponry as they advanced. "Prepare to fire."

Where would they go, once they boarded the ship? Justinian must know they'd destroyed the bridge and the secondary facilities, so...engineering? They hadn't landed anywhere near the engineering compartments, but perhaps they intended to secure the interior of the ship first. Boarding actions were rare, so Roman couldn't be sure; as it was, he couldn't recall a single example of a successful boarding action against a carrier or a superdreadnaught.

And this one's not going to be the first...not if I can help it, he thought.

The enemy battlecruisers were much closer now, their targeting sensors sweeping *Enterprise's* hull. Roman hoped that didn't mean they had missiles ready to fire. A single antimatter warhead would vaporize the entire carrier. He braced himself as the final seconds ticked down, keying the tactical console and uploading precise firing instructions. All four battlecruisers had to be targeted and destroyed in the opening barrage.

"I have a message from the damage control parties in the starboard flight decks," Sultana said. "They report that we can launch starfighters once they reroute power to the launch catapults. Many of the ready craft were destroyed when the ship was hit, but the remainder were held in their cradles and check out as being ready to fly."

"Tell them to get ready to launch," Roman ordered. He caught himself a moment later. "No, belay that; no power emissions until we open fire. We don't want to scare them off."

He looked back at the tactical console. The four enemy battlecruisers were just entering point-blank range. In terms of space travel, they were close enough to touch.

"Fire," he ordered, keying the switch.

Enterprise shuddered as missiles spat from her tubes, already hitting terminal engagement speeds. The enemy battlecruisers were hit directly and three of them exploded as antimatter warheads knocked down their shields and hit their hulls. The fourth staggered out of position, only to die after Roman launched a second spread of missiles before the enemy ship could recover and start firing back.

"Get the drives and shields up," he ordered. "Reroute power and launch fighters as soon as possible."

It crossed his mind that he'd just killed—directly—thousands of people. A standard battlecruiser had a crew of two thousand. Assuming the battlecruisers had been fully-manned, he'd just killed eight thousand people—and however many Marines had still been in their landing craft when *Enterprise's* point defense blew them out of space. RockRats knew death, understood it in all its forms, and yet...he swallowed hard, desperately trying not to be sick.

"The starfighters have been launched," Sultana informed him. "The Marines are reporting that they're holding, although the enemy are pressing them hard."

Roman allowed himself a moment of cold amusement. The enemy Marines had just lost all hope of escape, or even of victory.

"Bring up the active sensors and launch drones," he ordered. It dawned on him that he had forgotten something important. "Send a data package to Admiral Drake and update him on our situation. Inform him that we intend to rendezvous with his force as soon as possible."

Enterprise quivered as her drive came back online. With one drive unit destroyed—and another suffering from a dangerous drive harmonic—there was no way that they would be able to maintain the carrier's standard acceleration rate. They'd be easy meat for any enemy superdreadnaught that happened to get into missile range, yet at least they would be moving and heading towards help.

At least he hoped so, as the time delay hadn't allowed them to see what had happened to Admiral Drake—for all Roman knew, Admiral Drake might have been cut off from them, or destroyed. Seventy superdreadnaughts and over a hundred smaller craft wouldn't go easily, yet Admiral Justinian might have the firepower to destroy them. Roman might only have postponed the inevitable.

He scowled as the active sensors started to fill up the holographic tank. There were hundreds of enemy starships out there, including swarms of starfighters that appeared to be attacking another enemy force. It took the computers several minutes to isolate the friendly craft from the enemy ships, but it didn't look good. Admiral Drake's ships were under heavy attack. Roman tried to think of something they could do to help, but there was nothing. They could barely help themselves.

The sensor board *pinged*, altering the display. One of the enemy fleets was a decoy, composed of nothing more than decoy drones. Roman tapped a command into the console, ordering the data forwarded to Admiral Drake, even as he ordered *Enterprise* to alter course. The fake enemy fleet couldn't stop them from breaking through and escaping into interstellar space...

"Orders from the flag," Sultana said. "We are to shift course as directed and prepare to link up with the remainder of the fleet."

Roman grinned when he saw the projected course. It was the course he'd already ordered.

"Inform the admiral that we may require help evicting our unwelcome guests," he said. The enemy Marines were still clinging on, refusing to surrender or to be wiped out. "And perhaps some additional damage control teams."

✥ ✥

Even with the improvised StarCom network, Admiral Justinian hadn't the time to respond to the sudden change in his fortunes. *Enterprise* had somehow escaped capture—he had no illusions about how long his remaining Marines could hold out—and was heading towards one of his decoy fleets. The carrier's sensor drones had to have penetrated the ECM, an annoying development considering he'd hoped that Admiral Drake would not be able to isolate the real formations from the decoys; worse, it had allowed Admiral Drake to alter course and avoid interception by two of his forces, either one of which would have been sufficient to destroy the damned Senatorial lackeys once and for all.

"Redeploy Beta Force and Gamma Force," he ordered, wishing he had more troops available to deploy. But Delta Force was guarding the Asimov Point and couldn't be moved, unless he wanted to cope with the enemy fleet suddenly reversing course to dive for the Asimov Point and escape. And Alpha Force was too far out of position to intervene. "They must move to intercept the enemy fleet before it crosses the mass limit and escapes."

Once the computer projected the various fleet courses in front of him, he scowled. Apart from the starfighters and gunboats, there was no hope of a short-range missile duel, unless Drake's fleet could somehow be convinced to reduce speed. Of course, it was possible that Drake's lackeys would slow their speed long enough to escort their damaged ships out of the system, but he knew of Drake. The man was no fool, even though he was on the side of the Grand Senate, and would have to know better than that. Losing his entire force would be disastrous.

"And bring up the modified carriers," he added. "I want constant starfighter attacks, wearing down their defenses before Beta Force is within range to finish the job."

"Aye, sir," Caitlin said.

Justinian adjusted the display until he was looking at an overall vision of the Jefferson System. The enemy fleet was heading away from the Asimov Points, which meant they must intend to cross the mass limit and escape in stardrive. It wasn't a bad plan, but it had a big downside: they'd be exposed to missile fire for hours before they could escape. *His* ships could reload at will, while the enemy's supply train was—quite literally—six hundred light years away. They wouldn't be able to resupply until they escaped.

He allowed himself a smile. The battle hadn't gone entirely according to plan, but then—what battle ever went exactly as planned? At least the Senate's lackeys were on the run. All his forces had to do was keep piling on the pressure. Even if a handful of Drake's ships escaped, the so-called Retribution Force would be broken and disorganized.

Once they were, he would be able to capitalize on his victory and claim the throne that was his by right. After all, his backers had promised him their full support.

80 03

Marius skimmed through the report from *Enterprise* with a growing sense of disbelief. The carrier had been crippled by precision strikes—using a new weapon that needed to be identified and countered—and her captain had been killed, along with the admiral. A mere *lieutenant* had taken command, a very junior officer who was *nineteenth* in the chain of command. How badly had the ship been hit?

On the other hand, the young officer, Roman Garibaldi, had been lucky—and luck was a quality that Marius had learned to value. And besides, it wasn't as if he had time to appoint a new commander for the *Enterprise* and ship him over to the carrier.

And young Garibaldi might just have saved the entire fleet. By identifying one of the decoy fleets, he'd allowed Marius to alter course ahead of time, saving him from having to engage one of the enemy formations at close range while others came up behind his ships. Whatever else happened, Marius silently vowed, Garibaldi would receive the Navy Star—perhaps even the Federation Star—for his heroism. Under the circumstances, even the Senate couldn't disagree.

He turned back to study the display as the next wave of enemy starfighters screamed towards his ships. *Enterprise* would be a very welcome flight deck for his starfighters, whatever the inherent limitations of their design, as most of his carriers had been picked off or damaged by Justinian's forces. They weren't the only ones. Two superdreadnaughts had been destroyed, and several more were badly damaged. The *Zhan* was on the verge of falling out of formation and being destroyed by the enemy. And yet, he might just get the entire fleet out of the trap...

"Admiral, Bogey One and Bogey Two are altering course—ah, have altered course," the sensor officer reported. "They're moving to intercept us."

Marius swallowed a curse as the display updated. There could no longer be any doubt—somehow, Admiral Justinian was transmitting orders at FTL speeds. How, Marius had no idea. Perhaps he'd simply pulled every StarCom he could find into the system and used them to coordinate his fleets.

Marius sucked in a breath. Three converging lines met on the display, just beyond the mass limit. He saw no way of avoiding a long-range missile duel, at the very least, not with Justinian's starfighters snapping at their heels. He briefly considered turning and trying to tackle Bogey Four head-on, but Bogey Four had enough firepower to devastate his force if his maneuver didn't work. So the only way out was through.

He silently cursed Parkinson under his breath as he considered the situation. His tired crews were about to run another gauntlet.

"Launch another set of sensor drones," he ordered grimly. "And then arm half our fighters for antishipping strikes. Perhaps we can pay the bastards back in their own coin."

Chapter Fifteen

In the event of a stern chase, starships that fall out of formation are to be regarded as expendable.
-Federation Navy Regulations, 3900 A.D.

Jefferson System, 4092

"I have missile separation—multiple missile separation," the sensor officer sang out. "They're launching from extreme range—emptying external racks."

Marius nodded. There had been little respite for his battered Retribution Force over the last two hours. Admiral Justinian's forces had launched repeated fighter strikes against his ships, forcing him to cover the carriers at all costs. Five more superdreadnaughts had been blown into flaming debris, along with a dozen cruisers and destroyers. *Enterprise*, it seemed, was the luckiest carrier in the fleet. Four others had been destroyed, and every one of them—including *Enterprise*—was damaged. Only sheer luck had saved two carriers from destruction.

Justinian's fleet had been forced to close with the Retribution Force before they could start launching missile strikes, which was the only thing that gave the regular Navy a chance to escape. Marius had watched the enemy ships and their apparent courses and silently calculated the most likely moment when they would open fire. Their commanders had actually opened fire earlier than Marius had expected, in defiance of The Book and common sense. It would take nearly ten minutes for the missiles that had already been expended by Justinian's forces to reach his ships, which was more than enough time for his point defense systems to calculate interception solutions and gird their mechanical loins for battle. And their own missiles, once his forces started to return fire, wouldn't take nearly as long to reach their targets—Justinian's fleet was rushing towards them, not trying to run away.

"Retarget the point defense," Marius ordered.

He continued to study the enemy fleet's formation. Admiral Justinian was playing it carefully, choosing to open fire at extreme range rather than wait until they closed in. That again suggested a certain sensitivity to losses, which in turn suggested that Justinian was rather less confident of overall victory than it appeared. Or perhaps he expected another Sector Admiral to declare his independence? Whether another admiral did so to join Justinian, or just for his own purposes, it would tear the Federation apart.

"Prepare to launch missiles, full spread," he said calmly. He studied the trajectories, running through various possibilities in his mind. Starships, particularly capital ships, carried expendable external racks on their hulls that were loaded with missiles. This posed a considerable danger, particularly when antimatter warheads were involved, but it gave an opening salvo a far superior throw weight.

Up until now, his ships hadn't been able to launch their missiles, as there was no point in using shipkillers to swat starfighters, even if it were possible. Two of his superdreadnaughts had died because enemy starfighters had managed to detonate their warheads, using the Retribution Force's weaponry against itself.

But now, they could finally shoot back at their tormentors.

"Aim to disable rather than destroy," he ordered, assigning targeting priorities. If they could knock some of the enemy fleet out of formation, it would reduce the number of starships chasing them, perhaps even forcing the enemy to fall back. "Launch attack starfighters in the wake of the missiles, then launch a spread of ECM drones."

"Aye, sir," the tactical officer said.

There was a pause as the officer worked at his console frantically. The overall display updated, allowing Marius to see the weight of fire bearing down on his ships. The enemy had fired over ten *thousand* missiles towards his fleet. But most of them wouldn't get into attack range.

"Missiles armed and ready, admiral."

Marius smiled.

"Fire."

Magnificent shuddered as she vented her external racks in one smooth motion, followed by launching the first spread of missiles from her external tubes. Every superdreadnaught in the Retribution Fleet fired at the same time, creating a massive salvo that merged into one coordinated entity. The controlling missiles, each carrying a command and control system rather than a warhead, angled towards their targets, utterly ignoring the spread of enemy missiles. There was little chance of collision between both spreads of missiles, Marius knew; the point defense would have to stop as many of the incoming missiles as possible. His starfighters launched from the carriers and fell into position behind the missiles. If they were lucky, the ECM drones would confuse the enemy long enough for the starfighters to sneak into attack position without being detected.

"Enemy missiles will enter point defense engagement envelope in one minute, thirty seconds," the tactical officer informed him. "Point defense datanet is online and tracking targets."

"Good," Marius said. "You are cleared to engage at will."

He watched as Justinian's remaining forces fell back, leaving only Bogey One and Bogey Two to tackle his ships. It would have looked odd to a layman, but Marius had to admit that Admiral Justinian had no real choice. The other Bogeys could not have engaged his force, unless Drake decided to turn back and engage them himself. The battle had boiled down to one simple issue: either his Retribution Force crossed the mass limit and escaped, or they were hunted down and destroyed before they could flee the system. In the days before the continuous displacement drive, he knew, his fleet would have been doomed. Without a way to cross the interstellar desert, they would have had to punch their way through the Asimov Point, surrender—or die, once they were finally run down by the enemy.

"Enemy missiles now entering point defense range," the tactical officer said. "The point defense is engaging...now."

Unlike Justinian's starfighters, the actual missile bombardment seemed more focused on Drake's destroyers and smaller ships. Only an isolated handful of missiles were targeted on the capital ships.

Marius ground his teeth as he watched the projected trajectories and knew that Justinian was playing it smart as well as safe. The onrushing missiles would strip away the smaller—and less well-defended—point defense platforms first, ensuring that the following salvos had a greater chance of punching through to the capital ships. The blunt truth was that the destroyers and even the cruisers were expendable when compared to the remaining superdreadnaughts and fleet carriers, but in the long run the results would be fairly even. Justinian knew that he would have at least four hours to pound Drake's fleet to wreckage before they could safely escape.

Hundreds of ECM drones spilled out of *Magnificent*, set to deception mode. The missile sensors, not the brightest of computers, would be seeing thousands of possible targets, forcing many to expend themselves on useless drones rather than real starships. Thousands more were swatted out of space by the point defense network, which was constantly updating its projections in real time.

Marius allowed himself a moment of relief once he saw how the enemy missiles reacted to the point defense —normally. His worst fear had been that Admiral Justinian had somehow developed a small FTL communications system, capable of being installed in a warhead, but it obviously hadn't come to pass as he could tell that the missiles were on their own. The time delay made it impossible for the enemy to steer them directly.

Better yet, Justinian hadn't even launched gunboats to give his missiles some additional support.

And then—Marius clenched his fists in rage as hundreds of missiles broke through the point defense. Many died once his ships switched to self-defense and used short-ranged pulsars to destroy the missiles, but others made it to their targets and rammed home. Antimatter warheads detonated against shields, knocking them down and allowing the tearing power of matter-antimatter annihilation to hammer away at the naked hulls. Some of the targeted ships were lucky and survived, if damaged; others were destroyed before their crews had a chance to run for the lifepods and escape. He kept his face as expressionless as possible once the damage reports started to come in. Seventeen ships had been destroyed, and over thirty were damaged. Four were on the verge of losing their drives and falling out of formation.

"Admiral, *Rose Tyler* reports that her drive is failing," the communications officer reported. "Her commander is requesting permission to fall out of formation."

"Denied," Marius said. *Rose Tyler* was a light cruiser, armed and equipped as an additional point defense platform. On her own, however, she would be rapidly overwhelmed and destroyed—or worse, captured. Admiral Justinian had tried to capture the *Enterprise* and might try to board other ships, or force them to surrender. "All ships are to remain in formation as long as possible, and then attempt to surrender, following standard protocols."

He scowled. There was no way around it. Some ships were going to be lost. The standard protocols had been drawn up when humanity had first fought the Snakes and hadn't been revised since then, even during the Inheritance Wars. The crews would destroy the starship's computers and drives, rendering the ship useless for anything other than scrap. The classified data in the ship's computers would be lost, a vital consideration when fighting aliens who wouldn't know anything about the Federation's network of military bases and rapid reinforcement forces. Much of the data would already be known to Admiral Justinian, he knew, but there was no way to know what might help him plot his next move.

The enemy ships were already firing a second salvo of missiles, followed rapidly by a third. His own salvo was just entering attack range, forcing the enemy to concentrate on their own defense, just for a moment. He scowled as Bogey Two started to come within range as well, offering the threat of vastly increased missile salvos. At least his starfighters were having an impact, even though he knew that most of those fine young men would be lost. He quickly checked the mass limit reading, and scowled again. If they could just hold out for a few more hours, they would be able to escape. If...

"Multiple hits on Bogey One," the tactical officer reported. "Five of their super-dreadnaughts are falling out of formation."

Marius smiled tiredly. Maybe they could pull it off after all.

"Continue firing," he ordered. At this rate, they would shoot their magazines dry before too long, leaving his ships defenseless. The enemy would have the same problem, but standard doctrine insisted that superdreadnaughts be escorted by ammunition ships in battle. Transferring missiles from transports to superdreadnaughts at speed wasn't easy—and sane officers blanched at the dangers—but it could be done. "Knock as many of their ships out of formation as you can."

"Aye, sir," the tactical officer said.

ↄↃ

"The remaining invaders are surrendering, captain," Elf's voice said over the intercom. "Do you want us to secure the prisoners?"

Roman wondered absently if she knew how unlike a captain he was feeling. *Enterprise* might have linked up with the remainder of the fleet, yet they were still in battle—and still vulnerable. The carrier's point defense had taken a battering, and her drives were dangerously unstable.

"Captain?" she asked.

"Yes, go ahead," he ordered, even though he felt like a fool. Elf had vastly more combat experience than he did. "Confine them as best as you can and then report to the damage control master."

He clicked off the intercom and stared down at the internal systems display. *Enterprise* had been vastly overpowered for her size, something that had saved the ship's life. Commander Duggan had told him that certain admirals had wanted large starships to serve as their flagships, insisting that the ship be built to their personal specifications. The Federation Navy could have built four fleet carriers for the cost of one *Enterprise*, but that very overdesign had saved their lives when a standard fleet carrier would have been destroyed. The starship might look like Swiss cheese from the outside, yet she was still going strong.

Or maybe not, he thought sourly. One of the drives had been destroyed in the attack and two more were showing alarming harmonic fluctuations, which suggested they were on the verge of burning out. Losing one wouldn't be fatal; losing both of them would mean that *Enterprise* would have to drop out of formation, exposing her to the tender mercies of Admiral Justinian, who might not feel like taking prisoners. Roman's trick of waiting until the enemy battlecruisers had come within point-blank range would hardly encourage the enemy to accept an offer of surrender. They'd be more likely to put a missile in the carrier's hull instead.

He pulled up the starfighter display and shivered. There were no organized flight groups and squadrons, not any longer. Instead, pilots were flying with whatever wingmen they could find and rearming at whatever carrier could take them. The perfect organization of the Retribution Force was a thing of the past. If *Enterprise* fell out of formation…Admiral Drake hadn't mentioned it, but Roman knew what his orders would be. *Enterprise's* fighters would transfer to another carrier and the fleet's former flagship would make its final stand alone.

"The CAG is reporting that they're having trouble transferring supplies from the holding bays to the flight decks," Sultana reported. At least she sounded calm. Maybe she really was; Roman saw nothing more than a thin sheen of sweat on her forehead. "The damage control crews are asking for permission to cut through the bulkheads and transfer the supplies directly."

"Check with the engineer," he ordered. It felt like an abdication of responsibility, but he didn't know if cutting through the bulkheads risked damaging the ship. "If he agrees, tell them to go ahead with it."

He turned back to the main display. *Enterprise* wasn't being targeted directly—he suspected that Admiral Justinian still wanted the carrier intact—yet there was always a possibility that one missile would lose its target and lock onto *Enterprise* as a substitute. Or perhaps the admiral would change his mind and decide to end *Enterprise's* charmed life.

"Two hours to the mass limit," the helmsman reported. "Once we cross, we can escape."

Sultana looked over at him. "And go where? Can we double back and find a chain of Asimov Points leading home?"

Roman said nothing, as she was right. Asimov Points were far quicker than the stardrive. It would take years to get back to Earth without re-entering the Asimov Point network, which meant that Admiral Drake would have to head for another Asimov Point. And Admiral Justinian could certainly guess where he was going, and perhaps have a fleet in place to block their retreat…

"Stow it," he ordered sharply. "We will concentrate on getting out of here. The rest we leave to the admiral."

ഇഗ

Marius wanted a shower desperately as his fleet crawled towards the mass limit. It felt as if they had been fighting for days, not hours, and he was alarmingly aware of his own stink. The crew looked tired and worn, looking to him to get them out of this nightmare. He rubbed the side of his chin and felt stubble, taunting him. The only consolation was that Justinian's fleet had to be in the same condition.

"Admiral, they are launching starfighters," the tactical officer reported. He should have been relieved long ago, but the secondary tactical officer was needed on the secondary bridge. "They seem to be preparing a final strike."

"Prepare our own fighters for launch," Marius ordered slowly. The fighter jocks were exhausted. He'd given the order to have stimulants issued to the pilots, even though they knew that stimulants could impair judgement and coordination. There hadn't been any other choice, even when one of his remaining pilots had nearly killed a second one under the impression that he'd been an enemy. "Combine our squadrons and stand by to launch them on my command..."

The enemy fighters screamed in towards his ships and his own weary pilots went forward to meet them. Both sides were clearly tired—thankfully, their mechanical servants never got tired. Many of Justinian's fighters died as they were picked off by the point defense network, their reaction times clearly impaired. But two more of Drake's superdreadnaughts were blown apart before Justinian's fighters started to fall back, evading Drake's vengeful starfighters as they retreated.

Marius knew that it wouldn't be long before Justinian's starships opened fire again.

"Admiral," the sensor officer reported, "they're falling back!"

"What?" Marius demanded. "They're falling back?"

The display showed the enemy fleet reducing speed and recovering their fighters. If it was a trick, they gained nothing from it, not even a chance to convince Marius to slow his own ships at the same time. The distance between the two fleets widened sharply, until every bit of the remaining Retribution Force was safe. At this point, even Justinian's starfighters would have problems catching up with them before they crossed the mass limit and escaped...that is, if Justinian had any pilots left in any shape to fly.

"Bring up the stardrive on all ships as soon as we cross the mass limit," Marius said. He'd barely had any time to think about their course, but he had to pick something that might work once they went FTL. He pulled up a star chart—with bright white lines showing the Asimov Point network—and frowned. There weren't many options. "Set course for FAS-836393."

"Aye, sir," the helmsman said. He sounded relieved. "Stardrive activation in...seventeen minutes."

Chapter Sixteen

A star's value can be measured in three ways. Does it have a life-bearing planet or one that can be easily terraformed? Does it have a gas giant that can be mined for He3? And, most importantly of all, does it have any Asimov Points? A star with nothing but Asimov Points may be of immense significance to the astropolitical planner.
-Federation Navy Tactics and Strategy, 4000 A.D.

Jefferson System/FAS- 836393/Boskone System, 4092

"The enemy fleet has crossed the mass limit," Caitlin reported.

She was too much of a professional to show her surprise, but Justinian had known her long enough to guess what she was thinking. He hadn't given up the chance to destroy the Senatorial lackeys, no matter what it looked like. Yet he could have crippled or destroyed many more ships before the remainder escaped, so she had to be wondering why he didn't do it.

"They will be going FTL as soon as possible," she said.

"Leaving behind a number of cripples," Justinian said. He allowed himself a smile. Marius Drake had done well to extract most of his force from what had been intended as a death trap, but he'd had to abandon nearly thirty starships. "Pass on the message; I want the Marines to accept surrenders and take the ships intact."

"They'll blow the computers," Caitlin warned. "Sir, why...?"

Justinian smiled again, doing his best to project some warmth.

"We could have pressed our advantage and perhaps destroyed additional ships," he told her. "This way, however, those lackeys know that we *will* accept surrenders and may not be willing to fight to the death—not for the Senate."

He grinned up at her, and then looked back at the display. "And that way, we can regroup and advance against the nearest fleet base before Drake's forces can get back in contact with the rest of the Federation."

He stood up and strode to the airlock. "Stand the fleet down and start repair work at once," he added. "I want to be ready to move within seventy-two hours."

ဆာ

"Stardrive engaged, sir," the helmsman said. "We're clear."

Roman allowed himself a moment of pure relief. His mind had come up with all kinds of theories about what Admiral Justinian might be playing at when he allowed the remainder of the Retribution Force to escape. Justinian might be sending a force around outside the mass limit to intercept and destroy the fleeing ships, or he might have other plans...or he might even have run out of missiles. But whatever the reason, *Enterprise* was safe...at least for the moment.

Intercepting a starship under continuous displacement drive was almost impossible. The entire fleet had gone into FTL together—allowing them to communicate and even shuttle from one ship to another—but any pursuing forces would have to somehow insert themselves into the displacement field surrounding the fleet.

"Stand down from condition-one," he ordered. He was mildly surprised that Admiral Drake hadn't relieved him the moment he'd heard that a mere lieutenant had assumed command of the Federation's flagship. "The damage control crews can continue to make basic repairs; the tactical and conning crew can get some rest."

He turned and looked up at the ship's status display. The damage control teams had worked wonders, sealing off the damaged parts of the ship and ensuring that the ship's structural integrity would remain intact. It didn't take years of experience to know that *Enterprise* would need at least six months in a shipyard before she could be declared fully operational, but they'd make it home. Roman was in no doubt of that.

He flicked through the next part of the report and shook his head. They'd fired off most of their missiles in the final engagement, and needed to rearm. And they'd lost over three-fourths of their fighters.

"Sir," Sultana said slowly, "you need to get some sleep yourself."

Roman hesitated. He didn't want to leave the bridge. There might be another crisis that would require his personal intervention, at least until he was relieved of command. And then there was the problem that there were only a handful of command-track officers left alive. They *all* needed sleep. His tired mind refused to grapple with chain of command issues. He honestly couldn't place who was next in command and who didn't need sleep. The chief engineer wasn't in the chain of command, nor was the ship's doctor, or the intelligence officers who had been attached to Admiral Parkinson—those who remained alive. He made up his mind and scowled. Appointing someone outside the command track to take command, if only for a few hours, was a violation of regulations.

He keyed his console anyway.

"Chief engineer, this is Garibaldi," he said. *Captain* Garibaldi sounded pretentious and not a little absurd. "I need you to assume command for a few hours. You have full authority to command the damage control teams in repairing the ship."

"Understood," the chief engineer said. His voice was oddly reassuring. He'd had years of experience in engineering and damage control and that was what *Enterprise* needed. "I'll see you on the next watch."

Roman yawned as he stumbled off the bridge and staggered down towards the shared cabin. It crossed his mind that he was captain and really should sleep in the captain's cabin, but the thought felt absurd. Besides, the captain's cabin had been depressurised in the attack. The airlock hissed open and he almost fell. Once inside the cabin, he collapsed on his bunk, not even bothering to take off his shoes and uniform jacket. Tiredness overwhelmed him and he fell asleep.

He woke up a few hours later, shaking. He'd been in command of the ship—and he'd killed thousands of Justinian's soldiers. Former Federation Navy soldiers. Roman had known, intellectually, that he'd have to kill in the name of the Federation, and yet...he'd somehow never realized it, not really. And then he'd been in command... it was a miracle that the ship hadn't exploded the moment he'd assumed command. He'd given orders and somehow they'd survived, yet he had no clear memory of what he'd said or done. Everything was a blur.

There was no sign of Sultana, he noted, as he sat upright. It took everything he had to stumble to his feet, strip, and stagger into the fresher, cold water washing away the sweat and grime from the battle. As water ran down his body, he activated his communications implant and accessed the damage report. The damage control crews had managed to fix most of the easy problems, but the rest would have to wait until they reached a shipyard. It made him wonder when that would be, if ever. The only shipyards in this sector were controlled by Admiral Justinian.

Shaking his head, he stepped out of the fresher and started to dress. There was work to do.

ಬಿಡ

Marius ran his hand through his hair as he stared at the star chart, considering. "Once we get to FAS-836393"—the red giant had never been honored by a name—"take us through the Asimov Point at once to Delta Bannerman, and then through there to Golden Harbour."

He scowled, running through the possibilities in his head. The strange network of Asimov Points doubled back on themselves, leaving relatively few links to the Core Worlds, unless there was an uncharted Asimov Point somewhere in the sector. It wasn't impossible, but it wasn't something they could count on, not when Admiral Justinian would be preparing his forces for a rapid advance.

The olden days must have been easier, back before the continuous displacement drive. On the other hand, without the stardrive, the fleet would have been forced to surrender, or it would've been destroyed.

"From there, take us through the Gamma Chain to Boskone," he concluded unhappily. "We can link up with the Fleet Train there and use the base's facilities to reload and repair our ships."

"Aye, sir," the helmsman said. "I am relaying the course to the remainder of the fleet."

Marius barely heard him. He was still considering the implications. It would take at least ten days to reach FAS-836393 and slip into one of the red giant's Asimov Points. From there, it would take at least another twelve days to reach Boskone, while Admiral Justinian—if he pushed it—could be there in ten. In fact, if the Admiral was willing to gamble, he might be able to cut the remains of the Retribution Force off and destroy them. It wouldn't be a peaceful flight. If they beat Justinian to Boskone, they might be able to hold him until reinforcements could reach them from the Core Worlds. If...

He keyed his console, accessing the Marine channel.

"Toby, take a squad of Marines and get over to *Enterprise*," he ordered. "I want those prisoners transferred over here for ONI's interrogators. I need to know what they know."

"Understood," Vaughn said.

Marius released the console and studied the fleet's status. Seventy superdreadnaughts had entered the Jefferson System. Forty-eight had escaped, almost all of them damaged, some badly. And then there were the damaged carriers, cruisers and destroyers. Nearly half of his starfighters had been wiped out in the fighting, along with most of his gunboats and light support craft. He couldn't remember such a defeat in the years since the Blue Star War, even back when he'd been commanding the fleet stationed along the Rim. The pirates and Outsiders had never managed to inflict major losses on his ships. They'd preferred to avoid the Federation Navy and pillage undefended civilian ships and planets instead.

You need sleep, he told himself tiredly. There was no way around it. Taking stimulants would only come back to haunt him. Promising himself that he would sleep once he finished reorganizing his fleet, he studied the display. The senior CAG had been killed on *Illustrious*, leaving Commodore Mason in overall command of the starfighters. Marius barely knew Mason, but he had a good reputation as a hard-charging commander.

"I need you to reorganize the starfighter squadrons," Marius ordered without preamble once his communications officer had gotten him in touch with Mason. "Consider yourself promoted to Fleet CAG and start work after you have some sleep."

"Certainly, sir," Mason said. He sounded groggy.

Marius hated to think what *he* sounded like, but he doubted that it was reassuring.

"I have one issue to raise," Mason said. "I should move my flag to *Enterprise*, yet the ship is currently being commanded by a mere lieutenant..."

"He assumed command under Case Omega," Marius said sharply. It was very much a tenth-order issue at the moment. Besides, the young lieutenant was either very good, or very lucky. Both were traits worth encouraging. "I will review the matter when I have time. Until then, I expect you to treat him as you would any other captain..."

"But admiral..."

"Those are your orders," Marius said coldly. "Either follow them, or turn the command over to your successor and consider yourself relieved."

There was a pause.

"Understood. I will follow my orders," Mason said. "Over and out."

Marius rubbed his eyes, issued a few more orders, and then headed for his cabin. *Magnificent* had a truly magnificent suite fit for any admiral who might be aboard her, yet all he cared about was the bed. There were officers who brought their mistresses aboard—a practice officially disapproved of, although winked at in private—and even installed a private staff of their own. But Marius had never cared for such abuses of authority. Why set a bad example for the rest of the fleet?

He collapsed on the bed without even loosening his shirt or taking off his boots, and went to sleep.

₧₧

The first ten days of the transit went smoothly, much to Marius's relief. The fleet's ships shared engineers and repair crews, swapping out damaged components and repairing the ships as much as possible. Most would need a shipyard before they could be repaired properly, but they'd be able to fight or run if necessary. They wouldn't be able to fight for long, unfortunately, as they would run out of missiles very quickly. Marius had reluctantly decided to avoid action if possible, at least until they reached Boskone.

He'd checked up on *Enterprise* from time to time—Mason apparently had supporters in the fleet, who had attempted to bring the matter to Marius's attention—but everything seemed to be running smoothly. Besides, he didn't have a suitable commanding officer to put in Garibaldi's place. Mason himself might have been angling for the command—a poisoned chalice at the moment, although *Enterprise* would be repaired as soon as she was brought to a shipyard—yet normally he'd be outside the chain of command. Marius could override the regulations in an emergency, though he would have to account for his actions to a Board of Inquiry. The thought made him grimace. No matter what happened, there was going to be a Board of Inquiry and a Senate Commission inquiring into the defeat.

FAS-836393 had no planets, not even a cloud of asteroids or comets. As such, the system was deserted, without even a smuggler or pirate base. Marius didn't take chances—Admiral Justinian would probably have been able to deduce his destination—and ordered the liberal use of sensor drones to probe the Asimov Point prior to taking the fleet through to Delta Bannerman. The RockRat system—Delta Bannerman possessed no Earth-like worlds but it did have an abundance of asteroid belts, making it an ideal home for the asteroid-dwelling RockRats—was suspiciously quiet as the fleet crossed from one Asimov Point to the other. It was unlikely that Admiral Justinian had been able to subvert them, Marius told himself; it was far more likely that the fiercely independent RockRats had chosen to ignore his fleet. Marius had considered seeking their help to repair his ships, but it would only have given Justinian more time to cut them off even if the RockRats had agreed.

Golden Harbour was friendlier, although there was little they could do to aid his fleet. The twin planets were one of the strangest systems in the Federation, two water worlds orbiting surprisingly close together. The planets had been settled by mermen—humans who had undergone genetic modification to allow them to live and breathe underwater—and there were relatively few baseline humans in the system. Their handful of orbital facilities were barely sufficient to stand off a pirate attack, let alone a rebel fleet. Marius exchanged greetings with the planet's president, warned him of the danger and wished him luck. There was little else he could do.

"That bastard Parkinson led us into a trap," he said to Vaughn one evening. "What did the captives have to say for themselves?"

"Admiral Justinian was very keen to capture the *Enterprise*," Vaughn told him. "Justinian wanted the carrier intact to serve as his flagship. His Marines didn't know why."

"Ego, probably," Marius said. "Or perhaps he was making a point."

He closed his eyes. There was no way to avoid the consequences. ONI's private evaluation of the situation made grim reading. The Federation Navy had somehow devolved into factions over the past few decades, while he'd been out on the Rim chasing pirates. Admiral Justinian might be the first admiral to rebel, declare independence and perhaps attempt to make himself Emperor, but he wouldn't be the last. ONI suspected that at least a dozen more senior officers were considering rebelling themselves, either to ally with Justinian or betray him down the road—and the defeat at Jefferson would only embolden them. Even if they acted in isolation, without coordinating their forces, Marius's force would be in real danger.

The thought was bitter, but Marius forced himself to study the situation unflinchingly. He believed in the Federation, in the unity of the human race. Only unity protected humanity from countless alien enemies, or even from its own darker instincts. How many would wage war if the Federation didn't keep a lid on such conflicts? Too many, he was sure.

And that would tear the Federation apart.

The Inheritance Wars had come close to shattering humanity's fragile unity. What would Justinian's War—for want of a better name—do, with the Outsiders poised to take advantage of the Federation's weaknesses?

He shook his head. Whatever happened, whatever the price, the fundamental unity of the human race had to be protected. The Senate might be corrupt, the Federation might be unwieldy and far too complex and restrictive, but it was all they had.

The alternative was chaos. On a galactic scale.

ಬಿಂಡ

Roman had never visited Boskone, but he'd heard about the system. Quite apart from the fact that it served as a chokepoint along the Harmony Chain, it was unique in explored space. The system primary had one massive planet, a gas giant that might well have been a star if it had slightly more mass. Instead, it had given birth to a handful of moons, including an inhabitable planet. Life-bearing moons were rare, but Maskirovka was unique. No other moon had developed an intelligent race.

Even so, there was no time for sightseeing. They'd met up with the Fleet Train when they entered the system and started to reload the ships at once, while sending smaller ships back to the Core Worlds to request reinforcements. Roman had expected to be relieved, yet instead he found himself still in command as *Enterprise* struggled to prepare herself for the coming battle.

No one had any doubts that Admiral Justinian was on the way. If he punched through Boskone, he would be able to push out a defensive perimeter or drive on towards Earth. Either would be disastrous.

But attacking a strongly-held Asimov Point was a difficult task at the best of times. Pushing Justinian back would be costly.

Roman had hoped they would have several weeks to prepare before the system was attacked. Instead, the Retribution Force was still struggling when Justinian's first probes transited the Asimov Point.

Chapter Seventeen

A system with only two Asimov Points is a natural chokepoint, even after the invention of the continuous displacement drive. The enemy must attack through an Asimov Point in order to reach his target. The defenders have the advantage of massed firepower and—often—prior warning.
-Federation Navy Tactics and Strategy, 4000 A.D.

Boskone System, 4092

The display sparkled with red icons as alarms howled through the *Magnificent.*

"Admiral, we have recon drones transiting the Asimov Point," the tactical officer reported. "The CSP is moving to intercept."

"Order Mason to ready fighters and then prepare the remainder for antishipping strikes," Marius ordered calmly. Mason could handle it. He was competent, even if he'd been demanding that a superior officer take command of *Enterprise.* "Bring the entire fleet to alert and prepare to engage the enemy."

He settled back in his command chair. The Book insisted that all Asimov Point assaults had to be preceded by recon drones, just so the attacking force knew what it was about to face. It wasn't a bad idea, even though it was predictable; there was no way to know what was waiting for the attackers until they actually went through the Asimov Point. If Admiral Justinian had had a pre-placed ship in the Boskone System, it shouldn't have been able to pass through the Asimov Point with the latest updates.

One hundred and twenty enemy recon drones had jumped through the Asimov Point. Seventeen had interpenetrated and died in colossal explosions. The remainder were sweeping local space using active sensors, and had picked up the presence of superdreadnaughts and even a few of the Retribution Force's jury-rigged fortresses guarding the Asimov Point. The CSP was killing those drones as fast as possible, but Marius already knew they would be too late.

As he expected, a handful of drones flickered and vanished, skipping back to Admiral Justinian with their data. Marius wondered fatalistically if Admiral Justinian would launch the attack at once, or if he would decide to suspend operations until reinforcements arrived from the Harmony Sector in order to give the Retribution Force absolutely no chance of escape.

Marius had picked the Boskone System to make his stand with malice afore-thought. Boskone might have had only two Asimov Points, but it provided a place that Admiral Justinian would *have* to take in order to seize later nexuses in order to cut off a third of the Federation from the Core Worlds, or make another attempt on Earth. The crazed logic of the Asimov Points also made it difficult for Justinian to bypass the system using continuous displacement drive. Justinian could reach the Earth in a handful of months through the Asimov Points, but it would take him over ten *years* using stardrive.

No, Admiral Justinian *had* to take Boskone. There was no other alternative.

೮ೡಿ

"We are receiving the data download from the drones now," Caitlin said. "Drake's forces have secured the system."

Admiral Justinian nodded. There had been many delays while they'd been struggling to prepare for the grand offensive. Far too many of his superdreadnaughts had needed repairs before they could be sent back into action; even though the repairs hadn't taken long, they had gobbled up time. He'd lost his chance to cut Admiral Drake off from the Core Worlds, which was why he and his forces had come to Boskone instead.

He had to defeat Admiral Drake's force before he could achieve his overall objective: Earth.

"Launch the first assault wave," he ordered. By now, his entire fleet should have seen the sensor recordings taken by the drones. "They are cleared to engage at will."

℠ℛ

"Captain, we have multiple small contacts transiting the Asimov Point," Sultana reported. "The CSP is moving to intercept."

Roman nodded, feeling tension rise on the bridge. He hadn't expected to remain in command, not when Admiral Mason had made his attitude clear with every word he'd said. But by regulation, the captain was the supreme master of his own ship— and even a lowly ensign could issue orders to an admiral when he happened to be sitting in the Captain's Chair. And yet, it would be a brave or foolish ensign who presumed to issue too many orders to an admiral. If Admiral Mason had been in the command track, he would presumably have relieved Roman a long time ago.

"Launch the ready fighters upon command," he ordered. *Enterprise* was hanging well back from the Asimov Point, surrounded by a score of destroyers and the other fleet carriers. There was no point in exposing a carrier, even *Enterprise*, to the maelstrom that was about to envelop the Asimov Point. Besides, *Enterprise* wasn't in good fighting trim and wouldn't be until she saw a shipyard. "And then..."

"Admiral Mason is issuing orders for the fighters to withdraw," Sultana said suddenly. "They're pulling back from the Asimov Point..."

℠ℛ

Standard military doctrine stated that a single starship that transited into an Asimov Point would immediately find itself under fire from the point's defenders. The Federation Navy had learned that rule during the First Interstellar War, and then relearned it in the opening battles of the Blue Star War. Conventional doctrine, therefore, ordered the use of heavy antimatter bombardment to remove any mines and enemy starfighters covering the Asimov Point before sending the main body of the fleet through the gateway.

Marius watched as the brilliant white light of antimatter detonations started to flare out through the Asimov Point. He'd mined the point as much as possible— there had only been a small supply of mines on hand available to work with—but all of the mines were now being cleared by Justinian's forces, along with a handful of starfighters that hadn't swerved in time. He made a mental note to commend Admiral Mason for his quick reaction.

The bombardment was, if anything, growing in intensity. The constant barrage was wearing down his sensors and disrupting his plans, even before the battle proper began.

"Admiral, we're picking up superdreadnaughts transiting the point," the sensor officer reported. "I believe they're ECM drones."

Marius turned to look at him. "How can you be sure?"

"The sensor returns keep flickering," the sensor officer reported. "Real super-dreadnaughts don't flicker."

"Pass the word to the remaining mines," Marius ordered. "Hold them back from engaging the drones unless we're certain that they're real superdreadnaughts."

"Aye, sir," the sensor officer said.

It was one of the variants they'd rehearsed during the desperate struggle to pre-pare a defense strong enough to give Admiral Justinian pause. Even so, it carried its own risks. They might mistake a real superdreadnaught for a drone long enough to let it get its shields up and start launching missiles. On the other hand, once the new-comer did open fire, there would no longer be any doubt about its reality.

For a long moment, the intensity of the bombardment seemed to fade, winding down to nothing. And then the first starships appeared.

ЮCB

"Captain, we have multiple starships transiting the Point," Sultana reported. "They're definitely real this time; light cruisers and destroyers, opening fire on the remaining mines."

Roman nodded. The real battle had begun—and they were little more than help-less spectators. *Enterprise* was simply too far from the battle to take any meaningful role, at least as anything other than a fighter platform. The battle would be fought by others. He felt helpless...and guilty. Others were going into danger and he was safe, watching while they died.

ЮCB

The enemy light cruisers opened fire the moment they appeared, sweeping through the remaining mines before they could retarget themselves on the cruis-ers. A number died almost at once as automated weapons platforms opened fire, expending themselves frantically to kill the cruisers before they were picked off themselves. The CSP followed, flashing back into the combat zone and launching missiles towards the cruisers before the cruisers could bring up their datanets and fight as a single entity. All but three of the cruisers died in the first five minutes of the engagement, but in doing so they cleared the path for the heavier ships.

"Admiral, we have four heavy bulk freighters transiting through the Asimov Point," the sensor officer reported. "They're..."

Marius exchanged a puzzled glance with the tactical officer. Bulk freighters were hardly warships, although in the opening years of the Inheritance Wars they'd soaked up missile strikes from warships before the widespread use of compressed antimat-ter. There was no rhyme or reason to using them in the assault, which meant...what? Were they loaded with antimatter?

"Check that—they're carriers, sir," the sensor officer corrected himself. "They're launching starfighters now."

Marius scowled. Converting freighters into carriers was an old tactic, although the makeshift carriers were nowhere near as flexible as properly-designed carriers. Admiral Justinian clearly didn't want to risk his remaining carriers in a direct assault on the Asimov Point. It reminded Marius of his other actions, where conservation of force was placed ahead of tactical considerations, even the opportunity to destroy most of the Retribution Force.

"Order the CSP to move in and destroy," Marius ordered tightly. He studied the possibilities for a moment, then made up his mind. "The Forty-Fifth Squadron will advance and engage the enemy carriers."

"Aye, sir," the communications officer said.

Marius barely heard him. There was a second possible reason for using bulk freighters as starfighter carriers, to lure the superdreadnaughts forward where they could be engaged by antimatter-loaded drones or even superdreadnaughts jumping through the Asimov Point. If Marius lost his superdreadnaughts, his fleet would be defeated. There was no way around that, nor did he have the fixed defenses necessary to hold without his mobile units. The Core Worlds would only be hearing about the first defeat now—it would be weeks, at least, before they forwarded reinforcements to his fleet. If, of course, they sent any at all.

He watched coldly as the single superdreadnaught squadron moved forward and opened fire, targeting the bulk freighters before they could turn and escape through the Asimov Point. Once they were destroyed, the enemy starfighters would be trapped, unable to retreat without another carrier to carry them back through the Asimov Point. They'd have to surrender, or die once their life support ran out.

The final cruiser died as the superdreadnaughts moved closer, followed by two of the bulk freighters. A third was hit badly and heeled over, spewing out plasma before losing containment on its antimatter warheads and vaporizing into a fireball. The enemy fighters threw themselves on the superdreadnaughts, only to be engaged by the CSP and the supporting gunboats.

Marius allowed himself a brief moment of optimism. Perhaps they could hold after all.

"Sir, enemy superdreadnaughts are transiting the Asimov Point," the sensor officer reported. "I have at least five superdreadnaughts...no, seven..."

Marius watched as at least seven superdreadnaughts emerged from the Asimov Point in a tight stream of death and destruction. Admiral Justinian wasn't taking the chance of ordering simultaneous transits—not with ships that took two years to build—but he was funnelling them through as tightly as possible. As the earlier assaults had temporarily cleared the field, the superdreadnaughts were safe from immediate attack. The mines and automated platforms that should have engaged them were already destroyed.

"Send a signal to all ships," he ordered. One way or the other, the battle would be decided now. "The battle line will advance and engage the enemy."

෨෨౮෭

Flight Leader Elspeth Grey cursed as her starfighter flashed towards the newcomers, already spitting deadly plasma fire into space. They couldn't hope to hit a planet, let alone a starfighter, with random fire, but they were successfully disrupting the wave of incoming starfighters. The squadrons—hastily patched together after the Battle of Jefferson, although she called it the Fuck-Up of Jefferson—had drilled as hard as they could once the fleet had reached safe harbor, yet they weren't as disciplined as they had been at Jefferson. Half the pilots had never worked together before. The remainder had barely graduated from various training camps when they'd been scooped up and told to crew carriers from the Naval Reserve. It was typical of the brass to throw together a few scraps of meat and try to make a sausage out of them—and it wasn't very pleasant for the sausage.

"Form up on me," she ordered, swallowing her anger. She hadn't expected to be promoted to Flight Leader so quickly, but her former commander had bought the farm at Jefferson along with his second, leaving Elspeth as the most experienced pilot in the squadron. It was a sign, she told herself, of just how desperate they were to put her in command. Her experience had been limited to simulations and chasing down pirates, who often didn't have a clue how to use the equipment they'd somehow obtained from the Federation Navy.

She designated a superdreadnaught as a target and waited for her pilots to check in before issuing a second order: "Follow me!"

The enemy superdreadnaught grew larger in her HUD as her starfighter rocketed towards it. At least it wasn't protected by a CSP of its own, she reasoned, and the remainder of the enemy starfighters seemed to have been tied up by the Federation Navy's superdreadnaughts.

She led her flock towards the rear of the nearest superdreadnaught. The superdreadnaught's point defense was getting more and more accurate as they approached, picking off a handful of inexperienced pilots before they could evade. Elspeth barked orders and dire threats into the communications channel, reminding the remaining pilots that randomness was the key. A predictable flight path meant certain death.

"Hold on to your missiles," she ordered when several inexperienced pilots brought up their targeting systems too early. She didn't blame them—it was easy for inexperienced pilots to misjudge distances and fear a collision—but it wasn't the right time at all. They were only making themselves bigger targets. "Stand by...now!"

Her squadron of starfighters turned and fell into attack formation, shifting as a blizzard of plasma fire burned through space towards them. Two pilots—both men she barely knew, as they'd been assigned to the *Illustrious* before the carrier had been blown out of space—died as they were picked off by the enemy's point defense. The remainder did her proud, holding on to their missiles until she finally barked the order.

They fired in one great salvo. The great hulk of the superdreadnaught was pockmarked with balls of fire, which merged together into one great explosion that wiped the superdreadnaught from existence.

Elspeth laughed, picked off an unwary enemy fighter that had approached too closely, and led her flock back to the barn. They would rearm and return to the fray.

Grinning, she allowed herself the thought that perhaps the newcomers—maggots, as they were known—weren't so bad after all.

ഇരുജ

"Fire at will," Marius ordered.

Magnificent shuddered as she unleashed a swarm of missiles towards the remaining enemy superdreadnaughts. This time, the firepower advantage was on his side, and he used it ruthlessly. The massed fire of entire squadrons of superdreadnaughts were launched against isolated targets, forcing them to struggle to survive.

One by one, the enemy superdreadnaughts blew apart and died in the darkness of space. The remainder were fighting a losing battle.

He scowled. None of this made any sense, unless Admiral Justinian had one final trick up his sleeve.

ഇരുജ

Justinian forced himself to remain calm as the loss rates continued to mount. He hadn't led his fleet into the Boskone System personally, something that probably hadn't endeared him to men who were committing treason on his orders, but that had helped to save his life. He didn't have the force to punch through the Asimov Point without bleeding his fleet white, leaving them easy meat for a counterattack from Home Fleet or one of the other loyalist forces.

"Recall the remaining ships," he ordered. There was no point in forcing a victory that would ruin him and his cause. He had his shipyards, his newer innovations—and his backers on Earth. The game was far from over. "We'll concede this battle."

"Aye, sir," Caitlin said, sounding relieved. "Do you want to fall back on the Asimov Point?"

"Negative," Justinian said. He doubted that Admiral Drake had the firepower to punch through the Asimov Point. "If they come through, we will hold them here."

He settled back, watching as his surviving ships retreated through the Asimov Point. The Federation had to hold Boskone—that was a given. On the other hand, Justinian could fall back and make a stand closer to Jefferson, which allowed him a degree of flexibility the Federation lacked.

And yet, he knew he was pinned, at least until he rebuilt his forces and launched a second attack. The war had effectively stalemated.

ഇരുജ

"That's confirmed, admiral," the sensor officer said, "Their remaining ships have pulled out of the system. We won!"

"So it would seem," Marius agreed. There was no way to know what was going through Justinian's mind—which meant that Drake's forces would have to stay on the alert, knowing that a second attack could come at any time. "Admiral Mason, designate a fighter wing to serve as CSP and recall the remaining pilots. Hold them at condition-two, but let them get some rest. They deserve it."

He allowed himself a tight smile as the fleet slowly stood down. They'd held! They'd stopped Admiral Justinian dead in his tracks. Morale, which had been rock-bottom after the disaster at Jefferson, was going to skyrocket. And it wouldn't do his reputation any harm, either. The Senate would have problems trying to smear his reputation now.

"And pass a message on to all ships and personnel," he added. "Well done."

Chapter Eighteen

Federation Navy medals may be handed out by the commanding officer, once confirmed by the Admiralty—confirmation that is almost invariably forthcoming. Federation awards and decorations are the exclusive gift of the Senate, although a commanding officer may recommend a subordinate for them.
-An Irreverent Guide to the Federation, 4000 A.D.

FNS *Magnificent*, Boskone System, 4092
The summons to report to Admiral Drake onboard *Magnificent* had come nearly a week after the Battle of Boskone. Roman had spent nearly twenty minutes trying to decide what to wear while his shuttle was prepared for the flight. As a captain—even an acting captain—he had a right to wear dress whites, but somehow he doubted that Admiral Drake would be impressed by a lieutenant putting on airs. As a lieutenant, he should wear his dress uniform, yet very few people in the Federation Navy enjoyed wearing dress uniforms. The issue had been settled by the discovery that there were *no* captain's uniforms on *Enterprise*, so he'd reluctantly worn his more standard dress uniform. He was honest enough to admit to himself that worrying over the uniform was a substitute for worrying over what the admiral was going to say, considering the hostility of Admiral Mason. Roman was sure Mason had burned up the airwaves with his complaints about having to report to a very junior officer.

It wasn't the first time Roman had been onboard a superdreadnaught, but somehow it felt very different. No formal party met him when he disembarked from the shuttle, much to his relief, as he had no idea how to handle the protocol when one captain visited another. Yet everyone he met seemed to know his name. Officers, including some astronomically senior to him, found time to shake his hand and congratulate him, adding to the air of unreality. He was almost in a daze when the Marine guard opened the hatch to the admiral's office and motioned for him to step inside.

He'd never met Admiral Drake before, but he'd taken the opportunity to use his new command codes to read the classified section of the admiral's file. Drake was shorter than he had expected, reminding him of Major Shaklee, yet he was clearly in control of the situation. Short, dark hair framed a classically handsome face and brilliant dark eyes. Roman marched across to the desk, threw a perfect salute, and stood at attention. The only other admiral he'd encountered—briefly—was Admiral Parkinson, but he hadn't commanded this level of respect. Admiral Drake had pulled the entire fleet out of a deadly trap.

"At ease," Admiral Drake said. He had a faint Martian accent. "Cut the cadet crap. There's just the pair of us here."

Roman relaxed, very slightly.

"I said relax," Admiral Drake added dryly. "You're not in trouble, Mr. Garibaldi. I assure you of that."

Roman did his best to stand normally, as he would if he were around Sultana before he'd been so abruptly elevated to acting captain.

The admiral settled back and grinned, an expression which transformed his entire face. "First things first, Mr. Garibaldi. I have nominated you for the Navy Cross, with Gold Stars. I believe that it will be confirmed automatically by the Admiralty, but don't gloat too soon about being the youngest officer to win it in combat. They may feel that I have been too generous."

"Yes, sir," Roman said. The Navy Cross was *only* issued to personnel who had served with distinction in combat. The only officer below the rank of captain to win it had been a lieutenant-commander during the Blue Star War. The recipient had to show uncommon valor and skill. "I...thank you."

"I believe there may be other rewards coming your way," Admiral Drake said in an almost jovial manner.

Roman flushed, and then realized that he was being teased. But before he could respond, the admiral carried on.

"I recommended you for several Federation awards, although *those* will have to be granted by the Senate. You're also entitled to a cash reward for saving the *Enterprise* from certain destruction. The taxmen will probably try to take a bite out of it, but hire a good lawyer and they will discover that they don't have a leg to stand on."

He paused. "And you have my thanks as well," he added. "Many people showed uncommon valor in the Battle of Jefferson, but you stood out among the crowd. Your assumption of command was precisely the right thing to do, as were your actions when the enemy started to land troops on your ship. Allowing them to land on your ship will probably annoy the traditionalists—you didn't have any way of knowing if they were carrying an antimatter mine to destroy *Enterprise* if they couldn't take her intact—but it paid off. As a very old commander once said, it's better to be lucky than good."

"Yes, sir," Roman said carefully.

Admiral Drake leaned back in his chair. "You do realize that you won't be allowed to keep *Enterprise?*"

Roman nodded. It wasn't a surprise, even though part of him had dared to hope as the weeks went by without his being relieved of command. Traditionally, anyone who assumed the position of acting captain was automatically confirmed as captain, but he'd looked it up: The most junior officer to assume the position permanently had been a lieutenant-commander. And he'd only commanded a destroyer, not the Federation's flagship.

"You're too young and too inexperienced," Admiral Drake said seriously. "I did think hard about letting you take her back to Earth and transferring command there—she will have to go into a shipyard anyway, unless they decide to scrap her..."

"No," Roman said before he could stop himself.

"Your first command is always something special," Admiral Drake said, showing no sign of annoyance at the interruption. "I read your report—very professional, by the way—and she will need at least six months in a shipyard, perhaps longer. It depends on how many other ships need to be repaired—they may just dry-dock her for a few years until there's a slip free for an expensive and time-consuming repair job." He shrugged. "I'm going to be stripping out most of her crew to fill holes elsewhere—I think they'll probably give her a whole new crew and commander."

"Yes, sir," Roman said again.

"I understand how you feel," Admiral Drake said. He looked up, meeting and holding Roman's eyes. "The Navy doesn't usually bother to take account of its junior officers' preferences when it comes to assigning berths, but I'm going to give you a choice. The Navy Cross will ensure that you're promoted one full grade in any case. So. Captain Singh on the *Vengeance* needs a new tactical officer. You'd be promoted to lieutenant-commander and assigned to his command. You'd be on the fast track to a command of your own—you've certainly proved that you can handle it.

"The second possibility is the *Donna Noble*," he added. "She's a destroyer with seventy crew, under Captain Homchoudhury and she needs an XO. I've stolen both her XO and his second for filling in other holes. You'd be in the spotlight, but her captain has a good reputation for getting young officers ready for higher command. He'll even teach you what fork to use first at a banquet."

Roman blinked, and then realized that he was being teased again. Luna Academy hadn't taught many social graces beyond basic formality in the mess and how to act at the captain's table. Blake Raistlin, on the other hand, had introduced him to the concept of a whole upper-class social strata that excluded everyone who couldn't or wouldn't fit in. It hadn't occurred to him that a captain would *have* to fit in, but it made sense.

He smiled. A useful life lesson from Blake Raistlin. Who would have thought it?

"You get to choose," Admiral Drake said. "Whatever your choice, I will endorse it."

"Thank you, sir," Roman said. He was tempted to ask for advice, but suspected that it might be a test, not unlike some of the tests the cadets had undergone at the Luna Academy. "When do you need my decision?"

"As soon as possible," Admiral Drake said. "The fleet really doesn't have time to waste. *Enterprise* and a small escort will have to take our casualties back to the Core Worlds, along with my report on this battle. It might stop unreasoning panic and start more grounded panic."

He smiled at his weak joke. "But I can give you an hour or two. After that, I will have to assign you myself."

Roman considered it. He had to admit that he'd enjoyed command, once he'd gotten over the blind panic and crushing sense of responsibility. And he liked to think he'd done well for the *Enterprise*, besides saving her from total destruction. Losing command of her hurt, even though he'd expected it. Being a tactical officer would be exciting, but it was still a small fish in a big pond. An XO, even of a destroyer, had far more responsibility.

"I'll take the *Donna Noble*," he said finally.

"I thought you would," Admiral Drake said. He picked a chip off the desk and passed it to Roman. "Your promotion and official orders. Return to the *Enterprise*, enjoy command for the last time by ordering the stewards to pack your supplies, and then take a few days of leave on Maskirovka. I'm going to be rotating as many crew as I can through the shore leave facilities so they all get a chance for a rest."

He shrugged. "You can report to the *Donna Noble* after that. Be sure to enjoy your leave, as it will be the last chance for quite a long time."

"Yes, sir," Roman said.

"And please accept my congratulations as well," Admiral Drake said. "I expect to hear a great deal more about you in the future."

Roman stood to attention, saluted, and turned to leave through the hatch. If he had to lose *Enterprise*, serving as an XO on a destroyer would more than make up for it. And his name would be entered in *Enterprise's* Captain's List. He shook his head and headed towards the shuttlebay. Once he was back on *Enterprise*, he would ensure that his successor received a ship in as near to perfect condition as humanly possible before he went on leave.

₧⇛

"Was I ever that young?"

Vaughn did him the honor of considering the question seriously. "I don't think you were born wearing an admiral's uniform and a silly hat," he said after a long pause. "You were a young officer when we first met, a young man who'd earned a First and thought he knew everything."

Marius snorted. He'd arranged for Vaughn to watch the brief interview, trusting the Marine's sense of character to compensate for his own willingness to believe the best of someone with an excellent combat record. And Roman Garibaldi had accepted his semi-demotion calmly, without becoming upset or angry. Marius had demoted officers before for incompetence and some of them had lost their tempers completely.

"I was a young fool," he agreed. "I take it you like him, then?"

"From what I know of him," Vaughn said. "Major Shaklee spoke highly of him, as did a handful of his subordinates. He definitely shows promise."

"More than shows it," Marius pointed out. "He killed four battlecruisers and took the only prisoners that we got out of the whole war, at least until they came through the Asimov Point and tried to take us out."

The thought made him grimace. The attacking starships had all been destroyed, but a handful of starfighter pilots had surrendered once they realized they'd been abandoned. Their interrogations had been brief; the pilots knew little beyond their own roles in the battle, certainly nothing about Admiral Justinian's overall strategy. He'd hoped to learn about why they'd thrown themselves in with the rogue admiral, but they hadn't been forthcoming. ONI would have to use drugs or direct brain implantation to learn their secrets, and that didn't seem too likely under the circumstances.

"You're the admiral," Vaughn reminded him. "If you have doubts about him, act on them; if not..."

"Shit or get off the pot?" Marius guessed.

"Exactly," agreed Vaughn.

Marius shook his head, studying the display. "I'm giving the *Enterprise* to Captain Fowler. He'll be delighted to get out of the line of fire and he can certainly command her long enough to take her back to Earth..."

He snorted. Captain Fowler had somehow been promoted time and time again, mainly for looking like a 3D star, but it hadn't taken long for Marius to realize that the man had a soft, panicky interior. Fowler had never seen action before, at least not against an equal or superior force, and he'd come close to losing it completely during the Battle of Jefferson. Only the threat of being relieved of command from Commodore Sheridan had kept Fowler and his ship in line. If Fowler had fled, his ship would have been isolated and exposed to enemy fire. Her rapid destruction would have been a certainty.

Perhaps that, too, had kept Captain Fowler in formation.

"He won't hesitate to stab you in the back," Vaughn warned. "He'll whine to the Senate and his backers about how you mistreated him and threatened him with death or worse."

"Fuck him," Marius said tartly. "He's stupid enough to think that command of *Enterprise* is a reward, even now. He can take the carrier back home, along with my report on his fitness—and Commodore Sheridan's report. We'll see what the Admiralty makes of that."

"Make sure they're in an unbreakable code," Vaughn warned. "I'd bet you dinner at the Hotel Splendid that he'll read them as soon as he's out of reach, otherwise."

Marius nodded, then ran his hand through his hair. Legally, he could have relieved Fowler of command and sent him back on a civilian ship to face a court martial, but that would have opened him to attacks from the captain's backers and family. Sending him back on the *Enterprise* would reduce the number of attacks, at least until the Admiralty had a chance to decide if he should face a court martial or simply be transferred to an isolated mining station in the middle of nowhere. The Federation Navy had plenty of places to promote incompetent officers into command positions where they could do no harm.

"On a different note, the Governor of Maskirovka requested that you assign a pair of Marine Regiments to support the Planetary Guard," Vaughn said.

Marius frowned in surprise. The request was probably working its way through his inbox somewhere, but he hadn't seen it yet. Vaughn would have been copied into any requests for Marine support.

"He didn't say why," Vaughn went on, "but Maskirovka does have an intelligent race. Perhaps they're causing trouble for the settlers."

"Or perhaps the settlers are thinking about causing trouble themselves," Marius said. He'd been on the Rim too long to share the unthinking prejudice against aliens held by most of the human race, but when push came to shove it was humanity first, last, and always. "How long has it been since the Inheritance Wars? Long enough for us to forget the carnage?"

"Boskone wasn't involved in the wars," Vaughn pointed out. "The chances are good that the governor is just as deeply corrupt as any other politician. His subjects may feel that they have nothing to lose through rebellion, and the settlers may feel like throwing their lot in with Admiral Justinian. How can it get any worse for them?"

"It can always get worse," Marius said sourly. "Anyway, please go check it out. We can't advance through the Asimov Point without reinforcements, so if you think it's necessary, ship in a couple of regiments and deploy them as you see fit."

"They'll be pleased," Vaughn said. "Damage control isn't what we jarheads signed up to do."

Marius shrugged. Now that Admiral Justinian's forces had been beaten back, he'd taken the risk of carrying out more extensive repair work on some of his starships. ECM buoys would create the impression that his fleet was still on alert, watching the Asimov Point carefully. The CSP would keep any intruding recon drones from getting close enough to realize that they were being conned.

But even with the Fleet Train, the repair work was going slowly. Too slowly. He'd sent an urgent request to the Core Worlds for as many mobile repair yards as they could send forward, along with fortress components and additional crew. But he doubted he'd get everything he wanted, or even everything that he absolutely needed. He knew that the Senate would still be reeling from the disaster at Jefferson, and would be looking for someone to blame—him.

But he couldn't let that affect him, or his decision making, or this war would be over soon—and in a way the Grand Senate assuredly would not like.

"They may need to do more of it," Marius said after another long pause. "We can't leave this system without risking overall defeat."

"So who gets there first with the most wins," Vaughn said thoughtfully. "In the long run...can Justinian win?"

Marius studied the star chart. "If the other Sector Admirals and governors remain loyal, then no—he can and will be ground into powder once the massed Federation Navy is pointed at him. If not...the Federation could shatter into a myriad of competing powers. In that case, Justinian might win by default."

"Not a pleasant thought," Vaughn agreed. "One other point: I would like to deploy Marines to escort the younger officers and crew on Maskirovka. They won't have any experience of life on a settled world, and may get into real trouble."

"Babysitting," Marius said with a nod. "See to it. They won't like it, but it's for their own good. I can do without having to search for kidnapped crew—or bailing them out of jail."

"You could always send in the Marines and break them out of jail," Vaughn offered.

Marius allowed himself a moment to consider the image before dismissing it with a wave of his hand.

"Come on; it will be fun—and cheap." Vaughn's eyes twinkled.

"Be gone, tempter," Marius said with a laugh. "I have to write the report. If I'm really lucky, it won't get me summarily demoted when the Senate reads it."

"They won't do that, will they?" Vaughn asked. "You got us all out of the trap."

"Why not?" Marius asked. "Who else do they have to blame?"

Chapter Nineteen

The Human Race's Burden, according to the Federation, is to civilize every other intel-
ligent race. Toward this end, the human race assumes control of every other intelligent
race encountered by the Federation. Despite the propaganda, the overall intent is far
more sinister—by making other races dependent upon humanity, any threat they pose
is forever removed. Needless to say, this practice causes no end of resentment among the
client races...
-An Irreverent Guide to the Federation, 4000 A.D.

Maskirovka, Boskone System, 4092

"You see, all the Purples cannot be trusted," the man announced. Roman hadn't
caught his name when he'd turned up and bought the table of Navy personnel a
round of drinks. "We have to keep the boot on their necks for their own good..."

Roman shrugged, doing his best to conceal his disgust. After a day in Maskirovka
City—the unimaginatively named capital of Maskirovka—he'd decided to see some
local color and head to one of the alien cities on the gas giant's moon. There had
been little to see in Maskirovka City, just another spacer town with bars, broth-
els and overpriced souvenirs, trying to drive spacers and other visitors deeper into
debt. Merchant crewmen were generally paid in a lump sum whenever they reached
safe harbor and the planet's inhabitants were devoted to relieving them of as much
money as possible before they left. Not that most of them complained. After months
on merchant ships, breathing in each other's air and getting on each other's nerves,
the chance to get drunk and enjoy some female company had to be very welcome.

"They just can't be trusted," the man insisted, waving toward the bartender. "Can
you believe—they think they would have achieved greatness if not for us!"

Roman had seen aliens before, but he'd never previously encountered a native
of Maskirovka. But that shouldn't have been surprising. According to the files he'd
accessed on the way down to the surface, none had ever set foot off the planet, unless
they'd been lifted illegally by smugglers and taken to a hidden base.

The alien showed no sign of listening to the conversation. Like roughly half of
the aliens known to humanity, the Purples were humanoid, but there the resemblance ended. Their skins looked like gooseberry skins—although of a sickeningly
purple color—and their eyes were dark and lidless. The alien was clearly female—
she had prominent breasts, larger than the human norm—and was actually taller
than Roman. If he recalled the files correctly—his implants lacked a secure connection on the surface—the intelligent Purples were all female; the males weren't intelligent and lived only for food, fighting and fucking, perhaps not in that order. He'd
mentioned that to Elf, who was seated on the other side of the table with a bored
expression, and she'd quipped that they were just like humanity. Roman had blushed
scarlet before he realized that he was being teased.

He deliberately looked away from the alien—and their unwelcome entertainer—
and studied the bar itself. It had started life as an alien building and all the proportions

were odd, even though someone had insisted on modifying it to better suit humans. A display of alien artwork covered one wall, paintings that reminded him of some of the early rock carvings done by RockRat asteroid miners during the First Expansion Era. Many focused on humanity and while the overall tone was positive, there was something sinister about seeing his race portrayed as godlike entities.

But perhaps the natives considered them to be gods. Humans had changed the shape of their world forever.

Years ago, according to the files, the Purples—their name for themselves was unpronounceable by humans—had been on the verge of entering the computer age. The files claimed that they'd been loosely comparable to Earth of 1914, although they'd actually advanced faster in some areas than humanity had—a fact that had been carefully buried under a mountain of statistics and dry data. It had taken Roman several hours to work it out from the sparse hints in the files. In fact, he had a suspicion that if *Enterprise's* computers hadn't recognized him as her acting captain, he wouldn't have been able to access and download the complete file.

Their advancement hadn't helped when the Federation arrived. The human race had landed, made contact with the alien leaders and started supplying them with technology to help correct their problems. Free food had been provided for aliens on the verge of starvation, technological fixes had been offered for other issues…and the humans had eventually taken over the world. Over the years, the Purples had been systematically reduced to little more than zoo animals, seemingly for their own good.

But it hadn't taken long for Roman to realize the truth, even though the files had never stated it directly. The Federation's intervention—in the name of saving the Purples from themselves—had ensured that the Purples would never become a threat to humanity.

The irony was chilling. Humanity's first contact had almost been its last. The Snakes wouldn't have allowed a race as adaptable as humanity to live—they'd enslaved several races, but exterminated at least two others—and humanity had learned a hard lesson. No alien race could be allowed to become a threat. Even without the Imperialist Faction pushing the Federation into war, the Blue Star War might have taken place anyway. An alien race with a space navy, even a primitive and unreliable one, was a clear and present threat. It could not be tolerated, even if it meant reducing entire races to beggars, dependent on human charity.

Roman jumped as a hand landed on his shoulder.

"Don't think we're ungrateful because of your presence," the man who'd bought them drinks said. "You help keep the Purples in their place and…why, I hear that some of them are rejecting the benefits of civilization and are taking off to the wildness and hiding and…"

It took all the self-control Roman had not to put one of his fists next to the man's nose. It would have been easy. The man was half-drunk, and Roman had barely touched his beer—overpriced, tasting suspiciously like it had come out of the wrong end of a horse—and it was clear that the man had no formal fighting training. Yes, he'd been warned not to cause friction with the locals, but how much nonsense could he take?

"Thank you for your words of wisdom," Corporal Hastings said. Unlike Elf, the burly Marine exuded an air of menace. "Go away."

The man looked at him with wide eyes, and then stumbled away, tripping over a chair in his haste.

Roman watched him go, wondering just how much of that had been an act. The settlers had been very welcoming to the Navy crewmen on leave, but there was something unsettling about their demeanor. It occurred to Roman for the first time that the settlers were hugely outnumbered by the Purples. If the Purples had revolution and mass slaughter in mind, the only thing keeping them back was orbital bombardment…and Marine Regiments from the Federation Navy.

"Thank you," he said sincerely.

Hastings made a show of saluting. Traditionally, Marines only reported to captains and Roman was no longer even an acting captain. On the other hand, he'd earned respect from officers and men who were many years his senior.

"Why…?" Roman wasn't able to finish the thought.

"That's a fairly typical attitude for a settler," Elf said seriously. "They're the ones who don't feel like breaking the ground on a new planet, so they find their way to a system where the locals will do all the work—if they know what is good for them. And if they don't know, the settlers will be happy to break some heads until the locals realize where their best interests lie. Along the Rim, there are places where humans and aliens live together in perfect harmony—but not *here*, and certainly not formally. The aliens have no rights on their own planets."

Roman looked toward the bartender. She mopped the counter, seeming to pay no attention to them at all. A pair of males—smaller, nasty-looking humanoids—were running around in back, jumping onto the counter to look at the human visitors. Roman shuddered at the look on their faces, the complete absence of anything but rapidly shifting emotion. The females, according to the files, traded males, effectively as pets. And yet, when a female Purple entered mating season, she was compelled to submit to a creature that was little more than an animal. The females had even bred males in hopes of improving the breed, Roman had learned, although the human settlers had soon put a stop to that.

"Ah, forget them," Blake Raistlin said. Like Roman, he'd been promised promotion after heroic service on the superdreadnaught *Thunderous*. Unlike Roman, it hadn't come through yet, not even with his family connections. Roman had heard that Raistlin's father had been unable to secure him a posting to *Enterprise*—Admiral Parkinson had apparently hated Raistlin's father—and it might well have saved his life. "I could do with another round of drinks. Who's buying?"

Roman studied the pale yellow liquid that passed for beer and shook his head. "Not me," he said, thinking wistfully of battle. "How do you think they make this crap?"

"They taught us how to make it," an oddly musical voice said. Roman turned to see the alien bartender looming over him. Up close, she smelled of sweet flowers and something he couldn't identify, almost like human perfume. "We grow the plants for them in a poor field and then turn it into drink for them. They cannot get enough of it."

"Well, neither can we," Raistlin said quickly. "Another round of drinks, and don't spare the alcohol. We have a genuine set of war heroes at the table."

If the bartender was impressed, she didn't show it. Instead, she collected the empty glasses and headed back toward the bar. The twitch in her rear had to be an affectation she'd picked up from the settlers, Roman told himself. She couldn't be trying to tempt them with the possibility of alien sex, could she? Or perhaps she was—there were plenty of stories about human-alien sexual relationships, even though they were the last, great taboo. A poor settler, unable to afford a wife, might just be tempted by an alien...

He pushed the thought aside before it made him throw up. It was far more likely that some of the other rumors about settlers—and RockRats—were true. Back at the Academy, he'd discovered that some of Earth's citizens still believed that RockRats were all homosexuals, a stereotype that hadn't been true for almost two thousand years. If ever.

"You saved an entire ship," Raistlin said cheerfully. He made a show of lifting his glass. "Cheers, gentlemen; he served on *Enterprise*."

Roman flushed. "I need some air," he said, pulling himself to his feet. Why did his legs feel unsteady? "I'll see you back at the lodge."

"Unless you find someone and go home with her," Raistlin called. "Enjoy yourself!"

The Purple town was a strange mixture of human and alien styles. Roman took a deep breath as he stepped outside, enjoying the clear air. He couldn't help but realize that the human habitations were all prefabricated colony-style buildings, while the alien buildings were far more elegant. The ugly human buildings had been designed that way to encourage colonists to develop their building skills and eventually move out of the prefabricated buildings and into proper homes. But the settlers had never bothered to move any further, even in Maskirovka City. With an industrial node floating in orbit producing all the prefabricated buildings they could desire, they had no incentive to change.

The alien buildings bore no resemblance to human styles of architecture and design, at least at first glance. They looked to be constructed from a mixture of wood and stone, with earth pressed into the roofs and used to grow a grass-analogue. Roman recalled some of the genetically-engineered plants the RockRats had taken with them as they spread out among the stars and wondered, absently, if the Purples used something similar to help hold their buildings together.

He looked up at the gas giant hanging in the sky, and shivered. *You are mortal,* the gas giant seemed to say. *I am eternal. You puny mites and your tiny starships are nothing to me.*

A line of alien males ran past, squawking as they sighted a female target. Roman watched as the female dropped the bag she was carrying and knelt in front of the males, pressing her face into the dirt. The males surrounded her and began to fight savagely among themselves for the right to mate with the female. Roman wanted to look away, but he couldn't take his eyes off the scene. He guessed that the kneeling female had just entered mating season—her scent calling the males to her—and that none of the other females was ready to mate.

Once the victor in the fight had knocked the others down or out, he howled in triumph and then swept down on the female, lifting her ragged dress before entering her from behind. After a brief moment, the male pulled out, chattering happily. The female pulled herself to her feet, her expression unreadable, and gathered her possessions. No one stepped forward to help her—and none of the other males showed any sign of interest.

"They're not like us," a voice said from behind him.

He turned to see Elf.

"To us, that's a disturbing sight—a rape, perhaps even a gang rape. To them, that's normal. No one will think any less of her, while the males are doing what comes naturally to them. On the other hand, they may mock her for not being careful when she was on the verge of entering mating season. She should have been inside so she mated with the male *she* chose—if she chose any male."

Roman blinked. "Have you been here before?"

"I read the file as soon as we arrived in this system," Elf said with a wink. "Old Marine saying—learn everything you can, because you never know what might come in handy and you'll feel a damn fool if you don't know it when you need it."

Roman nodded sourly. But they had to ponder what they read to make any use of it.

He looked back at the alien female and saw her walking away, almost waddling. The other aliens seemed utterly unconcerned, although he saw a few casting their lidless eyes in the direction of the two humans. A handful of other humans—all teenage boys—had chortled to themselves at the show before heading back to one of the human buildings. They'd thought it was hilarious.

"What are we doing here, anyway?" Roman asked after a long pause.

"Shore leave," she said dryly. "I must say you've been a terrible disappointment to me as your escort. All you've done is drink, and you've visited an alien city. You should be being fleeced by a fast-talking dealer, or spending your credits in a brothel...I remember a young ensign who was reported missing during shore leave and we had to go track him down. It turned out that he'd been lured into a drug den, and honestly thought that it hadn't been more than a day."

Roman snorted. "And how long was it?"

"A month," Elf said. "The poor bastard was completely out of it, utterly zonked. At least they'd fed and watered him, or he would have died before we pulled him out."

"That wasn't what I meant," Roman said. He tried again, hoping she'd understand this time. "What is the Federation doing on Maskirovka?"

"We're here because we have no other choice," Elf said. "What are you going to do now?"

"I don't know," Roman admitted. He still had three days before he was supposed to report onboard the *Donna Noble*, leaving him at loose ends. He couldn't return to *Enterprise*, not now. "I just don't know."

"Come with me," Elf said, reaching over and taking his hand. "There's a place where we can dance—I love dancing—and then get some dinner, and more dancing... and who knows where it might lead?"

Roman looked up in surprise. He'd thought that she'd lost interest in him, if she'd ever had it.

"You're the hero of the hour," she said with a wink. "Relax and enjoy it—and all the free drinks you'll get when you tell your story. Tomorrow is another day of woe and misery, in a universe of woe and misery, where death and destruction stalk us like...two giant stalking things."

"Oh, shut up." Roman laughed. "Lead on, fair lady."

Chapter Twenty

In public, all members of the Senate regard their fellow Senators as rivals. In private, they are often far more friendly—after all, they have friends and family in common. The world of the Federation Senate is a largely closed one and few people are permitted to enter it, at least without pledging their loyalty. The few Senators who are not part of the Factions are rarely able to accomplish anything.
-An Irreverent Guide to the Federation, 4000 A.D.

Earth, Sol System, 4092

It would have surprised many of the residents of Earth—particularly the poor unfortunates who spent their entire lives in the cities that housed hundreds of millions of human beings—that there were parts of the planet that had returned to an almost pristine state. The Federation hadn't shared its predecessor's obsession over preserving the planet's ecosystem, but it had encouraged the development of off-planet industry and the transfer of as much manufacturing capability into orbit as possible. The development of fusion power, solar power satellites and other systems had reduced—and eventually eliminated—most of the sources of pollution that had so bedevilled earlier generations. As more and more people left the planet, or crowded into the growing network of interconnected cities, the planet had started to recover. Large portions of entire continents were slowly returning to a more natural state.

The citizens rarely saw any of it. The ones who managed to obtain a fairly good education and better themselves tended to emigrate, often finding work as contract labor, although their descendents might find citizenship on a colony world.

There were always rumors about tribes living in the wilderness, unaware or uncaring of the modern world, but no one took them seriously. Grand Senator Rupert McGillivray would have liked the rumors to be true, if only because they showed the indomitable nature of the human soul. No other race had achieved so much in so short a period of time.

He smiled as the first aircar—escorted by hovering gunships and private troops—settled down on the landing pad at the front of his mansion. Like almost all of the Senators, and all of the Senators who were part of the network of families that made up the Federation's political elite, he lived in the countryside, inhabiting a mansion that had been in his family for generations. The Senate Hall was the public place for debates, but the mansions had always served as the place for private deal-making, all the more so now when a political catfight between the Conservatives and the Socialists could spectacularly shift the balance of power. The two visiting him today who would eat his food and drink his wine would hate the thought of being beholden to the remains of the Imperialist Faction, but they had little choice. Admiral Justinian had knocked down far too many old certainties.

The second aircar floated in from the opposite direction, forcing his house's traffic control system to concentrate on keeping the two escorting forces separate. In these troubled times, Rupert wasn't surprised that they both had heavy escorts, yet doing so ran the risk of an argument turning into an actual battle. Perhaps they were intent on demonstrating their power in the hope that they wouldn't have to use it. There was nothing more worrying than a terrified member of the political elite.

He keyed the badge he used as a private terminal.

"Escort our guests to the Blue Room," he ordered as he turned and left his private room. "I will be along shortly."

Generations of his family had added their own improvements to the mansion. Examples of alien artwork—the loot of humanity's conquests—littered the walls, joined by hundreds of paintings that had been liberated from various art museums and storage vaults centuries ago. Some of them were believed lost by the remainder of the human race—for example, a painting of the Battle of Pearl Harbor that hung on his wall from when Chinese forces had stormed the American base in the opening days of World War Three had been reported destroyed after San Diego was decimated by a nuclear bomb—while others were held in trust for the day they would be returned to humanity.

He padded down the long corridor, shaking his head. Very few people on Earth, outside of people attending universities and of course the historians, knew there had once been nations called America or China. These days, when people thought of Americans, they thought of the American-ethnic planets that were part of the Core Worlds.

The Blue Room had been designed for conferences and was outfitted with the most sophisticated counter-surveillance tools known to the Federation. It was comfortable, rather than formal, with a small drinks dispenser and adjustable chairs, along with a processor that could connect to every database on Earth. Rupert took his seat and settled back, waiting for his household staff to escort the guests into the room. Their allies—the supporters and aides they'd brought to the meeting—would be placed elsewhere. The real meeting would take place here.

He stood up as Grand Senator The Honorable Carlton Brockington, Leader of the Conservative Faction, was escorted into the room. Brockington looked tired and worn. The shock of hearing about the defeat at Jefferson, much less the later battle at Boskone, had taken a toll on the Conservative Faction. Allegiances were being redrawn under the table, suggesting that Brockington might find himself replaced if the war continued to go badly. Grand Senator Alison Wallisch, Leader of the Socialist Faction, looked altogether more confident. She cast a nasty look at Rupert as she entered, reminding him that she—at least—hadn't forgotten how the Socialist Faction had been pushed into supporting the Blue Star War. The prospect of yet another alien race to civilize had proved too tempting to resist.

"Thank you for coming," Rupert said once the doors had closed. He had no doubts about the loyalty of his household staff, but the other two would be aware that his staff worked for *him*. "It is my pleasure to allow you to use my humble home for your talks."

Brockington scowled at him. He knew when he was being mocked.

The shifting political scene might not resurrect the Imperialist Faction, but Rupert controlled a handful of votes. They could be decisive if the two main factions fell out. Perversely, despite being the weakest of the three, Rupert knew that he was in the strongest position. He might not be able to win on his own, but he could determine who won—or lost.

"We need to consider the current situation," Brockington said after a long pause. "Parkinson failed us. The grand march to victory he promised turned into a disaster. The media...has been tearing away at our failure to secure the victory we guaranteed."

Rupert concealed a smile. The Senators controlled around a third of Earth's media, but the system of checks and balances the original writers of the Federation Constitution had worked into the system prevented them from controlling *all* of it. And that didn't include the independent media outlets off-planet; the Core Worlds would resist any attempt to slap controls on their media, threatening the position of their elected representatives. The net result, now that Admiral Justinian hadn't been squashed flat, had been the media turning on the Senate. Someone in whatever was left of Navy HQ had leaked the records of the battle and retired admirals had been happy to comment on Parkinson's many failings as a tactician, feeding the panic. Earth's citizens hadn't had to feel fear since the First Interstellar War. Now, after the attack on Earth itself, they were fearful and turning on the Senate.

"They've actually been demanding that we put Admiral Drake in charge," Alison said. "For all I know, he's the one who might have leaked the recordings to the media."

"I very much doubt it," Rupert pointed out mildly. "Admiral Drake has ordered the media out of the Boskone System, citing concerns about revealing too much information to the enemy."

"A clear abuse of his authority," Alison snapped.

Rupert thought about pointing out the hypocrisy in that statement—the Socialist Faction wanted to control the media completely, believing that the less the public knew, the happier they'd be—but declined the opportunity to score a point. Instead, he focused on the issue at hand.

"Admiral Drake has also given us a victory—both victories," he said. "And then he managed to extract most of the Retribution Force from Jefferson after it was ambushed. I submit to you that we cannot afford to lose him. We *have* to use him."

Alison snorted.

"And what happens if he turns his coat and goes over to Justinian, or sets up on his own? We are talking about giving him enough firepower to wreck several planets..."

"More like entire star clusters," Rupert said. "A single destroyer could wreck a planet or two if they weren't defended."

"The fact remains that he could turn on us," Brockington said. "He may be from Mars, but his family is not well-connected. They are certainly not connected to the Senate."

"We could find him a wife," Alison said slowly. "There are quite a few possible candidates for a marriage which would tie him to us by blood. There isn't even any reason why it has to be immediate. We could hold out the promise to him and delay things until Justinian is defeated—and then cancel the arrangements, if necessary."

"I have asked my researchers to draw up an extensive psychological file on Admiral Drake," Rupert said with a smile. He'd also spoken to Professor Kratman and some of his other allies, although that wasn't something he was about to mention in this company. "Their conclusions were quite encouraging."

He had their undivided attention.

"Marius Drake is a believer in the Federation; in duty, honor, loyalty...all the military virtues," Rupert continued. "His desperation to convince us to release additional units to the Rim didn't come from an urge to challenge us, or to encourage his own relief, but from a determination to protect the colonies from pirates and Outsiders. Drake may not be loyal to any of us, not personally, but he is loyal to the Federation—and we are the embodiment of the Federation. I believe we can count on him.

"He could have gone rogue along the Rim, or joined Admiral Justinian, or even led his ruined fleet to a different sector and set up as an independent warlord," he pointed out when they looked unconvinced. "Instead, he chose to make his stand and hold Admiral Justinian. That is not the record of a traitor, but of a very loyal man."

"We can use him," Alison agreed.

"The fact remains," Brockington growled, "that he isn't one of us. Even if we arrange him a marriage to one of our daughters, he won't be part of High Society."

"We could always put in another formal commander and inform him that he is to consider himself subordinate to Admiral Drake, whatever the chain of command might say," Alison said thoughtfully. "That would save us having to acknowledge that we owe him, at least publicly."

"I'm afraid that won't work." Rupert shook his head. "In fact, it would be asking for trouble."

"And why would that be the case?" Alison rounded on him.

"Let's face facts, shall we?" Rupert asked. "The bonds of loyalty that held the Federation Navy together are snapping. Admiral Justinian was merely the first to attempt to seize supreme power for himself. There are at least a dozen other admirals—or Sector Governors—who might launch their own bids for power. They're currently sitting on the fence, waiting to see what we do.

"Now tell me: how do you think they'd react when we keep replacing the one man who has bought us victories?" He smiled at their disgusted expressions. "We will be telling them that whatever grounds we use for promoting people, they don't include either loyalty or competence. The ones who don't have serious political connections will be wondering if they will be made to carry the can for failures or disasters caused by other people. The ones who are ambitious will start thinking how they can accomplish their aims without us, if we don't help them. We have to send them a message—and that message has to be that we will reward loyalty, and success. Or we may as well decide that we're going to lose most of the Federation."

The Socialist and the Conservative looked at each other.

"Very well," Brockington said, finally. "We will recognize Admiral Drake as he deserves."

Rupert nodded.

"And we also have to listen to his recommendations. You saw the report he sent back to Earth. We have to honor it as much as possible."

"He's asking for huge monetary expenditure at precisely the time we need to reduce spending," Brockington pointed out. "We cannot afford a new program of military construction."

"And you think that Admiral Justinian cannot afford it?" Alison demanded. "We increase the taxes on the industrialists—call it an emergency raise in taxation, to be repealed after the war—and use it to fund the program. We're fighting for them as well as ourselves."

Rupert smiled as they started arguing again. Brockington was opposed to all increases in taxation on principle, if only because the industrialists provided much of his Faction's backing. The Socialists, on the other hand, had wanted to hit the industrialists with higher tax rates for centuries. Brockington's supporters would not be happy, not the least because there was no guarantee that the Socialists wouldn't insist on keeping the higher tax rates after the war was over. If the Socialists used the wedge they'd been given and forced through *higher* taxes—and penalties, and regulations—they could cripple the economy. Worst of all, they'd be using the money they gained to buy votes by distributing government largesse into the Core Worlds, ensuring that they couldn't be easily removed from power. The results would not be pleasant.

"With very strict limits," Brockington said unhappily. "And we end the war as quickly as possible."

"That may take years," Rupert said flatly. "Admiral Drake was clear on that. We have to rebuild, train new people and produce an entire new fleet. And then we have to smash our way to Harmony and crush Admiral Justinian in his lair. All of that assumes that Admiral Justinian is the *only* one we have to deal with. If another admiral turns rogue, we could be looking at a nasty civil war that will last for decades."

"And put far too much military power in the hands of Admiral Drake," Alison observed. "There should be checks and balances."

"Interfering with his command could cause a disaster," Rupert reminded her. It was a point he had to keep repeating. The Senators had been absolute masters of the Federation for so long that they had problems realizing that might have changed. "We either trust him or we don't. There isn't a middle ground."

"Right," Brockington said. "We trust him—and we take a few precautions. My cousin's youngest son is going to be promoted; right, we will promote him to commander and assign him as Admiral Drake's aide. A Fleet Admiral needs an aide and that aide has to be well-connected himself, so he won't be able to argue. And when the time comes that Admiral Drake is no longer needed..."

He allowed his voice to trail off suggestively.

No one bothered to argue.

଼୨ ଓଷ

The banquet following the second round of meetings—when the decisions taken by the leaders were hammered out into formal proposals that would be presented to the Senate—was as elegant as Rupert could make it. His servants served a luxurious meal coupled with the finest wines from across the Federation. He allowed himself a second glass of Brigadoon Whiskey as he contemplated his success. The other two didn't realize it, as their Factions were currently occupied in sorting out the contracts for the new wave of military construction, all of which promised vast opportunities to skim from the government funds in all manner of barely-legal ways, but he'd gotten everything he wanted.

He turned back to the table and smiled as the desserts were finally served. His maids, like the maids in all of the other mansions, wore skimpy uniforms and bracelets that marked their status as brain-burned criminals. The brain-burned—a punishment reserved only for the very worst of criminals—had no rights, but using them as personal servants was illegal. Not that it really mattered; for High Society, laws were something that happened to other people. The brain-burned made ideal servants. as they did what they were told, without question, and never betrayed their masters.

It would have really upset his visitors, particularly the half-drunk youngster who was playing with one of his maids, to know that they weren't brain-burned at all. It was astonishing what someone would say in front of someone they *knew* couldn't understand them. The level of intelligence Rupert gathered was remarkable.

The maid put a plate of cheese and biscuits in front of him and he ate it slowly, considering his next move. So far, everything was going entirely to plan. All of the variables had been successfully predicted and countered. So far, he reminded himself; ultimate success was not guaranteed. Nothing was *ever* guaranteed in life.

Still, the Brotherhood *would* be pleased.

Interlude One

From: *The Chaos Years* (5023)

As we have seen in preceding chapters, unnoticed by most of its citizens, the Federation's moral authority was declining rapidly in the period following the Blue Star War. The social glue that held the Federation together was crumbling, creating an unrecognized state where corruption and ambition went hand-in-hand to shake the Federation to its foundations. Admiral Justinian was merely the first admiral to turn into an independent warlord; the Federation's failure to crush him quickly meant that others would be tempted to try their luck. The Senate—nervous about its grip on power—only made matters worse. Admirals and governors who might have sat on the fence saw the Senate's desperate attempts to shore up its power as a threat, one that might consume even the loyal.

So it was that the three years following the Battle of Boskone—and the stalemate between the loyalists and Admiral Justinian that resulted—saw the Federation stumble from crisis to crisis. No less than seven Sector Governors and nine admirals declared independence, or attempted to turn their sectors into autonomous regions within the Federation. Two went rogue and turned their fleets into pirate forces, or headed out beyond the Rim to set up pocket kingdoms of their own. The chaos kept spreading. No one was safe.

It was Admiral Lafarge who has been commonly credited with posing the worst threat to the Core Worlds. Lafarge, commander of a sector far too close to the Core Worlds for comfort, risked a drive on Earth, convinced that the Senate intended to recall and murder him. (No amount of historical research has provided convincing evidence that this belief was actually well-founded.) His incursion, destroyed by Home Fleet in the brief and bitter Battle of Terra Nova, only provided the impetus to the Senate to proceed with its plans for internal security—even at the cost of alienating other potential allies.

An outsider, looking at the Federation from a mythical objective vantage point, would have wondered if the edifice was going to collapse within years, perhaps months. Rogue and rebel admirals, Outsider raids and even rebellions on hundreds of human and alien worlds threatened its integrity. Had the Federation's many enemies succeeded in working together, its defeat and dismemberment would have been a certainty.

And so it was that Admiral Drake, now promoted to Fleet Admiral, set plans in motion to keep its enemies off-balance and suspicious of one another. It was the only hope of salvaging something of the Federation from disaster.

Chapter Twenty-One

Assault cruisers were designed to serve in a variety of roles, from intelligence gathering to commerce raiding and other roles. Although the class was originally designed in the years following the Blue Star War, the first examples only entered regular service during the Chaos War, after the Battle of Terra Nova.
-Jane's All The Universe's Starships, 4160 A.D.

FNS *Magnificent*, Boskone System, 4095
It was an older and more confident Roman Garibaldi that strode into Fleet Admiral Marius Drake's office on the superdreadnaught. He wore a captain's uniform as if he'd been born to wear it.

Marius accepted the younger man's salute and returned it before waving Garibaldi to a seat. The newly-minted captain took it without the hesitation he'd shown on their first meeting, three years ago. Marius smiled as he returned to his own seat. It wasn't the first time he had mentored a promising junior officer, but Garibaldi was something special. Very few people had the combination of skill and luck that Garibaldi displayed in abundance. The Promotion Board clearly agreed. At twenty-five, Garibaldi was the youngest captain in the Federation Navy—and in history.

The thought made Marius smile momentarily as he nodded to his steward, who had prepared cups of coffee for the admiral and his guest. Too many promising young officers had died since Admiral Justinian had started his rebellion, killed in battle or captured by one of a dozen factions that were tearing the Federation apart. Admiral Justinian's second attempt to punch through the Asimov Point and capture the system had been bad enough, but the revolution on Maskirovka had been bloody and futile...and the other rogues had been worse. Marius knew that he'd been lucky to get even the reinforcements he'd been given, not with too many other flashpoints requiring a permanent Federation Navy presence. The Senate's growing panic had ensured that large forces were kept on permanent standby around nodal points, limiting the ships that could be deployed on offensive operations. It was total bloody chaos.

"My congratulations on your promotion," Marius said as they sipped their coffee. "I read the citation. Your little stunt at Terra Nova could have gone spectacularly wrong."

"Yes, sir," Garibaldi said. "I believed that the risk was justified."

Marius had to smile. The younger man was more focused than he'd been as a junior officer. War did that to young officers, those who survived the first few years of their careers.

"So did the Promotion Board and your own captain," Marius agreed. "I read both his report and the more private message he forwarded to me. You nearly gave him a heart attack."

He smiled at Garibaldi's expression. "You deserve command of *Midway*, certainly," he added, changing the subject. "Command of the first of a new generation of starships! Not too shabby, not at your age."

Garibaldi hesitated, and then must have realized that he was being teased.

"Yes, sir," he said, an unmistakable note of pride in his voice. "I'm very proud of her."

"I read the readiness reports." Marius tapped the datapad on the table. "You're doing very well, certainly better than some believed. I think you have a bright future ahead."

He shrugged, dryly. "And since you've come all the way from Earth, do you have any personal messages for me?"

"There's a locked information store that I brought over to you from the Senate," Garibaldi informed him. "And Professor Kratman gave me a datachip that I was to place into your hands alone." He reached into a sealed pocket, produced the unmarked chip, and passed it over to Marius, who took it gingerly. A secure datachip would be rigged to disintegrate if someone tried to break into the encoded data store. "He sends you his regards."

"I served with him," Marius said absently. He placed the datachip in a secure drawer on his desk and closed it with an audible thump. "It's good to see you again."

"Thank you, sir," Garibaldi said, sounding excessively formal. "It is good to see you again too."

He wasn't used to the informality of higher-ranking officers, Marius noted, certainly not among those under his command. But he'd learn.

"You may change your mind," Marius told him, and smiled at his nonplussed expression. "I have a particular task for you and your ship. I'm afraid another tempting opportunity to get yourself killed in the line of duty beckons."

Garibaldi showed no overt reaction.

"Yes, sir," he said.

ॐ ∞ ☙

Admiral Drake, according to rumor, had been offered another Star Carrier—perhaps even the *Enterprise* herself—as a flagship, but had chosen to continue to fly his lights on the *Magnificent*. Roman had only been onboard her once, when he had been relieved from command of *Enterprise* and officially promoted for the first time, so he'd never seen the briefing room. It was large enough to hold every captain in the fleet, but only a handful of people were seated at the table today: a brown-skinned woman without any rank tabs, a very dark-skinned man he'd never seen before, a Marine Major General who looked oddly familiar...and Blake Raistlin, who turned towards Roman with a welcoming smile. He wore the tabs of a commander and the white and blue uniform of an admiral's aide, which struck Roman as odd. The Raistlin he remembered had been determined to win a command.

"My father didn't like the thought of me risking myself," Raistlin muttered when Roman asked. "I'm his only heir, you see, and he felt that I shouldn't be risked on board a smaller ship. I haven't told him that when the admiral takes us back on the offensive, I'll be on this superdreadnaught and under fire from enemy ships. It would only upset him."

"If we could all be seated," the brown-skinned woman said, "we can begin."

The room locked and sealed itself as Roman took his seat. Admiral Drake joined them, seated at the head of the table, along with a man Roman recognized; Admiral Mason, who looked as if he hadn't changed much from the days when he'd flown his flag on *Enterprise*. Mason gave him a thin nod.

Of course, back then, Mason hadn't thought much of his flagship's commander and hadn't hesitated to make his feelings known. Roman had been told that some officers had opposed his promotion to captain and wondered, absently, if Mason had been one of them. And what, precisely, was he doing at the briefing? The last Roman had heard, he was still in command of the fleet's starfighter force.

"I am Commodore Arunika, for those of you who don't know me," the brown-skinned woman said calmly. "My companion"—she indicated the black man—"is known as Uzi. His real name is highly-classified and he assures me that he has forgotten it himself. His precise role here will be explained in the privacy of this briefing room and may not be discussed outside a secure compartment. Anyone found leaking the data to any unauthorized person will be facing a court martial before they can blink."

She smiled thinly. "With the admiral's permission, I will review the current situation before going on to outline Operation Kidd," she said.

Drake nodded.

"Admiral Justinian has been content to play a waiting game since his failure to punch through the Asimov Point a second time and the defeat—the destruction—of the rebellion on Maskirovka," she told them. "The sudden upsurge of violence and rebellion all across the Federation—and the rise of the new warlords—may have helped encourage him to remain quiet, for now. We do not expect that happy state of affairs to last, nor are we able to go on the offensive. The bottom line is that we believe he is currently building up his forces with the aim of taking advantage of our weakness before we can overcome the other threats and crush him."

A holographic star chart appeared over the table, a number of stars blinking bright amber.

"Six months ago, Governor Pyotr Eustasovitch Hartkopf abandoned the pretense that he was a loyal and able servant of the Federation," she continued. "Hartkopf's name was a byword for corruption and decadence long before Admiral Justinian kicked off the war, but powerful friends in high places prevented him from being recalled to Earth to face an investigation. An investigatory commission was, in fact, being pulled together when Hartkopf, perhaps realizing that time was running out, chose to declare himself a warlord. He subverted or overcame loyal units of the Federation Navy and established himself in full control of the Zathras Sector.

"As you can see from the star chart, this poses us with a series of problems unseen since the Inheritance Wars. Hartkopf's positions are connected to Federation territory through an outstandingly long chain of Asimov Points and diverting the firepower necessary to crush him would mean leaving other bases and locations uncovered, for months at least. Worse, his territory effectively borders Admiral Justinian's and it is possible that the two will come to an alliance. While Hartkopf doesn't possess the level of firepower that Justinian has at his disposal, their alliance would open up new angles of attack for Justinian into Federation territory. Our psych profiles of Justinian do not suggest any great enthusiasm for an alliance with Hartkopf, but we feel that the possibilities would make his doubts moot."

She tapped her terminal and the star chart focused on a handful of stars along the borderline between the two warlords. "Our intelligence networks were torn apart during the first rebellions, both ONI and Federation Intelligence, but we have been working to pull them back together. That hasn't been an easy task. The Asimov Point in this system has been blocked and we are therefore forced to fall back on the longer paths into enemy space, making communication difficult. What we have been able to find out, however, is alarming. Hartkopf, who always had links with smuggler bands operating out of places like Hobson's Choice or Rawls, has been making alliances with pirates, mercenary groups and perhaps even Outsiders. I don't need to tell you, I suspect, that any such alliance could shift the balance of power quite remarkably."

Roman considered it, and then nodded. Hartkopf didn't have the firepower or industrial base to stand up to the Federation Navy, but if he hired mercenaries and made links with Outsiders, he might be able to trade on the advantages he did have to build up a more powerful fleet. And if Admiral Justinian gained unimpeded access to Hartkopf's space, the Federation's outer flanks could be exposed. And if the Outsiders got involved...

"Operation Kidd is intended to prevent that possibility from ever coming to pass," Arunika said, her voice calm and composed. "Like all operations, it has a substantial amount of risk, all the more so because we cannot commit overwhelming forces to the objective. The plus is that if it works, we will accomplish it without a major redeployment of mobile units."

"ONI has established—don't ask how—that the two warlords have been working on establishing supply chains running through Marx and The Hive." She nodded towards the star chart. "Neither system was surveyed properly when they were discovered and—at the time—the fact they were only twenty light years apart passed unnoticed. The Hive may be taboo space, but that doesn't bother the smugglers—it's the perfect place to transfer goods and supplies. The ships pop out of the Asimov Point in one system, travel to the other using stardrive, and then re-enter the Asimov Point network. The border between the two warlords isn't under control, not properly. We believe that it won't be long before pirates start to infest the region, once they realize that there are opportunities for loot there. We're going to get there first.

"Operation Kidd has three objectives," she added. "The first is to scout the area and draw up a rough outline of their operations within the border systems. We have some idea, but our data is very limited and often quite out of date. The second is to establish a secret operations base within the sector, one that can support a small squadron of light units. The third is twofold: first, to raid their ships and damage their supply lines, and second, to make each of them think that the other is responsible for the raids. Hartkopf's reputation goes ahead of him and he's precisely the kind of person who assumes that others have the same low motives as himself."

"Let's you and him fight," the Marine Major General said.

"Precisely," Arunika said. She paused. "Does anyone have any questions?"

"Yes," Roman said. It had occurred to him the moment she'd mentioned raiding their ships. "It strikes me, commodore, that they will think the only people who actually benefit from the raids are us, the Federation itself. They may not be fooled by us, whatever IFF signals we use..."

"That actually works in our favor," Arunika assured him. "If they don't realize what we're doing, that's great—they will break off relations and perhaps even go to war, which will give us the chance to crush the winner when he finally emerges. If they do realize the truth, they will have to divert scarce ships and resources to protect their convoys, a task that will require capital ships rather than light units. We win either way."

"I have a different question," the Marine said. "What are we going to do about Hobson's Choice?"

"For the moment, nothing," Admiral Drake said before Arunika could speak. "I know; we need to do something about them, even if it involves flying a battle squadron into their system to convince them to see reason. For the moment, however, the Senate has vetoed all operations against the world. They feel that it would set an uncomfortable precedent."

Roman frowned and accessed his implants. Hobson's Choice was barely rated as habitable and had only been settled because the founder had discovered the planet, claimed it and then realized that no colony developers were willing to buy the rights to settle there, on the grounds that hardly any colonists would willingly choose to emigrate. Even the Involuntary Settlement Department—which ran the hell-worlds the Federation used as a dumping ground for serious criminals—hadn't been interested. The founder had bought some tools, convinced a few of his friends to help out and established a small settlement. He'd styled himself a King and written a very loose body of laws; three hundred years later, the independent world had a thriving and thoroughly illegal economy as a base for smugglers, mercenary outfits and probably pirates. It was not, technically, a Federation member world, but that wouldn't protect it if the Federation Navy decided to come knocking.

The Senate's reluctance to move against the planet was odd. Perhaps some of the Senators had hidden interests on the world?

Admiral Drake cleared his throat. "We will proceed as follows," he said. "Captain Garibaldi will take his ship into the sector and start scouting. Admiral Mason and Task Force Kidd will follow him within a week and base themselves at FAS-382674, at least until they can locate a proper location for a base. Once the shipping routes have been charted, the Task Force will commence operations against their shipping."

Roman kept his face blank by force of will. Serving under Mason's command was not his idea of fun. He wouldn't put it past Mason to insist on flying his flag on the *Midway*...no, he couldn't, not if the *Midway* was intended to precede the main body of the fleet. If the truth were to be told, he wasn't entirely happy with orders to play pirate, even though he saw the underlying logic. Turning two of the Federation's enemies against each other would save lives in the long run, even if it meant going near The Hive. Mason would probably insist on using The Hive as a base of operations, the bastard. He wouldn't be gripped with the almost supernatural fear that pervaded the Federation. The Hivers were dead and gone, but the trauma they'd caused would never be forgotten.

"I have a question," Mason said flatly. He sounded as if he'd just bitten into a very rotten fruit. "You are talking about operating on the end of very long supply lines. How long do you expect us to keep even a relatively small task force up and running before we have to withdraw from the region?"

"For the first part, we will be sending a large Fleet Train with you," Arunika said. "For the second part, you will have to purchase supplies from Hobson's Choice. They will be happy to sell anything to you; they never have problems supplying Outsiders, or rebels, or even aliens. Uzi and his team will handle that part of the operation."

Roman frowned. Mason was right; he might be an asshole, but no one could call him incompetent. Relying on Hobson's Choice as a source for supplies struck him as absurd, even though the files backed Arunika up. The planet's natives would be happy to sell anything to everyone. There was no law or order, apart from a loose agreement not to fight in orbit around the planet.

He turned to look at Uzi and started in surprise as he saw the man's eyes. Uzi was enhanced, almost a cyborg. Fully-enhanced humans were rare, even on the most advanced Federation worlds; the RockRats were the only culture to embrace enhancement on a regular basis. Apart from The Hive...

"There is no reason to fear," Uzi said. He had a gravelly voice that reminded Roman of the first Instructor-NCO he'd encountered at Luna Academy. It was easy to see some of the enhancements flexing under his skin as he spoke. "We have operated in that region before. Obtaining the supplies you require will not be difficult."

"I don't have to remind you," Admiral Drake said softly, "that preventing the two warlords from linking up is a priority. If all of the warlords, or even most of them, learn to work together, the Federation is doomed. Consider that while you're preparing for this mission."

Chapter Twenty-Two

Military-grade encryption is, of course, banned for public use in the Federation. Naturally, attempts to prevent its dissemination have all failed. Everyone from the Senate to the poorest peon on a barely-settled world wants private communications. There is a thriving underground trade in encryption protocols and an ongoing battle between their creators and the various counter-intelligence agencies in the Federation.
-An Irreverent Guide to the Federation, 4000 A.D.

FNS *Magnificent*, Boskone System, 4095
"He has grown up a bit, hasn't he?"

Marius nodded as he poured glasses of wine. If there was one advantage to being—officially, at least—in the Senate's favor, it was that he was regularly sent gifts by people hoping to ingratiate themselves with him. Marius simply took them, distributed some of them to people who needed the gifts more than him, and never acknowledged any of it, hoping that the senders would get tired of wasting their money. So far, it hadn't worked. They'd sent very good wine, though.

"He has," he agreed, as he passed Admiral Mason his glass. He took his seat and tried to relax, even though it was difficult knowing that there was a hostile enemy fleet on the other side of the Asimov Point. Both sides had sent through recon drones from time to time, but neither had followed them up with a full-scale offensive...and nothing less would settle the issue. The defenses on Admiral Justinian's side of the Asimov Point were formidable. Even if Marius succeeded in breaking through with his fleet, he'd be bled white. "And I noticed that he was a little wary of you."

"Young upstart," Mason said without heat. "I guess that the whole incident at Terra Nova convinced most of us oldsters to give him a ship."

Marius snorted. Mason was fifty years old and, going by some of the pre-war standards, young for his current rank. He wouldn't have been given Task Force Kidd at all, were it not for the fact that he needed fleet command experience to be promoted higher. Marius expected him to do well, if only because getting in, hitting the target and getting out again were skills that fighter pilots excelled in. Mason hadn't flown a fighter in years—his leg had had to be replaced after an accident that had nearly killed him—but he still had the guts and determination that had taken him into the cockpit.

"He's brave," Marius said after another swallow of wine. "He'll do well, so don't attempt to relieve him without a very good cause."

"Your young protégé," Mason said dryly. "Why did you assign him to this operation? *Midway* is a good ship, perfect for the mission, but she's hardly essential."

"Everyone needs to learn by doing," Marius said. "They told us at the Academy that it was sink or swim time. Didn't they tell you something like that on Mars?"

Mason shrugged.

"I'm surprised you gave me *Golden Hind*," he said. "Didn't the Admiralty want you to keep her out of danger?"

"She's ideal for the mission," Marius said, scowling. "And I really cannot spare any of the fleet carriers I have to join you. The Admiralty keeps making noises about transferring some of my superdreadnaughts to face one of the other warlords and that would invite attack from Justinian if he realizes we've been weakened. I'd bet you anything you want to put forward that he has his spies in this system, watching us."

He scowled again. The Core Worlds were the greatest nexus of industrial power in the known universe, but gearing up to produce a vastly-expanded military took time and money. He hadn't heard much from the Senate, yet there were stories about production issues and work slowdowns that had been largely kept out of the media. Admiral Justinian had been preparing his own industrial base for ten years, and was still building it up. If the war lasted too long, God alone knew how many other warlords would be deploying their own industrial production nodes.

But then, the Bainbridge Protocols had ensured that every system had at least the basics in industrial production. That was something that had come back to bite the Federation on the behind. Hard.

"Losing her would be a public relations catastrophe," Mason said darkly. "You know that operations are not predictable."

"No," Marius agreed. *Golden Hind* was a star carrier, identical to *Enterprise*...and, just like her sister, was neither a fleet carrier nor a superdreadnaught. Using her as a mobile base for a raiding party made far more sense than risking her in battle, even though losing her would not amuse the Senate, or the Admiralty either. "I expect you to do as you see fit. I wish I could come with you, but..."

"I know exactly how you feel." Mason drained his wine and stood up, placing the empty glass on the small table. "I'll uplink my operational plans once my staff and I have drawn them up, admiral. And I won't relieve your young officer. Besides, most of the task force will be operating independently during the operation."

"I know," Marius said. Realistically, losing the entire task force—even *Golden Hind*—wouldn't affect the balance of power that much. The media, however, would go mad and demand answers—and he would shift from public hero to villain very quickly. "Good luck, admiral. Depart as soon as you are ready to go."

Marius settled back into the sofa as the hatch closed behind Mason. He didn't want to admit it, but he envied the man. Mason was going to be doing something, rather than floating near an Asimov Point that might at any moment disgorge an attacking fleet with blood in its eye. Marius had learned at the Academy about a politician who'd fancied himself a general; he'd arranged, perhaps by coincidence, that powerful armored forces would be drawn up on the border, facing his enemies. Eventually, the enemies had—like civilians living on a dormant volcano—started to grow used to the threat and to discount it. And then, when his enemy was lured into dangerous complacency, the politician-general had struck—and won.

Of course, if he'd folded his cards then, rather than choose to continue the war, he might have reshaped the world in his image.

There was a chime at the hatch. Marius sent a command through his implants; the hatch hissed open, revealing Commander Raistlin. Marius wasn't too happy with the thought of having a permanent aide, as he'd always been more comfortable with a tactical staff. But Fleet Admirals were always assigned aides. Marius' case had been unusual, though, as most senior officers above the rank of captain arranged aides for themselves—but he had to admit that Raistlin had thus far been very helpful. If only he didn't keep updating his superior on matters that were for junior eyes.

"I have the latest reports from Commodore Tsing," Raistlin said. He was always polite, but his manner conveyed an undertone of informality that reminded Marius of his exalted family. "He says that his squadron should be back in formation in three days at the latest."

"Good," Marius said.

Tsing's squadron—the One Hundred and Twenty-Third Superdreadnaught Squadron—was largely composed of new ships from the Jupiter Yards, but they'd been having teething problems since before they'd arrived and joined his command. Their engineers had reported that someone had skimped on the shielding, requiring several days of difficult and expensive repair. At least they'd managed to move a mobile dock and fabricator into the system—with the Senate complaining hugely about the cost, of course—and they hadn't had to send the ships back to the nearest Fleet Yard.

"Has there been any update from Commodore Lopez?" Marius asked.

"No, sir," Raistlin said. "His last update was at 0700. Since then, his squadron has not reported in to the flagship."

Marius stroked his chin while remembering that Lopez he hadn't been given orders to report in regularly. "Never mind, then. If there is no other business, I suggest that you hit your rack and get some sleep. We're going to have a long and busy day tomorrow."

He smiled while Raistlin saluted and left the cabin, but frowned as soon as Raistlin was gone. The commander's very presence was odd. He was good enough at his job, but it was clear that he hadn't *wanted* the position. And considering his father's political connections should've assured that Raistlin would've been able to get him transferred to a better position, it was even odder that Raistlin was here.

Raistlin's father was a powerful Senator. The Admiralty wouldn't pick a fight with him over something as minor as his son's position. A powerful Senator could cause a great deal of harm if he decided to attack the Navy...

He dropped that train of thought, then activated his implants and uploaded a very specific code into the room's processor. The hatch sealed with an audible *clunk*, and the monitors were turned off. No one else on the ship, apart from her captain, could deactivate the monitors at will; indeed, few were even aware they existed. It would only have upset the crew if they'd known that everything they did was recorded.

Once he'd performed a quick sweep for bugs, he unlocked the drawer in which he'd put the private datachip with his thumbprint, and then opened and removed both the datachip and a private terminal. Keeping a private system wasn't exactly against regulations, as it was tricky to enforce, but it would certainly raise eyebrows if anyone knew he had it.

Just as well they don't, then, he thought.

He inserted the secure chip into the terminal and waited impatiently while the machine checked it, then demanded his ID codes and retinal patterns. Annoyed, Marius supplied them while, wondering what could be worth this level of security. The datachip unlocked, accessed its opening file and displayed it automatically. A holographic image of Professor Kratman appeared in front of him.

"Good morning, Marius," Kratman said. He looked older than the last time Marius had seen him, although that could just be due to the tiny image. "Or is it evening where you are? I have no way of knowing, of course, but I like to think that it's morning there, too. You'll be pleased to hear that the latest crop of Academy graduates is coming along very well, although I may have to cut a few of them for the crime of not thinking about the subject matter. One of my more successful students is carrying this chip."

Marius frowned. The Professor was rarely so chatty. It had to be bad news.

"Bad news first," Kratman said, as if echoing Marius's thoughts. "The expanded training camps for new crewmen aren't producing anything like enough crew for the new construction. Now that the Naval Reserve has opened up all of their facilities, I fear that we may be looking at a shortfall in the required numbers of new crew. The ones we trained before the war—or should I say *wars* now, I wonder?—were the ones who actually *wanted* the positions, and we could weed through them at will. The expanded training camps are actually taking recruits we wouldn't have taken at all, back in the old days."

He shrugged. "It isn't a new problem, son. Earth's educational establishment has been producing ignorant kids for centuries. Kids who have the drive to learn can access the information they need, but no one kicks them in the ass and tells them to get moving. And most of them opt for easy courses and credentials before leaving school at eighteen and going on the dole and producing a few more stupid kids. Anyone smart enough to actually make something of himself is smart enough to emigrate—and God knows that anyone capable of doing that on Earth will be a success even on a hell-world. Mostly, the ones we have would normally become couch potatoes or gangsters—and die young.

"But this is the raw material we have to work with, so we need to turn them into crewmen. It isn't an easy task. Nine-tenths of Earth's population can't even read! We've had to open up remedial training centers for the youngsters, and it really isn't enough. They don't understand anything we tell them beyond the very basics, if that. The hell of it is that this will dumb down the entire fleet once they graduate. Honestly, I'd be afraid to sail on a ship maintained by some of the so-called recruits. And believe me, most of the Core Worlds are in the same state. The really smart ones emigrated generations ago.

"Matters aren't helped by the fact that the Senate has created a whole new series of security agencies," he added. "One of my contacts warned me that there is a movement afoot to start assigning political officers to your ships—and fortresses, and training centers...basically, they will have vast powers to seek out and destroy anti-Federation elements. You can probably imagine that it won't be long before their powers *really* start to expand. You need to be careful of this, Marius. The Senate is scared, and scared people do stupid things."

He chuckled. "Speaking of the Senate, they're *still* trying to find a bride for you. No, I don't think that you or she will have much choice in the matter. It isn't common for someone like yourself to marry into the political elite, but I think that some elements are determined to bind you strongly to them. It's odd, though; I've been telling every cadet who will listen that the political elite is barely a tiny fraction of a percentage of the trillions of human beings, yet they still haven't managed to find you a bride. If I had to guess, I'd say that they are either squabbling over who *won't* have to marry you, or they are stalling. Probably the latter—but seriously, I suspect that it won't be long before they produce someone and tell you to marry her. I've attached a list of possible brides, but there are no guarantees. Luckily, you don't have to love the woman. You don't even need to have sex with her, not to produce a kid or two. Pretty much all of High Society use artificial wombs these days.

"But back to the matter at hand. I'm afraid that there have been more...incidents at various construction yards than made it into the official reports. I wouldn't have heard anything if I'd just been dependent on the standard chains of communication. Going from what I heard, there have been everything from dangerous accidents caused by poor workers to strikes and perhaps even outright sabotage. I don't think that any of them are actually linked to the warlords, but it hasn't helped the Senate's sense of security. The last I heard, they were talking about sending in a military regiment and using force to impose order. I'm not convinced that that is going to work very well. If the workers are drawn from the same labor pool as the trainee crewmen, they're just going to be fearful as well as ignorant."

He stared down at his hands for a long moment. "I have heard through one of our mutual friends that Senator Chang Li has absconded from Earth. I had the pleasure of meeting her at one of the Academy's inspection tours and she struck me as impressive, perhaps the smartest political figure I have ever met. Quite ineffectual, of course, and I suspect that her departure is linked to the current series of...problems. The last I heard, just before she left, the Senate was talking about conscripting workers from the out-worlds and putting them to work on the construction yards, perhaps even recruiting them for the fleet. You know how nervous they've been about colonials in the Navy since the Inheritance Wars. It will be a disaster if they try to conscript unwilling recruits in large numbers. The last thing we need is a second round of colonial wars. At least they're not thinking about recruiting aliens."

"Or perhaps they are," he added, brow furrowing. "They're working on recruiting a specialised unit, and the security is quite phenomenal. The unit may be composed of specially-trained people from Earth, or maybe aliens. It isn't as if the Federation is short of aliens who would be interested in cracking human skulls for a living."

The Professor looked up. "I promised myself that I'd send you some cheerful news, but we have a slight shortage of it," he concluded. "There are rumors that at least three of the warlords are organizing themselves into a single unit—luckily, not an overwhelmingly powerful unit, but enough to be dangerous. And the Senate feels that it cannot rely on any senior officer, except you, perhaps. I'd be surprised if they trusted you completely. Watch your back."

He grinned, adding: "And a military victory would be good, too. Good luck."

His image vanished. Marius put the chip and his private terminal away, making sure to secure the drawer properly, then sat down again and thought about what he had been told. He'd rerun the message later, of course—it would run three times before it was automatically wiped from the chip—and read through the files the Professor had included, too, later at night when he'd not be disturbed. He wasn't too interested in any prospective bride; he'd never married, and had never intended to marry. And yet, the Senate was tempting him with the ultimate prize. His descendants would be part of the political elite that ruled the Federation.

And yet...who was really running the show? It wasn't hard to guess who Kratman worked for, besides the Federation Navy. His position was ideal for selecting and investigating prospective recruits. And he had access to information that a lowly professor, no matter how well-connected, should never have been able to access.

He keyed his intercom, unlocking the privacy shields. "Gary," he said when he was linked to the CIC. "I want you to find Commodore Arunika, wherever she is. When you find her, tell her to report to me in my cabin. I need to see her as soon as possible."

"Aye, sir," Lieutenant Owen said. "Fleet Com shows her on the fleet carrier *Helena Cain*. She should be with you within an hour."

"Thank you," Marius said. "I'll wait."

Chapter Twenty-Three

The Marine contingent on a Federation Navy starship reports directly to the ship's captain or acting captain. Junior officers are not entitled to issue commands to Marines, regardless of rank. This ensures that, if worst comes to worst, the captain has a loyal force at his disposal. However, friendly relationships between Marines and Navy crewmen are not unknown and there is a considerable amount of fraternisation.
-Observations on Federation Navy Regulations, 4056

FNS *Midway*, In Transit, 4095

"I noticed that you can't sleep," Elf said in the half-darkness of the captain's cabin. The artificial starfield thrown over the bed shone upon her, lending her features an otherworldly air. "The responsibilities of command pressing down on you?"

Roman nodded without moving the rest of his body. The captain's cabin onboard *Midway* was huge, far larger than anything he felt that he had a right to expect—or needed. Three years of service since graduating from Luna Academy hadn't left him with much in the way of possessions, although one wall was covered with some old-style printed books he'd picked up on shore leave. Admiral Drake, he'd been informed, was a keen book collector and so Roman had attempted to follow in his mentor's footsteps in that regard. He'd soon discovered that books were an overpowering habit and, somehow, they bred on his shelves.

"Yeah," he said after a long beat. "I don't want to fuck this up..."

Elf was now his best friend and his lover. But no one knew about it outside his cabin. Whenever she was on duty, most particularly when she was surrounded by others, she was all Marine. Their relationship didn't *quite* break any regulations, but if it became known, people would talk.

And he didn't want that for Elf. She was a damned good Marine. She'd earned every promotion she'd ever gotten.

So he kept it quiet. And hoped no one would figure it out, because there were times that Roman thought that the Federation Navy ran on chatter and rumors.

Elf snorted and poked one of her fingers into his stomach. "And when was the last time you fucked something up?"

"I wasn't in command then," Roman said. "I mean...I didn't know I was going to wind up in command of the *Enterprise*, so when I did, I hadn't had any time to think or plan. Here...the buck stops with me."

"And you know what you are doing, you know that it needs to be done, and you know that the Admiralty has faith in you," Elf said dryly. She poked him again, harder. "And if they didn't have faith in you, they wouldn't have given you the *Midway*. How many of your graduation class have their own newly-constructed assault cruiser to play with?"

"True," Roman agreed. He reached out and touched the bulkhead, marvelling at the faint vibration he felt as the ship's stardrive drove her on into the endless night.

Only three of his fellow year-mates from Luna Academy had been promoted to captain—two of them, like Roman himself, originally had been forced into a dead man's shoes. Several others had been killed in the incessant wars tearing the Federation apart. "Of course, we are also the test-bed for the whole concept. We fuck up, and the whole construction program goes to hell."

Midway was the latest design of assault cruiser, a cross between a heavy cruiser and a battlecruiser. She was fast enough to catch almost anything in known space—apart from a starfighter or gunboat—and armed to the teeth. He couldn't take her into battle against a battlecruiser or anything heavier, but *Midway* would have no difficulty evading anything powerful enough to punch her out. The designers had talked about using her as a fast scout, but the Admiralty had marked her and her sisters down for commerce raiders as soon as the potentials had percolated through their collective heads. And then there were the prospects for covert insertion missions and other interesting tasks.

Roman's appointment to command her was a sign that some very powerful and well-connected people had a great deal of faith in him.

And yet, although he hadn't wanted to admit it to Admiral Drake, he had his doubts about the mission. Not the part about sowing dissent between the two warlords—that clearly served the Federation's purposes, although that alone suggested the enemy would know who was to blame—but raiding commercial and industrial starships like simple pirates. His parents had been killed by pirates, long ago, and he'd hoped to be assigned to *hunt* pirates. The *Donna Noble* had spent the six months before the Battle of Terra Nova escorting convoys and chasing pirates, and he'd enjoyed every last moment of it. It felt as if he were avenging his parents every time he killed a pirate's ship.

But then, Federation Navy was tearing itself apart and, scenting an opportunity, the pirates had begun to press their efforts closer and closer to the Core Worlds. Roman hadn't been allowed—officially—to see accurate figures, but the ones he'd obtained from an old friend suggested that pirate activity had increased tenfold over the last three years. It didn't take much mental effort to deduce that their depredations were actually damaging the Federation's economy quite badly, particularly when the Federation Navy couldn't spare the ships to escort convoys and patrol the more vulnerable systems. How many more ships would be taken, their crews tortured and killed, before the civil wars ended and the Federation Navy resumed normal patrols?

"The sooner we win, the better," Elf said when he put his fears into words. "If what we're doing in this sector helps win the war, we need to do it. Besides, how many people legally visit The Hive anyway? The last I heard, the Senate had quarantined the entire system and banned all entry without special permission."

"The pirates don't pay attention to the Senate's orders," Roman pointed out. He threw back the covers and climbed out of bed, standing naked against the artificial starlight. Outside the hull, there was nothing more than the madness-inducing continuous displacement space. "I just wish I felt more comfortable with our orders."

"I shouldn't worry about it," Elf advised. She picked up a pillow and threw it at him with devastating accuracy. "We do have a few more hours before we are required to return to duty...unless you intend to whine some more?"

"Fuck you," Roman said without heat.

"You just did," Elf reminded him. "If you want my advice, you ought to keep a closer eye on the Delta Commandos and not worry so much about the pirates—or acting like a pirate. They may have orders that you won't like..."

Roman frowned. The Delta Commandos—Uzi and the nine enhanced soldiers along with him—had come on board just before *Midway* had departed the Boskone System. They'd been given a suite of cabins and kept to themselves, refusing to interact with the Marines or any of the other crewmen. If they were training behind closed bulkheads, Roman didn't know about it—or anything else they might be doing. The file he'd been given on them had been surprisingly thin, merely a brief outline of some of their capabilities and an order to take their requests and suggestions into account, if any were offered. Roman suspected that was actually a way of saying to treat any suggestions from Uzi as orders.

He looked over at her and lifted an eyebrow.

"Are you saying that they can't be trusted?"

Elf shrugged, which did interesting things to her breasts.

"I'm saying that they tend to do the dirty work—wet work—and that they have a very dark reputation among the Special Forces community. You cannot assume they will follow your orders, whatever regulations may say about a captain being the sole authority on his ship. Their superiors in the Senate may have given them specific orders, and told them to keep them from you. They report to the Senate Oversight Committee specifically."

She frowned. "The Colonel told me once that a team of Delta Commandos arrived on Luton when the rebellion against the ruling caste was underway. The rulers had begged their allies in the Senate for help and they sent the Delta Commandos, who somehow got into rebel territory and butchered the rebel leadership, along with their families and friends. They then manipulated the rebels into fighting each other with a program of planned assassination and black propaganda. This whole plan—putting the warlords at each other's throats—smacks of their work. God alone knows what they have in mind."

"So they definitely can't be trusted," Roman said. "Are they actually good fighters?"

"Individually, better than most Marines," Elf admitted. Roman could tell that that admission had cost her. "Their enhancements—each of which cost ten billion credits, by the way—make them formidable in any combat zone. On the other hand, they don't always play well together. And an enemy who refuses to panic, or assume that she's automatically beaten, is going to have a fair chance of defeating them."

She grinned. "But they're damn hard to kill. You could toss one of them into vacuum, and it wouldn't do more than piss him off.

"Anyway, enough doom and gloom." She reached for him and pulled him towards the bed, pushing him down and straddling him, her hands running over his chest and up towards his neck. "If you're not going to sleep, I have something else for you to do..."

ᏸᎧᏇᏣ

"Long night, sir?" Commander Janine Trojanskis, his executive officer, said as she offered him a mug of strong coffee.

Janine was several years older than Roman, and by all rights should've had her own command years ago. Yet a black mark on her record prevented her from being promoted past her current rank. Since her file was sealed, Roman had no idea what Janine might have done to annoy the Admiralty. It couldn't have been gross incompetence; she was a good officer, he'd seen that already. Roman's best guess was that she'd insulted an admiral in some way, and that personage must have decided that forcing her to serve under a younger man was sufficient punishment.

"Of course not," he said, knowing all the while he was lying. Elf had told him he needed to go see the doctor to get a sleep aid, but he'd declined; the story of Captain Trautman who'd accidentally slept through the Battle of Prince's Burg due to taking a drug to get to sleep was still well known throughout the Federation. "Ship's status?"

"All systems functioning nominally, sir," Janine assured him as he took the command chair. "The *Midway* is fully at your command. I stand relieved."

"I relieve you," Roman said, settling down into the command chair. "I suggest that you get some sleep. We'll be in the Tranter System soon enough, and I'll need you on the secondary bridge."

He settled back into the command chair, took another sip of coffee, and considered the engineering reports. Janine was right—they *were* all nominal—but he always checked them himself. After two weeks of travel—first through three Asimov Points, and then crossing the inky darkness of space—it paid to be careful. If the stardrive broke down while they were traveling between star systems, they would be stranded in interstellar space. It was a spacer's worst nightmare, apart from the Slowboaters—and they were just plain weird.

The hours ticked by slowly until *Midway* reached the mass limit and dropped down to Slower Than Light speeds. Roman knew the odds were vastly against an enemy picket ship having the sheer dumb luck to be lurking anywhere near their arrival point, but he launched a pair of stealth drones and kept *Midway* under cloak until he was sure. The Tranter System was effectively enemy territory, and discovery would force them to retreat into FTL and come at the target from another direction.

"Take us in," he ordered. "Tactical, continue to monitor the drones. Inform me if there is the slightest hint that we're not alone out here."

The Tranter System was fairly typical, as star systems went, although it lacked a gas giant that could be mined for He3. It had seven rocky worlds orbiting the system primary, one of them habitable and, like many other worlds, home to an intelligent race. Roman had seen holograms of the inhabitants and it was easy to see why they were called Trolls: they were huge, ugly and given to carrying clubs and swords around wherever they went. The human settlers had used their technology to convince the Trolls that the humans were gods—a few thunderbolts had ensured they would be worshipped with fervor—and started shipping Trolls out as slave labor. It might have been against any number of laws and regulations, but Trolls made good security guards and slaves, although they didn't possess the brainpower to handle advanced technology.

Or so the file claimed.

Personally, Roman wondered if that were actually true. The Trolls might prefer to be taken for dumb animals, only a step or two above cats and dogs. It would certainly be safer.

"Captain," the tactical officer said sharply. "I am picking up energy signatures from AP-1!"

"Go to tactical alert," Roman ordered calmly. Energy signatures on their own proved nothing—AP-1 was a good place to station a defense force—but if the defenders were on the alert, they might have picketed the entire system. "Can you get me a breakdown at this distance?"

There was a long pause.

"At least nine starships, all dreadnaught-sized," the tactical officer said, finally. "They're mounting modern scanners and tactical drives. I can't pick up anything else at this distance."

Roman nodded, thinking hard. The Federation Navy had only a handful of dreadnaughts in service—and none of them had been assigned to this sector. The dreadnaught design had been superseded by the superdreadnaughts, with the last dreadnaughts being built during the Inheritance Wars. After the wars, some had been sent to the Naval Reserve, while others had been decommissioned and sold as scrap. ONI had warned the Federation Navy that pirates and Outsiders were buying decommissioned ships for their own purposes, but no one had put a stop to the practice. Even a hull, without drives, weapons or sensors, was worth billions of credits.

It stood to reason that warlords would buy up every starship they could find, hiring mercenaries to help fight their wars and defend their worlds against the Federation Navy. It was rare to encounter a mercenary unit with anything larger than a heavy cruiser, but Roman couldn't think of any reason why one *couldn't* have nine dreadnaughts—apart from the crewing issue. A dreadnaught needed upwards of four thousand men to run effectively, although they could have modernized the ship and placed greater dependence on automated systems than the Federation Navy preferred.

Or perhaps one of the warlords had made a deal with the Outsiders and offered support in exchange for military assistance. Roman could see the sense in that, too.

"And AP-2?" Roman asked.

"Nothing, as far as I can tell," the tactical officer said. "They don't even have an ICN station on duty near the Asimov Point..."

"Unsurprising," Roman commented dryly. It wasn't as if the Marx System had anything to offer, apart from pirates and perhaps a black colony or two. The civil war that had literally destroyed the entire planet hadn't left much behind. "Still, we will be careful. Very careful."

Midway slipped towards AP-2 carefully, every passive sensor alert for a prowling starship. Logically, Roman told himself, there was no reason for Governor Hartkopf's forces to picket the Asimov Point, not when there was nothing to be gained by trying to hold it and no reason to expect anything to come out of it. On the other hand, the governor had to know that Admiral Justinian would turn on him one day and perhaps attempt to use AP-2 as a possible angle of attack. In that case, securing the Asimov Point might seem like a good idea...although there were more direct ways for Justinian to get at his enemy without a costly diversion.

"No sign of any cloaked ship," the tactical officer reported very quietly. There was no need to speak softly—sound didn't travel in the vacuum of space—but no one had been able to break crews of the habit. "Still...passive sensors only, sir."

Roman nodded. Passive sensors wouldn't give the ship away, but they also meant that *Midway's* sensor capability was grossly reduced. A cloaked enemy ship near the Asimov Point might spot them and launch a barrage before Roman's active sensors located her presence. It was risky, but it cut three weeks off their journey.

"Take us in," he ordered. *Midway* glided forwards, very gingerly, as if she expected an ambush at any second. They were within the Asimov Point... "Jump."

Space twisted around the cruiser, then they were suddenly in the Marx System.

"Report," Roman snapped. At least missiles weren't already being fired towards them. "Are we clear?"

"No sign of any watching picket ships, captain," the sensor officer reported. "The system might as well be deserted."

"Maybe," Roman said. It would take months of searching to locate a hidden colony or starship—if the task was even remotely possible. "Helm, take us towards the first waypoint. And then we will go pay a call on The Hive."

He smiled at their relief. If nothing else, the long trip was finally over.

"It's time to go hunting," he assured them. "Let's see what we can find, shall we?"

Chapter Twenty-Four

The Brotherhood is not a banned organization. This is because of several reasons: Senators have been known to find it useful, it helps promote human unity (and therefore Federation rule) and, perhaps most importantly, no one knows half—if that—of the members of the Brotherhood. The secret society's leaders are completely unknown. Anyone could be a Brother or Sister of Humanity. Anyone.
-The Dark Secrets of the Federation, 3999

FNS *Magnificent*, Boskone System, 4095
"I understand that you sent for me, admiral?"

Marius leaned back in his chair and contemplated Commodore Arunika. She was pretty, as pretty as she'd been the day they'd first met, back before the Retribution Force had set off on its ill-fated mission. That wasn't too surprising, considering modern anti-aging treatments—Arunika's file claimed she was over sixty years old—but what *was* surprising was that she was still a Commodore. ONI handled promotions internally—the Promotion Board didn't sit in judgement on Intelligence personnel—yet she should have been promoted long ago.

But then, that would have meant transferring her away from *Magnificent*. And that suggested all kinds of reasons why she might not have been promoted.

Her file had been remarkably thin, even for his clearance. Arunika had been born on Hindustan—the first world settled from India, back during the Second Expansion Era—and abandoned her caste to join the Federation Navy. She'd also abandoned her surname, a sign that she had turned her back completely on her homeworld. Hindustan wasn't known for being very tolerant of differences and Marius had heard, from a friend who had visited the planet, that some of its citizens knew little about the Federation and cared less. Some of them might even believe they were still on Earth. Arunika, at least, had known better. ONI had snapped her up during Basic Evaluation and trained her as an analyst, before allowing her to move up in the ranks during the purge that followed the Blue Star War. And, somewhere along the way, she'd been recruited into the Brotherhood.

Marius kept his face under tight control, considering his possible options. It wasn't common for a Brotherhood member to declare themselves openly, no matter what the situation. Arunika had probably been ordered to do so by her superiors, which suggested that part of their reasoning focused around Marius himself. The Brotherhood was supposed to have operatives and members at all levels of society—an outlook that would irritate parts of the Senate—and no one knew for sure who led the Brotherhood, if anyone did. It said something about their influence and reach that the various intelligence agencies hadn't tracked down the Brotherhood's leadership, although it was quite possible that the Brotherhood controlled Federation Intelligence. The Brotherhood was not exactly a banned organization, but if Marius had learned one thing in three years, it was that the Senate would respond harshly to *any* threat to their power—and they could conceivably regard the Brotherhood as a threat.

"Let's cut right to the chase," he said once he'd ensured that the cabin was sealed. "Why does the Brotherhood have an interest in me?"

Arunika leaned forward, her face expressionless. "What makes you think that the Brotherhood has an interest in you?"

"You're here," Marius countered. He had little patience for games. "You declared yourself to me—to everyone on this vessel—and you've stayed with me. Why would you do that unless you wanted me to know who you work for?"

"Point," Arunika conceded with a smile. "Although I don't actually *work* for the Brotherhood. We are more of a collective society than a top-down system. Those of us who are accepted have a say in our collective decision-making."

And I can believe as much of that as I like, Marius thought dryly. It seemed a cumbersome system, although perhaps it worked better in practice. The Brotherhood had been around since the First Interstellar War, and presumably had a great deal of practice in remaining underground and organizing themselves.

"But as for why we are interested in you, I would have thought that was obvious," she added. "You're the commanding officer of this fleet."

"Your interest in me started before the Battle of Jefferson," Marius pointed out. "I say again; why me?"

"You saved Earth," Arunika explained. "That alone marked you as a person of interest. When you were appointed to the Retribution Force, we decided that it would be better if one of us accompanied you, if only to share our view of the situation."

Marius's eyes narrowed. "Did you know that Admiral Justinian was planning a rebellion before the Battle of Earth?"

"I'm afraid not," Arunika admitted. "If we had known, we would have taken action to stop him before he launched his attempted coup. Sadly, Justinian and the other warlords are a symptom rather than the cause of the Federation's problems. The Federation had been falling apart for a long time before someone decided to take advantage of its weakness."

"As Captain—Professor—Kratman told me," Marius said. Something clicked in his mind. Professor Kratman had access to far more information than he should have been able to access. "He's one of you, isn't he?"

"He could be," Arunika said. "I don't get to know everyone in the Brotherhood."

"And how do you know, then, that I am not already part of the Brotherhood?"

"There are signs and countersigns," Arunika said. She touched the space between her breasts with one long, dark finger. "I'll lay our cards on the table. Our purpose is to keep humanity—which means the Federation—strong and supreme. A strong humanity is one that isn't threatened by alien invaders. This prolonged period of civil war risks shattering that unity and inviting aliens to try their luck. The Outsiders are already probing our borders, admiral. It will not be long before they start a full-scale invasion."

Marius sat back in his chair. "How do you know that's what they're planning to do?"

"We have our sources," Arunika said. "I'm afraid that we cannot give details, even to a prospective recruit, but we believe the Outsiders have been planning to invade for a long time. An alliance of Albans and aliens, an abomination against nature, will sweep down on the Rim and push in toward the Core Worlds. And if we keep fighting this civil war, we won't have the power to stop them."

Marius shivered, for her words conjured up a repulsive historical nightmare. Maurice Alban had been a Federation official back during the First Interstellar War who had either believed the lies the Snakes had told him or had sold out completely. Alban had made propaganda broadcasts to human worlds, attempted to organize human laborers working for the aliens and even acted as an advisor for the Snakes. He'd been assassinated four years after the war began, but his name lived on in infamy as a human stupid enough to believe that humans and aliens could coexist, or worse, that humans could submit to aliens. An alliance between Outsiders and unknown alien foes was the Federation's worst nightmare.

"As you are currently the Federation's foremost military officer, we have an interest in recruiting you," Arunika added. "We have information and support—and influence—that you would find useful. In exchange, we'd want you to advise us and perhaps act on our requests from time to time."

Marius considered it for a long moment. "I swore an oath to the Federation," he said finally. "I cannot act against orders, even for the Brotherhood..."

"We wouldn't expect you to betray your oath," Arunika assured him. "We swore similar oaths. You want to protect and defend the human race, as you swore when you were commissioned into the Federation Navy; we share the same goals and oaths. We would not ask you to commit treason on our behalf."

"I see," Marius said. "What happens now?"

"If you accept, I make contact with my superiors and you get welcomed into the Brotherhood," Arunika said. She held up her hand and displayed the silver ring. "If you refuse, you won't hear anything more from us. We're not going to assassinate you for daring to refuse."

"I'm glad to hear it," Marius said dryly. "Do I get time to think about it?"

It occurred to him that the Brotherhood simply didn't *need* to assassinate anyone. A person who accepted their offer would have his career path smoothed by unseen allies, to the point where he owed his position to the Brotherhood and would be willing to do anything for them. A person who refused simply wouldn't be able to harvest any of the benefits of membership. And the Brotherhood was *old*. They could have their people in all levels of the Federation Navy, perhaps even in the Senate.

But he had already risen as high as he could go in the Federation Navy...

"Take as much time to think about it as you need," Arunika said. She hesitated again. "Purely because your interests and ours coincide, I should tell you that we orchestrated the press campaign on Earth that ensured that the Senate couldn't simply dismiss you when your military victories turned you into a possible threat to them. You may wish to consider what else we could do—both for you and final victory—before you make your decision."

ഇ∞ൠ

Marius found Vaughn in Marine Country, watching as the latest regiment of Marines ran through their training exercises before being deployed to Maskirovka on a pacification mission. It wasn't the role that anyone wanted for the Marines, most particularly the Marine Corps itself, but it officially provided a training opportunity for the young soldiers. Unofficially, pacification battalions were in great demand throughout the Federation at the moment, so none could be spared for Maskirovka. It was butcher's work, and Vaughn had complained bitterly about it—fortunately in private. Marius was sure that any public complaints of this nature would not have been good for Vaughn's career.

The Marine General nodded after Vaughn realized Marius was there, but frowned when Marius gave him their private hand signal to ask for an immediate—and private—chat. Vaughn nodded again, and led Marius to Vaughn's own office, which should be clear of surveillance devices. Marine counter-surveillance teams made sure of that.

"So." Vaughn waved Marius to a seat in front of his desk. "What's eating you now?"

"The Brotherhood," Marius said.

He outlined everything that had happened since he'd heard the message from Professor Kratman. It wasn't something he would share with anyone else—the Brotherhood wouldn't react kindly if its secrets were spilled to outsiders—but he trusted Vaughn completely. That said, there was no way to know if the Marine wasn't a member of the Brotherhood. It would be easy to give into paranoia and assume that *everyone* was part of the Brotherhood.

He finished with, "I confess that I have no idea what to do."

"You always were too focused on space battles to see the more subtle political battlefield," Vaughn commented, when Marius had finished. "You should try running a counter-insurgency campaign once in your life. It will give you a whole new appreciation for politics—and teach you how to eat soup with a knife."

"I'm serious," Marius protested.

"So am I." Vaughn gave him a long, level look. "The Brotherhood relies upon secrecy, misdirection, and rumor to build its power. Reality doesn't matter, not compared to what people *think* the Brotherhood is, or about what it can do."

Marius contemplated this for a long moment, then set it aside. "Still, look what they're offering. How can I turn it down?"

"Do you have any real evidence that their claims are true?" Vaughn asked in return.

"They put an agent—probably more than one—into ONI," Marius pointed out. "And they can steer her career so it intersects with mine. I think they have a great deal of power and influence, even if it is behind the scenes."

Vaughn considered it for a long moment. "Now you know why I never followed my father into politics...well, that and I knew my father's name," he said.

Marius snorted humorlessly.

"Let's see." Vaughn steepled his fingers. "You have the choice between accepting the Brotherhood's help, which would give you access to far more influence than you have at the moment, or refusing their offer and carrying on without their help, right?"

Marius nodded.

"And what are they asking for in return?" Vaughn asked. "They're just asking for you to do your duty. It isn't as if they've ordered you to bombard Earth with antimatter bombs, is it?"

"So you think I should accept their offer?" Marius asked him.

"I didn't say that," Vaughn demurred with a smile.

"No, but I can tell you think it," Marius shot back. "What happens if the price is too high?"

"It's good to know, given what they're offering, that you consider some prices to be too high," he said.

Marius scowled, taking the point.

"I suppose it all comes down to trust, really," Vaughn said thoughtfully. "Do you trust the Brotherhood to have humanity's best interests in mind?"

"I'm not comfortable with it," Marius admitted. "I don't want an unelected elite dictating Federation policy."

"Oh? And what, exactly, is the Senate?" Vaughn shrugged. "You know as well as I do that decisions made light years away are never as good as decisions made on the spot. The Senate causes problems for colonists and out-worlds simply by insisting on unified regulations, or worse yet, levying taxes that the poor colonists are simply unable to pay. And it doesn't matter if the Senate actually means to cause harm or not—the fact of the matter is that the Senate *is* causing harm. The Senate isn't designed to respond to democratic pressure from the out-worlds, which provokes rebellion and revolt."

"Like the Inheritance Wars." Marius ran his hand through his hair. "I wish I knew what to do."

Vaughn laughed.

Marius gave him a quizzical look.

"I know you very well," Vaughn said. "You've already made up your mind; you just want me to help clarify it. You want to preserve the Federation, while the Brotherhood *also* wants to preserve the Federation. You want to beat the warlords before they become too entrenched to stop, and the Brotherhood also wants to beat the warlords before they become too entrenched to stop. You want to stop Outsider raiding fleets pillaging the Rim, and of course the Brotherhood--"

"I get the point," Marius said. "We have interests in common."

"I don't know enough about the Brotherhood to comment," Vaughn said. "I will say this; they're not going to leave you dangling on the edge of a long chain. You will probably end up being recruited into their senior leadership and becoming one of the people who set its course. You will have an opportunity to shape the future of the Brotherhood, and ensure that it doesn't end up as much a parasite as the Federation Senate."

"I see," Marius said. "Toby...are you one of the Brotherhood?"

"If I was, would I tell you?" Vaughn snorted.

Marius raised an eyebrow.

"No, I'm not one of their agents, or controllers," Vaughn said. "I used to know a couple of Marines who claimed to be in the Brotherhood—there aren't many in the Marine Corps, supposedly—but I never knew for sure. They could have just been bullshitting me."

He grinned. "One of the Marine Training Holograms has a program where an infiltrator from the Recon Force slips into a meeting of the rebel headquarters, only to discover that all of the rebels are, in fact, other infiltrators..."

"I take your point." Marius nodded slowly. "I'll watch my back."

"And so will I," Vaughn replied. "The Brotherhood might not want to threaten or kill a mere cadet, or lieutenant, but someone in your position...if they felt you were a threat, they might decide to deal with you permanently."

Marius gave him a questioning look.

"You have a fleet that is loyal to you and a certain *slight* reputation for tactical competence," Vaughn reminded him sardonically. "You could root out most of the Brotherhood if you tried. And I bet you anything you want to put forward that they've already considered the possibility."

෭෬

"The latest recon probes report that there are now nine hundred fortresses facing us," Commodore Arunika said several hours later at Marius Drake's normal daily briefing. "The best case estimate—worst case from our point of view—is that Admiral Justinian could not have produced more than two hundred fortresses, considering the limited amount of time on the one hand and the fact that if he'd tried for more, it would have required the diversion of most of his industrial output. Simple logic tells us, therefore, that most of the fortresses are actually nothing more than ECM buoys. But without actually charging into the system and seeing which ones fire on us, there is no way to tell the difference at this range."

"So in other words, we cannot launch an attack through the Asimov Point," he said with a nod. "Thank you for the briefing, Commodore. We will consider other alternatives after lunch."

He wasn't particularly surprised at her information. A full-force attack could be very costly, as Admiral Justinian had found out during his first and second offensives. Somehow, they needed to find another way to deal with Justinian before the Senate ordered them to launch a direct assault, even though it was against all military logic.

He waved for her to remain behind as the officers filed out of the briefing compartment.

"I've thought about your offer," he said once they were alone. "I accept."

"That's good to hear," Arunika said with a smile. Her smile grew wider as she held out her hand. "Welcome to the Brotherhood, admiral. I look forward to working with you."

Chapter Twenty-Five

When on detached duty, separated from higher command, a captain will handle matters as he sees fit. Naturally, different captains have interpreted these regulations in different ways.
-Observations on Federation Navy Regulations, 4056

FNS *Midway*, The Hive System, 4095
"Anything to report?"

"Negative, captain," the sensor officer said. "The system is as quiet and dark as the grave."

"It is a grave," Roman pointed out dryly. The *Midway* was floating in space, twelve light minutes from the single Asimov Point, cloaked and watching through every one of her passive sensors. "Maintain a steady watch and continue to deploy passive sensing platforms. Inform me once all of the platforms have been deployed."

He looked up at the star chart in the holographic tank and smiled. A fluke of astrometry had placed the Marx System alarmingly close to The Hive System, only a mere four light years apart. In the days before the continuous displacement drive, they might as well have been in separate galaxies, but now even a commercial-drive ship could cross that distance in a week.

It said something about the taboo most people felt regarding The Hive that relatively few shipping companies had taken advantage of the opportunity when the continuous displacement drive had been licensed for commercial starships. Even now, after so long, the system was abandoned. Or at least there were no signs of any habitats or starships. If some remnant of The Hive still existed, they were very well concealed. They knew what would happen if they showed themselves.

Just before the Inheritance Wars had begun, back during the political ferment that culminated in the Battle of Spider Bite and the start of the first war, a scout ship had stumbled through the Asimov Point and surveyed the system. Finding nothing of particular interest, the settlement rights had been sold to a development corporation, which had started to ship in settlers, industrial nodes and all the other equipment intended to help get a new colony settled and self-sustainable. The Bainbridge Protocols had been taken seriously in that age and the development company hadn't stinted, even with the wars weakening the economy. The Hive—it had been called Morning Glory at the time—should have been a success.

Instead, a little surprise the scouting parties had missed had destroyed the entire colony and threatened the entire Federation.

It was hardly unknown for a life-bearing world never to develop an intelligent race and the survey crew had almost been grateful, for an alien race would mean surrendering their settlement rights to the Federation Alien Development Agency. They hadn't noticed how...orderly the planet's small animals had been—the planet hadn't developed any larger animals—nor how they tended to stay well away from the human settlers. The animals might have been unintelligent, but the creatures that used them were alarmingly smart. The Hivers—tiny parasites that shared a group mind and infested living beings, controlling them once they took up residence in their brains—slowly took over the entire colony, and then the star system. The colony's low tech base helped; the infestation wasn't easy to detect and was impossible to remove.

By the time The Hive started sending out infection parties to other worlds, they owned the entire system. It was too late to do anything for the infected, even with the most advanced Federation medical technology.

They'd overplayed their hand, fortunately, and they'd been discovered long before they could infect most of the Federation. The Federation Navy had sealed the Asimov Point—luckily, The Hive hadn't had access to real warships—developed a nanotechnological counter to the alien infestation, and invaded the system. Once the pitifully small defense fleet had been brushed aside, The Hive—and every other world in the star system—had been bombarded with antimatter bombs. The entire star system had been sterilised. There were still rumors that some infected humans had escaped on a starship, somewhere in the void of interstellar space, but nothing had ever been proven. The Hive was dead.

Roman settled back in his command chair, waiting patiently. Once the survey of the system was complete, they would proceed to another system, and then another, until they returned to the rendezvous point. He wasn't expecting trouble, but he'd done everything he could to prepare for it. Besides, it kept the crew on their toes.

How quickly things could change, he mused. As a younger officer, he'd resented the endless drills, but as a captain, he appreciated them. He could not afford to allow his crew to become complacent.

Absently, he glanced down at the reports from the probes they'd launched towards The Hive, an action that had sent shivers of fear down the spines of some of his crew. RockRats didn't suffer from taboos (at least, not the same taboos) as planet-born spacers, but Roman had to admit that they might have a point. The Hive had given birth to a deadly threat, one that could have proven lethal if they'd managed to infect more star systems before being discovered, and one that touched on humanity's worst nightmares. It was one thing for humans to collaborate with alien invaders, but quite another to face the prospect of losing all individuality and merging into a hive mind.

"Captain," the communications officer said suddenly. "I'm picking up a distress beacon, bearing..."

Roman swung around in his command chair and scowled at the display. There hadn't been anything there a moment ago, but that proved nothing. The problem with passive sensors was that they could only pick up objects that were actually emitting energy signatures. A starship that shut down all its drives and sensors would be effectively invisible, a needle in a haystack the size of a planet. And if it was emitting a distress signal...his mind raced, considering possibilities. No warlord, he was sure, would stoop to the level of using a distress beacon to lure in an unwary starship, but pirates had been known to do so. They were already dead if they fell into Federation hands, so what did they have to lose?

And if it was a real distress beacon, they had a moral duty to respond.

"Helm, set course to home in on the beacon," he ordered. The distress beacon was nearly forty light-minutes away. Whatever had happened, he reminded himself, had taken place forty minutes ago. A battle between two starships would be very hard to detect at that range. "Keep us under cloak. I don't want them seeing us if it is a trap."

"Aye, sir," the helmsman said.

Midway hummed slightly as she turned in space and set a new course towards the source of the distress signal. It would take over an hour to reach the beacon, by which time it might all be over. The Federation insisted that all starships—particularly civilian craft—carried lifepods and emergency shuttles, but The Hive was almost always deserted. There shouldn't have been anyone to come to the rescue.

His XO's face appeared in the small display.

"Kind of an odd coincidence," Janine pointed out. "We get here, *then* something decides to happen."

Roman had been having similar thoughts, especially due to the nature of travel through the Asimov Points. It was theoretically possible to see a cloaked ship just as it came out of the Asimov Point, but whoever observed it would have to be in exactly the right place at the right time to do so, and the odds were vanishingly small.

"We were in the system for nearly a day before they set off the distress beacon," Roman countered, even though he appreciated Janine's thoughts and suggestions, as she had more practical experience than he did. "We have no idea what the traffic through this system is like in wartime."

ONI's intelligence had suggested, quite seriously, that The Hive was being used as a transit point for smugglers and pirates. Roman couldn't fault the logic, particularly if smugglers were working with the warlords. Even so, they'd have to be careful about operating *too* blatantly in the system, not when half the planets in the sector would refuse to allow them to dock if they knew that they'd been anywhere near The Hive. It wasn't particularly logical—not when there was little chance of infection unless they actually landed on the dead homeworld. Yet humans had never been logical creatures. Apart from the Hooded Sect, who tried to embrace lives of logic and reason, somewhere out on a hot desert world no one else wanted.

"True," Janine agreed. "Still, best to be careful. They may have no idea what they're trying to trap."

"No argument," Roman agreed. "We'll assume that we're heading into a trap and prepare to face the enemy when they show themselves."

The minutes ticked by slowly as *Midway* inched across the star system towards the squawking distress beacon. Roman had to fight the urge to stand up and pace on his bridge, knowing that it would upset the crew if they thought that the Old Man—which was a joke, given that he was the youngest captain in the Navy—was nervous or fearful. It struck him, not for the first time, just how vast space truly was, even though Asimov Points could take them from star system to star system virtually instantly. It could still take hours to respond to any emergency within a star's mass limit.

Roman ordered the launch of a stealth drone as soon as they entered range, trusting that the drone—using passive sensors—would pick up enough signs of a waiting ambush to allow the ship to escape before any trap might be sprung.

"I'm picking up residue traces of weapons fire," the sensor officer said suddenly. "It reads out as fairly standard plasma fire, perhaps from old-style pulse cannons. No trace of nuclear or antimatter warheads."

Roman looked up at Janine's face and knew that she shared the same thought. *Pirates.*

"Take us in," Roman ordered harshly. Images of his dead parents danced before his eyes. "Set condition-one throughout the ship. Prepare for engagement."

Alarms howled as *Midway* went to battle stations, ready for anything.

"Captain, the source of the distress beacon is coming into visual range," the sensor officer said. "She's no warship."

"All stop," Roman ordered. "Put her on the main display."

He sucked in his breath as the image appeared in front of him, a long, swan-like starship spinning helplessly in space. The *White Swan* liners were ships the Federation's rich and powerful took on holidays, sailing from star system to star system while enjoying the finest in food and hospitality. Roman had grown up hearing stories about how passengers were treated on such liners, stories that hadn't grown much in the telling. A third-class ticket on the liner would have cost more than he made in a decade. And now one of those liners was in front of his ship, its white hull marred by the dark scars of direct hits where energy beams had burned into the hull. She was dead in space.

"Helm, take us on a slow circuit around the ship," Roman ordered. If it was a trap—which looked increasingly unlikely—they'd spring it. "Sensors...report."

"Apart from the distress beacon, the ship appears to have lost all power and atmosphere," the sensor officer reported slowly. "There may be safe locks within the ship preserving some of the passengers and crew, but we can't detect them at this distance."

And they might well have run out of air, Roman thought. *What the hell were they doing in this system, for God's sake?*

"Hold us in position," he ordered. He keyed his intercom to the Marine channel. "Major Elf, are your men ready to board the stricken ship?"

"Aye, sir," Elf said. She sounded the same as always, but he knew she must be as hungry for vengeance as he was. Pirates and Marines were natural enemies; the latter were often the first to see what the former had left of their victims. "Request permission to launch."

"Permission granted," Roman said. "Good luck."

80CB

It took the Marines two hours to search the liner *Harmonious Repose*, out of Harmony, but they'd sent back images from their combat suits as soon as they entered the torn and battered hull. It was a sickening sight. Space combat was normally clean and sterile, yet the pirates hadn't been content to loot the hull and kill the passengers. They'd boarded, stormed the ship, and captured every surviving passenger and crewman. The male crew had been taken down to the ship's gym and summarily shot; the female crew had been raped, then shot. The liner's captain had been found, mutilated and castrated. There were no survivors.

For a time, Roman had held out hope that some of the passengers may have found refuge in a safe lock. But Elf reported that the pirates had burned through the armor and taken the passengers.

The mystery deepened when Roman looked up the service record of *Harmonious Repose*. According to the Federation Shipping Register, the *Harmonious Repose* had been in the Harmony System a few months before Admiral Justinian had launched his attack on Earth and had never been seen since. ONI's report had assumed that the liner—like other commercial ships in Admiral Justinian's territory—had been pressed into service as a supply ship. But the evidence now suggested otherwise.

It made no sense.

Why would Admiral Justinian allow a starship with wealthy passengers—and no military capability—to travel through the badlands of space? And, come to think of it, what was it doing anywhere near The Hive?

As the ship's computers had been destroyed, ostensibly by the pirates, Elf's Marines had to do some digging to find the ship's emergency datacore. Her best computer specialist used Federation Navy codes to break into the system. It wasn't particularly informative, at least on the surface, but the intelligence team working on the datastream uploaded by the Marines were able to draw some conclusions. The liner had been berthed in Harmony for the first two years of the war, and then she'd been pressed into service—finally sent on a route that would have, eventually, taken them out of Justinian's territory. The standard shipping logs, which should have held a full explanation, including a reason for their flight, hadn't been updated in years.

It was almost as if the ship had been retired, and then brought out of retirement for one last mission.

The forensic teams turned up another riddle. The ship's official crew had, of course, been listed in the Federation Shipping Registry. It didn't entirely surprise Roman to hear that most of the crewmen located by the Marines—their DNA sampled by remote drones—weren't on the crew manifest. Even odder, some of them had been Federation Navy personnel in the Harmony System who had—presumably—signed up with Admiral Justinian. Was he looking at the remains of an escape attempt, or something else? The handful of passengers located by the forensic teams—killed in the attack, Roman assumed, as wealthy passengers could be ransomed back to their relatives—were people he assumed would have supported Justinian, those who could be identified at all. And they'd clearly followed communication security protocols.

They hadn't written anything down about their mission, as far as the Marines could tell.

Under normal circumstances, Roman knew, the ship's hulk would have been towed to the nearest planet and the Federation Navy would begin a full investigation while notifying the relatives of the murdered crewmen. That was hardly a possibility at the moment, not with two warlords in the area who wouldn't be inclined to cooperate with the Federation Navy. It was possible that they could use the liner as a source of spare parts, but that would mean transporting her to the *Golden Hind* and the Fleet Train when Admiral Mason arrived. But that would have to wait.

"Elf, deactivate the distress beacon and pull back your teams," he ordered. Unpowered and silent, the hulk wouldn't be detected unless a patrolling ship literally stumbled over it. The odds were vastly against discovery. "We'll keep the records, perhaps relay them to the warlords if they are disposed to cooperate, or inform the shipping companies once we leave the sector."

"Understood," Elf said crisply. "We're on our way."

"The admiral won't approve of sending any kind of notification to the warlords," Janine's voice whispered through his earpiece. "We are at war with them, you know."

Roman nodded sourly. "I wasn't going to send them a message with an ID header," he told her. "We'll have to leave it until we leave the sector, or unless our presence is discovered. The hulk can wait..."

"Captain," the sensor officer said. "I'm picking up a single ship in the system, heading away from us!"

"Show me," Roman ordered.

A red icon blinked into life on the display.

"Why didn't you pick it up sooner?"

"They were lying doggo," the sensor officer reported. "They only just lit up their drive."

Roman did the math in his head. Elf had deactivated the distress beacon three minutes ago. The enemy craft had lit its drive just after it would have heard the distress signal terminate, tipping them off that someone had found the wreck. Distress beacons were designed to remain operational unless the hulk was completely vaporized.

"Helm, bring us about," he ordered. "Take us in pursuit."

Chapter Twenty-Six

The Federation Navy's position on piracy is quite clear. All pirates, regardless of their motivations, are to be interrogated—using truth drugs and brain probes—and then executed. Taking pirates alive is strongly discouraged. Rumors that some pirates have made deals with Federation Navy crewmen have been strongly denied.
-Observations on Federation Navy Regulations, 4056

FNS *Midway*, The Hive System, 4095

Roman gripped his command chair as *Midway* picked up speed, running the tactical position through his head, again and again. In many ways, this reminded him of what the Federation Navy had endured at the Battle of Jefferson, where their survival had depended upon crossing the mass limit and escaping into FTL before the enemy battered them into dust. The pirates, on the other hand, might not *know* that someone was chasing them; they might not even realize they had been detected.

For all the pirates knew, anyone could've stumbled across the dead luxury liner. And they shouldn't know *Midway* was in the system…should they?

"The pirate is picking up speed," the tactical officer reported. "I think I have an identification, sir; she's a *North Carolina*-class light cruiser. Several hundred of them were sold into self-defense forces or commercial shipping interests after the Inheritance Wars, and quite a few of them became pirate ships."

Roman nodded. The *North Carolina* ships had been withdrawn from service, according to his implant records, because they had major failings in their design that had become apparent when the Federation Navy tried to refit them. They operated fine with their original power cores, but more powerful fusion plants and drive fields had shaken several starships apart. The designers had rapidly produced a more suitable design, and the *North Carolinas* had been relegated to convoy escort before being decommissioned at the end of the war.

Unless the pirates *had* risked installing newer drive systems, she couldn't hope to outrun *Midway*.

He felt his lips draw back into a snarl as the distance between the two ships narrowed sharply. Admiral Drake's intelligence officers might want to encourage piracy in the hopes that it would set the two warlords at each other's throats, yet there was no way he was going to allow scum like that to live. There hadn't been any justice for his dead parents, not when pirates had killed them and vanished into the darkness of space, but there would be justice for the *Harmonious Repose* and her crew. The pirate ship would be obliterated.

"I think they know we're following them now," the sensor officer said as the main display flashed red. "They just swept us with high-powered, active sensors."

"Drop the cloak," Roman ordered. There was no point in attempting to hide now. Their pursuit had clearly created enough turbulence to allow their position to be located. "Bring up active sensors and lock onto them. Make sure they know that they can't escape."

He pushed his rage into the back of his mind and concentrated. How would the pirates play it? They might try to surrender and attempt to claim that they should be tried by a planetary court, or they might try to fight. It would be a very short battle, under normal circumstances, and yet...

Roman had standing orders to attempt to take pirate ships intact, if possible. The real problem with finding pirate bases was locating them. The intelligence officers wanted to brain-suck pirate crews to locate their bases and their support network within Federation space. Once they were found, a single battlecruiser would usually suffice to blow them to hell and gone.

"They're locking weapons on us," the sensor officer reported. There was a very brief pause. "Missile separation; I say again, missile separation! I count ten inbounds toward our location!"

"Bring up the point defense," Roman ordered, as tracking data flowed up in front of him. Compared to the massive salvos thrown around during the Battle of Jefferson, it was hardly impressive. And, given that the missiles were at least ninety years out of date, they weren't particularly threatening either. "Deploy ECM drones; take the missiles out only as a last resort."

His lips twitched as *Midway* flew through the missile salvo. The pirates hadn't invested in the latest counter-ECM technology, although few pirates wanted to tangle with a warship under any circumstances. Only one missile refused to be distracted and had to be picked off by a point defence pulse cannon; the remainder flew off into the endless void, completely harmless. Roman could have returned fire, fairly sure of a kill, but he chose not to do so. Besides, the closer they were when his ship opened fire, the greater the chance of scoring a quick kill.

"Open communications channels," he ordered. The communications officer nodded and activated the ship-to-ship frequencies. "Pirate vessel; this is the Federation Navy." Normally, he would have identified himself, but he had no idea who else might be listening in from cloak. "Cut your drives, lower your shields and prepare to be boarded. If you offer any resistance, we will destroy your vessel."

He waited as the message flashed to the pirate ship. It was a bluff, of sorts; even if the Federation Navy hadn't ordained the death of every pirate encountered while on patrol, he had no intention of letting them live. But if he could arrange for their interrogation first, it might allow him to salvage something from the disaster. Admiral Mason wouldn't be too pleased to discover that Roman had been chasing pirates instead of scouting their area of operations. His operations, no matter how strongly they aligned with tradition, might well have revealed their presence to prying eyes.

"No response, sir," the communications officer reported.

"I think they did respond," the tactical officer said. "I have another wave of missiles heading towards us."

"Deploy countermeasures," Roman ordered dispassionately. The targeting systems were systematically drawing a bead on the pirate ship. He'd be able to open fire and cripple her drives within minutes, and then she could be boarded at leisure. The only danger would be the pirates attempting to trigger the self-destruct once the Marines started to swarm over her, but that would have been surprisingly brave of them. Pirates were rarely the bravest of men. "Prepare to engage..."

"Navy ship, we have hostages," a male voice broke into the circuit. The pirate sounded terrified, and yet determined to hold on to his ship. "We have hundreds of well-connected civilians on this ship. If you fire, you'll kill them as well."

Roman ground his teeth. He'd known—*known*—that the pirates had captured the liner's passengers, and yet he hadn't thought about the danger in his desire to blow away the pirate ship and crew. Using the passengers as human shields was an old pirate tactic. Given that anyone wealthy enough to travel on a *White Swan* liner was clearly very rich and would have friends among the wealthy and powerful, destroying the ship would have unpleasant repercussions for his career. And even if he pushed that aside, he didn't *want* to kill hundreds of innocent people. They didn't deserve to die.

"Elf," he said, keying his private channel, "can you liberate the ship?"

"Not easily," Elf said grimly. "The bastards would see us coming. They'd be able to blow the ship or kill the hostages before we landed—it isn't as if they have a future now we've caught them. And what happens when you fire on the ship?"

Roman felt like screaming. She was right. A well-tended light cruiser would survive the crippling blow he'd planned to inflict, but a pirate ship might be destroyed, as pirates were notoriously sloppy about preventive maintenance. And considering there might be human shields on board the pirate ship...

He keyed the ship-to-ship intercom.

"Pirate ship, face facts," he said, hating what he was about to say. "You cannot escape. I will not let you take hostages over the mass limit. And if you start killing hostages, I'm simply going to put a missile in your hull. Now, you can try and delay matters, but I really don't have that much patience."

There was a long pause.

"But I am prepared to deal with you," he added reluctantly. "If you surrender without further ado, I will transport you to the nearest inhabited world. You will face trial there, rather than be summarily executed in space. I believe they will offer you the chance to pay your debt to society rather than execute you on the spot. That's the best offer I will make, and it will be withdrawn soon. I suggest that you choose quickly."

"Right," the pirate voice said. The pirate sounded as if he didn't believe the offer, but judging from the noises in the background, discipline on the pirate ship was starting to break down. The younger pirates, in particular, knew that they were looking at a very short and nasty future that would end with them taking a short walk out of an airlock without a pressure suit.

Roman smiled.

"And what guarantee do we have that you will keep your word?" the pirate asked.

"The word of a Federation Navy officer?" Roman offered. "The fact is, you really don't have a choice. You either take the chance at life I'm offering, or you die for certain when I run out of patience and blow your little ship into debris. Which do you choose?"

There were the sounds of more argument on the pirate bridge, followed by the unmistakable sound of a gunshot. Roman guessed that the previous captain had just been gunned down by his own crew.

"We wish to surrender, Navy," a new voice said. "What do you want us to do?"

Roman allowed himself a moment of relief before ordering them to lower their shields, deactivate their weapons and de-power their ship's drives. After they did so, he commanded, "Disarm your crew and have them wait for inspection in the rear hold. Any resistance of any kind will be met by lethal force. There will be no other warnings."

"Yes, sir," the pirate said, sounding relieved. "We will comply."

Roman scowled. The Federation Navy's policy on pirates wasn't in place just because it was logistically easier to execute the pirates on the spot rather than dragging them to the nearest planet for a trial. It was possible that the nearest planet's leadership might have agreements in place with the pirates, as poorer colonies needed supplies and weren't always too choosy about where they came from. Handing the pirates over to the local governor was sometimes a way to ensure that they'd be freed and allowed to return to piracy. And besides, they *knew* that the pirates were guilty. No Naval court would do anything other than stamp 'fully approved' on the execution certificates.

He keyed the intercom.

"Elf, we have some prisoners for you," he said. "Board and secure the ship, then check out the hostages. We'll set up care for them on board *Midway* if necessary."

"Aye, sir," Elf said. There was a dull *clunk* in the background as the Marine shuttles detached themselves from *Midway*. "We're on our way."

Roman braced himself for last-minute treachery as the Marines flew toward the pirate ship. They were protected by ECM and shields, but even weapons dating all the way back to the First Interstellar War would easily be able to pick off the Marine shuttles. The pirate ship would never survive the barrage Roman would throw at it in response, yet Elf and two platoons of Marines—and the hostages—would still be dead. The pirates might suspect that he meant to trick them, or believe that they'd never see the light of day again; anything could push them over the edge. Pirates were simply not rational.

"We're boarding now," Elf's voice said, in his ear. "No sign of resistance yet..."

"Good," Roman said.

On the live feed, pirates were swiftly secured by the Marines, their hands cuffed after a rough search and the removal of anything that could be used as a weapon. The remaining pirates—wonder of wonders—had followed orders. Elf and her team rapidly arrested them and left them to cool their heels in their own cargo bay. It didn't take any DNA testing to determine that these were the pirates responsible for the attack on the liner. The look on their faces was enough.

The Marines moved on to the hostages, who had been stowed into one of the other holds and a handful of cabins. Roman suspected that most of them were enthusiastic supporters of Admiral Justinian, but they'd probably be grateful to be rescued by anyone at this point. And if gratitude didn't make them talkative, ONI would inject them with truth drugs and strip them of anything worth knowing. There didn't seem to be any reason why some of the captives had been separated from the others. None of the female captives, at least, had been raped, although it was certain that they'd been threatened with it if they refused to cooperate, or if their relatives refused to pay the ransom. They would probably be *delighted* to see the Federation Navy.

Elf buzzed him on their private line.

"Captain, I believe that you should see this one personally," she said. There was something odd in her voice. "One of the captives is far more important than we thought."

"They didn't capture Admiral Justinian himself, did they?" Roman's eyes narrowed.

"Oh, no," Elf said. "They captured his *daughter.*"

"Pardon?" Roman blinked. "What the hell was *she* doing there?"

&ℭℨ

Over three hundred hostages had been rescued from the pirate ship *The Black Knife*, creating an immediate humanitarian crisis for Roman and his crew. Most of the hostages hadn't been injured or mistreated, but they did want to go home as soon as possible, particularly the ones who suspected that ONI wanted a few words with them. They couldn't all be accommodated on *Midway*, creating a minor problem until the engineering crew re-activated some of the space liner's passenger compartments. The *Harmonious Repose* might have been disabled, but she made an adequate passenger space—and a prison for the pirates. Roman wasn't about to leave them on their own vessel.

He looked through the monitor into the holding cell. Henrietta Beauregard-Justinian had been separated from the other hostages on the pirate ship—clearly, the pirates had known who she was—and Roman had ordered her kept in isolation. She was a remarkably pretty girl, barely out of her teens, with long blonde hair and an utterly perfect face. Her file stated that she had been engineered to fit the fashion of her birth time, a technique rarely available to anyone outside the upper class. The RockRats rarely engineered their children for looks.

And she was under sentence of death.

Roman scowled as he studied the oddly composed girl. The Senate had passed decrees ordering that anyone related to Admiral Justinian and the other warlords was to be killed on sight, with their properties seized and their personal effects confiscated. If he handed her over to Admiral Mason, Henrietta would be executed before she had a chance to beg for her life—indeed, Roman knew that his orders suggested that he should execute her himself. And yet, she was too young to be involved in her father's treachery. It wasn't *right* that she should die for his actions.

He looked over at Elf, to see her looking at him speculatively.

"I know what you're thinking," she said. There was no one else in the compartment. Henrietta was guarded by an armoured female Marine, but she was alone in the holding cell. Roman understood how she must feel. "You want to save her."

"Am I that predicable?" Roman snorted.

"You're a decent person," Elf said. She leaned forward until her lips were almost touching his lips. "Now tell me; are you willing to risk everything you've earned since you set foot on *Enterprise* to keep her alive?"

And that was the nub of it, Roman thought numbly. Refusing to execute her—or hand her over to Admiral Mason to be executed—would break the Senate's decree. The Senate would not be charmed with this challenge to their authority. It was true that starship commanders had wide latitude to decide how to interpret regulations, but Senatorial decrees left no room for maneuver. He swallowed, hard. Professor Kratman had warned them that there might be times when they had to choose between following orders blindly or risking court martial, but he'd never considered, even in his worst nightmares...he'd thought about choosing to refuse orders to bombard an inhabited planetary surface, not refusing to execute a slip of a girl. Bombarding an entire planet would be wrong.

And that was the answer, wasn't it?

"Yes," he said. He closed his eyes for a long moment, thinking hard. "How many people know that we took her alive?"

"Only you and I," Elf said. "The others don't know her identity. Her fellow travelers were separated from her as soon as the pirates figured out who she was."

"Good," Roman said. "We keep her here as a prisoner. No one is to know anything about her."

"As a pet?" Elf asked dryly. "What do you intend to do with her in the long run?"

"I'll figure something out." Roman shook his head slowly. At the moment, he didn't have the slightest idea what, though. Keeping her alive was bad enough, but should he report her death? The admiral would be furious if he knew that Roman had signed a lie into the ship's log, with good reason. "You never know. Having her alive might come in handy."

"We could always sell her back to her father," Elf said mischievously.

Roman gaped at her.

"Just kidding, but you do have to admit that it is an interesting point. What *would* his father do to get his daughter back?"

"That's one question," Roman agreed. "And here is the other. What was she doing on that ship in the first place?"

Chapter Twenty-Seven

An officer who knowingly lies to a superior officer, for whatever reason, can be court-martialled at the request of the victim. A Board of Inquiry will decide if the incident was justified or not. If not, the ultimate sentence is death.
-Observations on Federation Navy Regulations, 4056

FNS *Golden Hind*/FNS *Midway*, FAS-48237892, 4095

"I assume, young man," Admiral Mason said coldly, "that you have some kind of explanation for this?"

Roman kept his expression blank. The flight to the rendezvous point had been fraught with tension. A single assault cruiser might slip through an unguarded Asimov Point without anyone detecting its passage, but a star carrier was far larger—and *Golden Hind* was supported by seventeen older-model starships. The admiral had known the risks of detection and chosen to brave the passage anyway, even though it would put them out of direct contact with the loyalists for several months. He couldn't blame the admiral for feeling a little concerned. He *had* overstepped his orders, after all.

"Yes, sir," he said carefully. "I have a very good explanation."

"Really?" Admiral Mason said. His tone suggested that he didn't believe a word of it. "Let me see now, shall we? You were ordered to scout out enemy convoy routes and attempt to determine their numbers and strength in our area of operations. You were not ordered to engage their ships, or engage pirate ships. By doing so, you have imperilled the operation's chances of success. What do you have to say for yourself?"

Roman bit down on his temper. Shouting at a superior officer wouldn't help.

"The civilian ship was attacked by pirates and I chose to rescue her, knowing the risks," he said. "The pirate ship was nearby and I chose to engage her, capturing the crew and rescuing the hostages." Including one he wasn't going to mention to the admiral. "My actions were in line with the Federation Navy's very reason for being."

"An interesting argument," Admiral Mason said with a sneer. "And do you think that your mentor will accept it?"

"Yes, sir," Roman said.

"Oh," Admiral Mason said. "I know that captains have wide latitude in carrying out their orders, but very few captains have ever been granted the authority to rewrite their own orders—and I can assure you, Garibaldi, that *you* are not one of them. Please tell me, exactly, why you feel that this little bout of disobedience will not result in a court martial for gross insubordination in the face of the enemy?"

Roman gathered himself. "Because, as I stated in my report..."

"I am asking you, captain," Admiral Mason said. "I want to hear the answer from your own mouth."

"The pirates didn't board, storm and loot any old commercial ship," Roman said. "They boarded a *White Swan*-class liner with a very strange passenger manifest. The passengers we were able to identify, sir, were all from Admiral Justinian's government. We took the liberty of carrying out preliminary interrogations, and they sang like canaries under truth drugs."

"My," Admiral Mason said drolly. "And you feel that this stroke of luck makes up for disobeying orders?"

"Yes, sir," Roman said. "If I had chosen to ignore the wrecked ship, or blown the pirate craft into atoms, we wouldn't have had such an intelligence windfall drop into our laps."

"True," Admiral Mason agreed. He leaned forward, his dark eyes fixed on Roman's face. "I think you'd better tell me what you found."

Roman kept his face impassive. Had the admiral not read his report, or was he intent on giving Roman enough rope to hang himself with? Or was he just testing how his youngest captain handled himself under pressure?

"Admiral Justinian and Governor Hartkopf—he now styles himself Governor-General Hartkopf—are on the verge of concluding an alliance," Roman said. That, at least, hadn't been hard to discover. "The liner we discovered, the one that was attacked and pillaged by the pirates, was carrying the negotiating team to discuss the final terms of the treaty. It was also carrying"—and here he knew he was venturing into dangerous waters—"the admiral's daughter. She was to be given to Hartkopf in marriage."

Admiral Mason stroked his chin, thoughtfully. "Curious," he said finally. "I was under the impression that Hartkopf was already married."

"I looked it up," Roman said. "His wife was on the list of proscribed personages after the governor abandoned his claims of loyalty to the Federation. She may already be dead, executed by the Senate. In any case, they were not on speaking terms, and she was on Earth with her lover when her husband declared independence."

He smiled inwardly at the admiral's expression. It had been Blake Raistlin who'd introduced him to the underground news-sheets that followed Earth's political elite and their children, turning their doings into entertainment for the rest of the Federation. Roman was hardly a prude—RockRats were rarely prudes—but some of their activities shocked even him. Mistress Hartkopf had not only cheated on her husband, she'd blatantly flaunted her many affairs all over Earth when the war began. Roman could easily understand how the Governor-General might prefer a nubile teenage girl as a wife...and if his own wife was dead, so much the better. High Society tended to frown on bigamy, much to his surprise. It wasn't as if it frowned on many other deviant behaviors.

"It makes sense," Admiral Mason said slowly. He sounded as if having a tooth pulled out would be preferable to agreeing with Roman. "Admiral Justinian doesn't have much to offer that would actually prove his sincerity, but his daughter...yes, that makes sense. She'd be a hostage for her father's good behavior as well as an incentive for Hartkopf to cooperate. And besides, it isn't like he has much else in the way of legitimacy..."

"Sir?" Roman blinked.

"The Federation Senate is the elected government of the Federation," Admiral Mason said. "That very fact alone gives it legitimacy in the eyes of trillions of human beings, even those who hate and fear the Federation's power. Admiral Justinian, on the other hand, is a usurper. He has to rely on force and persuasion, threats and blandishments, to encourage people to cooperate with him."

"But humans have always been willing to follow monarchies in times of hardship," he added, eyes narrowing. "I wonder if Admiral Justinian intends to declare himself Emperor of Humanity? If so, Hartkopf would have a chance to become Emperor himself, or father the Heir to the Throne. In any case, your reckless disregard of your orders seems to have given us an opportunity. How best, I wonder, to make use of it?"

He looked up suddenly. "The daughter," he said. "What happened to her?"

Roman had, luckily, prepared for the question. There had been no way to hide the fact that Henrietta had been on the liner, not without arranging for the other prisoners to suffer an unfortunate accident. No one knew, apart from Elf and himself, that she was still alive and on the *Midway*. And, if he wanted to keep her safe, the admiral must never be allowed to find out.

"The pirates captured her," he said truthfully. There had been no way to hide that either, even though only a couple of pirates had known her identity and they'd both been killed during the brief confrontation, shot down by their own men. "We have been unable to locate her corpse. They may have handed her over to another ship that escaped detection, or they may simply have killed her and pushed the body out of the airlock."

"Shame," Admiral Mason commented. "It would have been nice to hand her over to the Senate along with the other prisoners."

"Sir," Roman said slowly, "I think we shouldn't do anything too hastily."

Admiral Mason lifted a single eyebrow, daring Roman to proceed further. "We're talking about men from the admiral's inner circle," Roman explained. "The level of intelligence they could give us would be very helpful..."

"ONI would get to interrogate them first, before they were handed over for execution," Admiral Mason pointed out.

"And there is also the possibility of sowing the seeds of suspicion and distrust between the two warlords," Roman said. He'd thought about little else since they'd started their flight to the Marx System, and then back to The Hive. "What if we attempted to convince Admiral Justinian that the pirates weren't pirates at all, but Hartkopf's forces?"

"And why, exactly, should Hartkopf decide to start a war with his fellow warlord?" Admiral Mason sneered. "Where is the logic in that?"

"Hartkopf knows—he must know—that if he allied with Admiral Justinian, he would always be the junior partner." Roman smiled. "According to the negotiators, Admiral Justinian was prepared to concede autonomy to Hartkopf, but very little else. What if we convinced Justinian that Hartkopf made a deal with the Federation, and arranged for the negotiating team to fall into our hands?"

"A turncoat can never be trusted, for he turned his coat once," Admiral Mason said thoughtfully. "It isn't as if your scenario is impossible, I suppose. On the other hand, *captain*, the inhabitants of the Marx System could have told you a few things about relying on too complex a plan. How many things do you think could go wrong?"

Roman nodded towards the holographic display, showing the nearby stars and Asimov Points.

"Sir, with all due respect, if the two warlords join forces, we will be hard pressed to defend the Federation's flank. The prisoners have confirmed that the treaty has already been drawn up and only awaits a royal marriage to seal it. I respectfully submit that *anything* that has a chance of disrupting that alliance is worth trying. We could hardly be in a worse position."

"Why is it," Admiral Mason enquired, "that when a person says 'with all due respect,' they mean without any respect at all?" He held up a hand before Roman could try to answer. "Never mind, captain. Very well; I concede your point. Now, how do you intend to turn our two enemies against one another?"

Roman had spent days thinking about the possibilities.

"Sir, Admiral Justinian has the Marx Asimov Point heavily fortified, but they have only a limited mobile component," he said. "We have the firepower necessary to blow that mobile component to hell and gone."

"Right," Admiral Mason agreed. "And assuming that I agreed to take the risk of direct confrontation with his forces—which, may I remind you, we were ordered to avoid if possible—what would it gain us?"

"We use our ECM to pretend to be from Hartkopf's forces," Roman said. "We demand a meeting well away from the Asimov Point and wait until the enemy cruisers come into firing range, at which point they'll open fire. We use the face of one of the prisoners to convince them to come up fat and happy."

"I doubt they'll be that willing to take anything on faith," Admiral Mason said slowly. "Three years of war will have weeded out the incompetents on his side...still, it might work. And dare I assume that you have an operational plan already drawn up?"

"Yes, sir," Roman said. He accessed his implants and shunted the encrypted file into the admiral's desktop processor.

"I will review it with my staff and consider it." Admiral Mason leaned back in his chair, apparently relaxed. "And now that that's over, perhaps you could give me your verbal impressions of our area of operations."

"Yes, sir," Roman said.

He sat back and started to outline his thoughts. *Midway's* probes had identified several convoy routes through the border space, although there was no way to know if they were serving the warlords or merely civilians trying to survive as the Federation tore itself apart. Roman's sensor section had identified one patrolling warship as actually belonging to a mercenary company out of Hobson's Choice, presumably hired to guard the freighters from pirate attacks—or even one or both of the warlords. The fleet would have good pickings, at least until the warlords started patrolling the sector more aggressively.

"Not too bad," Admiral Mason said after Roman was done. "One other thing, captain?"

Roman looked up.

"What do you intend to do with the pirate prisoners?" the admiral asked casually.

Roman scowled. He hadn't bothered to check on the prisoners he'd abandoned in the wreck of the *Harmonious Repose*. They had enough supplies to last them for several weeks without rescue, assuming they were careful. He wasn't going to shed any tears if they killed themselves instead, or if they were just never able to recover them. Besides, there was the issue of just how to deal with them. He'd given the pirates his word.

"I was going to have them interrogated to learn the location of their bases and other information, then transfer them to a penal colony," he said. "I gave them my word."

"So you did," Admiral Mason agreed. He leaned forward coldly. "Regulations are clear on this point, *captain*. Pirates captured in the act are to be executed once interrogated—no exceptions."

"Yes, sir," Roman said. "On the other hand, if I'd tried to storm the pirate vessel— or put a missile into her hull—there would have been a bloodbath. And we would have been denied the intelligence windfall I collected from the pirate ship. And we wouldn't have recovered the pirate ship. I think we could probably put that to use, sir."

"I'm sure." Admiral Mason sneered again. "You seem to have a knack of falling headfirst into a bucket of shit and coming out covered in diamonds. It won't last, and the first time your luck fails you will be the day your universe collapses. *Don't* disobey orders again, or even your mentor won't be able to stop you being busted down to Ensign and assigned to an isolated mining colony so far from Earth that they think FTL travel is a joke."

"Yes, sir," Roman said.

"Now get back to your ship," Admiral Mason ordered. "I'll read your plan and inform you of my decision."

ဆဝပ

It wasn't common for starships—even the superdreadnaughts and carriers—to have more than a handful of cells in the brig. If the starship did need, for whatever reason, to restrain more than a handful of prisoners, it was easy to seal off a section and use it as a makeshift jail. Without power tools or weapons, the prisoners couldn't hope to escape. Roman had turned one of *Midway's* holds into a prison for most of the prisoners—and they had complained non-stop about the accommodation, even though they weren't in danger of being tortured and raped—but he'd kept Henrietta separate. He'd have to transfer the other prisoners to *Golden Hind* and they couldn't be allowed to learn that she was still alive.

Midway's brig consisted of two sections. A Marine guard stood outside one section, under strict orders not to enter the brig or allow anyone else to enter without Roman's permission. Inside, there was a force field hemming the prisoner into a small cell, allowing visitors a chance to speak to the prisoner in private. Unlike a civilian jail cell, every moment in the brig was recorded by hidden sensors, but Roman had used his command authority to deactivate them. There would be no record of this prisoner.

Henrietta was lying on the bunk when he walked through the hatch and stopped outside the force field. She looked as if she had been sleeping, but her eyes were hollow when she pulled herself upright and stared at him. Elf had checked her thoroughly and reported that she was in good health, yet it would have surprised Roman if she wasn't a little traumatized. Her life had turned upside down several times since the war began. And she knew that if a senior officer learned of her presence on the ship, she'd be executed. She was completely at his mercy and she knew it.

"Thank you for coming," she said. Her voice was soft and weak, vulnerable. "I was running out of books."

Roman nodded. A prisoner, even a crewman placed in the brig for a brief spell, could not be allowed to access the ship's computers, even the recreational files open to all. In earlier days, he'd been told, computer-skilled personnel had hacked into the security systems and made their escape. That was supposed to be impossible now, but the regulation still remained in force.

"Tell me something," he said suddenly. "Did your father give you a choice when he sent you to marry Hartkopf?"

"What do you think?" She sneered. "My father is ambitious, and my mother is as bad as he is, if not worse. Girls are pawns to them, to be sold on the marriage market in order to improve their social position. I was told that I was going to marry him, and nothing I said changed their minds. Do you think I wanted to marry a man who's over ninety years old?"

"I don't know if you're any better off here." Roman shrugged. "I may have to quietly ship you elsewhere before the shit hits the fan."

"It's better than waiting for an old bastard to deflower me, just because Daddy wants access to his starships," she said. "You need to watch my father. He will do anything to satisfy his ambitions."

"I see," Roman said. He wished for a trained interrogator, but that wasn't a possibility. "And what does your father actually want from all this?"

"Empire, of course," Henrietta said. "He wants to be Lord and Master of All."

Her face twitched. "Compared to that," she added, "what is the happiness of a single daughter? He has four more."

Chapter Twenty-Eight

Humans have saddled themselves with many strange ideas about how best to govern humanity. Some believe in the value of monarchy, others in the voice of the people and still others in communism or fascism. The Federation wisely allowed the settlement of worlds that attempted to follow a designed governing system, rather than one that evolved by chance. Not all of the experiments, it should be noted, worked...

...The Federation, in fact, rarely interferes in a planet's internal affairs, as long as they follow the Federation Protocols...
-An Irreverent Guide to the Federation, 4000 A.D.

Marx System, 4095

"Commodore?"

Commodore Joseph Truing turned to face the young officer and—barely—refrained from rolling his eyes. Joseph was over a hundred years old, thanks to anti-aging treatments he'd accepted when he'd joined the Federation Navy, and Lieutenant Harwich looked as if he'd barely started to shave. He was eager enough, anyway, even if he did have a habit of reporting every random flicker on the detectors as an incoming enemy attack. It was hard to believe, Joseph thought to himself from time to time, that *he* had ever been that young.

"Yes, lieutenant? What have you detected this time?"

Admiral Justinian's military machine was, somewhat to his regret, less formal than the Federation Navy. Proper military discipline would come in time, Joseph was sure, but until then he'd just have to suffer. He didn't regret signing up with the admiral when his recruiters had found him on the colony he'd chosen as a retirement home, yet there were times when he wondered if Justinian's grand plan to reshape the Federation would succeed. The news from the war front, heavily censored through it was, was not good. The war had stalemated.

The youngster managed to look offended, even though he was also keen to show off. "We picked up a signal from a starship that just entered the system...ah, entered the system some hours ago," he reported. "The Governor-General is requesting a meeting between his ships and our squadron for transfer of classified material. There is also an ID header from Secretary Festal directing us to comply with the request."

"Interesting," Joseph said thoughtfully. A month ago, the Secretary and his staff—and the admiral's daughter—had entered the Marx System through the Asimov Point and headed off towards The Hive and the Asimov Point that would take them deeper into Hartkopf's territory. Joseph had strongly recommended an escort, but Hartkopf's ambassadors had warned that their superior would not accept armed ships in his territory before the treaty was signed. "Do they say why, I wonder?"

"No, sir," Harwich said. "They're just repeating the same message."

Joseph nodded. Admiral Justinian preferred to rely on military men in his government, but he'd had to accept a number of civilian experts, including the Secretary of

Foreign Affairs. The title was something of a joke, Joseph had privately concluded, yet it might have had a point. An alliance with Hartkopf might be just what Justinian needed to turn the tide of the war. And that meant that anything Joseph did wrong might imperil the alliance.

He looked down at the display. The admiral hadn't been able to spare any more units, leaving Joseph with nothing more than a squadron of heavy cruisers and a handful of gunboats, but the fortresses defending the Asimov Point were modern and powerful. They could hold it against anything less than a couple of squadrons of superdreadnaughts, backed up by assault carriers and starfighters. Even if his entire force was destroyed, the Asimov Point would be safe, and so would the inhabited planets through the distortion in time and space.

They might as well honor the request. Governor-General Hartkopf had to be coddled, for now at least.

"Order the helm to set us on an intercept course," he ordered. "We may as well take the opportunity to run a few tracking exercises while we're away from the fortresses."

"Yes, sir," the youngster said, turning back to his console.

"Thank you, lieutenant," he said. "Put it on the main display. I'll command from the flag bridge."

∞

"They've taken the bait, sir."

"It looks like it," Roman said. "Keep monitoring them with passive sensors only."

The sick feeling in his chest was growing stronger. He hadn't planned a fleet operation—technically, a squadron operation—before, and all nine ships in the fleet were under his command. Part of him wished that Admiral Mason had chosen to place a more experienced officer in command, but Mason had reminded him—not without a thoroughly sardonic smile—that the Federation Navy's tradition was very clear. The man who dreamed up the plan would be charged with actually turning it into reality.

He settled back in his command chair and tried to relax. It wasn't easy. Marx's Asimov Point was unusually close to the system's primary. They were actually deeper in the mass limit than they'd been in any of their prior engagements—even Jefferson—and if something went wrong, escape might prove to be tricky. The Marx System might not be as dead as The Hive, as there were small colonies scattered throughout the system and a gas giant operation orbiting the larger of the system's twin gas giants, and there might be enemy starships lurking elsewhere.

Centuries ago, before the dawn of spaceflight, a philosopher-prophet named Karl Marx had come up with what he called the ultimate destination of humanity: pure and perfect communism. His discovery had led to the creation of some of the darkest regimes in human history, despite which far too many people had continued to hold a faith in communism that was almost religious. The attempts to found communist planets had failed, but the settlers of Marx believed they had a solution. If

communism was too perfect for humanity, they would create a new breed of humanity that would be capable of accepting and following their tenets. They'd eventually started breeding modified humans—in defiance of Federation-wide law—with
altered brains.

At first, it had seemed like the whole project was succeeding, until some of the
older altered humans started to show an incredible number of instabilities. Even in
the Fortieth century, tampering with human brains was difficult and very dangerous.
It hadn't been long before the entire planet was torn apart by war and most of the
population exterminated. Their brains had simply been too warped to live.

He watched the display as the enemy ships crawled closer, praying that the
ECM worked. Admiral Justinian hadn't dispatched his modern ships to watch the
back door, so the ECM should be successfully mimicking ships known to belong to
Hartkopf, but if the developers were wrong they might be heading into a missile duel
at knife-range. In such a battle, the person who fired the first shot often fired the last
one. If they were really lucky, they would destroy the enemy ships before they managed to get a shot off.

"Captain," the communications officer said suddenly. "They're demanding verifi-
cation of our codes."

Roman frowned. They'd interrogated Admiral Justinian's Foreign Secretary and
he'd provided them with his authorization codes, but a paranoid mind would insist
on having other codes, ones that might have been lost with the *Harmonious Repose*.
The interrogators were convinced that the prisoners knew nothing of any other
codes, yet it was quite possible that the liner's commander had orders to keep his
codes apart. And he'd gone down with his ship.

"Repeat the message," he ordered. They'd created a computer simulation of the
Foreign Secretary, but it wouldn't hold up to more than casual scrutiny. If someone
on the other side actually knew the man personally, they'd be able to see through
the deception. "Inform them that we have to transfer certain classified components
as soon as possible."

"Aye, sir," the communications officer said.

ജ∞ക

Joseph had been a serving naval officer for over sixty years and, unlike some
officers he could mention, he hadn't shied away from the prospect of battle. He'd
earned his stripes, unlike the officers who were promoted merely for looking good
at inspection time, and every instinct he had was screaming a warning. He couldn't
put it in words, yet something was wrong. Why, exactly, would Hartkopf want to
transfer classified components to his ships?

His orders said that he had to be diplomatic when dealing with Hartkopf's starships, but they didn't say that he had to obey their every command, even if one
of them *was* carrying the Foreign Secretary. Besides, even if they were perfectly
innocent, the exercise would do them good. Admiral Justinian had been a fleet commander himself. He'd understand.

"Inform them that they are to reduce speed, hold position and cut their shields," he ordered. "I want to board them and inspect their cargo before we allow them any closer to us."

"Aye, sir," the lieutenant said.

Joseph barely heard him, considering the tactical situation. Two squadrons of cruisers were racing towards each other, already within missile range. His ships were using their active sensors; the enemy—and he was already thinking of them as enemy ships—weren't. That proved very little, he knew. They could track his ships through their emissions.

"They're not responding," the lieutenant told him.

Joseph scowled. Something was *very* wrong.

"Send a message to the fortresses," he ordered. "Give them a full update and warn them that Hartkopf might be trying something..."

He broke off. The unknown starships had just opened fire.

ಏಲಿಛ

"Fire," Roman ordered. *Midway* shuddered as she vented her external racks, and then unleashed a full broadside from her internal tubes. The other cruisers followed suit, slipping to rapid fire as the enemy ships came within range. Firing so many missiles was chancy—an alert operator might notice that his ships had fired more missiles than they were supposed to be able to fire—but there was little choice. Nine heavy cruisers—even outdated ships—were nasty customers. "Shift to rapid fire, and keep firing."

The display frantically updated as command missiles took control and angled their charges toward their targets. The enemy ships hadn't been completely fooled—or perhaps someone over on the other side had decided to run all kinds of drills—because their point defense opened fire at once, raking great holes in the formation of missiles. Their return fire was much slower off the mark, suggesting that they hadn't had their missiles armed and ready to fire.

Roman allowed himself a moment of relief. All they had to do now was survive and destroy the enemy ships. This far from the fortresses, the crews would never be able to tell that it hadn't been Hartkopf who had attacked the cruisers. The report they'd make to their superiors would be exactly what Roman wanted it to be, as if he'd dictated it to them personally.

"First wave shifting to terminal assault," the tactical officer reported grimly. They'd fired off enough missiles to destroy the heavy cruisers, but the enemy point defense was taking a heavy toll on the missiles. "Second wave preparing to follow up the first wave; command missiles taking control now."

Roman nodded as the first missiles started to strike home.

ಏಲಿಛ

Joseph cursed as the first volley of missiles started to slam into his units. By sheer luck—or the whim of a mad god—*Haven* was barely targeted by the first wave, suggesting that the enemy hadn't realized that the cruiser was the flagship. But then, part of his mind whispered, the *Planet*-class cruisers were virtually impossible to distinguish from the *Archer*-class cruisers that made up most of his force. The enemy wouldn't have been able to tell the difference until his ships started spitting missiles back at them, and by then they wouldn't have been able to retarget the first wave of missiles.

"Spread our fire," he ordered, ignoring the lieutenant's shock. Luna Academy— much less the facilities Justinian had set up as training camps since his defection— would have been horrified at the decision, for spreading their fire ensured that no enemy craft would be destroyed.

On the other hand, if they were lucky, they might disable a few starships and prevent them from escaping before reinforcements arrived. The fortresses would have already fired courier drones through the Asimov Point, summoning reinforcements from the terminus.

"Link our ships into the datanet and coordinate our point defense," Joseph ordered.

He cursed his own complacency under his breath as ships started to die. The *Power* vanished in a ball of fire as her shields were knocked down by the tearing force of antimatter detonations; the *Pocahontas* followed her a moment later, a missile slipping through a brief chink in her shields and detonating against the hull. If he'd had the datanet up and running...but no, that could have been taken as a hostile act. Governor-General Hartkopf—the title was ashes in his thoughts—had sucked his cruisers in, and they were all going to die.

"They're shifting their fire," the tactical officer said.

Joseph nodded grimly. The datanet was collapsing almost as quickly as it was being put up, with starships falling out of the network or being destroyed outright.

"Transmit an emergency signal, then drop a stealth beacon," he ordered. "I want the admiral to know what happened here."

"Sir...incoming fire."

The savage missile swarm fell on his remaining starships. *Robert Graves* exploded in a ball of fire, followed rapidly by *Spider Bite* and *Tunbridge Wells*. And then the missiles sought out *Haven*. There was no time to say anything, no time to react, before the missiles started striking the hull and blew the entire starship and crew to vapor.

⁎⌘

Midway rocked violently as a missile—one of the last fired by the enemy cruisers before they died—exploded against her shields. Roman allowed himself a small moment of hope as the cruiser absorbed the blow, before contemplating the damage report from two of his ships. He'd had the great advantage that his datanet, at least, had been ready for instant action when he'd opened fire and he'd used it unmercifully. Only a handful of missiles had broken through his defenses and overall damage was minimal.

"All enemy ships destroyed, sir," the tactical officer said. "There are a handful of lifepods floating in space..."

"Ignore them," Roman ordered. Some of the warlords had ordered their starships to fire on unarmed and helpless lifepods, but he wasn't going to commit such an atrocity. Besides, the survivors could only testify that Governor-General Hartkopf's ships had opened fire on them, without warning or provocation. It would certainly sour relationships between the two warlords. "Helm, break us away from the Asimov Point and set course for the mass limit, best possible speed."

"Aye, sir," the tactical officer said. *Midway* rolled in space and started to head away from the Asimov Point, followed by her consorts. The starfighters launched by the fortresses—too little, too late—were simply ignored. They could perhaps catch up with the starships, but their life support packs wouldn't last long enough for them to inflict real damage.

But perhaps the enemy thought differently. A rational foe would have broken off the pursuit, yet the starfighters were still following them.

"New contacts," the sensor officer reported, his voice rising in alarm. "Twelve starships just transited the Asimov Point!"

Roman scowled. All of a sudden, the enemy seemed a great deal more rational. "Identify them," he ordered.

If he understood what he was seeing, the enemy fleet would certainly include a carrier that would recover the starfighters before they ran out of life support. They had to have had a reaction force on the other side of the Asimov Point, one that had been alerted as soon as the first missile was launched. The enemy—he acknowledged ruefully—had reacted with astonishing speed.

"Nine battlecruisers, two starships of indeterminate class and one bulk freighter," the sensor officer said. Roman remembered how Admiral Justinian had turned freighters into carriers and put two and two together. If that ship wasn't a converted carrier, he'd be astonished. "The unknown ships may be a new design of cruiser. Their power curves are roughly compatible with *Darwin*-class starships."

"Launch a stealth probe towards them," Roman ordered. Obtaining information on a new class of enemy ships was greatly to be desired. It would certainly help avoid surprises when Federation ships encountered the newcomer in formal combat. "Helm, continue to maneuver until we are clear of the starfighters."

He sat back and watched as the enemy ships started to pick up speed, running through the vectors in his head. Unless the starfighters could delay them, they'd escape without needing to engage the newcomers, even in a long-range missile duel. And yet, there was almost no way to prevent the starfighters from engaging them... was there?

"Launch a spread of antimatter missiles," he ordered. Shipkillers were never spent on starfighters; everyone knew that. And if they were lucky, the enemy starfighters wouldn't recognize the threat. "Detonate them at closest approach to the enemy craft."

"Aye, sir," the tactical officer said.

Roman watched the results grimly. Only a handful of enemy craft were destroyed in the blasts—antimatter detonations were tiny in the vacuum of space—but the remainder scattered, convinced they were fighting madmen. The tactic wasn't normally considered to be reliable, if only because it expended too many missiles, weakening the cruiser if she encountered another starship. And as long as starfighters were scattered, the threat they posed was greatly reduced.

"Sir...?"

"Keep us on course," Roman ordered harshly. They couldn't fight the enemy ships in a straight battle. "Once we cross the mass limit, take us into FTL and aim us towards the first waypoint."

"Aye, sir," the helmsman said.

Two hours later, with the enemy having given up the chase, *Midway* and her consorts crossed the mass limit and vanished from the Marx System. They left behind nothing but chaos.

Chapter Twenty-Nine

"The Enemy of My Enemy is My Friend" is a common truism. Like many other truisms, it is true only as far as it goes. In reality, the truism might read better as, "The enemy of my enemy is my enemy's enemy," as a shared enmity does not automatically translate to shared interests, let alone friendship.
-Sayings of the Federation Marine Corps, 3757.

Jefferson System/The Hive System/Tranter System, 4095

The benefit to having access to an Asimov Point nexus, Captain Caitlin Bowery reminded herself as armoured Marines escorted her through the drop tube into Admiral Justinian's private habitat, was that it gave the defenders the advantage of interior lines. Admiral Justinian could shift his forces to intercept any Federation thrust into his territory, even if the Federation managed to discover a previously undetected Asimov Point along the Rim that led into civilized space. It had allowed him to pull back most of his fighting units into Jefferson and prepare them for the grand offensive that would take him into the heart of the Federation, once the new units were built, crewed and worked up to fighting trim.

She allowed herself a smile as she passed through a series of airlocks, each one reinforced with a force field capable of standing off a nuclear warhead at point-blank range. All over the Harmony Sector, Admiral Justinian's recruiters were enlisting young men and women into the armed force that would eventually break through to Earth. There was no longer any need for the artificial restrictions of Luna Academy, nor was there any need to discourage mustangs from rising to commissioned ranks, not when the entire social order was being turned upside down. Admiral Justinian— soon to be *Emperor* Justinian—had made the colonies certain promises. Once he was Emperor, the economic rape of their worlds by the Core Worlds would come to an end. The restructured Senate would recognize the out-worlds, like Harmony and Jefferson, as equal to Earth or Terra Nova. And the colonists had responded to his words.

"Captain Bowery, here to see the admiral," one of her escorts said as they reached the final airlock. Admiral Justinian had become more than a little paranoid after the failure of his first and second attempts to break through into Federation-held space. He'd moved his headquarters to Jefferson—leaving his wife and daughters on Harmony, apart from the poor bitch who was being married off to seal a treaty between the admiral and another warlord—and started insisting on strict security. Caitlin had been strip-searched before she'd been allowed through the security cordon—and she was his most trusted associate. Very few people were allowed to see the admiral in person. "She's clean, sir."

There was a long pause. Caitlin had a moment to wonder if the security teams would insist on searching her again, or sending her in to visit the admiral minus her clothes and personal terminal, before the hatch hissed open and allowed her access.

The Marines inside the hatch waved her in and pointed her to a more standard airlock at the end of a metal corridor. The entire complex was silent, so silent that she could hear her footsteps as she walked down the hallway and keyed the entry coder. There was a brief pause, then the airlock clicked open, allowing her into the admiral's presence.

"Captain Bowery reporting as ordered, sir," she said.

The admiral looked dreadful, his face pale and tired. She had only a moment to realize that something was wrong before he picked up a bottle and offered her a swig. He actually meant for her to drink straight out of the bottle.

"Sir...?" Caitlin had no idea what he was thinking, or even if he was thinking at all. It felt as if she were about to be called on the carpet for some imagined offense, yet if he'd doubted her loyalty she would never have been allowed to meet with him in person.

"Sit down," Admiral Justinian said. His voice was bleak, yet coldly determined and fixed on something. "The forces in the Marx System were attacked."

Only the ease of long practice kept Caitlin's face blank. The Marx System should have been effectively impregnable, if only because of the long distance between the Federation loyalists and Admiral Justinian's flank. A starship under stardrive from the nearest Federation-held star system would take—she checked her implants to be sure that the answer was right—over two years to reach Marx. The implications were not encouraging. No pirate or mercenary company would dare tangle with warships if it could be avoided. There was no profit in having one's ships blown out of space.

The conclusion was inescapable.

"Governor Hartkopf has turned on us."

"So it would appear," Justinian agreed. He took a long swig from the bottle and sat back in his chair. Caitlin scowled at the display, wondering when her commander had turned to drink. He'd never shown any desire to drink himself senseless before. "And Henrietta is missing."

Caitlin listened to the remainder of the story silently. The ships that had attacked the cruisers at Marx had used Admiral Justinian's codes—the ones issued to his Foreign Secretary—to lure the cruisers away from the covering fire of the Asimov Point fortresses. That in itself had disturbing implications. The Foreign Secretary had either been taken prisoner and interrogated, or he'd turned his coat. Either way, the admiral's daughter was in enemy hands, and all hell was about to break loose.

It had taken weeks of persuasion for his wife—Millicent Beauregard-Justinian, a woman whose ambition far outstripped her husband's—to convince him to allow his daughter to be used to seal the treaty. And now it looked as if he'd sent her into enemy hands. The young girl didn't know anything that could be used against her father, but her mere presence would be used against him. Caitlin forced herself to think coldly and rationally.

"Hartkopf isn't insane," she pointed out. "He may have convinced himself that we will let it pass, but his subordinates have to know better. I think he might have come to an agreement with the Federation to safeguard his life, in exchange for using his territory as a base. They could have moved a fleet up into his sector and pushed him into launching an attack on us."

Carefully, she considered the possibilities. The Federation possessed vast industrial strength, even in its diminished state. And then there was the Naval Reserve… given enough time, the Federation could out-build all of the warlords and crush them to powder, although no one knew if they had the determination to risk economic collapse by carrying on the war. Even if they won, they wouldn't recoup what they'd lost, even if they declared all of the various territories of the warlords as war prizes, as they'd done after the Inheritance Wars. And yet, she knew just how deeply the Senate depended upon its ability to ravage the colonies at will. If they gave it up, the rump Federation would suffer an economic shockwave. The entire system might collapse into flaming debris.

And with that in mind, the Federation might well agree to make a deal with Governor Hartkopf. Allowing the treacherous bastard to keep his head on his shoulders—perhaps by sending him into a comfortable exile somewhere out along the Rim—would be a small price to pay for the easy recovery of his sector. And once they had their fleet there, they could move through Marx and into Justinian's soft underbelly. The war might be within shouting distance of being won outright.

"Perhaps," Admiral Justinian agreed, when she outlined her thoughts. He smiled humorlessly. "We did offer him more, didn't we?"

"I think he decided that we were the losing side," she said with a shrug. "A guarantee that he won't be executed would look better than the promise of an entire sector—if the Federation took it off him regardless."

"No doubt," Admiral Justinian agreed. He looked up at the star chart floating over his desk. "We have to make it clear that the attack on Marx will not go unpunished…"

"But we don't know if Hartkopf or the loyalists launched the attack," she objected. "Who do we target?"

"Hartkopf allowed them to move through his territory," Admiral Justinian said firmly. "You will take direct command of a squadron of battlecruisers and take them through The Hive into the Tranter System. You will destroy his defenses in that system and then withdraw, once you broadcast a message from me. The message will make it clear that I will not tolerate treachery, and that any further attacks on my forces will be seen as a declaration of war."

"Yes, sir," Caitlin said. She didn't want to object and risk a sudden mood swing, but it had to be said. "If we do get into an all-out war with Hartkopf, sir, what is to stop the Federation taking advantage of it to stab us in the back?"

"If the Federation is already working with him, or controlling his sector, we're at war anyway," Justinian pointed out mildly. "If he's prodding us to find out what kind of reaction he'll get from us, we'll give him a bloody nose to convince him to look elsewhere for his prey. Do you know what he demanded as part of Henrietta's dowry? Four entire star systems!"

"Yes, sir," Caitlin said. Privately, she was shocked. If someone could demand such a dowry, it suggested that that person's grip on reality wasn't particularly strong. "And what do we do about her?"

"You will recover her if possible," Admiral Justinian said. "My note will include a demand for her immediate return. And if she can't be returned—if they've killed her—he will pay for it. Personally."

ᛞᚳᛇ

Two weeks later, Caitlin stood on the bridge of *Avenger* as she dropped out of stardrive on the edge of The Hive's mass limit. The nine battlecruisers, four fast freighters and two of the converted starfighter-carriers that she'd brought with her held their position for a long moment, and then started to advance into the system towards the Asimov Point.

Caitlin had never visited The Hive System before, and she felt a shiver crawling down her back as the battlecruisers drove deeper into the system, although she knew that it was purely psychosomatic. Certainly, none of the more exotic stories about The Hive having converted itself to a creature of pure energy—or even hidden colonies within the system, undetected by the vengeful Federation Navy—had any basis in reality.

"The system appears to be clear, Commodore," Captain Lachlan said. "If Hartkopf has any forces present within the system, they are lying doggo."

Lachlan gave her the courtesy promotion out of habit, for there was only one captain on a vessel. Besides, although Caitlin wasn't a real squadron commander, she spoke for the admiral himself and, as such, she had wide authority.

"Good," Caitlin said. "Take us to the Asimov Point and prepare to launch recon drones. I want to know what we're facing on the other side before we jump in and open fire."

She'd had time to think, during the frantic struggle to prepare the battlecruiser squadron and launch the mission before the Federation launched a second attack, and she'd started to wonder what was *really* going on. The attack on Marx had been... odd. Why would Governor Hartkopf do something to declare his enmity in a way no one could ignore?

Further, if he'd actually concluded a deal with the Federation loyalists, why not string Admiral Justinian along while the Federation prepared a counterattack of its own? Even now, the undefended flank was being strengthened, with starships and fortresses being dispatched from Harmony to slow down any would-be invader. An offensive would rapidly become much harder. So who really benefited from attacking Marx?

They'd rejected the possibility of the Federation Navy launching the attack without Hartkopf's permission because it would have been difficult for the Federation to get an assault force in place. But difficult wasn't the same as impossible. Hartkopf's regime was known for being even more corrupt than the Senate—an achievement that Caitlin would have previously considered impossible—and it was quite possible that some devious Federation Navy Admiral had merely applied a large infusion of cash. His ships could then have passed through the Asimov Points without being reported to superior authority, allowing them to launch the attack on Marx in the certain knowledge that Hartkopf would be blamed.

And yet, if they hadn't had Hartkopf's assistance, how had they obtained the codes?

She was still mulling the possibilities over in her mind when the small squadron reached the Asimov Point and launched recon drones into the gravimetric distortion directly ahead of them.

"Commodore, the recon drones have just returned," Captain Lachlan informed her. "There are no hostile fortifications on the other side of the Asimov Point."

Caitlin studied the results in disbelief. In the days before stardrive, there was little point in defending an Asimov Point everyone *knew* to be a dead end, but the continuous displacement drive had turned interstellar defense doctrine upside down. Governor Hartkopf had to *know* that it was easy for ships to cross the light years between Marx and The Hive—he collected money from smuggling ventures—so why had he left the system undefended?

Something was very wrong...she considered, just for a moment, aborting the mission until they received new orders from Admiral Justinian, but they'd been given no leeway at all. They had to launch the raid.

"Cloak us," she ordered. If there were no defenders, no one would notice as her ships flickered into existence in Tranter. And then they could sneak up on their targets and blow them to hell. "Take us through the Asimov Point."

୫୦ଓଔ

"Now *that's* interesting," the sensor officer said slowly. "Captain, I think you should see this."

Roman tapped his console and brought up the feed from the sensor department. The task force had found a suitable hiding place within The Hive system—a large asteroid that had been mined out and abandoned some time before the apocalypse had destroyed the entire system—and the engineers had been turning it into a base. *Midway* and her consorts had returned to find themselves briefly assigned to cloaked defense and scouting duties until the base was complete, not something that pleased him. Admiral Mason, it seemed, wanted to keep a close eye on *Midway* and her young commander.

The nine enemy battlecruisers didn't seem to be heading for their current location; in fact, they were heading straight towards the Asimov Point. And the report from the passive sensor platforms was showing that their weapons and shields were fully charged. They were looking for trouble.

"I think we must have annoyed someone," he said. "Alert the flag and prepare to move out of formation."

The enemy battlecruisers didn't slow until they reached the Asimov Point, at which point they came to a halt and waited. Roman wished—not for the first time—that the Federation Navy had developed the kind of sensors they saw in entertainment dramas, where it was possible to not only watch targets halfway across the system in real time, but determine what they were carrying and if they were hostile with ease. The enemy ships could be doing anything from sealing the Asimov Point to preparing to transit through with bad intentions; there was no way to tell at such a distance.

Admiral Mason's face popped into existence on his private display. "Captain," he said coldly. "I believe that your actions at Marx have sparked a response. I do not wish you to engage the enemy ships or even to scout after them."

Roman frowned. "Sir, this is an opportunity to..."

"That is an order, captain," Admiral Mason said. "In fact..."

"Captain, enemy starships are transiting the Asimov Point," the sensor officer reported, suddenly. "They're leaving the system."

"It would appear that you succeeded," Admiral Mason said. "We will keep our heads down and watch what happens from a distance. Might I remind you, captain, that you have already threatened the secrecy of this mission?"

"Yes, sir," Roman said. It was frustrating, but Mason was in command. "I understand."

೮೦ ಅಕ್ಷ

Caitlin's sense that something was very wrong only grew stronger as the fleet—still hidden under cloak—crossed the Tranter System, heading right towards the other Asimov Point. The system's sole inhabited planet was barely defended, but there was a squadron of old-style dreadnaughts on guard at the Asimov Point. They could deter her from carrying through with her offensive—if she meant to take the system permanently—but they couldn't stop her from launching an attack and then beating feet back home. Governor Hartkopf did not seem to have prepared for an attack.

"Start rolling missile pods," she ordered as the squadron slowed to barely within engagement range. She wasn't going to take battlecruisers any closer to the dreadnaughts than necessary, not with the dreadnaughts clearly refitted with the latest in weapons and shields—and sensors. Missile pods were rare in ship-to-ship combat, but attacking from cloak...they were workable. They just couldn't be towed behind a ship travelling at full combat speed. "Prepare to engage."

She pushed her misgivings away, knowing that she might well be about to open a two-front war between her superior and Hartkopf. The governor was a weasel, everyone knew that, yet he might just be able to bite Admiral Justinian to death. They didn't dare pull too much combat power away from the Asimov Points linking Admiral Jefferson's territory to the Federation. The Federation wouldn't hesitate to take advantage of such weakness.

One by one, the battlecruisers checked in. "All ships report ready, Commodore," the squadron coordinator reported. "Weapons hot; I say again, weapons hot."

"Fire," Caitlin ordered.

Chapter Thirty

As the Federation considers itself to be charged with ensuring the fundamental unity of the human race, it comes as no surprise that it disapproves intensely of independent worlds. The few settlements that have no ties to the Federation often find themselves pressured into associate membership, even if they have nothing that the Federation actually wants or needs. When a world manages to maintain even a semblance of independence, it only occurs because the world is protected by powerful allies from the Federation.
-An Irreverent Guide to the Federation, 4000 A.D.

Hobson's Choice, 4095

"We're not being challenged at all?" Captain Roman Garibaldi asked.

"No, sir," Uzi said. The enhanced human looked as if he was enjoying himself. "Did you really think that they'd stop us coming into orbit? As far as they're concerned, we're just another pirate ship."

Roman wrinkled his nose. The pirate ship—hastily renamed the *Wildflower*—stank. It was clear that the pirates hadn't bothered to do much, if any, preventative maintenance. Roman knew that if Federation Navy ships had routinely been left in such a state, the entire Navy would literally have rotted away. His first commander would have exploded with rage if he'd discovered his crew urinating in the passageways and clogging up the tubes with rubbish, yet that's exactly what the pirates appeared to have done. In the end, the repair crews had vented the entire ship, just to kill the cockroaches and rats infesting most of the ship. God alone knew how many pirate ships lost life support or internal power because a rat had chewed the wrong piece of wiring.

Even now, after the ship had been put back into near-working order, Roman was still nervous. *Midway* was following them into the system, hidden under cloak, but if Janine had to recover them, their cover would be blown wide open.

Hobson's Choice had no government or System Traffic Command. Starships—smugglers, pirates and rebels—clustered the system, taking whatever orbits that suited them and ignoring protests from other starships. Roman would have expected a mass outburst of fighting among pirate crews, but everything seemed to be remarkably civilized. Fighting, the briefing files had stated, wasn't good for business.

Hobson's Choice served as a clearing house for pirates and smugglers, where anything could be sold and few—if any—questions were asked about where it had been originally found. The planet should have been shut down years ago, but it seemed that various interests in nearby sector governments had their own ties to the planet. They quietly ensured the Federation Navy never raided the place. Or, better yet, bombarded it from orbit.

He scowled as the helmsman—a volunteer, like everyone else on the undermanned ship—carefully guided her into orbit. Hobson's Choice was a dull brown world, her surface unbroken by oceans or greenery. The briefing had claimed that most of the planet's water was actually below the surface, with plants adapted to live in near-desert conditions growing roots that reached down towards the great aquifers. There were no official settlements, either; the handful of small communities were purely nominal, serving as places for crews to land and sell their products. Very few people would choose to live on the planet permanently, apart from Hobson himself. He'd built himself a small farm in the north and refused to have anything to do with most of the visitors.

"Orbit achieved, sir," the helmsman said. The pirates, for reasons that doubtless made sense to them, had combined the helm and tactical consoles into one. Roman would never have allowed it if he'd been crewing a ship, for the two roles could not be effectively carried out by a single man. "We've been pinged by a number of other ships, but nothing from the surface."

"They don't bother," Uzi said. He stood up and grinned at the bridge crew. "Do you still want to see the planet, captain?"

"Yes, I do," Roman said.

The data they'd recovered from the pirate ship stated that the prisoners would have been brought to Hobson's Choice, at least until the ransoms were paid. And if they weren't, Elf had pointed out, they'd be in the right position for being sold as slaves. There were plenty of credible stories about that, or worse, people simply being executed outright; the lucky ones were rescued by the Federation Navy. "Besides, I have to make sure everything goes properly."

"Don't worry about us," Uzi told him. "You just make sure that you and your companions don't blow your covers. Discovery here could mean death."

ଚ୦ଠଃ

The shuttle flew down to the settlement, its passage barely troubling the hot air surrounding it. Roman watched through the shuttle's sensors as it flew over the settlement and turned to land, coming down on a patch of ground on which someone must have used a fusion flame to bake it as hard as rock. The settlement looked rather like a shantytown to him, with hundreds of prefabricated shelters and apartments scattered around without rhyme or reason. There were no wooden shelters, due to the fact that Hobson's Choice had no forests, but there were a number of buildings constructed from stone. He guessed there had to be a quarry somewhere nearby.

"Just remember," Uzi said as the shuttle came in to land, "you're *not* Federation Navy officers and you're *definitely* not Marines. You're mercenaries from the Free Ship *Wildflower* sampling the booze and other entertainments here. Even if someone recognizes the *Wildflower*, they won't say anything. They'll just assume that the bastards lost a fight and their ship was taken as a prize. Don't fuck up and you'll be fine."

The shuttle's hatch cracked open, allowing a wave of hot air to come streaming into the compartment, bringing with it a sandy smell mingled with something unpleasantly human. Roman scowled, resisting the urge to cough as the dry air invaded his lungs, and followed Uzi out into the open air. The sunlight beat down from high above, a mocking reminder that the planet had no ozone layer to protect visitors from the star's rays. Roman and his crew had been treated to prevent skin cancer—it was a fairly simple genetic modification—but he didn't want to think about what might happen to anyone who hadn't been treated. If there were children on the planet...he pushed the thought aside. There couldn't be children on the planet.

Elf caught his arm as they started to walk towards the settlement in the distance. "Slouch," she ordered firmly.

Roman nodded and tried to take the Academy out of his walk. It didn't work very well, but she seemed satisfied. Or perhaps she was hiding her opinion, even though she'd called him crazy in private. A captain shouldn't risk himself on a landing party in hostile territory.

The settlement had been marked in the files, but it had no name. Up close, it was a sandy mass of small makeshift buildings, prefabricated dumpsters and small shacks. Roman heard the music of a dozen bars, while there was a large market set up in the center of the settlement. He almost stopped dead as he took in the mass of humans and aliens plying the market, buying or selling as the fancy took them. They didn't seem to care that—officially—aliens were second-class citizens everywhere in the Federation. Here, the scum of the galaxy coexisted in an uneasy peace. He saw men holding guns and swaggering around, sometimes followed by older—beaten—men and women who were clearly slaves. Elf put a hand on his arm as a half-naked girl— with all of her teeth knocked out—walked past, following a tall man with a cruel glint in his eye.

He shuddered inwardly, wondering how anyone could manage to remain indifferent in the face of such suffering. Now that he knew to look, he saw hundreds of slaves, mainly young and female. One of the dumpsters had been turned into a brothel, with girls outside waving to customers and inviting them to come inside for some fun and games. The youngest he saw couldn't be older than twelve, perhaps younger. Or perhaps she'd been engineered to meet a particular demand...no, that wasn't possible. Hobson's Choice didn't have the medical tools to engineer a person's body for a given specification.

His nose twitched as the wind caught a smell of cooking meat and blew it his way. Someone was cooking a dinner for a pirate crew and showing off the loot they'd taken from their victims. He almost stopped dead as he saw the people following them, nine girls and five boys, their hands manacled in front of them. They had to be captives and, judging by their state, not ones worth ransoming. He saw their fate in the eyes of the people watching them, studying the captives as a farmer would study a cow or a horse, and shivered. The Federation Navy needed to stomp on the pirates, hard. Perhaps, after the war, the corrupt governors would be deposed and Hobson's Choice could be invaded and crushed.

"This way," Uzi said. He led them towards a small bar. There was no music coming from inside, thankfully. "I suggest that we all have a drink here before you go back to the ship."

Roman said nothing as they found a table and ordered drinks. The bar seemed to be marginally civilized, although the waitress was topless and had the tired expression of a person who had seen too much too young. The scars covering her breasts and arms made Roman look away in a hurry. He studied the drink she placed in front of him, but decided not to try it. A pint glass of foaming green liquid didn't look particularly appetizing.

"May I join you?" a new voice asked.

Roman looked up to see a man who was blatantly out of place, wearing a black business suit and tie even in the heat. He was a man who didn't want to remain unnoticed, he realized. He wanted the planet's inhabitants to know who he was, and why.

"You're off the *Wildflower*, are you not? A free company ship?"

"That we are," Uzi said in a bored tone. He'd warned them that there might be a "chance" meeting with a recruiter and, if so, they were to keep their mouths shut. Roman was happy to obey.

"My unit just worked out our last contract," Uzi continued. "And who might you be?"

"I am Devon," the man said. "My employers have a particular interest in hiring men of the free companies."

He reminded Roman of the man who'd tried to sell him a used aircar. There was something greasy about him. But there was an odd sort of contempt behind the man's smile that didn't add up; what was this man doing here?

"And we happen to be in need of a new contract," Uzi said. He pulled out a chair for Devon and waved to the waitress. "Another beer for my new friend here, love!"

Devon settled himself down with the grace and poise of a visiting aristocrat slumming it among the common herd. Roman was privately surprised that the man had lasted so long on such a lawless planet, but perhaps he had the money—or connections—to keep him alive. If he was willing to make an approach to a ship no one had seen before, at least as a mercenary ship, he was clearly rolling in cash.

Or perhaps he was an idiot. There was no way to know.

"Thank you, my friend," Devon said with a rather sardonic smile. "I'll get right to the point. What do you have to offer my employers?"

Uzi pretended to consider it. "I would be more interested in knowing what you can pay us. There are plenty of possible employers out there looking to hire combat veterans. My crew and I were on Paradise, and several of us were on Romulus during the civil war. We're not exactly desperate for cash, you know."

There was, just for a second, a brief flash of anger on Devon's face.

"Nor are my employers," he said evenly. "They are prepared to offer very competitive rates to any starship crews or groundpounders that are prepared to sign up with them. They will even throw in a limited budget for repairs and spare parts, or even training if you feel it necessary. And there may be other incentives, should you perform well."

"I see," Uzi said. "And who might we be fighting?"

Roman saw his expression alter, slightly. It was a good offer, perhaps too good.

"Ideally, you won't be fighting anyone at all," Devon said.

Uzi didn't bother to hide his disbelief.

"If it does come down to a fight, your exact roles will depend upon your capabilities," Devon explained. "You have a light cruiser. You may be asked to escort convoys, or even take part in small actions. You may even..."

Roman listened with carefully-hidden amusement as Devon and Uzi bartered. He'd learned a great deal over the past few years about the economics of mercenary service. Mercenaries weren't cowards, far from it, but they were often reluctant to risk their ships in direct combat. An even fight, particularly against the Federation Navy, might see those valuable investments destroyed in battle. They tended to prefer groundside actions, where their valuable starships wouldn't be at risk.

And that raised the question of just who Uzi and his team would be working for. The obvious answer was one of the warlords, yet Roman wondered if that were actually true. There was something about the whole arrangement that puzzled him. The two warlords might have been at daggers drawn over the last few weeks—the raid on Tranter had been repaid by a raid on Marx, which had led to another raid, and another—and yet, there was no sense of urgency. Devon was bartering carefully, rather than desperately, as if he had all the time in the world. Or it could all be an act.

He looked up sharply as a pair of hulking green aliens advanced into the bar. They both wore nothing more than loincloths and weapons bandoleers, each one carrying a full-sized plasma cannon on their backs. The aliens were known for serving as mercenaries and enforcers for the criminal underworld, although they were rarely seen near the Core Worlds. They were followed by another alien—a cross between a human and an octopus—and several humans, all of whom looked tired and worn.

Uzi paid them no attention. "You want, then, for us to go into your service without knowing precisely whom we may be serving? Do you suppose we are that trusting?"

Devon smiled. "You will be paid a formidable retainer," he pointed out, with surprising calm. "And even if the cause doesn't come to blows, you will be paid combat rates."

"Doubtless," Uzi said. "And what happens if our noble benefactors refuse to pay?"

"We will place the first year's worth of wages in an escrow account for you," Devon said. He made a show of consulting his watch, and then looking over towards the newcomers. "I have little more time. Will you accept the contract?"

Uzi made a show of considering it. "Subject to a get-out clause, yes," he said finally. "I will have to consult with my senior crew, and then I believe that we are yours."

෴෴

"Well," Uzi said, when they were back onboard the shuttle. "Did you find the trip enlightening?"

"Yes," Roman said. "And what, exactly, did it gain us?"

Uzi smiled, but it didn't touch his eyes.

"Here's where we part ways," he said. "My crew and I take the *Wildflower* and accept the contract. Whoever is hiring so many mercenaries—and it isn't either of the warlords—will eventually be revealed, at which point we get the information back to the Federation. The information should help the Federation Navy deal with the problem before it is too late."

"You're going to be alone..." Roman frowned.

"Not a problem," Uzi assured him, as the shuttle took off and climbed into the sky, heading for the captured ship high overhead. "We've done it before, captain."

"If they're not warlords, then they have to be Outsiders," Elf said. She'd been very quiet during the meeting on Hobson's Choice. "I was listening carefully. They want you to train people as well, and the only reason to do that is if they want to build a larger army."

"Then we need to identify the people behind it before the shit really hits the fan," Uzi said firmly. "As I will say in my report to the admiral, whoever is behind this is pouring out money like water. That alone makes them a major threat, for who has that sort of money to hire mercenaries on spec? He didn't even ask for major credentials or references, or even some guarantee of our good conduct."

"Maybe he's just really stupid," Elf said dryly. She held up a hand before Uzi could say anything. "I know; wishful thinking."

"Very wishful," Uzi agreed, equally dry. He looked over at Roman. "I hope you enjoyed the visit to Hobson's Choice, captain. That planet is what life is like without the Federation. No law and order, no common decency; nothing but the rule of the strong."

Roman nodded slowly, privately resolving to convince Admiral Mason—or better yet, Admiral Drake—to pay a call on the system once the war with Admiral Justinian was over. Even if most of the pirates escaped before the Federation Navy could seal off the planet, they'd be able to liberate the slaves and shut down the fences. The pirates would need time to regroup. Perhaps by then the Navy would be able to provide more escorts to civilian shipping.

He clung to that thought as they returned to *Midway*, remembering the slaves and how the pirates had acted. Whatever it took, he swore to himself, he would return with the Federation Navy behind him. Destroying the pirate operation would be worth the price.

Chapter Thirty-One

With the increasing return to aristocratic rule by a political elite—the Senate—arranged marriages have become far more common. The prospective partners get very little say in the matter as the arrangements are made by the parents after careful considerations of the advantages of the match. It is perhaps not surprising that High Society also has the greatest level of adultery and divorce in history.
-An Irreverent Guide to the Federation, 4000 A.D.

Earth/Sol System, 4095

"But I don't *want* to marry him!"

Lady Tiffany Eleanor Diana Katherine d'Artagnan faced her father, Senator William d'Artagnan, and pushed all of her determination into her words. "I don't know him, I don't want him and I am sure as hell not going to marry him!"

At twenty-nine, Tiffany had grown out of altering her body to suit convention and had returned to her natural appearance. Long red hair cascaded down her back, framing a heart-shaped face and bright green eyes. Unlike most of the other young ladies in High Society, she eschewed the long formal dresses that had come back into fashion, choosing instead to wear a basic tunic and shorts. She preferred being active to being indolent, even if it meant risking her father's wrath by having adventures and even slipping out into the vast cities of Earth. It would be decades yet before she could become a Senator—if she even wanted to run for office, for it all looked like a crock to her—and she wanted to keep herself from becoming an indolent child. Too many High Society children, unable to displace their parents as their parents lived for hundreds of years, had become nothing more than wasted souls, seeking nothing but entertainment. The current fashion was for direct brain alteration to produce a permanent state of orgasm, but that sickened Tiffany to her core.

Her father produced a truly impressive sigh. He was pushing one hundred years old but looked around forty, at least by the standards of pre-rejuvenation Earth. Tiffany was actually his youngest child—he'd had five, with different mothers—and he tended to ignore her as much as possible. He'd only married his wives—and then separated from them—for political advantage. If he'd loved any of them, Tiffany had never seen any sign of it. His children, too, were just pawns in his political games. After all, he'd been a Senator for nearly fifty years, following his father, grandfather and great-grandfather in an unbroken chain that reached back all the way to the dawn of the Federation. What did one young girl matter compared to such a legacy? d'Artagnan might be the current Senator, but he had no intention of being the last.

"I would prefer it if you accepted him willingly," her father said firmly. "It took several years of horse-trading to arrange your marriage. You knew that you would be marrying one day and that day has finally come. As my daughter..."

Tiffany would have stamped her foot if she hadn't grown out of such childish gestures.

"But I don't love him," Tiffany protested. "How am I supposed to leave everything and go with him to some barbaric posting on the other side of the universe?"

Her father didn't seem impressed by her arguments.

"You grew up in a world where you lacked for nothing," he said. "When there were people starving, you had plenty; when there were people dying because of poor medical care, you were healthy; when people lived without any sense of safety, you were safe. The only danger you've faced in your life was the danger you brought upon yourself when you had the insane idea of abandoning your security team and heading into an untamed city. And even then, you were rescued before anything bad could happen."

"I know, father," Tiffany said, "and I am grateful..."

"And there is a price to be paid for such luxury," her father said, overriding her protests. "The family that gives you your position, your wealth and your access to things banned to the vast majority of the population comes first, always. You exist to serve the family, so the family can survive and prosper in its rightful place. Your happiness comes second, as does mine. I had to give up the girl I loved because her family was part of the Imperialist Faction and disgraced. Her descendants are the laughing stock of High Society. Do you understand me?"

Tiffany bowed her head. "Yes, father," she said as submissively as she could. "I understand."

She was already thinking about escape. She had access to a private shuttle and a space yacht. She didn't have a stardrive, but she could navigate through the Gateway and escape, perhaps changing ships at the commercial yards at Terra Nova and heading to the Rim.

Her father wasn't fooled.

"I know what you're thinking. I thought the same when they brought Sally to me and told me she was going to be my first wife. I thought of nothing but escape, until my father told me that if I refused to marry her, I would be cut off completely from the family. Tell me something, Tiffany: could you survive without the family's protection? Without the influence that saved your life, or allowed you to bend and break flight control rules at will, or ensured that there would be no lasting repercussions from your crazy stunts?"

Tiffany clenched her fists, but said nothing.

"And this marriage is very important, both to the family and to the Faction," her father continued. "We cannot allow the Socialist Faction to gain unwarranted influence over Admiral Drake. And who is in the best position to influence a man? His wife, the charming girl he married and allows into his bed. That wife has to be one of us."

Tiffany blushed bright red, knowing that her father would see. "Father, with all due respect, I am not a virgin," she pointed out. "I am unsuited to a formal marriage."

"Do you think I was a virgin when I married your mother?" Her father laughed.

"You were married before," she pointed out, fighting down an insane urge to giggle—or scream. Her blush deepened. "You had four wives!"

"And my first wife wasn't my first woman, and I wasn't her first man," her father said bluntly. "I assure you that virginity isn't a factor in an arranged marriage. If it was, they'd have put that bitch Lola Pond forward as a possible candidate. She's so frigid that any man who tried to have sex with her would freeze his cock and it would snap off."

"Dad!"

Her father laughed.

There were times when Tiffany found his bitter attacks on the Socialists amusing—not least because, outside the Senate, there was little infighting among High Society—but this wasn't funny. There were some things that no child wanted to discuss with her parents, and sex was very definitely one of them. She knew, intellectually, that her parents had to have had sex in order to produce her—and that her father must have had sex with at least four other women when he'd produced her half-siblings—but she didn't want to think about it.

"Tiffany," he said with a cold finality, "I understand how you're feeling. You've been a child, but now it is time to take on adult responsibilities. The family needs your sacrifice and I'm afraid the wedding will happen, regardless of your feelings on the matter."

She turned away and said nothing. This could not be happening!

"You will take your vows even if I have to march you to the altar in handcuffs and chains," he said, "and hold a gun to your head to force you to speak. This is too important—both for you personally and for the family—to allow you to refuse. I am very sorry."

Tiffany felt angry, but didn't know what to do or what to say. Yes, she'd had lovers; she'd had plenty of lovers. And yet, she'd chosen them all, even the ones who had disappointed her. The thought of allowing someone she didn't know and didn't want to sleep with her was horrifying. She had known, intellectually, that it happened, yet she hadn't realized that it could happen to her. She was a fifth child, after all, inherently less important than her older siblings. Her father shouldn't have had to use her for decades yet.

She thought, bitterly, about some of the other marriages she'd seen in High Society. Some had worked out fine, with the couples growing to love one another and remaining close even after they'd separated. Long-life made it harder to spend one's life with another until death did them part, although there were a few who did live together until the end of their lives. Others were very formal, with the partners having their children in artificial wombs and never going near one another otherwise; some went very bad. Even then, the partners were on Earth in High Society. They had a place to run.

But if she accompanied Admiral Drake back to his command on a starship, she would be completely alone.

Her father took a glass of wine from one of the servants and passed it to her, an odd compassion in his eyes. Tiffany took it gratefully and sipped it slowly, hoping that it would help clear her head. She thought, again, of escape, but if her father had anticipated the possibility, he would have guards set on her private ship and probably an entire security team escorting her. The guards on the estate reported to her father, she reminded herself; even her own servants couldn't be trusted.

"It won't be that bad," her father said seriously. "The admiral's psych profile shows him to be a good man..."

"I recall that *my* profile once claimed that I was a pathological liar," Tiffany snapped. "You insisted that I visit one of those psych morons when I started writing fiction about living in an alternate world where magic, not science, ruled the universe. *You* thought that it was a psychological problem, rather than a young girl exercising her imagination."

"You were at the age where making things up is common," her father said. He stood up in one smooth motion and turned towards the door. "Tiffany, this marriage won't be for very long. You won't have to stay with him for more than a decade and you have a century of life ahead of you. And if you want to choose your next husband yourself, or remain unattached, I will honor your desire."

"*Thank* you," Tiffany said sourly. "Now please, father, get out!"

Her father stepped through the door and closed it behind him.

Tiffany looked at the maid rearranging her bed and ordered her out of the room too. The brain-burned always sent shivers down her spine, if only because there were some people in High Society who would have happily brain-burned everyone else merely to ensure that their rule was never challenged. It was a nightmarish thought and, back in the days when it had first occurred to her, she'd had problems sleeping because she feared that she'd wake up a brain-burned slave, or worse.

The folder her father had given her had landed on the floor somewhere. She reached around for it and picked it off the floor, placing it on the bed before opening it. Admiral Marius Drake, her unwanted husband, stared back at her, the unmoving photograph a mocking reminder of her fate. He wasn't the most handsome man, but she had to admit that that spoke well of him. A man in his position could have had himself reshaped into a living god, so perfect as to be inhuman. Instead, he was pug-ugly.

She skimmed through the file and knew that some of her friends in High Society would never talk to her again. Marius Drake had been born on Mars to middle-class parents, not to High Society; indeed, she understood now why it had taken so long to find him a bride. His kids wouldn't be part of High Society—at least not completely—and few people nearer his age would be willing to tolerate that for their children. Tiffany was already on the lower rung of High Society, so marrying a man from outside High Society wouldn't reflect too badly on her family. And besides, having influence over the admiral, as her father had said, would be worth any amount of social shunning.

"Damn you," she muttered, and turned to her terminal. It took only thirty minutes to realize that her father had locked her out of every secure system and cancelled all of her authorization codes. The only thing she could access was Drake's service record. She wouldn't be able to escape, either on her yacht or by booking a ticket off-planet on a commercial starship. The walls of her father's mansion—one of the largest on Earth—were closing in around her. She was trapped. "Damn you to hell."

Picking up the file, she keyed her terminal and started to record a message. If she had to be miserable, she saw no reason why the misery couldn't be shared.

𝕤𝕠𝕔𝕤

The Gateway defenses, Marius was relieved to see, had been strongly augmented in the wake of Admiral Justinian's first attack on Earth. Newly built fortresses surrounded the Asimov Point, bristling with weapons, while four entire squadrons of superdreadnaughts backed them up. Nor had the Admiralty neglected the defenses of Mars, Jupiter or Earth itself. Home Fleet had been strongly reinforced and new squadrons were working up on the other side of the Dead End. There might have been hundreds of problems with a sudden massive increase in production, but the Federation was responding to the challenge.

"Admiral, we are approaching Earth," Captain Sinclair informed him. Marius had been tempted to ride back to Earth in *Magnificent*, but the superdreadnaught had been needed back at Boskone. Instead, he'd borrowed the battlecruiser *Swift*, which had been due for a refit at the Jupiter Yards. "Would you like to take command of the approach?"

"No, thank you," Marius said. Strictly speaking, he shouldn't have been on the bridge at all, but he missed the days when he commanded his own starship, *Master under God*. Commanding a fleet deployment—even the largest deployment made since the Blue Star War—wasn't quite the same. "The ship is yours."

He settled back as the battlecruiser reduced speed, heading into the Earth-Luna Sphere. Prior to the war, Home Fleet hadn't stationed a sizable force near Earth. Now, a dozen superdreadnaught squadrons orbited Luna, with hundreds of smaller ships zipping around, scanning space for cloaked starships or other unpleasant surprises.

Their mere presence was a sore spot, for if those ships had been released to join his fleet, he could have punched through the Asimov Point and broken into Admiral Justinian's inner worlds. The Senate, however, felt differently, and in the wake of the Battle of Terra Nova, it was hard to blame them. Victory over one warlord might mean defeat by another. Indeed, the Senate was fortifying other Asimov Points and organizing nodal forces at nexus stars. By the time the war was over, it should be possible to start a large-scale operation against the Outsiders.

If, of course, the Outsiders let them have the time.

He'd read, carefully, the report from Admiral Mason and the shorter report from Captain Garibaldi. Someone was recruiting with an intensity that surprised him, which suggested that they had something in mind. Who? The warlords wouldn't have needed to hire so many mercenaries, but the Outsiders would definitely have wanted to learn from people who had been at the sharp end of the military operations over the last century.

There was little doubt in Marius's mind that the war against Admiral Justinian was only the precursor to a long and bloody war against the Outsiders. They'd never have a better chance to topple the Federation.

"Admiral," the communications officer said, "we have picked up a recorded message for your eyes only."

Marius nodded slowly. The communications officer was so *young*! The war had brought a great many accelerated promotions to deserving young officers, while killing a great many more.

"I'll take it in my cabin," he said. "Pipe it down to my private terminal."

Once he was in his cabin, it was a simple matter to decode the message. A hologram formed in front of him, showing a red-haired young lady. Marius frowned, uncertain of who she was or why she would be sending a message to him. It was hard to read the emotions of the tiny figure, but she didn't look happy.

"Admiral Drake," the woman said. Her voice was curt, very formal. "Please accept my salutations. I am Lady Tiffany Eleanor Diana Katherine d'Artagnan, your bride—to-be. My father has ordered me to marry you for the sake of the family and the Conservative Faction. I trust that I meet with your approval"—her voice darkened—"as it seems that neither of us have much of a choice in the matter."

Marius started. He'd known that the Senate intended to find him a bride, but he hadn't realized that it would be someone unwilling.

"I have argued against it, but my family have refused to even consider my pleas," Tiffany continued. "I think that even if you find the prospect of marrying me terrifying, you won't have any choice either. I think we should try and make the best of it. I don't bite—much. I'll see you on the planet's surface in a few hours, where we may have some time alone together. Or maybe not. It seems that my father thinks I might run away."

She looked up and smiled. "I wonder where he might have picked up that idea?"

Marius had to laugh.

"I'll see you soon," the message concluded. Her voice broke down into bitter laughter. "And if you don't like me, tough!"

Chapter Thirty-Two

When a marriage takes place in High Society, it is rarely—if ever—about love. Couples are married by their parents to bind together agreements, resources or even political influence. There is no marriage without careful consideration of the pros and cons of a match. A High Society person who marries outside High Society may be shunned by the remainder of High Society and their children mocked and teased at school...

...Such marriages are, in fact, arranged very quickly and may not last longer than a few months...

-An Irreverent Guide to the Federation, 4000 A.D.

Luna Academy, Sol System, 4095

"But I don't *want* to marry her!"

Professor Kratman snorted. They sat alone in a secure room, studying the blank grey walls that blocked any eavesdropping devices from sending a signal outside the tiny compartment. Its very blandness seemed to mock the turmoil of Marius' mind. For the first time since he'd been a young Ensign, he didn't know what to do.

"And what," Professor Kratman asked dryly, "do you think that that has to do with anything?"

Marius stared at his former commander.

"I don't know her," he pointed out. "I couldn't marry Amy because she knew I'd always put the Navy before her. I certainly couldn't offer Lady Tiffany anything more solid, or personal. And I don't love her."

"You're from a society where couples are encouraged to marry for love," Professor Kratman said evenly. "High Society, on the other hand, doesn't frown on pre-marital sex, but only allows actual alliances between couples when the marriage benefits the overall families. You don't have anything to offer them—family-wise—but you are in a position where they need a great deal of influence over you personally."

He paused. "As I'm sure I have told you before, you're old enough to know that the Senate can be very cold-blooded at times. And they're scared."

Marius nodded in understanding. Admiral Justinian was only the first of many warlords who'd declared their independence and had set up their own fiefdoms. If they ever allied together, they might be able to bring down the Federation—but fortunately, most of them only seemed to want to hold on to what they had. But ONI's long-term predictions were not hopeful. If Admiral Justinian wasn't beaten within five years, nothing could save the Federation from collapse. And that would be the end of humanity's unity.

Marius had asked Arunika, in private, what would follow the end of the Federation. She had tried to project it out, but the results hadn't been precise. She thought there would be clumps of human worlds that would inherit much of the remaining military force, alien worlds declaring independence and attempting to build up their own starships, the Outsiders pushing into the Rim and setting up their own empires...it would spark an endless series of galactic wars before some new authority managed to reunite humanity.

But the worst-case projection showed humanity being exterminated or enslaved by alien overlords.

"Scared?" he asked Kratman after a long pause. "Maybe they should be. But why be scared of me?"

Professor Kratman grinned.

"Think of this marriage as a gesture of their faith in you. They lost control of Admiral Justinian when he went rogue because he wasn't really bound to them. You, on the other hand, will be offered the chance to add your genes to High Society. Your long-term interests will be united with theirs."

"Right," Marius said. "And if the marriage isn't a happy one?"

"You do realize that all you are really being called upon is to produce children, which you could grow in an artificial womb if you wish," the Professor pointed out. "There's no reason for you to spend any more time with her after the wedding, even if they insist on her going back with you to your command. High Society might even expect that, because many of their marriages are in name only."

"That's heartless," Marius protested without energy. "Why...?"

"They've been the lords and masters of all of known space for centuries," the Professor reminded him tartly. "They know that their methods work. It's quite natural for them to stick with something they know has worked in the past. What's the happiness of one young girl—who will have a chance to find happiness later, perhaps in the arms of a lover—compared to ruling the galaxy?"

Marius closed his eyes for a long moment.

"I assume that I don't have much choice in the matter," he said finally.

Professor Kratman nodded.

"Very well, then." Marius switched topics. "I want to know why the Brotherhood is so interested in me."

The Professor said nothing for a long moment. "And have you agreed to join?" he finally wondered.

"You made a very convincing offer," Marius said flatly. "As I told Arunika, I have agreed to join the Brotherhood. She sent me to you."

The Professor looked at him for a long moment.

"It goes without saying, I hope, that the Brotherhood values its secrecy very highly. Disclosure of anything relating to the Brotherhood without permission will result in your termination, along with anyone you might have shared any information with. Do you understand me?"

"Yes," Marius said. "I won't betray you."

"You have secure implants already," the Professor said. "You won't betray us willingly, but you understand that we are more than a little paranoid with new members. You are unusual because you already possessed a high rank when we contacted you, one that you don't owe to us—well, not directly."

"Your messenger claimed that you orchestrated the press campaign in my favor," Marius pointed out.

"We did," Professor Kratman admitted. "It was fairly easy, to be honest. We've controlled many of Earth's foremost media outlets for centuries. We use them to make sure that the Brotherhood's agenda is put forward at all times, helping to ensure that the Federation doesn't follow us, but walks in the direction we want it to go. We constantly remind people of how aliens can never be trusted, ensuring that the idealists who intend to revoke the anti-alien laws never get a chance at a fair hearing. We also bolster the position of the Senate to some extent, ensuring that wild cards are rarely elected into power."

Marius considered it. Wouldn't that have played a role in the Senate's corruption?

"The Brotherhood sees the rise of the warlords as the greatest threat to human unity and supremacy since the Inheritance Wars," Kratman went on. "If they succeed in shattering the Federation, the human race will be weakened, leaving us vulnerable to the Outsiders. Worse, if the Senate succeeds in clamping down and pushing the entire Federation into lockdown, the Federation will rot apart from within. There will be yet another round of Inheritance Wars as the colonies strive to break away from the dying center of human civilization. We cannot allow such an outcome, Marius, and you are in a good position to assist us in deflecting it."

Marius considered for a long moment. He knew that the Professor was right, at least to some extent. The Core Worlds had been draining the colonies for a long time, while making it harder for their citizens to get a decent education and therefore crippling themselves in the long run. The Federation had been quietly discouraging innovation and scientific research for centuries, turning universities and research labs into places where the status quo was maintained and nothing else. The Federation had been stagnating for a very long time and stagnation meant eventual death. There was no hope of reinvigorating the Federation without something to help force through the reforms.

"Maybe we should act to limit the primacy of Earth," he offered after a long pause. "If we could break down the voting system..."

"We might cause a civil war," the Professor said. "Do you think that everyone who has vested interests based on the current system would accept its collapse without a fight?"

"We already have a civil war," Marius pointed out. He turned and focused on the professor. "What does the Brotherhood want from me?"

"We want you to win the war," Professor Kratman said. "The longer the current stalemate lasts, the greater the possibility of the Federation tottering and falling apart. Admiral Justinian may win by default."

Marius snorted.

"I have been trying to win the war since it was declared," he said sarcastically. "We're not going to be able to beat him without breaking through into Jefferson and then into Harmony—and doing that requires a far greater commitment of mobile firepower than I have. Can the Brotherhood convince the Senate to cut loose half of Home Fleet and allow me to use it on an extended mission?"

"Maybe," the Professor said. "Could you guarantee them a victory?"

"Nothing is certain in war, as you know very well," Marius reminded him. "Tell me something—how much influence does the Brotherhood actually have?"

"A considerable amount in some places, and none whatsoever in others," the Professor said dryly. "You'll understand if I refuse to give details."

Marius nodded. "How much influence do you have in the Zathras Sector?"

"A fair number of agents, including several who remained at their posts during the coup," the Professor said. "What would you like us to do with them?"

Marius looked down at his hands. The idea was only half-formed and he knew, from experience, that trying to push an idea out too quickly meant that it often refused to form perfectly.

"If we could send the sector into chaos, or even make an agreement with Hartkopf, we could send a fleet through the sector and into Admiral Justinian's territory," he said as the idea started to slowly come together. "Stab at Harmony through Jefferson—or, perhaps, cross the gulfs of space and hit him from behind. And then we'd have him on the run. We could win the war within two years, providing the Senate agreed to cut loose the mobile firepower and agreed to give me authority to negotiate."

"Tricky," Professor Kratman observed. "You're talking about convincing them to leave his head on his shoulders. And then you'd have to do something about Hartkopf..."

"If we can't make a deal with him," Marius said, "could the Brotherhood assassinate him?"

"I'd have to consult with my superiors," the Professor said. "Direct action is always dangerous because it risks exposing the Brotherhood. The Senate might start taking us seriously and perhaps even trying to hunt us down. The prospect of someone with that kind of power not under their control...well, I'm sure you can understand that that would make them panic."

"Yes," Marius said. He grinned. "But I thought you wanted to win the war?"

৪০ড়৪

It had been three years since Marius had set foot in Luna Academy, but he'd privately decided to visit and inspect the new facilities even before Arunika had asked him to meet with the Professor. The five thousand new cadets seemed less focused and determined than they had been when he'd been a student there, although that might just have been because of his own, poor memory. The thought made him smile as he passed a group of cadets cleaning the floors as punishment duty. Every generation thought that the younger generation didn't have what it took.

He looked in on the history class and frowned when he heard the speaker. She was a newcomer, wearing a uniform that somehow didn't look right on her, even though it had been perfectly tailored. Her sallow face promised trouble for anyone who didn't listen carefully to her and answer the questions perfectly. Her lecture was nothing more than political indoctrination, teaching the cadets that they had a duty to the Federation Senate more than anything else. They were being encouraged to rat on their friends, fellow cadets and even superior officers if they heard them making disloyal statements. Marius was horrified and walked away, wondering just how they meant to maintain a chain of command if junior officers were ordered to inform on senior officers.

It got worse in the next class. The cadets were being taught a very different version of the rules of war. The Federation Navy took prisoners where possible, but now the cadets were being told that rebels and warlords—and their followers— were owed nothing, not even food and water. They were traitors, after all, and traitors deserved nothing more than death. The lecturer even spoke about bombarding worlds like Jefferson—which had had no choice but to serve Justinian—back into the Stone Age. And then there was the discourse on political traitors, such as the colonists who wanted independence from the Federation.

Absently, Marius used his implants to call up a class roster and swore under his breath. The entire class—every cadet who had entered Luna Academy in the last two years—was from the Core Worlds. There wasn't a single colonial.

"It's been getting worse over the last two years," Professor Kratman said when he found Marius watching a space combat simulation. The combat simulations didn't seem to have changed much, thankfully. "The Senate has been ordering the incorporation of political courses into both the Academy and the training camps. Those cadets who don't have a perfect measure of political reliability will not be allowed to graduate as Firsts. I suspect that in the long run, cadets without a perfect measure will not be permitted to graduate at all."

"How can you allow this?" Marius turned to look at him.

"Do you think that we were given much of a choice?" The Professor shrugged and shook his head.

"But..." Marius wasn't sure how to finish that question, not without offending the Professor and the Brotherhood. What good were they if they allowed this travesty?

"That isn't the worst of it," he added. "You'll see men in black suits down on the surface; I suggest that you avoid them. They're the new Internal Security Division, with authority to question anyone they think might be hiding rebel sympathies and to detain—without trial—anyone who fails the interrogation. Several very good retired officers have vanished into holding cells and never been seen again after being picked up by the Blackshirts."

"The Blackshirts?" Marius stared at him.

"It seems to be a common feature of every internal security unit that they wear black uniforms," Professor Kratman said, irony heavy in his tone. "I wonder if they know that they're merely the latest in a long line of repressive organizations. Humans have been forming secret police groups ever since we discovered fire." He frowned. "Incidentally, be careful how much encryption you use, even on Federation Navy channels. They're hacking into some communications and could consider the heavy use of encryption to be a sign of disloyalty."

"Disloyalty," Marius repeated. The whole concept was absurd. "I couldn't think of anything more likely to make people disloyal, Professor."

"No," Professor Kratman agreed. "I can't either. But the Senate is scared, and scared people do stupid things. I think you'll probably wind up with political officers on your ships watching your every move. I'd be surprised if you didn't already have a spy or two beside you, keeping an eye on you. As I've said before, watch your back."

His eyes narrowed. "There are some of us who believe that the Senate intends to move into a complete lockdown on the entire Federation once the war ends...and that will really blow up any hope of a stable Federation. There will be a thousand rebellions, if that happens, and the Federation Navy will schism. Again. It will destroy us. Win the war quickly, admiral."

"I'll try, sir," Marius said, and nodded. For a moment, they were captain and lieutenant again. "Thank you."

"You'll need this," Professor Kratman said, pulling a small box out of his pocket and passing it to Marius.

Marius opened the box. It held a simple silver ring, like the one Arunika had worn when they'd first met.

"I suggest that you keep it somewhere very secure and *don't* let anyone else wear it. It will kill anyone but you." Kratman smiled at Marius's expression. "We take our security seriously, as I told you. Anyone who has a ring and refuses to put it on at request is probably a ringer. You have been warned."

He stood up and slapped Marius on the shoulder. "Go and get married, young man. You deserve a break before you go back to the war." His voice lowered. "And by then, we might know what we can do to help you with Governor Hartkopf."

"Thank you," Marius said. He pocketed the ring and held out a hand. The Professor took it and they shook firmly. "Can I invite you to the wedding?"

"I'm only a mere professor these days," Kratman said dryly. "Don't you think it would attract attention?"

Chapter Thirty-Three

As a High Society marriage is more about the politics than the young couple, it isn't unknown for the wedding to be a place for private deal-making and political planning. -An Irreverent Guide to the Federation, 4000 A.D.

Earth, Sol System, 4095

"You must be Marius," the girl said. She sounded oddly reluctant to talk. "I am Tiffany."

"Yes," Marius said. His mouth felt dry. "It's nice to meet you."

"It would have been nicer if Daddy Dearest had given me more than a day's warning," she said, eyes flashing. "I could probably have bypassed the lock-outs and escaped to the Rim before you reached Earth."

Marius found himself, again, at a loss for words.

"Don't worry about it," she said seriously. "You didn't choose me and I didn't choose you." She stepped back and gave him a frank inspection. "At least you're not as ugly as Senator Montgomery. Seventy years old if he's a day, and he looks five hundred. He needs to spend more money on improving his appearance."

"I think it's part of his charm," Marius said, and snorted.

Senator Montgomery was thrifty and utterly impossible to shift from the Senate, mainly because he knew where all of the bodies were buried. It took a very special person to make the Conservative Faction look like a bunch of raving progressives, but Montgomery managed it, somehow. Any change at all was anathema to him and his enemies had been heard to joke that the only reason he wasn't richer was because he was determined not to change his finances.

His wife-to-be snorted too. "What charm?"

"Precisely my point," Marius said. "Look, I didn't ask for this..."

"I know." Tiffany winked at him. "I'm sure you would have chosen someone much prettier if you had a free choice."

She made a show of spinning around in front of him. Marius had to admire her, for there was nothing artificial about her looks. She *was* young. He knew that it wasn't uncommon for Senators to have vast age differences between them and their brides, but Tiffany was nearly sixty years younger than him. Her long red hair set off her white dress nicely, while the dress itself pinched her body in all the right places. If they'd met while he'd been on leave, without his responsibilities to worry about, he might have tried to pick her up.

"You're beautiful," he said truthfully. Her face wasn't as inhumanly perfect as some of the joy-girls he'd known as a younger officer, but the few defects added character. Tiffany might grow up into a very strong woman if her family didn't cut her down first, or High Society show its traditional resentment of anyone trying to rise above their station, but he didn't know how to say that to her. "I think...we might do well after all."

He cringed, feeling like a young officer again. *That* had sounded lame.

Tiffany sobered quickly.

"I know that this wasn't your choice," she said, holding out a hand. "Let's make the best of it, shall we?"

"Why not?" Marius took her hand.

He felt strange, holding the hand of his arranged bride, yet he also felt oddly comfortable in her presence. She was showing a remarkable amount of calm. If he'd been told that he had to marry a complete stranger—and a stranger so much older than himself—he would have been throwing himself at the walls.

"Just know that I'll do my best for you," Marius said, not sure why he cared all of a sudden. "But—if you want children—"

"I think," Tiffany said cynically, "that they don't really care about your performance in the bedchamber." Her face fell for a second. "If you have someone...special... already in your life, I won't complain if you spend time with her instead of me."

"I don't," Marius said. That thought hadn't crossed his mind. "And do you have someone special?"

"Not at the moment," Tiffany admitted. "I thought that there would be enough time to find someone. Instead..." She shrugged expressively. "I'll do my duty, admiral, and as long as you do yours, your superiors will be happy."

There was something in her voice that broke Marius's heart.

"I've never been a husband before," he said, "but I'll do my best."

"I saw that in your file." Tiffany smiled. "You never chose to marry before now?"

"My first serious lover didn't want to spend her life following a young officer around the Rim, while the second didn't want to leave Mars or spend long months apart from her husband," Marius admitted. "After that, I gave up and decided to focus on my career. The Navy was my bride."

"I think you'd have difficulty taking a superdreadnaught to bed," Tiffany said archly. "Which missile tube would you use..."

Marius found himself chuckling as she giggled.

There was a knock at the door. It opened without waiting for any answer. Granny Sampson, one of Tiffany's oldest relations through a complex network of family ties Marius hadn't been able to fathom, bustled through the door and winked at them. Unlike most of the older members of High Society, she didn't bother to hide her age and grey hair topped her very aristocratic head. Marius had only met her briefly, but he'd seen enough to discern that she was very influential behind the scenes and was most likely one of the people who had helped arrange his marriage. He had wondered, at first, what she got out of it, before realizing that the old woman wanted nothing more than influence and the chance to shape the future.

"Not very active, are you?" she asked, as she closed the door behind her. "Good heavens; when I was a girl, the entire world was shocked to discover the happy couple pressed against the wall, getting a sneak preview of the honeymoon. Mind you, everyone was shocked because they hadn't thought the guy had it in him. He was a bit of a weed and a wet, and no one even thought he could get it up in a joy-house with nine joy-girls devoting themselves to his pleasure..."

"*Granny*," Tiffany protested, blushing furiously. "What are you doing here?"

Granny Sampson made a show of checking her watch.

"Why, the ceremony is about to start, my dear," she said. "I wouldn't want you to be late for your first wedding. First times are always special..."

"She's been married to nine husbands and outlived them all," Tiffany explained to Marius.

"Cheeky brat," Granny Sampson said. She didn't sound offended in the slightest. "I haven't forgotten the shocking story of a man who showed up late to his wedding because he was too busy getting it on with the best man. Everyone in High Society will be talking about this wedding—I mean, you actually met *before* the wedding. That's no good, is it? You might have run away in horror."

She gave Marius a wink. "Don't worry about a thing," she assured him. "The ceremony itself is very simple, afterward you just have to endure the reception and then you can rush off and enjoy yourself."

Tiffany let go of his hand—Marius had somehow never realized that she was still holding onto him—and rolled her eyes when Granny Sampson looked away.

"All you young folk are all the same," Granny Sampson said without turning back. "You think of tradition as an impediment. It wasn't like that in my day."

"When dinosaurs ruled the Earth?" Tiffany asked sweetly. "I'll see you at the reception, Granny."

She gave Marius a wink and walked out the door, followed rapidly by Granny Sampson. Marius consulted his internal chronometer and sighed. The wedding was about to begin, which meant...in an hour, he would be a husband. He shook his head. He'd never imagined, in his worst nightmares, that his own wedding would be such a farce.

⁎⌘⁂

The Great Hall was large enough to accommodate thousands of people, enough to allow all of High Society to attend without crowding. As Marius and his best man—chosen from among the bride's family, a distant cousin of his wife—walked up to the altar, he was acutely aware of the gazes fixed on him. He'd chosen to wear his dress uniform—though it had been the only choice he'd been allowed to make—and he could sense the collective shock and astonishment running through High Society. Marius found it hard to care. If they'd arranged the marriage to bind him to them, they might at least know what they were clasping to their collective bosom.

He had to admit, despite himself, that the Great Hall was impressive. The first Federation President had been inaugurated within its walls and all successive presidents, no matter how weak the office had become, had followed in his footsteps. It was lit by the glow of thousands of candles and decorated in a fashion that harkened back to the days of old, long before mankind had mastered space travel and gone out to create the Federation. He caught sight of the statues lining the walls and smiled grimly. Each of the statues represented an alien race that had been brought—willingly or otherwise—into the Federation. A couple of the statues had outlasted the races they were supposed to represent.

There were no live aliens at the wedding, of course. Aliens were banned from Earth and most of the Core Worlds, although there were some very small alien communities on a handful of them. It wasn't unknown for some aliens to be allowed to travel without supervision, although they tended to have a hard time at customs. The crowd was all human—at least for a certain value of human—and High Society. Marius hadn't been allowed to invite any of his family, even the ones living on Mars, let alone his friends. The cluster of admirals and generals at the rear of the room were all from High Society.

He sucked in his breath as the music began to play. *Courage*, he told himself. *You've endured a thousand battles with humans and aliens. You can endure your own wedding.*

Yes, his thoughts rattled on, *but you're not allowed to blow up your own wedding, are you? Regulations can be such a nuisance...*

His best man caught his arm as Tiffany advanced into the chamber wearing a long, white dress and carrying a bunch of flowers. She looked as if she was trying hard to be demure, but Marius could tell that she was nervous. Her bridesmaids, suitable young woman chosen from among her family, seemed to be laughing at her. Marius wondered, with a sudden flash of anger he refused to show on his face, if they were married themselves. Or, perhaps, if they knew that *they* wouldn't be married off to a complete stranger. He wondered, just for a moment, how many deals had been struck behind the scenes to arrange his marriage.

Tiffany stopped beside him, her head bowed, and didn't look up.

"Dearly beloved," the Speaker said, "we are gathered here today to bind together two of our children, who have chosen to give their lives to one another in matrimony."

Marius shuddered inwardly. Neither of them had chosen their partners.

"If there is anyone who can show just reason as to why they should not marry, let him speak now or forever hold his peace."

There was a long, nerve-wracking pause.

"No one has spoken," the Speaker said. He looked down at Marius and Tiffany. "You may join hands."

Marius reached for Tiffany's hand and held it gently.

"Both hands," the Speaker prompted.

A thin ripple of amusement echoed around the room. Marius turned to face Tiffany and took her other hand.

A moment later, the Speaker wrapped a thin golden cord around their hands, binding them together. "Admiral Marius Drake, do you take Tiffany as your lawful bride, to have and to hold, to cherish and protect, until death do you part?"

A farce, part of Marius's mind echoed bitterly. The divorce rates in High Society were astronomical. He wondered, in a moment of black humor, if that explained why the murder rates were so low.

"I do," he said. Tiffany looked up at him, her green eyes sparkling with dark amusement, and they shared a smile.

"Lady Tiffany, do you take Marius as your lawful wedded husband, to have and to hold, to cherish and protect, until death do you part?"

"I do," Tiffany said. She caught Marius's eyes again and they almost started giggling.

"I therefore pronounce you man and wife," the Speaker said with a smile. "You may now kiss the bride."

Marius hesitated, before Tiffany leaned up and pressed her lips against his. She felt warm and soft to the touch. He prolonged the kiss, long enough to make the Speaker clear his throat in irritation.

She'd had the same thought, he realized as they separated. If nothing else, they could annoy the Speaker and the people who had arranged the marriage.

"Together, you will start on a long journey," the Speaker intoned. He carefully undid the cord binding them together, speaking all the while about how they would be bound together by love and mutual respect. Marius had to look away from his bride, for fear that they would both start giggling again. "We wish you all the best in the future."

And the entire crowd applauded as they walked out the door.

಄ೞ

The reception was, in its own way, just as much of a farce as the wedding itself.

Marius had heard that a wedding reception was meant to be for the bride, but it was clear after only a few moments that it was really for the guests. Senators mingled with their political enemies, men they would never speak to in a civil tone in the Senate, making deals and swapping inside information. The bride's family seemed to be the focus of attention, apart from the Senators, although Marius couldn't tell if their visitors were congratulating her relatives or commiserating with them. It didn't take long for him to realize that many of the younger men and women were shunning Tiffany, although he couldn't tell if it bothered his bride or not. He felt an odd surge of protectiveness and thought wistfully of the sword on his belt. Traditionally, it should have been a harmless one, but he'd ordered a real sword.

None of these people seemed to know the difference.

"Allow me to extend my most fulsome congratulations," a voice said. He turned to see Grand Senator Rupert McGillivray standing behind him, holding an empty glass. "I think that the two of you will be good together."

He caught Marius's arm and pulled him into a corner. "Take care of her," he added. "She's probably the smartest person in the room."

"Including you?" Marius smiled.

"Oh, definitely," McGillivray assured him. He changed the topic as he saw Granny Sampson walking over to join them. "What news of the war?"

"Well, I have hopes that we can break through the Asimov Point and knock Admiral Justinian for six," Marius informed him. He wasn't going to go into detail, not here. "And then we can put an end to the remaining warlords and restore the Federation."

"Good," McGillivray said. He slapped him on the back. "Oh, look; the speeches are about to begin."

Tiffany joined him for the speeches. Very few of them, Marius noted, had anything to do with either Tiffany or himself. The speakers seemed more determined to offer florid tributes to themselves and the great wisdom of the Senate in dealing with rebels, traitors and domestic enemies. Their prattling was giving him a headache by the time the speaking was finally over and they were allowed to leave.

Tiffany pulled him into a black aircar, festooned with bunting, and ordered the autopilot to take them to the Grand Hotel.

Marius stared at his bride, feeling—again—the odd surge of protectiveness. Tiffany's eyes were bright, too bright. He recognized the symptoms of tiredness and stress and wondered how many of them he was showing. He'd once commanded during a battle that had lasted for two days, but that had been years ago, when he'd been a younger man.

"I'm sorry," he said, and meant it.

"Don't be," Tiffany said. She reached for him and placed her hand on his heart. "It wasn't your fault."

She snorted then and started to undo her dress. "I think someone designed this purposely to be uncomfortable so we'd want to get out of them quickly."

Marius stopped her. "You don't have to..."

"Yes, I do," Tiffany said. Her eyes narrowed. "The wedding has to be consummated, doesn't it?"

Marius hesitated, unsure of what to say. In an aircar, of all places?

"Besides, everyone was cheerfully predicting that the marriage would fall apart within a week. I thought we might try to make it last ten days."

"Oh," Marius said, and then realized that he was being teased. "Should we try for a month, or is that too ambitious?"

Tiffany laughed and reached for him. By the time the aircar reached the Grand Hotel's honeymoon suite and landed outside the private entrance, they were too occupied to notice until the aircar's autopilot hooted at them. Marius picked Tiffany up and carried her into the honeymoon suite, laying her down on the bed. A moment later, as the aircar departed into the night, he started kissing her again.

Afterwards, they toasted each other with champagne before returning to bed. As he drifted off to sleep, holding her in his arms, Marius allowed himself one final thought.

Perhaps marriage wouldn't be so bad after all.

Chapter Thirty-Four

The Senate's security levels often leave something to be desired. While the Senators them-selves are meant to be above suspicion, they are often quite willing to leak sensitive data to the media for their own reasons. Even if the Senators themselves do not leak the data, they have a habit of informing their subordinates, who might happily leak the informa-tion for their own reasons...

...What this means, in effect, is that anything told to the Senate may not remain secret for very long...
-An Irreverent Guide to the Federation, 4000 A.D.

Earth, Sol System, 4095

Marius whistled cheerfully as he was escorted by one of the Senatorial aides into the classified briefing room just outside the Senate Hall. Based on five days of mar-riage, part of him insisted that he would enjoy it all, even though they barely knew one another and there was no time for a proper honeymoon. They'd spent four days in the Honeymoon Suite, with no one intruding on their privacy, and a fifth day vis-iting the underwater grottos at the North Pole. Marius knew from history that the North Pole had once had an icecap, but it had melted down long ago, causing the sea level to rise dramatically. That ecological disaster had had a major impact on human-ity's determination to move out into space.

"Watch your back," Tiffany had warned him when they'd parted. "You may be High Society now, legally, but not all of the young bucks and blades are going to accept you."

Marius had taken her words to heart when he'd visited the Admiralty, but no one there had personally doubted him. A few old women of both genders had raised objections to his operational plans—at least the plans he'd chosen to share with them—and it had taken hours of arguing to convince them to accept the plans with-out major modifications. He had to admit that they had a point—the plans he'd shared with them were not particularly imaginative and therefore they would be predictable—but that was part of the point. If anything leaked back to Admiral Justinian or the other warlords, they'd be misled.

Or so he hoped.

He was awed at the level of firepower the Federation had created. Once the expanded training camps had finished turning out the next few graduating classes, it would be possible to man and deploy new construction very quickly. A few more weeks to work up the ships, and the Federation Navy would hold a decisive advan-tage over the warlords.

Of course, if the warlords did manage to work together, the advantage wouldn't be as decisive as Marius hoped, but it should suffice to weaken them. Once Admiral Justinian was defeated, the other warlords could be crushed one by one. They lacked the firepower to be a strategic threat. The real danger lay beyond the Rim.

"The room is now sealed," Grand Senator Brockington said. "The Senate Subcommittee on the Conduct of the War is now in session."

Marius nodded. The Leader of the Conservative Faction had been one of the few senior Senators to offer congratulations to Marius and Tiffany. Marius had had the odd feeling that he'd meant every word, unlike some of the others, who'd acted like Marius smelled bad.

"Thank you, Senator," Grand Senator Alison Wallisch said. "There are many questions that need to be raised."

Marius sighed. The Leader of the Socialist Faction *hadn't* offered sincere congratulations to the newlyweds, but Marius had already deduced that there were limits to her socialism. The Socialist Faction might insist on gifting alien races with the benefits of human technology, yet doing so also had the effect of permanently neutralizing any threat those aliens might pose to humanity. Anything they might create for themselves was automatically branded as inferior.

He sat back and watched as the Senators sparred, sometimes calling on Admiral Fallon—the CO of Earth's defense network—to answer specific questions. It seemed that there were accusations of war profiteering, although he couldn't tell if the Senators were annoyed over the war profiteering itself or if they were merely upset that they weren't skimming off the cream themselves. Judging from the messages he'd received from Professor Kratman, Marius would have bet good money that every Senator was profiting from the war, although it was an open question how long they could do so before there was an economic collapse. The Federation's economy had been badly weakened by the war.

Other questions focused on operations against other warlords. General Williamston, who had carved out a vest-pocket kingdom of four stars and nine planets, had been defeated in a short and bloody campaign. The General had somehow failed to realize that his little Kingdom didn't have the firepower to prevent the Federation Navy from sending a squadron of superdreadnaughts through the Asimov Point and punching out his orbital fortresses, or that the Senate was desperate and ruthless enough to order planetary bombardment as a response to his refusal to surrender.

Marius hadn't been involved in that campaign—he'd been watching Admiral Justinian—but he'd been sickened by the reports. The Federation Navy hadn't quite bombed the planet back to the Stone Age, yet that had only been avoided because the General's subordinates shot him in the head and surrendered unconditionally.

That example boded ill for the worlds Admiral Justinian had brought under his banner. Some worlds had followed him willingly, but others—like Jefferson—hadn't been given much of a choice in the matter. But that might not matter to the Senate, not when Jefferson was a money-maker for whoever owned the system. They'd be happy to remove the old government, put a Federation Governor in place and milk it for all that it was worth, along with a secret police to ferret out all independence movements and revisionists.

No matter what happened with Jefferson, Marius knew, it wasn't going to end well.

"Admiral Drake," Brockington said.

Marius looked up.

"I understand that you have a proposal to put before the Committee."

"Yes, Senator," Marius said, and avoided saying what he was thinking: *Finally!* "I believe the operational plan I have drawn up will lead to the quick defeat of Admiral Justinian and the end of the war."

He stood up and keyed the room's terminal. He'd uploaded the operational plan into it as soon as he entered the room. The Senate's computer network was supposed to be inaccessible from the outside, but Marius had long since stopped taking such statements for granted. The chances were good that one of Admiral Justinian's allies had slipped a tap onto the network before they were exposed or executed—if they had been discovered.

"Senators, here's the situation at present," he announced. "As you can see"—he'd discovered that most of the Senators couldn't read a tactical display, so he had to use simple concepts—"we remain on guard in the Boskone System, the shortest line between Earth and Harmony. We have also positioned forces here, here and here"—he keyed the systems as he mentioned them—"to prevent the enemy from trying to bypass our blockade and take us from the rear. So far, Admiral Justinian has not attempted to launch such an offensive."

"That's good," Alison said. "Do you have any explanation as to why?"

Marius smiled. ONI had turned up several, but only one was significant.

"All three alternate routes to Earth would add several months to the journey," he pointed out. "If the admiral did shift forces through them, we would be able to counter him before he reached anywhere significant. His great advantage is that he holds the interior lines of defense, but if he attacks us away from Boskone, that advantage shifts back to us. With the advantage of the superior firepower we possess, it would ensure his certain defeat.

"The important detail is that we have fortified Boskone to the point where we can be confident of holding the system even without the mobile units," he continued. He pointed to the fortresses on the display. "We have shipped in additional starfighters and fortress components, secured the planetary network and even fortified the other Asimov Point in the system. That allows us to take the risk of withdrawing our mobile units, combining them with the new-build units, and launching an offensive of our own."

"I beg your pardon, admiral," a Senator that Marius didn't recognize interrupted. "I understood that you refused to consider attacking through the Boskone Asimov Point because the rogue warlord had heavily fortified it."

"Yes, Senator," Marius agreed. "That would be a very costly offensive for little reward. The key to winning this campaign is to reduce the enemy's mobile units to the point where we can isolate his systems and reduce them one by one. Pitting our own mobile units against his fortresses would be asking for trouble. I do, however, have another plan."

He keyed the console and the star chart shifted, displaying the links between Justinian and Governor Hartkopf. "As you were all briefed in confidence, Admiral Justinian has been tricked into a shooting war with Governor Hartkopf, who occupies the stars here. It was a fortunate turn of events for us, as we have good reason to believe that they were on the verge of signing an alliance when they started fighting each other. So far, the war hasn't been significant as neither warlord dares devote most of his firepower to dealing with the other, but that may change. I intend to use Governor Hartkopf's space to launch a major operation against Admiral Justinian's unprotected underbelly."

A low murmur ran through the room, but no one said anything, allowing Marius to proceed.

"The combined fleet will proceed through the governor's space to The Hive and cross the interstellar void to Marx," he continued. "Once there, they will break through the defenses and advance on Jefferson. Assuming that everything goes to plan, the warlord will not be able to shift his forces to mount a defense of the Asimov Point before we reach Jefferson. We will meet his fleet in open space, where we can maneuver and crush his ships away from his fixed defenses. Once we occupy Jefferson, we will seal the Asimov Point to Harmony and demand his surrender. If he refuses to surrender, we will punch through to Harmony and destroy his government. His remaining forces will be scattered, no longer able to coordinate their actions, and we will be able to mop them up at leisure."

There was a long pause.

"It sounds very nice," Alison said, finally, "but weren't we given predictions of an easy victory before?"

"Yes, Senator," Marius said. "Admiral Parkinson promised you an easy victory."

Most of the Senators chuckled.

"I don't promise that this will be easy," Marius admitted. "I think that there is going to be a great deal of hard fighting before we punch into enemy territory and neutralize him. It is going to be very costly. I do believe, however, that this is our best chance to win the war before the other warlords manage to build themselves up into significant threats."

"It is an interesting concept," Grand Senator Rupert McGillivray said warmly. He locked his eyes on Marius's face. "But I have a question. You're claiming that you can get through Hartkopf's space. How do you intend to do that without fighting?"

"He slipped a small squadron through without fighting," the unnamed Senator pointed out dryly. "Why not a whole fleet of superdreadnaughts?"

"It won't be easy," Marius said, taking a breath. If they were going to balk, it would be now. "I propose that we offer Governor Hartkopf amnesty if he surrenders without further ado."

There was instant uproar.

"Are you mad?" Alison demanded angrily. "It is the position of the Senate that all warlords, their families and their allies must answer for their crimes against the Federation! Do you propose to change that on your authority? How dare you, admiral! How dare you?"

"It is certainly a provocative suggestion," Brockington agreed. "And quite against the stated policy of the Senate. On the other hand, we did select the admiral in the belief that he actually knew what he was doing."

He threw Alison an unreadable look. "Admiral, please expound on your suggestion for the benefit of the Senate."

Marius kept his expression blank while he organized his thoughts.

"It is a basic principle of military tactics that one should always leave the enemy a line of retreat," Marius said. "If the enemy can escape, they are less likely to fight hard and cost your forces heavily to defeat them. If the Snakes had offered to accept surrenders in the First Interstellar War, would we have been so determined to hold the line, liberate the occupied worlds and eventually destroy their ability to make war on us? We never accepted surrenders in the later years of that war, and it cost us badly.

"In this case, you—the Senate—have ordered the death of Admiral Justinian and his family and friends. It gives him nowhere to run, so he will fight. Why not? He might win—and even if he doesn't win, he'll hurt us badly. A man may accept his own death calmly, with composure, but what about his family and friends? What about those who took no part in the rebellion?

"So if we offer amnesty to Governor Hartkopf and his allies—with due steps taken to ensure that they are never in a position to rebel again—we will send a powerful message to our enemies. That message states that they can leave the war and keep their lives—and their families, and their children. And if the governor refuses to accept our terms, someone in his government will see the advantages in assassinating him and taking command himself, just so he can surrender promptly."

He smiled. "If we gain access to Hartkopf's space without fighting, Admiral Justinian won't know about our advance until our missiles strike his bases in Marx. And by then it will be too late for him to react effectively. He will have to fight us on our terms—the one thing he has consistently refused to do—and he will lose that battle."

"You seem very sure that he will lose," Alison pointed out.

"I *am* confident," Marius admitted. "We have worked our crews hard, training them and preparing for the grand offensive. The admiral cannot have massed the same level of mobile firepower. It all comes down to sheer mass and firepower, Senator, and we will have the advantage."

For once, he was grateful for their limited understanding of military affairs. The bare bones of the plan were sound, but he'd altered several details. If Admiral Justinian did receive warning—perhaps even a detailed copy of the operational plan—he'd be misled. It would work either way; if the admiral took precautions, it would divert him from the *real* target, and if he failed to catch wind of the plan, he would miss the preparations entirely.

And, best of all, there would *be* no leaks because the only person who knew the real plan was Marius himself.

"We will consider your proposal," Brockington said after another long pause. "We wish, however, to detail another operational change."

Here it comes, Marius thought.

"It is regrettably true that many units of the Federation Navy have shown remarkable disloyalty in this time of chaos," Brockington said smoothly. "We have had entire squadrons going over to warlords, or turning to piracy and carrying out depredations on entire planets. This cannot be tolerated.

"It has therefore been enacted that all starships will carry with them as part of their crews a Senatorial Commissioner, whose task will be to ferret out disloyalty and corruption wherever it might fester. The larger starships will also carry with them a company of Internal Security Division troopers, who will provide the muscle to deal with any disloyal officers and crew. The Marine detachments who would have normally provided internal security will be reconfigured into landing parties for the conquest of warlord-held worlds."

Marius kept his face impassive, but he knew Vaughn wouldn't be happy. Nor would anyone else.

"Furthermore, as there will be delays in communicating with the Senate, the commissioners will have command authority, with standing orders to overrule any orders that suggest disloyalty," Brockington said. "We trust, admiral, that you will make their introduction as smooth as possible."

If he hadn't been warned, Marius knew, he would probably have been staring in horror.

"Senator," he said carefully, "while I understand the need to ferret out disloyalty, I must protest at granting commissioners command authority. It is a principle of the Federation Navy that only the captain possesses absolute authority onboard his vessel. Adding in a separate source of command authority would only cause confusion at the worst possible time..."

"The commissioners are loyal," Brockington said flatly. "It is that loyalty that makes them suitable for their role."

"But do they know what they are doing in a war zone?" Marius asked angrily. "A person issuing orders without the right military background could..."

"Enough," Brockington said sharply. "We have enacted their function into law. Further arguments are counter-productive. We will consider your proposal, admiral. Until then, I must ask you to wait outside."

Marius nodded, saluted, and left the room.

⋅⋅⋅

"A very dangerous man," Alison observed after the door closed behind the admiral. "Did you see his reaction to the commissioners? Why would he have such a reaction unless he had something to hide?"

"His concerns are valid," Rupert pointed out dryly. "An untrained man could do a great deal of harm with a starship at his command."

"But he was willing to offer Hartkopf the chance to live," Alison countered. "How can we trust him to know where his best interests lie?"

"They lie with his wife, now," Rupert said. "We chose carefully. They will not be able to help falling in love. Despite their different ages, they have a great many things in common."

"Enough," Brockington said. "We agreed to use Drake and we have no alternative, not now. We need to agree to his proposal and allow him to approach Hartkopf. We can always go back on it later."

He stared down at his hands. "And when the war ends...?"

"We remove Drake," Alison said flatly. Her voice, cold and ruthless, would have shocked many of her constituents. "We can deal with the other warlords without him."

Rupert wasn't too surprised. Like all of the Senators, Alison was more interested in maintaining her power than anything resembling fairness and justice.

Rupert allowed himself a cold smile. "And what about Lady Tiffany's feelings?"

"Not our problem," Alison said sharply. "The feelings of one little girl are of no concern to us, not when the entire Federation is at stake. She will find someone else."

"Agreed," Brockington said. "A trial would be too dangerous, not with the degree of loyalty Drake has built up over three years. We have the tools on hand. I'll issue the orders personally. Once the war is over, Admiral Drake will be a dead man."

Interlude Two

From: *The Chaos Years* (5023)

Admiral Drake's grand plan to terminate the war, once approved, went ahead at considerable speed. New warships were fitted out, new crews were trained and put into position and research into new weapons and tactics went on apace. In the meantime, the shooting war between the two rogue warlords continued, although neither side launched a major offensive.

The Senate's paranoia, however, was growing ever stronger. The assignment of political commissioners to the Federation Navy was only the start. New Internal Security Divisions were created and sent to garrison worlds that were even mildly suspected of disloyalty. Thousands of undercover agents were infiltrated into every spectrum of society. The penal worlds soon started receiving thousands of unwilling colonists who had been accused—often with very flimsy evidence—of disloyalty.

It wasn't long before the first effects were seen on Earth, or the Core Worlds. Historically, the Senate had been more careful, for the citizens of Earth and the Core Worlds could vote the Senators out of office. But now, the Senate was willing to flex its collective muscle on Earth, using its power to crack down on all kinds of discontent. Striking workers were arrested and jailed at their command—without trial—and the military was used to maintain order. Would-be politicians were arrested, charged with pro-rebel sentiments and exiled from Earth. Planetary Governments, historically autonomous, were overruled at will. Press freedoms, long held inviolate by the Senate, were slowly weakened until most media outlets became nothing more than mouthpieces for the Senate. Protest groups, always swift to form when the Senate overstepped itself, were harassed and broken.

And the tighter the Senate cracked down, the greater the cracks that appeared within the Federation...

Chapter Thirty-Five

The Federation Foreign Department is actually the smallest department in the Federation Government, a remarkable achievement given how long the Federation has been in existence and how inflated many of its institutions have become. The reason for that is simple: the Federation rarely uses diplomacy. Humans deal with the State Department, while negotiations with alien powers tend to take the form of demonstration strikes against the planet's surface.
-An Irreverent Guide to the Federation, 4000 A.D.

Bester, Zathras System, 4097

"Jump!"

Roman braced himself as space twisted around *Midway*. Despite all the promises, despite the underhanded diplomatic discussions between the loyalists and Governor Hartkopf, Roman had little faith in the man's promises. Worse, *Midway* was alone, though an assault force was waiting to cover her withdrawal in the Vane System; the enemy fortresses guarding the Asimov Point could have blown her into dust before the drive recycled and she slipped back through the Asimov Point.

"Report," he barked. "Tactical?"

"Nine fortresses on active duty, scanning us," the tactical officer reported. He sounded tense, yet reassured. "They're not locking weapons on us, or shooting."

Roman allowed himself a tight smile. *Midway* was alarmingly close to the fortresses, so close that weapons lock would hardly be required to target and destroy them. But the fortresses could have tracked *Midway* with passive sensors alone, targeting her without revealing their intent until it was far too late.

The tactical display in front of him updated rapidly, revealing mine layers covering the Asimov Point itself and the fortresses—and a large battle squadron within easy reach of the gateway. The governor wasn't taking chances with his safety.

"Transmit our IFF codes," he ordered. If the governor had treachery in mind...he'd pay for it, eventually, but that would be small comfort to Roman's crew. "Let them know who we are."

Roman would have refused this mission if he'd been able to think of a better way to deliver a personal emissary to the rogue governor. But Admiral Drake had ordered it personally, which made Roman feel a little better. Besides, he didn't want to let the admiral down.

He looked up at the admiral's personal representative, his wife, Lady Tiffany. She looked calm and composed, although Roman knew it was at least partly an act. Her hands, clasped in front of her, betrayed her nervousness. It would be her first real diplomatic mission.

And if the governor planned treachery, she was walking right into his hands.

He couldn't blame Hartkopf for wanting to keep the whole meeting under the tightest of wraps, but still...he had agreed to allow *Midway* to enter his capital system without opposition. Roman had agreed to refrain from active scanning, yet both sides knew that passive sensors could pick up a hell of a lot of information.

"They're responding, captain," the communications officer said. "They're giving us a path to follow through the mines." He paused. "Apparently, if we deviate from it, we will be destroyed."

"No sense of humor, then," Roman commented drolly. "Helm, follow their course and try not to bump into one of the mines."

His crew laughed.

It didn't help their captain, who sat back and watched as the system display rapidly updated, with the battle computers adding their own tags to further complicate the display. Multiple spacecraft—they looked like asteroid miners—plied courses between the asteroid belts and Bester, the primary planet in the system, with several large energy signatures orbiting the planet. And that didn't count the dozens of warships, apparently waiting for an enemy to appear in the system, either.

It struck Roman that the governor had given up on any chance of securing additional territory for himself, a direct result of their operations near The Hive and Marx. A set of raids had kept Hartkopf and Admiral Justinian sniping at one another long enough to allow Admiral Drake the chance to build up the firepower to take them both out.

Bester was unusual in the Federation as the planet had actually been terraformed by the first settlers. It wasn't common to terraform a planet when there were so many inhabitable worlds in the galaxy, but Bester had possessed five gas giants and enough asteroid belts to create a powerful industrial node. The first settlers had started the terraforming project, only to go bankrupt when the galactic economy went through a major crisis in the run-up to the Inheritance Wars. Afterwards, the banks were reluctant to invest in the system and while Governor Hartkopf's predecessors had completed the terraforming project, they'd been unable to spark further economic growth.

Governor Hartkopf, ironically, might have been the first to succeed, if only because he was trying to produce a whole new war fleet. Given time, he could have built really scary defenses and a superdreadnaught fleet capable of taking on the Federation Navy.

Roman kept his expression blank, but he couldn't help feeling some satisfaction. The warlord's time had run out. Either he came to an agreement with the Federation, or he died when the Federation Navy forced its way through the defense and occupied Bester's orbitals. He doubted that any of the governor's allies would hesitate to kill their leader when the Federation Navy had them at gunpoint.

He glanced down at his console, and then up at Lady Tiffany.

"They're coming to meet us in a space liner, My Lady," he said, scanning the encoded message. "Do you want them to come onboard this ship?"

"If you don't mind," Tiffany said. "We may as well make it clear that we are talking from a position of strength."

She was sharp. Roman had to give her that.

Rumor had it that she and the admiral were besotted with one another. Roman hoped that was the case. When *Midway* had heard the news, her senior officers had lifted a loyal glass of brandy and then returned to planning their next operation, a ceremony repeated across the fleet.

Roman kept his own counsel on the issue, but he knew that the governor didn't have to travel in a superdreadnaught to make his point. Hartkopf had enough fire-power to prevent *Midway* from escaping intact and to bleed the Federation Navy when it came looking for revenge. It said something about the governor's willingness to meet with them that he'd actually come into interplanetary space.

Roman suspected that the governor was desperate to avoid admitting that he was meeting with the Federation. Or, perhaps, he was reluctant to allow Roman to bring his ship closer to Bester and the defenses he would have built as a matter of course.

The communications officer looked up.

"Captain, they're demanding that Lady Tiffany goes to meet with them on their ship," he reported. "They sound pretty insistent, sir."

"I bet they are," Roman said. He exchanged a long look with Tiffany, then looked back at the communications officer. "Inform them that they will be meeting with us on my ship. If they refuse, we'll turn around and head back through the Asimov Point."

There was a long pause.

"The governor has conceded the point," the communications officer said. "He says that he'll be on board in an hour."

Roman allowed himself a relieved smile. He hadn't decided if he'd been bluffing.

"Probably getting his finest uniform on," Tiffany commented, and a wry chuckle ran around the bridge. "Is he bringing an escort?" Tiffany asked.

"I'd be surprised if he didn't insist on one," Roman said. "We may as well honor him as much as possible. It will be the last time."

He smiled. Elf had already deployed her Marines to cover the negotiating team. If the governor believed he could bring a hijacking team onboard *Midway*, he was in for a very nasty surprise.

He settled back in his chair and concentrated on looking calm. Inwardly, he felt like panicking. Far too much could go wrong...and, of course, the admiral's wife was on his ship. If the governor decided to launch a suicide attack...

He pushed the thought aside and focused on his duty. Soon enough, time would tell.

&ℭℬ

Tiffany rose to her feet as Governor Hartkopf was shown into the briefing room. His team had been quietly dissuaded from coming any further, something that had been absurdly easy as it had been obvious that most of his team were enhanced bodyguards with implanted weapons and other augmentations. It seemed that the governor didn't trust his subordinates to handle the negotiations, although Tiffany could hardly blame him for that. Treachery was an easy habit to grow into and a hard one to abandon.

Governor Hartkopf was immensely fat, a sign of a complete lack of concern about what anyone else thought of him, particularly when he could have used nanites to remove most of the fat. His face was chubby, with three chins and an expression that suggested he'd been swallowing laxatives and needed to go to the head desperately. The oily hair that hung over his forehead was cut in the formal style of the Edo Monarchy, a mocking reminder of his claims to supreme power. And he was known for corruption on a scale that would have daunted the Senate; his vast personal wealth, amassed without a shred of concern for legality, could have purchased a star system or two.

She took his hand and shook it, keeping her expression under control with the ease of long practice. The governor, she reminded herself, had no known military skill, but he was a skilled political operator. He'd certainly managed to parlay a temporary advantage into a small empire, even if it was about to come crashing down into the dust. It would be a terminal mistake to underestimate him.

"Governor," she said, ignoring the way his eyes lingered on her. If half of the reports were true, the destruction of his government would be warmly welcomed by the populations under his control. "Thank you for coming."

"It is always a pleasure to meet such a charming young lady," Hartkopf said. Even his voice was oily. "I am...gratified that my concerns were recognized."

Tiffany allowed herself a neutral smile. Hartkopf had insisted, not unreasonably, that a person from High Society speak for the Federation. He wouldn't have accepted her husband, but his wife was a different matter...unless, of course, it was a trap.

Tiffany pushed that thought aside as hard as she could. The governor wouldn't benefit from killing her, not in the long run, and her value as a hostage was limited. Her father had enough children not to worry about losing one.

"With your permission, governor, I will get right to the point," Tiffany said. She settled back in her chair. "You committed treason against the Federation when you believed that the Federation didn't have long to live. You have discovered that the Federation is more resilient than you realized and your empire, carved out of Federation space, may not have long to live. Furthermore, you are facing Admiral Justinian's forces as well and *he* is unlikely to allow you to live. You did kill his daughter, after all."

Governor Hartkopf's face purpled.

"I did *not* kill his daughter. I wanted to make an alliance with Justinian!"

Oddly, Tiffany believed him. It was hard to see how he profited from a war on two fronts. Plus, she'd read the reports from Admiral Mason's task force, and it had been impossible to overcome the suspicion that more had happened than anyone had committed to a datachip.

"Regardless, you are caught between two fires." She settled her elbows on the table, striving for a nonchalance she did not feel. "I'm here to offer you a way out of your dilemma."

"So I was led to understand," Hartkopf agreed. "And what, precisely, does the Federation have to offer me? They've been executing people like me, in case you haven't noticed."

The fear in his eyes convinced her that her husband had been right. Hartkopf would happily switch sides again if he was given assurances of amnesty.

But even if he refused, it was likely that one of his subordinates would stick a knife in Hartkopf's back if they were given the same sort of assurances. She knew that the Senate's decree that had ordered their deaths was a mistake. It forced Hartkopf and others like him to fight to the last, in the desperate hope that they might pull something from the disaster.

"Here are our terms," Tiffany said. She'd been given some room to negotiate, but not much. The Senate's desire for revenge, pure and simple, had limited their options. "You will stand down your forces and surrender your planet. Your personal safety and that of your family, friends and chief subordinates will be guaranteed. You will no longer be governor of this sector"—she saw his face darken for a second and wondered if that would be a deal-breaker—"but you will be allowed to retire, unmolested, to one of the isolated pleasure worlds. Your subordinates who wish to join you will, of course, be allowed to do so."

His sneer showed her just what he thought of his subordinates.

"You will have your life and your fortune, which will be included in the amnesty," Tiffany concluded. "If you refuse our terms, there won't be a second chance. We'll come through the Asimov Point, destroy your defenses and take you by force. And, if we take you alive, you will suffer the full weight of the penalties for treason against the Federation."

Hartkopf fixed her with an unwavering glare.

"I want to remain governor of this sector," he countered. "That's my price for ending the war."

"Unacceptable," Tiffany said flatly. "Understand this, governor: the Federation will *not* permit you to remain in a position of power and influence. We will offer you your life and your fortune. If you choose to refuse our offer, it won't be repeated."

His face showed none of his true feelings, but she knew he had to be struggling to make up his mind. If he accepted, the Federation could break the agreement and execute him once the sector was safely in loyalist hands. If he refused, perhaps he could stand off the Federation Navy...and yet, cold logic suggested otherwise. The Federation Navy outmassed his private fleet a thousand to one.

"I have come here to listen to serious offers," Hartkopf said. "Instead, a mere slip of a girl offers me an insulting deal that will leave me a penniless pauper. I spit on your offer..."

"Think carefully," Tiffany said sharply. "You can't stand against the Federation Navy for long..."

"I will ally with Admiral Justinian and bring his fleet into the sector," Hartkopf said as he stood up. "I suggest that unless you want this ship to be blown to atoms, you should let me return to my ship. Now."

Tiffany didn't move.

"Are you rejecting our offer?"

"Yes," Hartkopf snarled. His voice darkened. "Do you think that I would give up all this just for a life as an internal exile?"

"Just remember, we offered," Tiffany said sadly. "I trust you'll understand if I don't bother to wish you good luck?"

The governor didn't bother to reply.

༄༅

"He rejected the offer?" Roman asked incredulously. As soon as Hartkopf had returned to his ship, the space liner—a twin for the *Harmonious Repose*, an irony that wasn't lost on Roman—had turned and headed back towards the planet. But he'd still had hopes that Hartkopf might listen. No one had opened fire, after all.

"I'm afraid so," Lady Tiffany said. "I suggest that we get out of the system before he turns on us."

Roman nodded, keying his console.

"Elf, launch the special package," he ordered. The enemy ships were too far away to detect the launch, luckily. "Communications: did you record the meeting?"

"Aye, sir," the communications officer said. "Plan B?"

"Plan B," Roman agreed, and smiled. "Launch the drone."

"Drone away, sir," the communications officer said. "Direct data link established. If something happens to us, the drone will be updated automatically."

"Helm, take us back to the Asimov Point," Roman ordered. "Best possible speed."

He'd expected Governor Hartkopf to order his defenses to attempt to intercept *Midway* as she headed towards the Asimov Point, but no one attempted to bar their way. *Midway* vanished through the Asimov Point and was gone.

"We're clear, sir," the helmsman reported.

Roman grinned. It had been Lady Tiffany who'd suggested a slight alteration to the original plan, one that her husband had enthusiastically endorsed. If Hartkopf refused to negotiate—if he prevented anyone else from learning about the negotiations—the Federation would make sure that the entire *system* learned the truth. The drone would start broadcasting a complete recording of the meeting and the governor's rejection, right across the entire system. By the time the drone was destroyed—as it would be easy to locate—it would be far too late. And then Governor Hartkopf would discover how his subordinates felt about losing their last chance for safety.

Admiral Drake had even improved the offer carried by the drone. If someone took the governor's head, the remainder of his subordinates could still claim amnesty.

"We've put the cat amongst the pigeons," he said with a grin. "Helm, take us back to the admiral. Best possible speed."

Chapter Thirty-Six

It is rare for the Senate to offer command of a sizable force to a single man. The reason for that is quite simple. An admiral has command of a force that will, as a general rule, obey him without question, perhaps following orders that end with a coup and the destruction of the Federation Senate. The more powerful the fleet, the more intrusive Senate interference becomes, something that was not unimportant during the opening battles of the Blue Star War...
-An Irreverent Guide to the Federation, 4000 A.D.

FNS *Magnificent*, Eddore, Zathras Sector, 4097
    From the observation blister, Marius could see his fleet, the greatest force assembled since the Blue Star War. The sight never failed to impress him.
    It was surprisingly rare for entire fleets to be visible using the naked eye. Even the closest of formations allowed plenty of room between starships that could be up to six kilometres long, and the only time that starships flew closer together was during reviews. Now, however, the Federation Navy's Grand Fleet—Marius had suggested the name and the Senate hadn't demurred—hung in orbit around a red dwarf, running lights illuminating them for all to see.
    Two hundred superdreadnaughts provided a solid core of firepower, backed up by nearly a thousand cruisers and destroyers. Ninety fleet carriers, seventy assault carriers and a hundred escort carriers provided over ten *thousand* starfighters to cover the fleet against enemy starfighters and missile fire. Behind the warships, the Fleet Train—two thousand freighters loaded with everything from missiles to crated starfighters—waited, providing all the supplies the fleet could need for a year of campaigning.
    Marius wasn't blind to the level of trust the Senate had placed in him. And he had no intention of losing the campaign. He knew just how weak the Senate was, as a government, but it was better than the alternative. Without a strong central authority, humanity would fall apart into chaos and the aliens would win.
    He had no intention of losing. Anything.
    He thought of Tiffany and found himself smiling. He'd been doing that a lot since he'd discovered that he and his young wife had so much in common. So far, they'd managed to build a life together, even if it wasn't exactly what he would have chosen. Tiffany's pithy observations on the Senate and High Society had helped to shape his own thoughts. He'd once regarded her, to his shame, as an encumbrance, but now... he found himself oddly terrified by the thought of losing her.
    And he'd sent her into deadly danger.
    "I saw that look," Vaughn said. His oldest friend smiled at him. "You're in love."
    "I suppose I am," Marius admitted. It was odd how easy it was to say. "I wonder if you will be getting married, too."
    "Two years of marriage and he thinks he can tell us all to get married," Vaughn said dryly. "I'm married to the Corps, as you know very well. And besides, I'm not the

latest political sensation, for which we should all be grateful."

Marius nodded sourly. "And what if you were?"

"I don't think that I will ever be quite that important." Vaughn frowned and abruptly changed the subject. "You do realize that nothing will ever be the same again?"

Marius quirked an eyebrow at him.

"The Federation almost came apart five years ago," Vaughn explained. "The warlords came close to destroying what little unity we had left. When this war ends—when the last warlord surrenders or is blown away—what will we have then? A weakened Federation, and Outsiders threatening our borders."

Marius stared at him. He'd never heard his friend sound so defeatist.

"What brought this on?"

"I have a child," Vaughn admitted.

Marius gaped. It was news to him.

"A little girl," Vaughn told him. "Her mother, when she realized that I would never be around, refused to allow me to spend much time with my daughter. And yet, she still wants to follow her daddy into the Marine Corps. What sort of universe is she going to inherit?"

"The very best one we can make," Marius said. He pressed a hand against the transparent covering, staring up at his fleet. "When we crush Justinian, we can force the other warlords to surrender, and then..."

"We get caught up in a war against the Outsiders," Vaughn pointed out. "The Senate is deluding itself if it thinks we can avoid it. The Inheritance Wars were bad enough, but this is going to be worse. All those races out there that have no choice but to grow up in a human universe, where we will only let them live if we restructure their society to fit our mold, and prevent them from becoming a threat to us."

"I know. But this is the best we can do." Marius wished he had a better answer, but he didn't.

Vaughn nodded impatiently.

"Still. We're on the eve of the greatest war in human history, and the Senate is acting like there's nothing to worry about, not really."

Somehow, Marius had to deflect this conversation.

"We can beat the warlords and we can beat the Outsiders too," he said with a smile. "Once we start preparing for war..."

"That's the question," Vaughn said. "*When* are we going to start preparing for war?"

The hatch opened before Marius could answer. Blake Raistlin popped through the hatch and saluted.

"Admiral," he reported, "*Midway* just transited the Asimov Point from Greenwich. They're sending a data download now..."

Marius had to smile. "And the results?"

Raistlin managed to do a good job of pretending to be innocent.

"Come on," Marius insisted. "Reading the data downloads is an easy trick..."

Raistlin would have flushed if his skin allowed it. "The negotiations failed, admiral," he admitted. "The governor rejected our demands."

"Well," Marius said after a long moment. "I guess that means we will have to do it the hard way, won't we?"

ᛒᛂᚳᛃ

Marius disliked face-to-face briefings. The logistics of bringing so many superior officers onto one superdreadnaught—even if protocol was cut to the bare minimum—were nightmarish. Even the *Magnificent*, lovely lady though she was, didn't have a compartment large enough for all the officers who believed they should be invited to the briefing as a matter of course. Indeed, coordinating so many starships was a tricky task in itself.

Part of the six-month delay in bringing war to Admiral Justinian and all of Justinian's allies had been because Marius had wanted to ensure that his men knew what they were doing. If nothing else, war was a great teacher and many of the incompetents in the Federation Navy had been shuffled somewhere harmless—or had been killed in action.

He'd solved the problem by inviting his subordinate admiral—and all of his Commissioners, as he couldn't avoid inviting them—his Marine Generals and a handful of other advisors to the physical meeting, while the remainder of his officers watched through the datanet. It was an innovation that had some of the traditionalists muttering darkly—standard etiquette for holographic presence was that holograms were rarely acknowledged or treated as genuine visitors—but he'd overruled them. It was his fleet. Besides, the old ways hadn't always worked out perfectly.

He allowed himself a wink at Tiffany—the mere sight of her hologram warmed his heart—and took his seat at the front of the table.

"Gentlemen, be seated," he ordered.

He allowed his gaze to slip around the table as the assembled officers took their seats. Admiral Mason had returned from The Hive to take command of his starfighter groups, a task that had diverted most of his formidable energy into solving the problems of operating so many starfighters at once. Vaughn, of course, would command the Marine detachment. Vice Admiral Arunika—she'd finally been promoted for good service—controlled ONI's resources that had been attached to the mission, as well as a handful of covert assets from the Brotherhood. He carefully did not show his genuine opinion of Commissioner Walter Williams—his Political Commissioner— to show on his face. Williams, at least, was smart enough to refrain from outright interference, although it had taken Tiffany to convince him that Marius had access to more of the levers of power than a mere Political Commissioner. The other starship commanders and senior officers weren't nearly so lucky.

"As you know by now, the mission to Bester was not successful," he began. "Governor Hartkopf refused to accept amnesty on our terms and appears to be completely deluded about the relative balance of power between the Federation and his rebels. We may—I say *may*—have upset the apple cart in his vest-pocket kingdom by broadcasting details of the negotiations to his allies, but we cannot rely on it. That

is all the more...*inconvenient*...as we are required to pass through the Bester System."
He waited for that to sink in, then allowed himself a smile. *That* hadn't been on
the original operations plan.

"We are now isolated from the Federation," he informed them. "The ICN is broken
in this sector. I—and I alone—will determine what messages are important enough
to be transported to an ICN hub in a destroyer." His gaze swept the room. "We are
under *total* information blackout. I do not want one *word* of our plan to leak out, not
to Hartkopf and not to Admiral Justinian. If any of you, directly or indirectly, leaks
the information to *anyone*, I will execute you under General Order Fifteen. If any of
you wish to protest now, you may do so. It will be noted in my log. Any such protests
may even be produced as evidence at my court martial."

Marius wanted to smile at their astonished reaction, but he somehow kept his face
calm and dispassionate. General Order Fifteen referred to mutiny and granted the
fleet's legitimate CO vast powers to investigate and punish any mutinous crewmen—
or officers. It had been forced on the Navy during the early days of the Inheritance
Wars. Somehow, it had never been repealed. The powers under General Order
Fifteen were so vast that Marius could have had them all shot, and they knew it.

Of course, by invoking General Order Fifteen, Marius would probably face a
court martial afterwards anyway, once the fleet returned to Federation space. But
that wouldn't make any difference to the dead.

"The Operations Plan we discussed when we were drawing up the orders for the
fleet was a sham," he continued. "I chose to develop it for two reasons: first, because
it could easily be adapted to what I actually had in mind, and second, because I knew
it would be leaked to Admiral Justinian. The warlord has already shifted his forces
back to Jefferson to meet us when we advance from Marx—as planned. Therefore,
we are not going to Marx. We're going to Sphinx, and will advance from there."

He watched their faces as they accessed their implants, working through the new
concept. Marius had chosen it with extreme care, trusting that Justinian had enough
faith in Hartkopf not to realize that there was a gaping hole in his defenses. If Bester
fell, if the fleet passed through Hartkopf's core systems unmolested, they could enter
a new chain of Asimov Points that would allow them to enter Justinian's forces by
the back door. *If...*

But it didn't take too much imagination to realize just how many things could go
spectacularly wrong. Fortunately, few officers would raise questions in front of the
commissioners.

"We will proceed at once to Bester," he informed them. "I believe that our psychological operations will produce fruit. But if they don't, we will punch our way
into the system and then cross to the other Asimov Point. We will not attempt to
recapture Bester at present. It would only cost us greatly, for very little in return."

He stood up, his gaze sweeping the compartment. "I trust that you all understand
exactly why I had to maintain secrecy," he concluded. "If Justinian gets a *hint* of our
plans before we are in his backyard, we may find ourselves in a position where we are
forced to retreat and impale ourselves on Hartkopf's forces. If we lose here, it will be

years before we can rebuild the fleet—and we will all be dead, of course."

He let that sink in for a long moment.

"*Do not* attempt to leak the plan ahead of time. You have been warned." He smiled coldly. "Now, are there any questions?"

There was a long pause. Several officers looked as though they wanted to raise issues, but the commissioners were still there.

"None, it seems," he said, answering his own question. "The details of the operation have been forwarded to you. Consider them carefully, then contact me if you feel that we should discuss possibilities. Other than that, gentlemen...good luck to us all."

He watched as the holograms popped out of existence. There were some details he'd been careful not to mention. The Brotherhood's agent in the Bester System, for example, and the "secret package" Captain Garibaldi had delivered while departing the system. But they didn't need to know *all* of the details.

Marius allowed himself an internal sigh as Commissioner Walters came over to him, his grey uniform matching his face. If he'd spent a day on a warship before being appointed as a political commissioner, Marius would have been astonished. The man seemed to have no concept of how a warship functioned. There were some people, even two thousand years after the birth of the Federation, who never really developed their space legs. Marius had been curious as to what Walters had been doing prior to his appointment to his ship, but the files had been carefully sealed. Even his access permissions hadn't been able to open them.

"Admiral," Walters said. His voice was thin, almost reedy. "The orders you presented today were not the ones my...ah...superiors forwarded to me."

"Of course not, William," Marius said. He was damned if he was going to call the little weasel "sir." "I knew that the original orders would have been intercepted by the enemy."

"The Senate is above suspicion," Walters protested angrily. "Refusing to follow their orders...

"Are the Senatorial Aides above suspicion?" Marius asked mildly.

Walters flushed.

Marius pressed his advantage. "What about their families? Or the industrialists or investors who watch the war carefully? Can you guarantee that the secret wouldn't have leaked?"

Walters ignored the questions. "But you're exceeding your authority by a very long way..."

"Actually, I'm not," Marius said pleasantly. He keyed his terminal and brought up the Senate's instructions. "You will notice, when you read my orders from the Senate, that they include a line about carrying out offensive operations as I see fit. Should you feel that I am still exceeding my orders, you are welcome to drop a line to the Senate about it—after we hit Sphinx and start hammering our way up to Jefferson."

He watched the Commissioner's face; it was obvious he was trying to do the math.

"It will be at least three months before you receive a reply," he said, taking pity on the younger man. "And that assumes that they send one back at once. My backers may refuse to say anything until they learn if the operation has succeeded. You might end up looking like an idiot."

Walters allowed that to slip past him. "Admiral, I must insist..."

"If you want to allow this opportunity to slip past us, you are free to do so," Marius said. "You would, of course, have to explain it to the Senate—after all, you will have prolonged the war. I'm not going to call the operation off, William. If you want to cancel it, you can cancel it on your own authority."

He had to smile as Walters wilted in front of him. The Commissioner had to know that Marius had powerful allies—and his wife had powerful relations. If he could talk Marius out of launching the operation, it wouldn't rebound on him, but Marius wasn't going to give him the easy option.

Besides, if Walters wanted to protect his skin so much, he shouldn't have accepted transfer to a warship going into harm's way.

"I will make an official protest," Walters said as he stood up. His voice sharpened, although it still had the same unpleasant twang. "I believe that you have exceeded your authority, and that will be reflected in my official report to the Senate."

Marius watched him storm out of the compartment, passing Tiffany as she walked into the room. His wife wasn't smiling.

"You should arrange an accident for him," she said flatly.

Marius gave her a surprised look. He'd known that Tiffany had a ruthless side, but he hadn't known that she was *that* ruthless.

"He's a small man," she explained. "And if there's one thing a small man can't abide, it's something that makes him look small. He's too much of a coward to strike at you directly, but I'd bet anything you care to put forward that his dispatch back home will accuse you of everything from fornicating in public to high treason."

"Fornicating in public and high treason," Marius repeated. He allowed himself a slight grin, cracking a weak joke. "How will I ever get a job with a record like that?"

"I'm serious," Tiffany said. She walked over to him and placed his hand on his shoulder. "You have to do something about him."

He relaxed into her touch, wondering how he'd lived without a partner for so long.

"And the next one will probably be worse," he predicted dryly. "But if the offensive fails, there is a good chance that we will all die, so his report will go nowhere. If we succeed, he'll look like a moron."

Tiffany snorted. "Do you think that that will stop him?"

"Not really, no," Marius admitted.

He pushed the issue of Walters aside and smiled at her. "In two hours, the fleet will depart and head through the Asimov Point toward Bester. Do you think we can find something to do to pass the time?"

She pretended to consider it.

"I suppose." Tiffany leaned down to kiss him deeply. Her hands reached down and stroked his chest. "I'm sure we can think of something."

Chapter Thirty-Seven

The Federation has complete freedom of the press, at least in theory. Ironically, it is the one promise that the Senate has never been able to subvert completely, although they have tried hard over the years. The sheer complexity of planetary datanets makes it very hard for the Senate—or a local government—to prevent the spread of information. This does not stop them from trying, of course.
-An Irreverent Guide to the Federation, 4000 A.D.

Bester, Zathras System, 4097

"Two kilometers to target…"

Alicia allowed herself a faint smile as she drifted towards the massive fortress. It said something about Governor Hartkopf's fear of his own people that he chose a mammoth orbital fortress as his command post. The fortress was armed to the teeth, with more weapons and defenses than the average superdreadnaught, yet it made him vulnerable. And never more so than now. Alicia's secondary processor had been scanning news reports from the planet below, and it was clear that the governor was hanging on by the skin of his teeth. It wouldn't be long before someone overthrew him, providing they managed to gain access to his fortress. The man's paranoia was quite unbelievable, but not necessarily misplaced.

The average defense system was designed to track fast incoming targets, like missiles. They weren't designed to track a single person in a tiny, completely silent combat suit. Alicia had been drifting in for four days, relying on her suit and augmentations to keep her on course while she allowed her mind to slip into a trance. Even a hardened vacuum-jockey would have hesitated to undertake such a mission, but Alicia had been enhanced far beyond the standard—or even legal—conventions. She didn't have to worry about the sensory deprivation the average person would suffer after four days in a suit. It was, in a way, just another day at the office.

She kept a careful eye on her passive sensors. She had to be as careful as she could, considering the fortress looming directly in front of her, filling the sky. It was just possible that a man as paranoid as Hartkopf would have taken a few additional precautions, perhaps adding additional sensor networks or even having some men in suits patrolling the hull. That would have been taking paranoia a step too far, she thought to herself, and most security personnel would have objected strongly.

On the other hand, if she did pass through the sensor nets undetected, manned patrols were the only thing that would have a prayer of intercepting her short of her target.

No security guards appeared to stop her as she drifted the final few meters to the fortress's hull. Her imagination filled in the *clang* as she touched down on the surface, even though she knew that no one would hear any sound of her presence. She checked around her automatically, activating the weapons built into her combat suit, before relaxing. No one was moving anywhere near her. The entire hull was abandoned.

Alicia grinned. She loved missions when she appeared right out of the target's blind spot.

She walked toward the nearest airlock. It wouldn't be long before she was safety inside the fortress. Then the real work could begin.

ONI hadn't been able to provide her with any plans for the fortress, as it had been built after Hartkopf had declared independence from the Federation, but Alicia was used to going in blind. Indeed, the better the intelligence, the greater the complacency—and the chance for something to go spectacularly wrong.

She doubted that Hartkopf would have produced a completely new design of airlock and so it proved. The airlock waiting for her was Federation-standard. By law, she knew, each airlock was supposed to allow anyone to enter manually—in case of an emergency—but if Hartkopf hadn't rigged up an alarm circuit, she would have been astonished. Hell, he might have seen fit to remove the manual overrides.

She studied the panel thoughtfully and allowed herself a tight smile. So far, so good.

She paced around the airlock until she located the command node and flipped it open. Placing her armoured hand against the panel, she extruded a small wire from her suit into the command node, hacking into its tiny brain. If the governor had been *very* paranoid, she'd just set off an alarm, but he would have to be clinically insane to even consider the possibility.

No alarms sounded.

She allowed herself a moment of relief before hacking deeper into the command node and rewriting the software to her specifications. As she had expected, there was an alarm circuit, which she bypassed, then dumped altogether. If she had to leave in a hurry, it was easier to have a way out that she knew was unguarded.

Swinging over to the airlock itself, she pulled the manual override and stepped into the airlock. A moment later, the other door hissed open automatically, and she was in. The easy part of the mission was over.

Hartkopf hadn't realized it, but his paranoia had actually weakened his position. He'd set up hundreds of computer programs to watch his subordinates, yet he didn't realize that those programs could be subverted. No one knew how Hartkopf had built the system, but Alicia had quickly discovered that he hadn't developed something new or even—as the Colonial Alliance had done during the Inheritance Wars—worked an alien computer system into his network.

Her implanted processors accessed the nearest communications node, slipped into the system and raped it, inserting a series of comforting lies into the network. No one would detect a trace of her presence.

Unless, of course, the paranoid asshole had added a secondary security system. Detecting *that* would be tricky.

Finding a small compartment, Alicia started to undress, removing her combat suit. As much as she loved it, it would stick out like a sore thumb if someone saw her. The uniform she wore below it stank—the result of four days in the suit—but it would pass for one of Hartkopf's uniforms at a distance.

Accessing her implants, she transferred the hacking link from the suit to her internal systems, before running through a quick weapons check. She might look like a normal aide, very unlike a soldier, but her implanted weapons and systems were deadly dangerous—and unseen.

The security systems insisted there were only seven hundred people on the fortress, although Alicia knew better than to take that for granted. If *she'd* been programming the security network, she would have programmed it to ignore security officers.

The hacked link told her that one of Hartkopf's female officers was four compartments away, so she stepped out of her compartment—locking it behind her—and walked down the corridor, watching carefully for anyone who might see her. Hartkopf, it seemed, had stripped the fortress's crew down to the bare minimum, thankfully.

She keyed an override code into the door's processor and stepped through while the room's occupant was still turning to face her. Alicia saw the surprise on her face—she *loved* that moment—as she shot her neatly with a stun bolt. The woman crashed to the floor and lay still.

Alicia picked her up effortlessly, rolled her over onto her back and started to undress her. Governor Hartkopf's uniform designer, she decided, had been insane or blind or both. The uniform was bright green, with yellow and black markings that reminded her of a Terra Nova Wasp. When Alicia donned it, after having a quick session in the fresher, it pinched her in uncomfortable places. If nothing else, she decided as she studied her uniform in the mirror, males would be distracted from her face. It was a shame that she couldn't mimic the stunned woman's face and figure, but even the most advanced implants couldn't do that quickly.

Picking up the naked woman, she tied her hands and feet quickly before stuffing a sock in her mouth. By the time she was discovered, it would be far too late.

Leaving the stunned woman behind, she walked down the corridor, avoiding cameras and security nodes whenever possible. When it wasn't possible, her hacking programs simply edited her appearance out of the sensors, leaving the security staff blind. They wouldn't see her even if they were watching the monitors. But she knew better than to assume that she would pass completely unmolested.

As she turned into the governor's private quarters, she almost ran into two burly security officers. Alicia braced herself, carefully activating some of her combat implants. If they realized that she was a fake...

"Lieutenant Brogan, here to see the governor," she said quickly. She'd taken a brief look at her victim's ID before abandoning her. There was no way to know if the governor would send for a sexual partner, or if he would prey on the women serving under him, but she knew his reputation. "I've been told it is priority business..."

"I'll bet," the older of the guards said gruffly. He exchanged a wink with his comrade that Alicia pretended not to see. "I'll have to run your implant through the scanner anyway, I'm afraid. Please place your hand against the panel."

Alicia prepared herself as she pressed her hand against the panel. A standard ID chip was buried in the palm of an officer's right hand; she, as it happened, had a processor that should feed another series of comforting lies to the scanner. If it failed, however, she would have to kill the two guards quickly and then get inside before the system registered her presence and sounded the alarm. She didn't want to do that, but she'd have no choice; once the fortress went into lockdown, finding and assassinating the governor would be much harder. She might even have to detonate the fusion cell built into her implants and take out the entire fortress.

"Access granted," the guard said. Alicia pretended that the issue had never been in doubt. "Have fun with the governor."

The armoured airlock hissed open and Alicia stepped into the governor's private sanctum. She hadn't been certain what to expect, but it was clear that rumors of Hartkopf's depravity hadn't been exaggerated. It reminded her of a high-class brothel on Paradise that she'd visited once, while waiting for a target to show his ugly face. The room was filled with comfortable cushions, the walls were decorated with erotic paintings and one corner was entirely devoted to pleasure tools.

Alicia wrinkled her nose in disgust as she prowled through the piles of cushions, looking for her target. She'd lost her hacking line as soon as the airlock closed, and no processor within the room responded to her pings. The governor had probably programmed them to respond only to him. Given time, she could have hacked in anyway, but she had the uneasy feeling that time was running out.

"Who's there?" a querulous voice demanded. Her implants checked it against the record she'd been given. It was Hartkopf.

Alicia stepped around the corner and saw the governor sitting at a desk, studying a tactical map of the sector. The horde of red icons in a nearby system had to be the Grand Fleet. She allowed herself a small cough as the governor turned and stared at her.

"Who are you?" he asked, lunging for a button on his desk.

Alicia shot him neatly through one eye, and watched as his body flopped down on the deck. He was heavy enough to make lifting him difficult, even with her enhanced strength, but eventually she got him onto the bed. A moment later, she had beheaded him.

She artistically placed his head on her forehead. His computer system still responded to the ID chip in his palm and it was a simple matter to program it to transmit a message right across the system. She didn't intend to speak, but it wouldn't be necessary. The image of Hartkopf's dead body would be all that was needed. She hoped that his subordinates would see sense and surrender to the Federation, or perhaps they'd start a civil war within the Bester System instead. But either way, her work was done.

Absently picking up a small and valuable statue from the outer room, she checked her uniform for blood and then headed for the airlock. She had only ten minutes before the message started to transmit, and by then she had to be off the station. Or else they might catch her before she could escape.

It would be a shame to die while *leaving* the station.

ꕤ

This time, *Midway* wasn't alone; an entire assault flotilla had escorted her through the Asimov Points, the transits as tight as possible without risking interpenetration. Twelve assault cruisers, nine assault carriers and fifteen destroyers faced nine fortresses and their escorting craft.

"Captain, we have multiple weapons firing," the sensor officer reported, as *Midway* flickered into existence in the Asimov Point. "Sir, they're firing at each other!"

Roman leaned forward in surprise. It was clear that *something* had happened within the Bester System. The passive sensors were picking up nuclear and antimatter explosions all over the system, while the fortresses were actually being attacked by dreadnaughts that should have been on their side. No one was attempting to engage his ship, which was against all tactical doctrine.

"Report," he ordered. "Analysis?"

"Civil war, sir," the tactical officer said. "I can't pick out sides at this distance..."

Roman nodded slowly. The enemy had given up their best chance to slap his fleet back through the Asimov Point when they'd first arrived. Instead, they were shooting at each other.

"There's no point," Roman told him. "Communications, contact the nearest fortresses and ask them to surrender. Promise them the same amnesty as everyone else if they surrender right now."

"Aye, sir," the communications officer said. "Transmitting now...sir, should we hold the drones?"

"Hold them on standby," Roman ordered. "No, belay that. Launch one drone with an update and send it back to the Grand Fleet. Inform them that we are attempting to sort friends from enemies."

"If we have any friends here," the tactical officer muttered.

Roman couldn't disagree. It was clear that *something*—either the message drone they'd released into the system or the assassination attempt—had sparked off a civil war, but there was no way to know who was on what side. Or even if there were any sides at all.

"There are several different factions," the tactical officer said. "I suspect some of the ships are even having internal struggles."

"Good," Roman said, curtly.

"We're picking up a laser communication from one of the fortresses," the communications officer said. "He claims to be a Commodore Lu and wishes to speak to Admiral Drake."

"Who happens to be on the other side of the Asimov Point," Roman said dryly. "Patch him through. I will speak to him personally."

He used his implants to scan Navy records. There was no Commodore Lu listed, but *Commander* Lu had been in Fortress Command in the Bester System just prior to the Battle of Earth. His service record didn't look very accomplished, but that might not mean much.

Commodore Lu's face appeared in front of him. He was a young Oriental officer with a short goatee and a shaven head. He looked desperately worried, as if he knew that whatever happened, his life would never be the same again. He was right; if he surrendered, he would probably end up going into exile rather than being allowed to return to his homeworld. He'd chosen the wrong side in a civil war.

Or the side had been chosen for him. Roman forced himself to remember that.

"Captain," Lu said flatly. "I would like to surrender. I also request assistance against the reactionaries, if we can agree on suitable terms."

Roman concealed a smile. The fortresses were being hammered by enemy super-dreadnaughts and dreadnaughts. Only their heavy firepower and armor had kept them from being crushed before the Grand Fleet's scouting elements arrived in the system. Lu didn't have much to bargain with, and he knew it.

"The terms are simple," he said. "You will surrender your fortresses and any star-ships under your command to Federation authority. We will guarantee your lives and personal possessions, providing you behave yourselves. Depending on your conduct, you may be pushed into internal exile or barred from serving in the Federation Navy."

Lu didn't look happy.

"Very well," he said, finally. "Call your ships. Tell them to hurry. We can't hold out for long."

"Of course," Roman said. He signalled for the communications officer to launch another drone. The force of superdreadnaughts attacking the fortresses was impressive, but the Grand Fleet was far more powerful. "Hold on. We're on our way."

He watched as the first of the superdreadnaughts appeared in the Asimov Point and linked up with the fortresses. The fortress ECM was sufficient to keep the enemy from realizing that they were being reinforced until it was too late. As the superdreadnaughts advanced, they opened fire on Hartkopf's ships and drove them away from the Asimov Point, allowing the remainder of the Grand Fleet to enter the system. It took nearly an hour, but the outcome was never in doubt.

"We have one squadron of dreadnaughts fleeing towards the mass limit," the sen-sor officer reported. "Another looks as if it is either contemplating a last stand, or maybe it intends to surrender. I think we broke them, sir."

"Let's hope so," Roman said. He looked up at the tactical display. "This is only the first system we have to take before we reach Jefferson."

Chapter Thirty-Eight

The treatment of political prisoners tends to vary by rank. Prisoners who were nothing more than grunts tend to be treated lightly, unless they committed atrocities while fighting the Federation. The senior leadership is either executed, transported to a hellish penal planet or sent into exile. It should be noted that exile, while better than a penal planet, is still a very real punishment. They will be placed on a planet of their choice and will not be allowed to go back into space again. They can never leave their new homeworld.
-An Irreverent Guide to the Federation, 4000AD.

Bester/In Transit, 4097

"The system is secure, sir," Commander Blake Raistlin reported. "The fleeing ships have crossed the mass limit and vanished."

"Very good," Marius said. He keyed his intercom, trying to ignore the commissioner sitting next to him. "Toby, launch your Marines and secure those fortresses and the surrendered ships. The prisoners can be moved to Bester until we decide what to do with them."

"Understood, sir," Vaughn said. "We'll get right on it."

Marius allowed himself a brief smile, and then turned back to the display. Once Bester's high orbitals were in his hands, the locals—and anyone who still wanted to rebel against the Federation—would have no choice but to surrender...or be stamped flat with precision strikes from orbit. Working out what to do with the warlord-controlled worlds would be up to the Senate—going by the Inheritance Wars, the Senate would probably assign a new governor and bleed the worlds white as punishment for their disobedience—but whatever they decided wouldn't affect his fleet. The planetary government could take control of the surface or abandon it to chaos. It wasn't his concern.

Thankfully, the fight had been brief and relatively painless, at least with regards to the Federation forces. None of Commodore Lu's men had continued the fight once the late and unlamented Governor Hartkopf had met his end. The governor, it seemed, hadn't convinced his men to be loyal to him, let alone his memory.

"Contact Admiral Hoskins and order him to bring his ships into the system," he ordered as the fortresses were secured. "Once the Fleet Train is in the system, I want him to start rearming the ships at once."

"Aye, sir," Raistlin said.

"Detach the *Queen Elizabeth* and her squadron and order them to secure the third Asimov Point in this system," Marius added. The fast superdreadnaughts—built to his personal specifications, including a reworked drive that gave them a combat speed nearly ten percent above average—would be able to beat any starship that left Bester and attempted to race to the Asimov Point. "Once there, they are to launch recon drones into the next system and confirm that it is clear of enemy starships."

He tapped his console, scanning the squadrons that formed the Grand Fleet. "And then detach the *Midway* and her fellow assault cruisers and order them to scout towards Sphinx," he concluded. "I want to make sure that our path is clear all the way."

"Aye, sir," Raistlin said, sounding stunned by the barrage of orders.

Marius suspected that Raistlin wasn't entirely happy serving as an aide, not when he should be able to command a ship of his own, yet that was all to the good. He'd seen too many officers who became comfortable as uniformed bureaucrats. But Raistlin, at least, still wanted ship command.

"*Midway* and her escorts took part in the battle, sir," Raistlin reported. "They fired off their external racks."

"That shouldn't be a problem," Marius said shortly. "We can rearm them before we launch the offensive."

Speed was of the essence now, speed and stealth. Admiral Justinian might well be keeping an eye on his fellow warlord. With some good luck, word of the governor's death might have already left the system before the Grand Fleet arrived. He wondered briefly what might happen on the other worlds that had been part of the warlord's little kingdom, before dismissing the issue. They could be mopped up later, once the other warlord had been crushed.

He watched as the Marines occupied the high orbitals and secured the surrendered starships. In a bad entertainment vid the Marines would have been able to turn the surrendered ships into usable starships instantly, but it was never that easy in real life. The tugs would tow the starships back to the nearest shipyard, where trained yard dogs would survey the ships and decide if they should be scrapped or refitted to meet Federation Navy standards. If they were scrapped, Marius hoped they'd be broken up this time. He'd seen far too many ex-Navy ships become pirate vessels.

"Detail a squadron of destroyers and a gunboat carrier to remain in the system," he ordered. "Detach one of the Internal Security divisions and assign it to maintaining control in orbit. The remainder of the system will have to wait."

"That is unacceptable," Walters said. "Powerful interests, admiral; powerful interests want this entire system secured as soon as possible."

Marius resisted the temptation to roll his eyes. He'd been surprised when the political commissioner had insisted on joining him on the flag bridge when the fleet made transit into danger, and even more surprised when the commissioner had kept his mouth shut during the fighting.

Before Walters could say anything further, Marius cut him off with a short, sharp gesture.

"You know full well that they shouldn't have expected anything. They shouldn't even know about it yet—unless you told them?"

"No, admiral," Walters assured him quickly. "I just feel that those interests would be pleased if we were to secure the system and hand it over to them..."

Marius clapped him on the shoulder, affecting a false bonhomie.

"Let's wait for the chicken to lay eggs before we scramble and eat them, shall we?" He grinned. "I'd hate to lose the system again because we didn't defeat the real enemy."

"And using the Internal Security troopers to hold the planet..."

"It's what they are there for," Marius reminded him, with the private thought that it would get them out of his hair. "No doubt their commander is fully aware of the political requirements, but I am sure that you will wish to speak to him personally before we depart this system."

"Thank you, admiral," Walters said. He turned and started towards the hatch. "I assume that I will have access to a private communications link?"

"Of course," Marius said. Walters would have a chance to put the interests of his masters first, just as he wanted. "Good luck."

He turned back to his console as Walters left the compartment and allowed himself a satisfied smile. The reloading was going quickly; soon, he'd be able to send most of his fleet through the Asimov Point and into the Wanaka System. From there, they would cross the system and hop into the Farnham System. And from there, they would cross the interstellar void and reach Sphinx.

If everything went according to plan, Admiral Justinian was in for a very nasty surprise.

"Angle the decoy squadrons over to the Tranter System," he ordered as he returned to contemplating the strategic display. "We don't want to disappoint Admiral Justinian when he starts looking for us, do we?"

⁖∳

Forty years into the Inheritance Wars, a madman called Wanaka had created a new religion in Earth's teeming undercity. His faith, which promised earthly salvation to the believers, had claimed that once Wanaka and his closest companions took control of Earth, there would be a new paradise for the oppressed masses. Whatever his grip on reality, Wanaka had been a gifted speaker and within ten years had raised an army that attempted to seize the mega-cities that made up most of Earth's population centers. It hadn't lasted, not least because his divinely-inspired plans hadn't taken into account little things like the orbital fortresses, or the fact that the Senate—already fighting one war for survival—wouldn't be inclined to handle the uprising with kid gloves. What *had* been planned as an easy takeover was mercilessly crushed and scattered by the Federation's security forces. Wanaka himself had been captured, along with most of his followers.

Realizing that creating a legend might lead to more instability, the Federation had offered Wanaka and his followers a deal. The Federation would transport him and his followers to a new world, where they would be free to live as they chose. The world the Federation had picked for them had been chosen with malice aforethought; Wanaka had no gas giant, few natural resources and plenty of vegetation that was completely incompatible with human biochemistry. It said something about the determination of the man's followers that they'd tamed the world at all, although they had very little intercourse with the rest of the Federation.

Roman and Elf stood together in the observation blister, looking down at the world as it receded. *Midway* and her consorts had made one pass, confirmed that the world had hardly any high technology, and then headed for the Asimov Point.

Making the entire journey under cloak would drain the ship's power, but Admiral Drake had specifically ordered it. The sector had never been surveyed properly; for all the admiral knew, there might well be an undetected Asimov Point out there leading to the heart of Admiral Justinian's territory.

Roman suspected that the Federation wouldn't bother trying to extract punitive damages from Wanaka. What did a planet of religious fanatics have to offer the Federation?

"You do realize that you're going to have to tell your guest something," Elf pointed out. "We're on our way to kick Justinian's head in."

"I know," Roman said. Truthfully, he had no idea *what* to tell Henrietta. He'd kept her on the ship for two years, without hope of freedom. Elf had suggested giving her a new identity and dumping her on a newly-colonized world—where she would have a chance to build a new life for herself—but if he put her down somewhere, she might have betrayed them, willingly or otherwise. If the Marines hadn't been loyal to Elf— and if the commissioner hadn't been an idiot, and if they hadn't managed to avoid a detachment of Internal Security troops—keeping her presence a secret would have been impossible. "What do you think we should tell her?"

Elf shrugged, crossing her arms under her breasts. "If Justinian accepts the offer of amnesty, there is no reason why she couldn't be included in it."

Roman swallowed a curse.

"But if so, she might betray us," he pointed out.

"You're quite the white knight," Elf mocked lightly. She uncrossed her arms and pressed her fingers against the transparent bulkhead. "You have two choices: you can kill her, dump her body into space and swear blind that you never saw her...or you keep her alive and accept the risk of betrayal. And if you don't want to murder a young girl who didn't ask to be born to the galaxy's worst traitor since the Convention of Arbroath, you *have* to accept the risks."

"I know," Roman said and nodded. He sighed heavily. "I'll talk to her."

"There is another option," Elf offered. "You could dump her on Wanaka. No one from the Federation can be bothered visiting the planet; it isn't as if they run the handful of newcomers through DNA scans to check their identity. She could make a good living for herself on the planet's surface."

"I doubt it," Roman said. Wanaka was hardly a testament to female equality. Life on the planet's surface was nasty, brutish and short. There was no modern medical care, save for medical packages imported by smugglers and reserved for high-ranking personages. "I'll ask her anyway, and see what she says."

"Better decide quickly," Elf said as Roman turned to go. "I think that time is running out for all of us."

∞〇ᗄ

It had taken some creative modification of bulkheads—and not a little barefaced lying—to create a compartment in which Henrietta could hide. Luckily, *Midway* and her sisters had been built to allow a considerable degree of internal reconfiguration without actually threatening the starship's structural integrity. The young prisoner—if she was a prisoner; Roman was never actually sure in his own mind—had a bunk, a living room, a food processor and a bathroom. Indeed, she had better quarters than some of his junior officers.

She had had to live in them for the last two years.

She was lying on the bed when Roman entered through the sealed airlock in Marine Country. Few crewmen entered Marine Country willingly, at least without permission, and the hatchway was carefully sealed. An inspection would probably reveal her presence, but Roman had, so far, managed to avoid it. Besides, he'd reconfigured the interior quite a bit, remembering what happened to the *Enterprise*. The reconfigured command stations had saved the ship from capture and conversion into Admiral Justinian's flagship.

"Good afternoon," Roman said, taking a seat near to her bunk.

Henrietta didn't look up from the terminal she was spooling through, studying history and politics. Roman had found her hundreds of books to read that he'd stored within the terminal, as she couldn't be allowed access to the starship's computer network.

When she didn't respond, he added, "We need to talk."

Henrietta had lost weight during her captivity and dark bags surrounded her eyes. Elf had told him that even though Henrietta was well-treated, it was impossible to avoid the fact that she was a captive. Being trapped in the small compartment would slowly drive her mad. Roman had felt more than a little guilty when Elf had pointed that out, even though if he'd handed Henrietta over to his superiors, she would have been executed along with most of the captured personnel, as the Senate hadn't been feeling merciful. Once ONI had drained those prisoners of everything they knew, they'd been formally executed by firing squad.

"Sure," she said after a long beat. "What can I do for you?"

"We're on a mission," Roman told her flatly. "We're heading right towards your father's homeworld. Once we get there..."

"You're going to kill him," Henrietta said in a matter-of-fact tone.

"I don't know." Roman took a breath. "The Senate has agreed to provide Admiral Justinian—your father—and his supporters with a limited form of amnesty. If they surrender without ado, they will be sent into exile rather than being killed outright. I believe that will apply to you as well. I can slip you into the transport so you would go into exile with your father."

"The Senate never keeps its word." Henrietta snorted. "Why should I trust them?"

"You do have a choice," Roman pointed out. "You can stay with us, at least until your father surrenders, or we can dump you on the planet below. It's called Wanaka. The Senate wouldn't find you there, even if they had a reason to go looking."

Henrietta's face took on the vagueness of someone consulting her implants. Even without access to the computers, she would still have a basic planetary database.

"A barbaric place," she said finally. "I'll take my chances with you."

"I had to offer." Roman stood up. "I'll chat with you again as soon as I can."

"Please stay," Henrietta said. She sounded lonely. "I just want to talk, I promise." Roman hesitated, then sat down again.

ഇരുഖ

The fleet passed through the Wanaka System without incident and made transit into the Farnham System. The settlers there hadn't wanted more than an agricultural economy, and had been reluctant to sell mining rights to their gas giants to anyone. The Federation Senate had ended the issue—after a great deal of pressure from a couple of interstellar corporations—by rewriting the law to allow the corporations to set up mining cloudscoops without permission. The local settlers had retaliated by refusing to provide any rest and relaxation for the mining engineers, so the system had rapidly become known as a hardship posting for mining crews.

Because the system had been cut off by the rebellion, ONI had no hard evidence on what might be taking place in the Farnham System. It was something of a relief for Admiral Drake to discover that the mining stations had been shut down, at least temporarily. But Marius hadn't been inclined to take anything for granted, so he'd dispatched a squadron of destroyers to check out the mining stations.

"The Marines confirm that the bases have been placed on standby and abandoned," Raistlin reported. "There are no signs that anyone has visited the stations since the shutdown."

"Good," Marius told him. He studied the display, wondering if Admiral Justinian had placed a single starship within the system. The Grand Fleet was cloaked, but the turbulence caused by the fleet's maneuvers would probably be detected, cloak or no cloak. "Recall the squadron, then tell the fleet to resume course for the mass limit. We need to keep moving before some unhelpful bastard picks us up and blows the whistle."

"Aye, sir," Raistlin said.

He settled back into his command chair and allowed himself a droll smile. Unless they'd missed something, the Grand Fleet's passage had been undetected and the back door was wide open. All that remained was to kick the door down as hard as possible and keep moving. If they were lucky, they'd get halfway to Jefferson before Justinian even realized they were coming.

"And get me Captain Garibaldi," Marius added. "I want to discuss opportunities for us in the Sphinx System."

"Yes, sir," Raistlin said. He paused, considering. "Do you wish him to report onboard *Magnificent?*"

"No," Marius said. Convention dictated that the junior officer visited the senior, but convention could go hang. And even though it was an aide's job to keep reminding his admiral about protocol, Marius didn't want to hear it. "I will settle for electronic transmission. Make sure that it is a secure link. We don't want just anyone listening in."

Chapter Thirty-Nine

The problem of interstellar communications has vexed humanity—and every other known race—since humanity first discovered the Asimov Points. Where there is a chain of Asimov Points from sender to receiver, it can take hours—or days—to send a message over hundreds of light years. Where there is a gap in the chain, it can delay the message by weeks or months. As can be imagined, this communications delay adds a certain amount of confusion to military operations...
-An Irreverent Guide to the Federation, 4000 A.D.

Jefferson System/Bester System, 4097

"The intelligence is remarkably precise," Admiral Justinian said, "and that worries me. How do we know that it isn't a trick?"

Caitlin considered the question seriously. The admiral had spent years building up an intelligence network on Earth—everyone who was anyone or wanted to be someone had their own intelligence network—but the Senate's hasty counter-measures had wiped out most of his better-informed sources, along with hundreds of people whose only crime had been annoying one of the Senators charged with overseeing the purge. His few remaining sources had chosen to remain in deep cover and were very careful what they forwarded to the admiral.

She sighed. Like most governments, the Senate had shown a much more dangerous side of itself when its power was genuinely threatened. Their reign of terror, as unpleasant as it had been, had definitely produced results.

"You must admit that it holds up under scrutiny," she pointed out after a long pause. "They only have two choices if they want to win within the year: reinforce Boskone to the maximum possible extent and attack from there, or push their ships through hostile space."

"And take us up the backside," Justinian agreed.

He stared up at the holographic display, studying the twin icons representing Marx and The Hive. Tactical icons orbited the two stars, the data already out of date. And yet, he was still more informed than the Grand Senate—or Admiral Drake. Admiral Justinian's one advantage over the Federation was faster communications, and he used it ruthlessly.

"If you were in command of the fleet, Caitlin, which way would you go?"

"Marx," Caitlin said automatically.

Justinian gave her a questioning look.

"It doesn't matter how they look at it," she explained. "A direct assault into a defended Asimov Point is going to bleed them white. It might cost them dearly enough to allow us to launch a counter-attack. If possible, they will seek to avoid such an offensive."

Justinian bowed his head in thought.

"I cannot disagree with your logic," he said after a long beat. "Look."

He keyed the console and the holographic chart zoomed out. Admiral Justinian's space was centered on Jefferson, the star that served as the terminus for nine Asimov Chains. Harmony, his capital, was at the end of one Asimov Point, but the others led to other parts of his empire, each one a nightmare to secure. The admiral had used most of his resources to build new starships rather than fortresses, and he hadn't paid anything like as much attention to the Marx Chain as he should have.

In hindsight, Caitlin knew they should have been more concerned with blocking access to The Hive.

"If we send ships to Marx, they will be out of position if the enemy does try to mount an assault from Boskone," he said.

Caitlin nodded impatiently. Justinian liked to outline and expound upon his thoughts, but she found it a little tiring.

"If we ignore the threat from Marx," Justinian went on, "we face the risk of a powerful enemy force getting loose in our rear. How many worlds would dearly love to switch sides if the Senate gave them the opportunity?"

Caitlin scowled. Admiral Justinian had repealed most of the Federation Law that colonists and settlers saw as an imposition by grey men thousands of light years away, but he hadn't put anything in its place. His rule was a military rule, and while a starship could be commanded by a draconian man, it wasn't so easy to command an entire economy in the same fashion.

It hadn't helped that he'd been diverting all his resources into building up his war fleet, which had caused shortages for the remainder of his empire. Planetary governments were going along with him, for now, but she had no illusions. Their professed loyalty would last until the Federation offered them a viable alternative.

Justinian pressed the point.

"Seriously, Caitlin—how many do you think would defect, given the chance?"

"Too many," she said. "Maybe if we moved our ships to here—" she tapped the icon representing Samovar, a dull world orbiting a dim red star "—and held them in position? If there is a threat from Marx, we'll know about it in time for the fleet to take up defensive positions and block the Asimov Point. If the enemy does intend to punch through from Boskone, we can move the fleet back to reinforce the defenses..."

"Workable," Admiral Justinian agreed. He looked over at her. "And yet, something tells me that there's something we have missed."

Caitlin studied the display for a long moment. "And what might that be?"

"If I knew, I wouldn't have missed it," Justinian told her sarcastically.

She recognized the stress in his voice and refrained from saying anything.

"Cut the operations orders and move the fleet into Samovar, but order them to remain near the origin Asimov Point," the admiral ordered. "We may as well hedge our bets as much as possible."

"Aye, sir," Caitlin said. She grinned at him. "We will certainly receive warning before the enemy starts crossing the gulf between The Hive and Marx."

"Let's hope so," Justinian said with a scowl. "My enemy is devious. I miss Admiral Parkinson. Perhaps I should have thought of that before I killed him."

"Doubtless," Caitlin agreed dryly. "At least we can be sure that Hartkopf won't allow them to transit the Bester System."

"You can always count on a weasel to weasel," Justinian reminded her. "I trust Hartkopf about as far as I can pick up and throw an entire superdreadnaught."

ଚ୍ଚର୍ଷ

Colonel Scudder allowed himself a moment to study the governor's private compartment, and then snapped his fingers for two of his men. When they arrived, he gave them orders to clear out everything in the compartment and to have it fumigated before anyone else tried to move into the section. He had no way of knowing just what Hartkopf had been doing in his private compartment, but the cushions, the filthy paintings and the vast array of expensive liqueurs suggested a number of possible answers. Hartkopf's tastes, it seemed, ran towards the gross rather than the subtle.

To a man like Scudder, who had deliberately cultivated his thin and pinched appearance, complete with a sallow face and pale complexion, it was disgraceful. A Sector Governor should have more dignity instead of playing the sybarite while plotting rebellion.

He marched up to the fortress's command center in a vile mood, which wasn't lessened by the discovery that Hartkopf's body—along with some of his most trusted subordinates—had vanished after he was assassinated. The people who might have known what had happened to the body had also vanished, although it seemed that they might have been killed in the fighting that had torn the system apart before the Grand Fleet arrived to restore order. He checked the list of remaining prisoners, compared them to the lists he'd been given before he'd left Earth, and allowed himself a relieved smile. His orders from the Senate had been clear and unambiguous. There would be rewards for those who followed orders, but those who disobeyed—even if they couldn't carry out the orders—would regret it.

The Senate wouldn't thank him for being insufficiently thorough when it came to reclaiming the system for the Federation. He knew that his superiors had their own business interests in the sector, which would only be boosted by control of Bester, and he intended to present them with a tamed planet.

"Ship the senior prisoners to the barge," he ordered when he'd finished skimming the list. It hardly mattered that not all of the senior prisoners were on the proscribed list. "I want them well away from the planet's surface."

The young lieutenant turned from the console. "Sir, the admiral specifically ordered that the prisoners were to be held..."

Scudder cut him off sharply. "Does the admiral outrank the Senate?" he demanded angrily. "I have instructions to secure and pacify this system, and that is what I will do. If you have a problem with that, place yourself under arrest. One of your subordinates will have your posting..."

"No, sir," the lieutenant said. He turned back to his console and started to issue orders, doubtless aware of Scudder's eyes drilling into his ramrod-straight back.

Scudder had no idea how the lieutenant been assigned to Internal Security, an organization where following orders, no matter how insane or absurd, was highly commended. Perhaps the youngster had highly-placed relatives who had secured him an easy position, although nothing Scudder did was ever *easy*, or safe. Whatever else could be said of him, he was no coward; he led his men from the front, shared their rations and ensured that few questions were asked about their conduct while on leave.

"The marshals want you to know that the prisoners are protesting..." the lieutenant started.

"Tell them to apply the treatment we applied to those protesters on Mars if they keep it up," Scudder ordered. Back then, he'd led his men, wearing full combat armor and carrying shock-rods and stunners, against men and women who might as well have been naked. The result had been a bloody end to the protest. "I want them all on the barge yesterday, if not sooner."

He turned away from the lieutenant and stared down at the tactical display showing Bester and the orbital defenses surrounding the planet. His men had relieved the Marines who'd taken and secured the facilities, and promptly shipped the junior prisoners down to the planet's surface. The senior prisoners were still on the station, but it wouldn't be long before they, too, were transferred to the barge. In the meantime, his forces would occupy the planet's vital locations and purge the government of all undesirable elements.

The Colonel was still contemplating this happy thought when he received a call from the barge.

"Colonel, all of the senior prisoners are aboard," the officer in charge reported. "I'm afraid that many of their family members insisted on accompanying them."

"No matter," Scudder said. "I'll be there in ten minutes."

He shrugged. The Senate's orders were clear, regardless of what the admiral had said. If they gave amnesty to snakes like the men who had betrayed their sworn oaths, they would just rise up again and launch a second coup. He knew how to deal with them, and the Senate's orders overrode the admiral's instructions. Besides, the Grand Fleet was already on its way towards its target. Whatever minor tactical considerations were involved, the battles would be over by the time the news of what Scudder had done reached Admiral Drake.

Some of his men—the ones he relied on for the truly dirty work—would be disappointed. Personally, Scudder didn't care. It was just a job. Besides, there was an entire planet of women just below them and Scudder had a reputation for being liberal with leave cards once the mission was complete. They'd be at Bester long enough to enjoy themselves, once the planet had been pacified and reinforcements arrived. The latest Internal Security divisions would already be on their way.

ଽୠେଔ

The barge—no one had ever bothered to name it—had started life as a bulk freighter, back in the days before the stardrive. Internal Security hadn't been concerned about the freighter's limited choice of destinations, as they'd converted the freighter into a prison barge. It would be difficult, if not impossible, for anyone to rescue the prisoners and if they rioted and overthrew their guards, the barge couldn't hope to outrun even a crippled destroyer. The ship was, naturally, completely unarmed.

Scudder had no time to gaze upon the planet below as his shuttle docked with the barge. He pulled himself through the airlock into the crew compartment. Most of the original automation had been pulled out and replaced with modern equipment, ensuring that only five crewmen were actually needed to run the vessel. The crew compartment and control systems were also separated from the prisoner compartments by a layer of battle steel that was completely impenetrable, at least to anything the prisoners might have on hand. If worst came to worst, the crew compartment could separate from the main body of the ship and abandon the prisoners in space.

"Welcome aboard, colonel," the barge's captain said.

Scudder had picked the man personally; he was small, unpleasant and thoroughly unimaginative. He was the ideal tool for Internal Security, if only because he didn't have the imagination to be disloyal. And he would do anything if ordered, no matter how vile. He'd been on suspension from the Federation Penal Service when Internal Security had recruited him.

"Can I say how pleased I am to see you?" the man added.

"No," Scudder growled. The sooner he completed his task, the better. "Show me the prisoners."

The crew compartment was cramped, even with the new computers and control systems. At the rear of the compartment, there was a set of nine monitors. Scudder flicked through them one by one, examining the prisoners thoughtfully. Many of them looked despondent, clearly wondering what was going to happen to them, while others had already realized the truth. Some of them—he caught sight of a number of young girls who had chosen to stay with their families—shouldn't really be there at all.

Not that Scudder gave a damn. The Senate had ordered the execution of all rebels, along with their families, and Scudder intended to give them exactly what they had ordered.

"I have command," he said.

The captain blinked at him, but nodded.

Scudder keyed a switch and accessed the intercom. His words would be heard throughout the prisoner compartments.

"Rebels: by Senatorial Decree, you have been found guilty of treason, mutiny against lawful authority and various other charges. The penalty for your crimes is death."

He keyed a second switch, opening the air vents. The prisoner sections would start to decompress slowly, but surely. The rebels would have plenty of time to realize what awaited them before they died. It would be interesting to see how they reacted when they realized the truth. He'd seen men fighting each other for the last gasp of air, and others trying to give their own lives to save other men. Perhaps it would be the latter here. There were families at stake.

"Make sure this is prepared for transmission," he ordered. "I want the entire system to see what happened to them."

The rebels were trying desperately to block the air vents, a tactic that might have worked if some of the air vents hadn't been out of reach. But the air was running out. Men and women started to turn purple as they stumbled around, gasping for air. A child—she couldn't have been more than six—stumbled to the deck and lay still. Other children had been killed by their parents to spare them the pain of suffocation and death.

Scudder allowed himself a tight smile as the final drops of air flew out of the compartment, leaving only death behind. How could such a sight fail to chill the heart of even the harshest rebel?

"Transmit the recording to the planetary datanet," he said, once it was all over. "I want them all to see."

ഇൗഇ

The tiny scout ship had watched from afar as the Grand Fleet had trashed what was left of the system, but they'd been sneaking back to the Asimov Point to reach The Hive when they'd picked up the broadcast. Admiral Justinian had ordered Lieutenant Suzan Bones and her crew to watch the planet and report back if anything occurred that might affect his interests. An invasion—and then a slaughter—definitely counted.

"Those lousy, murdering..."

"Quiet," Lieutenant Bones ordered. "We need to get this back to the admiral."

The scout was barely large enough for the four who occupied it. They'd been living in one another's fumes for weeks, and tempers had been riding high. Even so, they knew their duty; all they had to do was get back to Marx with the data.

And then, Suzan thought mordantly, *Admiral Justinian will know just what happened to people stupid enough to surrender to the Federation.*

She ran through the situation in her head while cursing under her breath. They'd never counted on Hartkopf being assassinated and his little kingdom falling apart. All of a sudden, new options had opened up for the Federation lickspittles. The admiral had to be warned.

"Entering Asimov Point now," the helmsman reported.

Suzan nodded.

"Get us out of here!"

Chapter Forty

Even with the stardrive, systems on the end of long, gangly chains of Asimov Points tend to be cut off from the remainder of the Federation. This tends to hamper their development and limit their immediate opportunities for economic expansion.
-An Irreverent Guide to the Federation, 4000 A.D.

Sphinx/Hawthorne System, 4097

"Nothing to report?"

"No, captain," the sensor officer said. "The sensor board is clear."

Captain Keller nodded impatiently, and then shook his head. Taking his frustration out on his officers was the mark of a poor commander and he liked to think that he was better than that. Still, it had been three months since *Percival* had been assigned to the system, and being at Sphinx was not the most glorious of postings. The system was at the end of a chain of Asimov Points that led back to Jefferson, and systems like that tended to worry planners.

It was true that the system had little beyond a handful of RockRat colonies and a tiny independent mining operation. It didn't really need a picket. The Book, however, insisted that there had to be a picket in all systems. Even without the stardrive, it was possible that a barely-surveyed system might hide a second, undetected Asimov Point.

And if that Asimov Point led into enemy space, the strategic situation would turn upside down, instantly.

It had been a long posting, and he was uneasily aware that he was running out of drills for his crew. They all needed some leave, but there was little hope of finding anything worth enjoying in the Sphinx System. Perhaps he should allow a handful of crewmen to take one of the gunboats and go through the Asimov Point to Hawthorne. The Hawthorne System was nearly as poor and deserted, but at least it had an Earth-like planet and the promise of female company.

"Never mind," he said, settling back down in his command chair. "Perhaps we should run a few tracking exercises, just to make sure that we don't get bored."

ഇറ

The blue icon representing the Asimov Point leading to Hawthorne, blinked on and off on the display. The red icon for the cruiser remained firmly in place, glaring down at Roman coldly, as if it was just waiting for him to come closer. The ship's commander had actually ordered his ship to remain on station within the Asimov Point itself, a gutsy move when an interpenetration event could destroy his ship before his crew even realized that they were dead.

The cruiser—pre-war databases listed her as the *Percival*—didn't have her shields and weapons up, ready to hit a target as soon as one showed itself. If she'd detected *Midway* and the remainder of the squadron, she would either have transited the Asimov Point and escaped, or opened fire. Unless her captain was insanely brave, he reminded himself. It was quite possible that he was quietly tracking them through passive sensors while lining his weapons up on Roman's ship.

Roman spoke softly, even though sound couldn't travel through space.

"Report."

"One *Gamma*-class light cruiser and two gunboats," the sensor officer said, equally quietly. "There's no sign that they have detected our presence."

"No," Roman agreed. "Weapons?"

"We can take her out before she even sees us, sir," the tactical officer assured him. "The gunboats may be a little trickier. One of them is currently looping around, out of range; it may be able to jump back through the Asimov Point before we destroy it."

"Yeah," Roman said. The problem with cloaking devices was that they were far from perfect. The longer they floated near their target, the greater the chance of being detected. "Lock weapons on target."

"Weapons locked, sir," the tactical officer said.

Roman sat down in the command chair and straightened his tunic. "On my command," he ordered. "Fire!"

Midway lurched as she flushed her external racks towards the enemy ship. It was overkill, by at least a factor of ten, but they had to take her out with the first shot. If *Percival* managed to bring up her drive and transit out, the entire chain would be alerted before the Grand Fleet reached its target.

He watched as the cruiser's point defense started to lash out—barely coordinated and far too little, too late—and then the missiles struck home. *Percival* vanished in an eye-tearing blast of light, followed rapidly by one of her gunboats. The second twitched and then started to race towards the Asimov Point, just before an anti-fighter missile launched from *Midway* killed her.

"Target destroyed, sir," the tactical officer reported calmly. "She didn't pass a message through the Asimov Point."

"Good," Roman ordered. "Signal Admiral Drake. Inform him that the point is secure."

ॐ

"Admiral," the communications officer said, "Captain Garibaldi is signalling that the point is secure. The picket ship was destroyed before she could get off a message drone."

Marius smiled. So far, so good. He had no illusions about how far they'd get before Admiral Justinian realized they were on their way, but the longer they could keep him in the dark, the better. If they had to punch their way through a defended Asimov Point, the Grand Fleet would be badly damaged in the struggle.

"Deploy the assault fleet," he ordered. "Signal Commodore Goldberg that he may begin the assault when ready."

He leaned back in his chair and relaxed.

"And send an additional signal to Captain Garibaldi," he added. "Well done."

ॐ

"Captain, Admiral Goldberg is preparing to launch his drones."

Roman nodded. Jumping blind was something that no naval commander would do if it could be avoided.

"Good," he said. "Prepare for transition."

The drones flickered, vanishing from the display. Roman counted silently down in his mind. The latest model of recon drones took two minutes to recycle their drives—assuming they survived the transit and whatever the enemy threw at them—before jumping back to their masters. In that time, their sensors would scan the surrounding area of space and identify enemy fortresses, minefields and starships. The pre-war reports claimed that there was nothing stronger than a pair of fortresses that dated all the way back to the Inheritance Wars, but ONI hadn't been able to get a lock on what might have been put in place after the current war began.

The seconds counted down. And then four drones reappeared on the display.

Four out of seventy, Roman noted. The defenders were clearly on the alert.

"Drone data downloading now," the sensor officer said.

The main display lit up like a Christmas tree. There were five fortresses guarding the Asimov Point, backed up by a squadron of dreadnaughts and a handful of smaller ships. Roman suspected that it was already too late to preserve secrecy, but if they were lucky...

"The Commodore is launching assault drones now," the tactical officer reported. "The jump countdown has begun."

A pair of red numbers appeared in the main display. Roman took a breath, knowing that the defenders would be being hammered by the fury of uncontrolled antimatter. Driving into an Asimov Point was a far cry from the stately space battles he'd fought against pirates and enemy warships; indeed, there was a slight chance that *Midway* would interpenetrate with one of her sisters and both ships would vanish in colossal fireballs. Even in friendly territory, it still struck him as somehow *unnatural*.

"Ten seconds," the helmsman said.

Roman waited, knowing that there was no point in issuing further orders.

"Five seconds...three...two...one..."

The universe *lurched* around Midway as she jumped into the Hawthorne System.

"Bring up the tactical sensors," Roman snapped. Without sensors, his ship would be blind and helpless. "Locate the enemy ships!"

He'd hoped that one of the antimatter pods would have taken out a fortress, but he hadn't been so lucky. The defenders would have been surprised when the first recon drones had appeared within the system, yet they hadn't let their surprise slow down their response. They'd started launching missiles as soon as the first assault units appeared in their sights, trusting in the minefields to slow down the Federation Navy's starships as they started to deploy.

"Bring up the point defense datanet," Roman ordered. The admiral would be designating targets for the cruiser's missiles. "Lock weapons at the admiral's command..."

"Weapons locked, sir," the tactical officer said. "We're targeting the closest fortress..."

Midway shuddered as she unleashed a full barrage at the enemy fortifications, which returned fire savagely. They'd clearly been modified extensively since the start of the war. Moments later, four assault carriers materialized in the system and immediately launched their starfighters, throwing them out of the ships as fast as possible while the carriers added their missile batteries and point defense to the datanet.

Oddly, Roman realized, the enemy didn't seem to have any starfighters. Perhaps they'd felt that the system was too remote to rate starfighters. They didn't have unlimited resources, after all.

Midway rang like a bell as the first enemy missile slammed into her shields, followed rapidly by a second missile. Roman cursed as his ship was blown backwards by the force of the explosion, but the shields held long enough for their comrades to take out the following missiles.

A moment later, one of the enemy fortresses, battered beyond endurance, exploded in a colossal fireball, throwing waves of debris across the system. A second fortress went dark, but the remaining two continued to fight, while the enemy dreadnaughts advanced on the Asimov Point. With the minefields taken out, they could sit on the point and hammer anything that materialized in the area before it could orient itself and open fire.

They were too late. The first giant superdreadnaught materialized in front of them, followed by the remainder of its squadron. Orders were exchanged between the admiral and the commodore in command of the squadron and the massive ships belched missiles towards the two remaining fortresses. As a second and third squadron of superdreadnaughts made their appearance, the enemy diverted their fire from the remains of the assault squadron and concentrated on the giants.

"The third fortress has been destroyed," the tactical officer reported. "The fourth is continuing to fight."

Roman scowled. *Midway* was small fry in such a battle, now that five more superdreadnaught squadrons had arrived. The smart thing for the enemy to do would be to signal up the chain, and then try to surrender. Instead, they were fighting grimly, trying to inflict as much damage as they could before they were killed. It didn't bode well for the future.

∞∞

Magnificent emerged into a universe of fire and rage. Marius had bare seconds to access the datanet and download the tactical situation report before the first missile slammed into the superdreadnaught's shields. It chilled him to the bone to realize just how close they had come to total disaster. A few microseconds later, and they would have interpenetrated with an armed antimatter missile.

"The enemy dreadnaughts are starting to break off from the Asimov Point," Blake Raistlin reported. Marius heard the excitement in his voice and wished, for a moment, that he was young again. "I think they're preparing to run for their lives, sir."

"Probably," Marius agreed. It wasn't something he could allow to happen, either. Luckily, he had two aces up his sleeves. "Detach the fast superdreadnaughts and order them to run the bastards down before they reach the Asimov Point, and then assign two assault carriers to their support."

"Aye, sir," Raistlin said.

Marius sat back as another missile rocked the superdreadnaught. It was impossible to tell if the enemy had realized that *Magnificent* was the command vessel, or if it were simple bad luck. No, it had to be the latter; if *he'd* been able to identify the enemy flagship, he would have engaged her with every missile and beam at his command.

The one remaining enemy fortress was fighting hard, but her shields kept failing and missiles were slamming against her bare hull. She couldn't last much longer...

The display blinked and cleared, with the icon of the fortress replaced by an expanding icon signifying a cloud of debris. The fortress had oddly refused all offers to accept surrender. Marius doubted that anyone on the fortress had been on the proscribed lists...and even if they had been, they'd only go into exile. He'd shown the universe how merciful the Federation could be at Bester.

He allowed himself to relax as the battle started to draw down to a close. The remaining enemy dreadnaughts were trying to escape now, but they wouldn't be able to reach the other Asimov Point before they were run down and destroyed. If they kept trying to flee, his starfighters would hammer them into submission; if they tried to fight, his superdreadnaughts would destroy them. He hoped they'd have the sense to surrender before it was too late. There was no point in slaughtering people for nothing.

"Detach a destroyer squadron and a Marine Transport," he ordered. "I want them to occupy the Hawthorne Orbitals and secure the planet. Inform the planetary government"—such as it was, assuming Admiral Justinian hadn't replaced the pre-war government with his own men—"that we do not intend to harm them provided they behave themselves. Once the war is over, normal trade can resume."

"Aye, sir," Raistlin said. "Sir, the enemy dreadnaughts are surrendering."

"Good," Marius said with a nod. "Order the superdreadnaughts to launch Marine parties to secure the ships, then continue on to the Asimov Point. They are to demand the surrender of any further fortifications and secure the Asimov Point itself."

He turned back to the display and studied it. There hadn't been any pre-war fortifications on the other Asimov Point, but Admiral Justinian might have changed that during his time as the undisputed emperor of this sector. The Asimov Points toward the Rim were sometimes quite heavily fortified, but sometimes were rarely guarded at all. Hell, they might not even have been charted properly!

It was one of the reasons why the Outsiders were so dangerous. The Federation made navigational data free for all, but the Outsiders had never shared any of their data with the Federation. And with the Survey Service practically moribund, there was little hope of updating charts, let alone placing navigational buoys near new Asimov Points.

As soon as the battle ended, Marius ordered his ships to rearm from the fleet train before resuming the advance. He'd lost twenty-seven ships in the battle and seventeen more had been damaged, some quite seriously. The mobile repair yards would do what they could before the damaged ships started to limp home (or, if the ship was too badly damaged, hid in the captured system until the end of the war). He was gratified—and somewhat amused—to discover that Captain Garibaldi's luck hadn't deserted him. *Midway* had been hit hard, but her shields had held and she'd barely been scratched.

"Sir, *Mohammad* and *Argus* report that they're ready to rejoin their squadrons," Raistlin said as the hours wore on. "*Harrington's* captain insists that his ship is also battle-ready, but the yard dogs disagree; they want more time."

"They always want more time," Marius commented. "Inform Captain Weber that if he trusts his ship is in fighting trim, he may rejoin the squadron. If not, assign him to Commodore Seiko's command and *Harrington* can add her fire to her squadron."

He smiled at the thought. Commodore Seiko commanded the covering force that would escort any damaged warships back to safe harbor. It wasn't regarded as a prestigious position, but it was a vitally important role. She'd find a superdreadnaught, even a damaged one, very helpful. If nothing else, *Harrington* could tow some of the cripples home.

"Aye, sir," Raistlin said.

"As soon as we are ready, the Grand Fleet is to advance," Marius ordered. They'd be advancing blind, again, and this time the enemy would have to know they were coming. If the fortresses hadn't screamed for help and fired off message drones, he'd be astonished. "We're going to take them at a run."

He ran through it again in his head. Assuming that a message had been sent as soon as the recon drones had transited the Asimov Point, it would be nearly two days before Admiral Justinian heard about the advance. If Marius made the further assumption that Admiral Justinian would react at once, it would mean roughly two weeks—perhaps twenty days—before Justinian got a blocking force into position. It would be longer if Justinian had kept most of his fleet facing Boskone or defending Marx, but Marius didn't dare count on it. The further he got up the chain towards Jefferson, the better.

And what if there was something he'd missed?

He shook his head slowly. His doubts—and doubts were a natural part of such an ambitious operation—weren't important. All that mattered now was speed—and victory.

Chapter Forty-One

Sun Tzu, thousands of years ago, laid down the basic rules that we still follow today. When an enemy is weak, advance; when strong, fall back. We think of terrain as being Asimov Points, planets and stars, instead of the wily Chinese General's land and seas, but the principles remain the same.
-Observations on Military Tactics, 3500 A.D.

Jefferson/Lombardi System, 4097

"Shit! They came through the back door. Damn them."

Caitlin had rarely seen Admiral Justinian so rattled, but the news was shocking enough to worry the strongest of men.

Her commander turned and studied the display. The Federation Navy was—presumably—advancing as fast as possible up the chain towards Jefferson. It would have to punch its way through four Asimov Points to reach the nexus star, but none of them were heavily defended. They certainly wouldn't be taken by surprise, not once the warning had been passed up the chain, yet it wouldn't really matter. The Federation Navy wouldn't have launched such an offensive unless they believed that they possessed a crushing superiority.

"The report was vague as to their strength," she said, scanning the final sensor readings the destroyer *Danton* had taken before she'd fled back to Jefferson. The ship's captain had nearly burned out his drives trying to reach Jefferson before it was too late. The hell of it was that it might be futile anyway. "We only saw forty-odd superdreadnaughts."

"They'll have more," Justinian said, dismissing her optimistic projection. "We need to stop them before they break into Jefferson."

He was right, she knew. Local commanders would do what they could to parse—and then delay—the full strength of the attacking force before it reached Jefferson, but Caitlin knew that they couldn't do much. Admiral Drake would hardly repeat the mistakes of the Retribution Force.

Jefferson and its nine Asimov Points served as the nexus for Admiral Justinian's empire. If the Federation Navy contested the system—let alone captured it—they would break the chains holding the empire together. Some of Justinian's more reluctant allies would switch sides, his junior commanders might turn into warlords on their own...it would be the end.

They couldn't allow the Federation Navy into Jefferson.

Admiral Justinian considered the overall picture, thoughtfully. "At least we have the combined fleet in a position to make transit back to Jefferson fairly quickly."

Caitlin nodded. She'd already sent orders along the ICN to alert the fleet to be prepared to move.

"We bring them back into Jefferson and then advance along the Chain to"—he studied the display, apparently trying to gauge how fast the Federation Navy could move—"Lombardi, I think. I doubt we'll get much further unless Admiral Drake feels like resting on his laurels."

"He won't," Caitlin said. "He had the imagination to blaze right through Bester..."

"True," Admiral Justinian agreed. "If we get the fleet into place before the enemy enters the system, we'll set up a defense on the Asimov Point and stop them cold. If not, we will have to contest the system and force them to assault the other Asimov Point."

He keyed his console. "In the meantime, I want tugs moving fortresses from the other Asimov Points to the terminus of the Sphinx Chain," he added. "Even if the fleet fails, we can try to hold the Jefferson System."

Caitlin considered it.

"It will take weeks to move enough fortresses over to the Asimov Point to make a difference," she told him. Towing a multimillion ton fortress wasn't an easy task at the best of times. "We could hold the fleet in Jefferson itself and force them to come to us."

"Maybe, but we might lose control of the outer system," Justinian pointed out. "And there is another concern."

His hands danced over the console. "As you can see, a hostile attacker who takes Lombardi will be able to cross interstellar space and reach Harmony," he explained. "There's only forty light years between the two stars and if they secure Lombardi, they don't need to attack Jefferson at all."

"Unless they want to link up with the forces defending Boskone," Caitlin reminded him. "If they opened up the Asimov Point chain for shipping, they could reinforce their fleet remarkably quickly..."

"I know," Admiral Justinian said. "There's little else that we can do."

Caitlin felt a flicker of sympathy, for he was facing the same dilemma he'd inflicted on the Federation. He had too many places to defend, and far too few ships and fortresses to cover them all. Most of his mobile firepower was badly out of position and it would take weeks to concentrate it to reinforce his reserves. A loss now could cost him the entire war.

On the other hand, the Federation had had space to trade for time. Admiral Justinian didn't have many stars he could trade for time, not now.

He suddenly looked up at her. "I will command the fleet, of course," he said.

At her concerned look, he added, "It's necessary. My men need to know I'll die beside them, if need be."

She nodded.

"I'll let my wife know," he told her. "Then we can depart on the *Rampant Lion.*"

Caitlin nodded, feeling a second flicker of sympathy. His wife had had dreams of being Empress since the day she'd been old enough to take part in High Society's endless rounds of social backstabbing, character assassination and metaphorical bloodbaths. The Court she'd set up on Harmony had always amused Caitlin, even though she knew that Millicent Beauregard-Justinian took it far too seriously. The woman wouldn't respond well to hearing that she would either have to flee, or be executed by the Senate.

"Yes, sir," she said. "I expected no less of you."

⁊ᘒ

Through heroic effort, the main body of the fleet was brought back into the Jefferson System, just in time to hear that another star system had been taken by the advancing Federation Navy. Admiral Justinian waited long enough to make certain of his supplies, and then led the fleet through the Asimov Point and up the Sphinx Chain. If they were lucky, they would intercept the enemy fleet well short of Lombardi and Harmony.

Caitlin tried to convince herself that they were bound to succeed—the last time the Federation Navy had tried to reach Jefferson, they'd been smashed—but no amount of mental argument convinced her that their success was guaranteed.

⁊ᘒ

Marius watched as tumbling wreckage drifted past his fleet, the remains of a pair of fortresses that had tried to bar the fleet's passage to Jefferson. Admiral Justinian had left the outdated fortresses in position and all they had been able to do, despite the advance warning of his coming, was die bravely. They hadn't even surrendered, although he was fairly sure that they'd been damaged and destroyed before their commanders had realized just how badly the odds were stacked against them.

"All ships report that they're secure, sir," Raistlin reported. "The Marine unit dispatched to the planet has reported that the planet has surrendered and is awaiting occupation."

"There's no time," Marius said firmly. "Order them to destroy the planet's defenses, and then return to the fleet."

He ignored Williams' surprised look. The political commissioner had been determined to occupy all the worlds the fleet passed as it advanced up the chain, and Marius had been happy to oblige, but they'd run out of Internal Security troopers to detach from the fleet. Besides, the further they advanced up the chain, the greater the chance they would run into something hard enough to stop them, and he needed all of his destroyers with the fleet.

He keyed his console as he checked the reports from his officers. The battle hadn't been very costly, at least in men and starships, although he was sure that the bean-counters at the Admiralty would complain about the number of assault pods he'd wasted on the outdated fortresses. Marius found it hard to care. Assault pods could be turned out easily by industrial nodes, but starships and trained crewmen took longer to produce. There was no point in spending lives like water when there was an alternative.

Sixteen starfighters, two destroyers and one heavy cruiser had been blown to atoms in the brief and furious battle. A handful of other ships were slightly damaged. They could carry out their repairs underway.

"The fleet is to resume its course toward the Lombardi Asimov Point," he ordered. "We will reunite with the Marines and assault cruisers before we charge into the next system. Deploy scout gunboats to cover our flanks and don't hesitate to launch sensor probes if you think you have a ghost of a target."

He smiled as he cut the channel. The last system had seemed undefended until a handful of destroyers had appeared from cloak and cut into a pair of his ammunition freighters. It wasn't a bad tactic if the enemy merely wanted to slow down his advance, as he'd been forced to redeploy some of his destroyers and escort carriers to protect the freighters. The farther they advanced up the chain, the more firepower the enemy would be able to hide under cloak until the time was right.

Magnificent shivered slightly as her main drive went to full power. "The captain's compliments, sir," Raistlin reported, "and he wishes to report that we will be at the Asimov Point within twelve hours."

Marius had to grin at the formality.

"Tell him and his bridge crew to get some rest," he ordered. "The remainder of the fleet can stand down to condition-two unless the enemy shows his face."

He'd need some rest himself, although he knew that he wouldn't sleep well, even in Tiffany's arms. Bringing her along was in some ways a breach of regulations, and he'd thought long and hard about it as it also risked exposing her to enemy fire. But she'd pointed out that he'd let her go into the Bester System without a second thought, and won the argument.

He turned back to the display, silently counting down the hours until the moment they encountered the enemy fleet. There were just too many unknowns; what had seemed like an excellent—indeed, brilliant—plan when he'd drawn it up in the privacy of his own head now seemed like an act of madness.

Where was Admiral Justinian's battle fleet? If he'd kept it at Jefferson, the Grand Fleet would have encountered it by now, but they'd seen nothing apart from a handful of light squadrons.

And where was the admiral? It was too much to hope that he'd scattered his fleet all over his little empire, but had he been taken in by the deceptions? Or had he simply not seen the false intelligence at all? Had Marius overestimated his intelligence apparatus on Earth?

"You seem concerned, admiral," Williams said. "Is the enemy not dancing to your tune?"

The political commissioner had come up behind him, moving silently across the deck. Marius would have been impressed under other circumstances.

"The enemy will do whatever he can to frustrate me, as I will do whatever I can to frustrate him," Marius quoted from a book of Navy proverbs. "That's why he's called the enemy."

He shrugged. "How much, commissioner, does the enemy know about us?"

"I thought you fed him your fake plan, hook, line and sinker," Williams protested. "You told me he was fooled."

Marius shrugged again. He'd exaggerated a little to keep the Commissioner happy, or at least quiet. "The enemy now knows that we are on our way, hammering our way up the chain towards Jefferson," he said.

He grinned at the commissioner's sallow face.

"He *has* to know, because they had plenty of time to get a message out," Marius explained. "But...does he know our strength? We've kept parts of the fleet under cloak, or used ECM to exaggerate our strength...how much does he know? Does he think that we only have fifty superdreadnaughts, or did one of his skippers have the guts to slip close enough to peer though the ECM?"

"I thought you could always detect a ship under cloak if it came close enough to read the letters on the hull," Williams said.

Marius sighed, concealing his irritation. Whatever criteria the Senate had used when it came to selecting commissioners, it hadn't included any military background, let alone experience.

"Or are our sensors worse than you suggested?" Williams pushed.

"The enemy may have left a ship in our path, lying doggo," Marius said. "Risky, very risky; if we detected the ship, we could pop off a single missile and vaporize her. On the other hand, very little chance of detection unless we used full-power active sensors. And her passive sensors would be enough to give them an accurate count of our ships."

He made a show of checking his wrist terminal. "As there's no way to know what is going through Justinian's mind right now, I suggest that you get some sleep, commissioner. In twelve hours, we go through it all again...unless we run into the enemy first."

�����

Midway and her consorts had been racing toward the Asimov Point that led into the Lombardi System. There were no fortresses guarding that end of the gravitational distortion, but there was a single light cruiser, watching the loyalist fleet as it advanced.

"Captain, the light cruiser is retreating," the sensor officer said.

"Pity," Roman said. "I wonder if..."

The icon blinked once—the yellow flash that signified a successful transit—and vanished.

"She went down the rabbit hole, sir," the sensor officer reported. "There are no other enemy ships detected within the general area."

Unless they're cloaked, or lying doggo, Roman reminded himself. The last two systems had been nightmarish; the cloaked enemy ships hadn't been able to do more than sting, but they'd stung hard. *Midway* had accounted for two enemy destroyers and what his tactical officer had believed was a converted freighter, yet it hadn't been enough. If the fleet had been operating with a long fleet train, they might have been in real trouble. Losing the supply lines would be disastrous.

"Launch recon probes," he ordered. "Let's see what's on the other side of the rabbit hole."

Only one of the probes returned, but the news it brought back was very encouraging. There was only one fortress facing the loyalists, another outdated design that dated all the way back to the Inheritance Wars. It would suffice to stop pirates and rebels in peacetime, but it wasn't designed to stand up to a frontal assault. The hast-ily-laid minefield on top of the Asimov Point was clearly unprepared for action, but that wouldn't stop it from being deadly. Roman conferred with his fellow captains and the commodore in charge of the assault force, and then checked with Admiral Drake. As he'd anticipated, the order was simple: attack.

Midway transited into the system hard on the heels of the first set of assault pods. Most of the minefield had been destroyed by the assault pods, allowing his point defense crews a chance to pick off the remaining mines before they recovered from the assault and started to target the attacking ships. The commander of the fortress, he was relieved to discover, was a realist. Once he'd updated his superiors on the composition of the fleet that had forced the Asimov Point, he surrendered. A small team of Marines was sent to secure the fortress while the remainder of the Grand Fleet transited in, one by one.

"New orders from the flag, sir," the communications officer said. "We are to pro-ceed at once to the Roslyn Point and secure it."

Roman felt a tingle run down his spine. Roslyn wasn't just a fully-developed sys-tem with a vast array of space-based industries and a formidable planetary defense network; it was the final stop on the way to Jefferson. If they could get into the system before the enemy reacted, they could threaten Jefferson from two Asimov Points at once...

He shook his head, reminding himself that the attempt to coordinate two assaults over interstellar distances at the same time had doomed the Federation Navy's attempt to seize Sapphire during the Blue Star War. Admiral Drake would not want to repeat that particular mistake.

"Helm, lay in a course," he ordered. "Maximum safe speed."

Midway hummed as she accelerated through space, heading right at the Asimov Point. The Lombardi System reminded Roman of his home system, even though his home system possessed no Asimov Points and had remained undiscovered until the Federation had developed the stardrive and used it to survey the worlds near Earth that had been settled via interstellar slowboats. The RockRats who'd settled the system had been astonished to discover that Earth had not only cracked the FTL problem, but had been exploring interstellar space for generations through the Asimov Points.

"Captain," the sensor officer said, "I think we have a problem."

"Show me," Roman ordered.

"There's a fleet coming through the Asimov Point," the sensor officer reported. New red icons flashed on the display. "I think that Admiral Justinian has sent his fleet to intercept us."

"I think you're right," Roman agreed. "Take us into cloak. Communications, signal the admiral and inform him that the enemy fleet has arrived, and that we will con-tinue to forward data as long as we can."

"Aye, sir," the communications officer said.

Chapter Forty-Two

When encountering one another in interplanetary space, two fleets may spend longer developing their formations and attack plans than they do actually fighting. Even so, a battle between two fleets is a slow, stately affair. If the fleets are evenly matched, the fight can go on for days.
-Observations on Military Tactics, 3500 A.D.

Lombardi System, 4097

"Showtime," Marius said.

He watched as the enemy fleet slowly shook itself down into formation. It was evident from their deployments that they'd intended to reach the other Asimov Point first, allowing them to take up positions on top of the Asimov Point and hammer him when he tried to emerge. But they'd been too late by roughly an hour. Now, they had to make the best of a bad lot and get into an aggressive formation.

The full might of the Grand Fleet was in-system now, but if they were lucky, the enemy would think that the Grand Fleet was weaker that it actually was. Of course, if they didn't, the enemy might find a way to put together a fleet that could conceivably wreck the Grand Fleet, which would force Marius and his forces to withdraw.

"Keep the ECM running," he ordered. "Launch additional probes into the enemy ships—no need to use stealth. We want them to see the probes."

He smiled. Captain Garibaldi was trying to slip closer to the enemy ships, yet the enemy should be watching for anyone gutsy enough to try it. Launching the probes at such an extreme range might convince them that he didn't have anyone in position close enough to try to count their ships before it was too late.

But they might be careful and know to watch for turbulence anyway. There was no way for him to know.

"Admiral," Williams said, "shouldn't we be launching starfighters?"

"No point," Marius informed him cheerfully. He felt better now that the enemy fleet had finally shown itself. "It will be six hours, at least, before we come into missile range. The pilots will be getting some chow and needed rest before we launch them to do battle against the foe."

"How powerful is the enemy fleet?" Williams swallowed visibly.

"It's hard to say at this distance," Marius admitted. "The first counts weren't too precise. Of course, they're screwed."

Williams stared at him, speechless.

"In this system," Marius explained, "they have to stop us—and they *know* they have to stop us. If they fail to do so, we can cross the interstellar void to Harmony and take out Justinian's capital world and all the industries he's been building up over the years."

"Industries that our superiors wish to take intact," Williams reminded him. "They feel that adding those industrial nodes to the Federation would help make up for shortfalls elsewhere..."

Shortfalls caused by profit-seeking and a lack of basic maintenance, Marius thought coldly.

The problem wasn't with the workers, although the workers often barely had the education necessary to read a book or operate expensive and valuable equipment. The problem was with the industrialists who owned the industrial nodes instead. They pushed the limits as much as possible, trying to earn as many contracts as they could before the war came to an end. The civil war might have killed millions of people, but it had profited a handful of industrialists immensely.

"We'll do what we can," he said tightly. It was a pity there was no way to claim the industrial nodes for the Federation Navy, but that was outside his control. At least the workers would be safe. They'd be needed to run the industrial nodes once they'd been captured. "In the meantime..."

He turned back to the display, stroking his chin in the hopes of conveying an expression of deep thought. It might stop the commissioner from interrupting Marius before he was ready to outline his tactical plan. The Lombardi System had once been a worthless system with one tiny gas giant and four rocky and lifeless worlds orbiting a bright star. The Federation Navy had somehow been convinced—Marius suspected by enormous bribes—to test the latest planet-cracking antimatter bombs on the four useless worlds. The bombs had worked as specified; all four planets had been blown into clouds of asteroids, which had been mined to help supply the sector with the rare ores that were normally only found deep under a planet's surface.

Every space entertainment vid he'd seen as a young man had featured an implausible asteroid belt that forced starfighter pilots to dodge like maniacs as they raced through the asteroid field at maximum speed. Such asteroid fields were rare in real life, but the remains of the four worlds would make for tricky flying, even for super-dreadnaughts. He preferred to remain well away from the asteroids as long as possible. As well as having to deal with the asteroids themselves, there was also the possibility of ambush, as it was very difficult to differentiate a starship from an asteroid when all drives, weapons and sensors were shut down.

Fortunately, it looked as if his fleet was going to encounter the enemy fleet well below the system plane, away from the asteroids, unless the enemy decided to avoid action.

He scowled. The irony was that he *could* break loose and cross interstellar space to Harmony, but the enemy would follow him at once. If the Grand Fleet lost there, it would be the end of them, and probably would spell the end of the Federation into the bargain. On the other hand, if he smashed the enemy fleet now—especially considering that Admiral Justinian couldn't be keeping many starships in reserve—the war would be as good as won. And then the Federation could mop up the other warlords and restore peace and harmony to the universe.

"Inform the fleet that I want to slip into Formation Omega-Nine when we approach," he ordered after a long pause. "We will start by launching starfighter strikes, and then we will follow them up with the new gunboats. We'll weaken the enemy ships before we close with them."

"It sounds impressive," Williams said, "but can we win?"

"War is a democracy, Commissioner," Marius said, shrugging. "The enemy gets a vote, too."

☜∞☞

"We're too late," Caitlin said.

"It looks that way," Admiral Justinian agreed.

Caitlin was pleased to note that the admiral sounded much more confident now that he'd finally come to grips with the enemy. The Federation Navy had beaten them to Lombardi, which meant that they couldn't be allowed to leave the system. It wouldn't be an easy contest, but it would be decisive.

"Launch probes towards the enemy ships and prepare for engagement," the admiral ordered.

Caitlin followed his gaze as he turned to study the main display. The Federation Navy was too far away for them to track properly, even using gravimetric sensors. She wished, suddenly, for the StarCom trick they'd used once in Jefferson, but not even throwing money at the researchers had allowed them to build a smaller and cheaper system. FTL communications, even on a tactical level, remained largely a pipe dream.

The only good news was that the Federation Navy was definitely aiming to engage Justinian's ships, rather than heading toward Harmony or even charging at the Asimov Point and attempting to secure it. They wouldn't have to worry about the enemy refusing battle, although the darker part of her mind whispered that was the least of their worries.

On the other hand, the Federation Navy might win the coming battle...and that would be the end. For her, as well as for the fleet.

Caitlin had no illusions about her fate. She'd allowed Admiral Justinian to lead her into treason and, if the Federation won, she'd be on the wrong side of the war—the one that lost. She still believed that Admiral Justinian was right, that the Senate was corrupt and power-hungry. Eventually, the Senate itself would tear the Federation apart—but that hardly mattered. If they lost, she'd never see a universe without the Federation Senate.

"Aye, sir," she said finally. "Should we prepare a fallback plan?"

"No need," Admiral Justinian assured her. He sounded remarkably cheerful. "We live or die today."

☜∞☞

Roman felt—again—the absurd urge to whisper as the enemy fleet swept towards *Midway*. The tracks shown on the main display suggested that Justinian's fleet would pass far too close to *Midway*, close enough for Justinian's ships' passive sensors to pick up his own ship, if the opposition was lucky. The cloaking device emitted a tiny level of turbulence, after all, and the enemy might well detect their presence. And if that happened, Roman would have to be very lucky and skilful to get his ship away before the enemy blew her into dust.

"One hundred and seventeen superdreadnaughts," the sensor officer said. His voice was very low, as if he could avoid being overheard. "Seventy carriers of various designs. Two hundred heavy cruisers, including some that seem to be of a new class we haven't logged before. Four hundred destroyers, and over a thousand gunboats. That's enough firepower to punch out the defenses of pretty much any star system apart from Earth."

"Log it and transmit the data back to *Magnificent*," Roman ordered. The laser beams they used for communication were impossible to detect unless a starship accidentally crossed the beam's path, something that was very unlikely. "Are they trying to use ECM to fool us into believing that they're stronger than they actually are?"

"They have some fuzzy ECM up and running," the sensor officer said slowly. "The level of drive turbulence matches the ship count, however, which suggests that the count is fairly accurate."

Roman winced. All drive fields emitted a certain amount of gravimetric distortion, allowing a starship's class to be determined even outside active sensor range. A superdreadnaught couldn't pretend to be a destroyer without some fairly radical and expensive drive modifications, but the reverse was an easy task. A destroyer *could* pretend to be a superdreadnaught and get away with it, provided no one scanned the ship with active sensors. But an active sensor scan would reveal the truth very quickly—and reveal the ship scanning them very quickly as well.

Roman couldn't risk that, not so close to the enemy fleet.

"Update the transmission with that information," he ordered. One way or another, Admiral Drake had to have that data. "And then..."

He broke off as the tactical console sounded the alert.

"They just saw us," the tactical officer reported. "They swept us with targeting sensors and locked on to the hull."

Roman swallowed a curse. "Helm, swing us around and get us out of here. Tactical, deploy ECM drones to confuse them; set them to maximum power, now!"

Midway's internal gravity shivered as the starship spun around and accelerated away from the enemy fleet. Unlike a ponderous superdreadnaught, *Midway* could accelerate at an astonishing rate; nothing larger than a starfighter or a gunboat could hope to catch her if she had a reasonable head start.

The display sounded a second alarm as the enemy CSP rotated and came after the cruiser, but *Midway* was already well on her way. The starfighters in pursuit posed a very real threat, yet before Roman really started to worry about them, they turned and fell back to their carriers. While he wasn't sure why they had done that, Roman allowed himself a sigh of relief.

"Signal Admiral Drake," he ordered. "Transmit the final data we collected, then request orders. We can watch them from this position, or we can rejoin the other ships, whatever he wishes..."

Roman settled back into his chair. It would be hours before they heard from the admiral and, until then, Roman's duty was clear. They would continue to observe the enemy fleet from a safe distance and keep the admiral updated. The admiral would need all the data Roman's people could produce.

"Deploy a shell of drones to surround us," he added, addressing the sensor officer. "If they feel like trying to sneak up on us, I want to detect them before they get too close."

ဆဝၰ

Commissioner Williams looked dreadfully tired, the malicious part of Marius's mind noted, even though he'd convinced the commissioner to get some sleep before the battle began. In fact, it looked as if the man hadn't slept at all, something Marius remembered from his days as a very junior officer. He hadn't been able to sleep on the eve of a major battle either. The Blue Star War had cured him of that, at least.

"Commissioner," he said, by way of greeting. "We are approaching the outer edge of the engagement sphere."

He waved a hand at the display. The enemy fleet—and his own—was surrounded by a transparent holographic sphere that marked out the moment when both fleets could open fire. One advantage of fighting a civil war—although it wasn't something he was going to point out to the Senate—was that it was easy to categorize the other side's forces...although they could obviously do the same. Unless Admiral Justinian's research programs had borne fruit, there wouldn't be any real surprises in store. The Federation's own research programs, which had been given a sudden boost by the war, held out the promise of new hardware, but nothing new had really been developed.

He did have a couple of surprises up his sleeve, yet they were really just improvements on current technology. The Senate's freeze on technological development had cost the human race dearly.

"Thank you," Williams said. He sounded tired, as if he were struggling to hold back a yawn. "How long until we launch starfighters?"

"Ten minutes," Marius informed him. "We don't want to strain their life support packs too much."

He settled back to watch the final approach. The enemy ships were turning slightly, presenting their broadsides to the Federation Navy. That wasn't too surprising—indeed, he'd ordered his own ships to begin a comparable motion—and it suggested that Admiral Justinian was thinking along conventional lines. If Captain Garibaldi's estimate of their strength was accurate, Admiral Justinian was outnumbered and outgunned. The question was simple: did he understand his weakness? A weakness could be turned into a strength if used properly.

"Record," he ordered the communications officer. "Admiral Justinian, this is Admiral Drake. You are outnumbered and outgunned. In order to spare the lives of our crews who will die in the coming battle, I wish to offer you a chance to surrender. I am authorized to offer you and your senior staff a chance to go into exile, along with your families, if you surrender now. Your junior crews will receive a full pardon. You have five minutes to respond."

He looked up at Williams, who nodded. "Transmit the message," Marius ordered. "Wide-band transmission. I want them all to hear it."

ഇഌ

"Admiral, we're picking up a message," the communications officer said. "It's a wide-band transmission, direct from the enemy fleet."

"Trace the source," Admiral Justinian ordered. "Let's hear it."

They listened to the message in silence.

"Do you want to surrender?" Caitlin asked, finally. "Your family could live..."

Justinian shook his head. His backers had warned him that the Senate would make many false promises to gain victory. He wasn't blind to the use of the wide-band transmission either, or what it implied. One of his junior officers would get a free pardon if he stuck a knife between his ribs. And yet, he'd picked all of his subordinates for loyalty. They'd stick with him.

"No," he said sharply. The enemy ships were just coming into engagement range. "Launch starfighters. All batteries lock weapons on target and prepare to commence firing."

"I can't trace the source," the communications officer reported. "They relayed it from all of their ships, sir."

Justinian nodded, unsurprised. The Book said to keep the flagship's identity concealed as long as possible, after all, and it was one piece of wisdom that everyone followed. They'd learned from Admiral Parkinson ...

"Starfighters away, sir," Caitlin reported. "They're falling into attack patterns now."

"Good," Justinian said. He'd win the battle yet. "Order them to press the offensive as hard as they can. No mercy."

ഇഌ

"There was no response, sir," the communications officer reported.

"I think they're going for the old boot in the head response," Marius said and smiled. The display was sparkling with new icons as the enemy starfighters launched from their carriers, turning towards his fleet and preparing to attack. "Launching starfighters is a pretty good way of saying *fuck off.*"

He looked over at the communications officer. "Record a second message," he ordered. "This is Admiral Drake, Commanding Officer of the Grand Fleet. Your admiral has rejected a demand for his surrender, even though we offered to guarantee his personal safety and that of his subordinates. I am extending the offer to his entire fleet. Cut your drives and weapons and stand down; we will accept your surrender and treat you as honourable foes under the Articles of War. I say again; surrender now and live..."

"No response," the communications officer said after a moment.

"Are they insane?" Williams frowned.

"Perhaps they're loyal, or perhaps they don't believe us, or perhaps...they're not in a position to surrender," Marius countered. "He could have loyal troopers on the bridge of every one of those ships, enforcing his orders."

"But they'll die, too," Williams protested.

"Of course they will," Marius agreed tiredly. "It doesn't really need that many idiots to turn a brief confrontation into a raging war. Just ask the admiral who lost the Battle of Spider Bite."

He snorted at Williams' expression. Evidently the man hadn't believed that Admiral Justinian would stand and fight.

"Launch all starfighters," Marius ordered Admiral Mason, "but hold the CSP in reserve, as planned. It's time to test out what the new units can do."

"Aye, sir," the CAG said through the intercom. Admiral Mason had drilled the starfighter pilots extensively and it showed; they were responding at astonishing speed. "Permission to launch fighter strikes?"

"Granted," Marius said. "Just make sure that you avoid our engagement envelope."

He allowed himself a tight smile as the two clouds of starfighters raced away from their respective fleets. In a few moments, no less, he'd know if his gamble had paid off...or if he was about to command the greatest disaster since the Battle of Athens.

His lips twitched. After everything else, there was one important point to recall about that battle: Despite how bad the Battle of Athens had seemed at the time, the Federation Navy had actually won the day.

Chapter Forty-Three

Individually, starfighters aren't dangerous opponents to a starship. But when operating in sufficient numbers they can be deadly.
-Observations on Military Tactics, 3500 A.D.

Lombardi System, 4097

Flight Leader Joe Buckley was not a happy man.

First, he had allowed himself to be seduced into joining Admiral Justinian years ago, lured by the promise of merit-based promotion and a fairer deal for the newly-settled colonies, such as the one his family lived on. Second, the admiral had lost the opening battles of the war and had found himself condemned to a war of attrition, a war that Joe was convinced the admiral couldn't win. And finally, Joe was leading a strike force right into the teeth of enemy firepower.

Joe was no coward—no one who flew a starfighter into combat could be called a coward—but the odds were badly against the rebels, and he knew it. The sane course of action would be to fall back to Harmony or Jefferson, daring the lickspittles to do their worst.

"All wings, form up on me and prepare to kick some serious ass," he ordered. The Senate's lapdogs had formed a fairly typical formation, with the lighter units moving into position to shield their bigger brothers from oncoming starfighters and missiles. They'd probably charge in, launch their missiles and then charge out again. "Prepare to..."

He broke off in surprise. He'd expected the enemy starfighters to move out to counter his men's strike in order to engage them in a brutal dogfight. Instead, they were moving *away*, as if they intended to dogleg around his force and attack the carriers and superdreadnaughts.

For a few seconds, he puzzled over their tactics, and then decided that the scumbags thought their point defense would suffice to deal with his strike. The thought made his lips curl back into a pitiless smile. His pilots had been drilling constantly since the war had stalemated and knew everything there was to know about their craft. They were the most experienced pilots in the universe. If the sons of bitches wanted to give them a free shot at their hulls without having to worry about opposing starfighters, it was fine by Joe.

"Prepare to engage," he ordered. "On my mark...go!"

The starfighters wheeled around, rocketing at their new targets. It would have been more amusing if the enemy fleet had been turning and trying to escape, but no superdreadnaught could hope to outrun a fighter, at least in the short term. In the longer term, they'd have their chance to escape while the fighters returned to their motherships for rest and replenishment...yet oddly, they weren't even trying to run.

He frowned as his HUD illuminated with new search radars and active sensors, wondering just what the enemy had in mind. The starfighters, ducking and weaving as they were, presented an almost impossible target. Any hits to any of the ships under Joe's command would be made at least partly through sheer luck.

"Leaders, designate your targets," he ordered as the enemy ships grew closer. They still weren't engaging his ships with point defense, something that made almost no sense at all. Even if they didn't hit a single fighter, they would still scatter his formation and make it impossible for Joe and his men to launch a coordinated strike.

Superdreadnaughts flashed red in front of his eyes as he marked targets, knowing that the ugly ships couldn't hope to escape. An individual starfighter, even one armed with antimatter missiles, wasn't that dangerous, but the swarm would kill. He ignored anything smaller, knowing it could be mopped up later.

"Prepare to separate..." Joe ordered, but then broke off. "*Jesus Christ!*"

The small enemy ships, the ones he'd dismissed, opened fire. They put out an impossible rate of fire, thousands of plasma bolts, pulsar bursts and antifighter missiles blazing from their hull, straight into the teeth of Joe and his men. He and his fighter jocks were well-trained and aware of the dangers of enemy point defense, but they'd never—not even in their worst nightmares—dreamed of such a savage defense.

His formation scattered as some of his starfighters began to explode, picked off by Federation ships...*dear God*, he realized, *they must have packed the ships full of antifighter weaponry and nothing else.* The Book frowned on single-purpose ships, yet it was clear that the designer of this little stratagem, probably Admiral Drake, hadn't read The Book. Or hadn't paid attention. And it had paid off for him handsomely.

"All units, abandon current strike plan," Joe ordered. "Form up on me and hit those point defense ships!"

He desperately threw his starfighter into a series of twists and turns that should make it impossible to track and hit his craft. Even so, the assholes might score a hit on his ship by pure luck; as no one had ever built a starfighter that could carry shields, a single hit would destroy his ship. If he were lucky, he might manage to eject into space before the ship went critical.

He cursed under his breath as his formation gradually reassembled. Squadrons and wings had been scattered by the point defense storm, leaving each starfighter's assigned unit well under strength. His squadron had lost five pilots—*five* out of twelve—and few of the others were in any better shape. No wonder the enemy starfighters had refused to engage; they'd known precisely what kind of shit-storm Joe Buckley and his pilots were about to encounter.

As the fighters formed up on him, he barked orders. He knew, without consulting with the CAG, that they had to take out the new starships first. Their point defense would be even more effective against missiles, which meant that Admiral Justinian's fleet would be fighting at a severe disadvantage. On the other hand, taking the starships—the battle computers rated them as nothing more than cruisers—would cost the lives of hundreds of his pilots.

But there was no choice, he realized. One look at the overall tactical display revealed that the two fleets were too close together to avoid engagement.

"All units, designate your targets and follow me in," he ordered, hoping he sounded more confident than he felt. "Here we go..."

The starfighter tilted and dived at its target, a light cruiser spitting fire and death. His pilots followed him, carefully keeping their trajectories random, although that didn't save a dozen more of his pilots from being blown out of space in the first few seconds. Joe mourned their deaths with one part of his mind, even as another part tracked the enemy craft and silently plotted revenge. A cruiser couldn't hope to soak up the same amount of fire as a superdreadnaught, so only a handful of missiles would be needed to blow the bastard out of the sky.

He selected his missiles, flew straight for as long as he dared—about four seconds—and fired two shipkillers at his target, just before yanking his craft out of the path of a plasma bolt that would have wiped him out of existence. The enemy computers, tracking the battle as best as they could, were *good*.

He had the satisfaction of watching seven missiles strike home. The cruiser begin to disintegrate into a ball of fire and light.

And then an errant plasma bolt scored a glancing hit on his fighter's drive array. The starfighter spun out of control, right for one of the other anti-starfighter cruisers. He reached for the ejection handle and started to pull it, hoping he could get out in time.

But it was too late. He didn't even have time to curse before a second plasma bolt struck his ship, vaporizing it instantly.

ဆဏ

"Admiral, their fighter assault has been blunted," Raistlin reported. "They're preparing to launch missiles."

Marius studied the display. He'd had to use all of his clout to get the anti-starfighter cruisers into production, fighting against an entrenched design bureaucracy, but it had been worth it. Half of the enemy starfighters had been destroyed before they had a chance to launch their missiles. And he knew that Justinian's fleet would have to strip away the Grand Fleet's cruisers first, before Justinian's men could even try to take out the heavier ships. That should give Marius time to act.

"They don't have much of a choice," Marius reminded him dryly. "Send a general signal to all ships; fire at will."

Magnificent shook violently as she flushed her external racks toward the enemy ships. Every other superdreadnaught in the formation followed her lead, launching their own missiles to strike at the enemy in the wake of the starfighter assault. Hundreds of thousands of missiles flew at the enemy ships, which were grossly outnumbered by Marius Drake's own forces.

Admiral Justinian's forces returned fire at once, flushing their own external racks to prevent the missiles from being destroyed or detonated by incoming fire, adding thousands of icons to the display. It was the greatest single number of missiles in action that Marius had seen during his long career, although he'd read that some of the battles during the Inheritance Wars had involved more missiles and superdreadnaughts.

Admiral Justinian's researchers hadn't been entirely idle, he realized, as the recon drones he'd launched with the missiles started to report back. They didn't seem to have the rumored miniaturized FTL communications system that the Senate had believed—or feared—Justinian possessed, but their ECM was greatly improved. A hundred phantom superdreadnaughts and carriers shimmered into view, tricking hundreds of missiles into wasting themselves on nonexistent targets. Their ECM was actually better than the ECM the ships of the Grand Fleet carried. It wasn't good enough to fool recon drones or shipboard sensors, but it was more than good enough to fool the tiny missile seeker heads.

He allowed himself a cold smile as the missiles entered terminal engagement range and roared down on their targets. With so many missiles, he'd had the luxury of spreading his fire over every enemy superdreadnaught and carrier, capital ships already weakened by the starfighter pass that had left nine superdreadnaughts and a dozen carriers nothing more than burning debris. Justinian would have to defend all of his ships or risk losing them, which weakened his defense still further.

Marius smiled. Vaughn had taught him an old Marine proverb—*he who would be strong everywhere is strong nowhere*—and it applied, even in space warfare.

"We've taken out at least thirty ships," Raistlin reported. "Nineteen more have been badly damaged..."

The intercom blared a warning. "All hands, brace for impact; I say again, all hands..."

Magnificent shook violently, twice. Red icons flared on the damage control screen, then faded as the computers realized that the ship wasn't badly damaged.

Marius muttered a curse under his breath as he realized that other ships hadn't been so lucky. Five superdreadnaughts were gone, while *General Sampson* had been blown out of formation and was now streaming air as her crew fought desperately to save the ship. It was too late; before her captain could issue the order to abandon ship, her fusion plant blew and she vanished inside a ball of expanding plasma.

A number of the anti-starfighter cruisers had been destroyed as well, he saw. The enemy had either decided to take them out prior to hammering the superdreadnaughts or they'd simply been picked at random by missile brains. No one would ever know for sure.

"Minor damage to sections 4623G and 4878F," the damage control officer reported to the captain.

Marius overheard the transmission through the datanet and allowed himself a moment of relief. *Magnificent* could still fly and energize a beam. With the two fleets converging, they would be entering energy range shortly...and then the real slaughter would begin.

"Signal to all ships," he ordered the ops officer. "I am hereby authorizing rapid fire. I say again, rapid fire."

"Aye, sir," Raistlin said.

A dull thunder could be heard, even within the flag bridge, as the superdreadnaught switched to rapid fire, launching missiles in sprint mode. Justinian's men would find it much harder to intercept them before they reached their targets, although the targeting wouldn't be so accurate.

"Sir, Admiral Mason is asking for orders," Raistlin informed him.

"Tell him to concentrate on the enemy carriers," Marius said with a nod. "The superdreadnaughts are to continue firing on the enemy superdreadnaughts."

Most of Admiral Justinian's carriers had been taken out, leaving Justinian with only a handful of ships that were able to rearm their starfighters. Once the rest of them were taken out, the enemy starfighters would be deprived of a base. They'd be fucked, completely. And then they'd have no choice, but to surrender—or die.

He kept his face impassive as two of his superdreadnaughts exploded in quick succession. And then *Admiral Rodney* died when a missile pulsed through her shields, speared through one of her fusion plants and detonated the antimatter warheads in her magazines. *Admiral Yamamoto* staggered out of formation, seemingly unhurt, but something had blown inside her hull; she vaporized. He barely noticed the death of the battlecruiser *Triumph* or the heavy cruiser *Kimball Kingston*. When superdreadnaughts were dying, each one taking over three thousand trained spacers and officers with her, the lighter ships seemed like small change.

"Arunika," he said, keying his wristcom, "have you located the enemy flagship?"

"Negative," Arunika said. "The enemy have their datanet locked tight."

Marius doubted that it would be easy to locate Justinian's flagship, so they'd just have to hope they destroyed her soon. The only proof he had that the enemy flagship was still intact was that their formation hadn't shown any signs of panic or disintegration. Even under the best of circumstances, transfer of command wasn't easy—and the middle of a battle was hardly the best of circumstances. The chaos that had followed Admiral Parkinson's death bore mute witness to that.

"Understood," Marius said, breaking the connection. He looked over at Raistlin, who was obviously waiting for orders. "Tell all ships to continue firing."

ഇരുഗ

Rampant Lion screamed as another missile slammed against her shields and raw energy burned through to her hull. The admiral's flagship had led a charmed life, almost, until now. With the escorting carriers gone and most of the smaller ships destroyed in the crossfire, the remaining superdreadnaughts were almost alone.

Caitlin looked over at Admiral Justinian. She wondered if he realized that the battle was lost. Charging into the teeth of the enemy formation, energy weapons blazing, would inflict vast damage, but it would also lead to the complete destruction of his fleet.

"Pull us back from the enemy fleet," Admiral Justinian ordered finally. His voice held the bitter tinge of defeat. "Order the remaining starfighters to cover our retreat."

Caitlin knew that the admiral now realized that his fleet had been savaged and that he wouldn't have much chance to extract even the surviving units from the disaster, and that was good. But the math didn't add up. They would have to alter course and head to the mass limit, as they'd never make it back to the Asimov Point, and flee to Harmony with a much larger fleet snapping at their heels. This did not seem like sound strategy, especially as it reminded her of the Battle of Jefferson...

except back then, they'd forced the Federation lickspittles to flee. Now the boot was on the other foot and she didn't like it.

The superdreadnaught rocked again as another missile slammed through her shields. A second later, a dull *thud* echoed through the ship, a harbinger of doom. Caitlin didn't need the brief report from damage control to know that they'd just lost one of the drive compartments. The superdreadnaught could no longer accelerate to her full speed, which left her helplessly trapped within enemy missile range. It wouldn't be long before the enemy fleet blew the cripple into plasma, or attempted to force her to surrender.

And Admiral Justinian could not be allowed to fall into enemy hands.

"Admiral," she said, checking her console, "the *Apollo* is within range for a transfer..."

"I'm going to die with my ship," the admiral said firmly. "I will not leave her."

"Admiral, you are the face of the movement," Caitlin said sharply. "If you die here, the cause ends. You *have* to survive. Once you leave this ship, the remaining cripples can surrender in good conscience while the intact ships escape to the mass limit and vanish."

Her logic was impeccable, but Admiral Justinian continued to hesitate.

Caitlin couldn't wait any longer. Hoping he'd forgive her for this someday, she drew her stunner from her belt and stunned him before he could object. He'd be furious when he awoke, perhaps even order her execution, but at least he'd be alive.

And the cause wouldn't die with him.

"Take him down to the shuttlebay and order them to transfer him to the *Apollo*," she ordered the admiral's personal guards curtly. Surprisingly, they didn't shoot her; they simply nodded as one, then grabbed the admiral and got him out of there.

Caitlin sat down in the command chair with her stunner on her lap and watched the battle. Nearly half of the remaining ships were too badly crippled to hope of escape, even if the enemy stopped firing and let them go. And that wasn't going to happen.

Her console buzzed.

"This is Shuttlebay One," Lieutenant Gomez said. "The admiral is on his way."

Caitlin watched the tiny shuttle as it fled towards the *Apollo*, praying that no marauding starfighter would intercept and destroy the shuttle. They were in luck. The battlecruiser picked up the shuttle, then turned to flee.

Godspeed, admiral, she thought. *And pull a rabbit out of your hat once you get to Harmony. You're going to need it.*

Caitlin keyed her console and started to issue orders, all in the admiral's name. The intact ships were to go to full military power and attempt to escape, while the cripples would cover them as long as possible before surrendering.

And then a second direct hit on her ship took out the remaining drive units, leaving the ship a drifting wreck. She watched the tactical display, eyes fixed on the Apollo, silently urging it to escape the system. Once she saw it safely beyond the mass limit, she turned to her communications officer.

"Raise the Federation Admiral. Inform him that we would like to surrender."

Chapter Forty-Four

It is a curious artefact, caused by the idiosyncratic warp and weft of the Asimov Point Chains, that your enemy may be on the end of a shorter communications and supply line than your own. Consider, for example, the case of the Buckhannon Campaign during the Inheritance Wars. It took the Federation months to send a message from one front to another; the Colonial Alliance could do it in a week.
-Observations on Military Tactics, 3500 A.D.

Lombardi/Harmony System, 4097

Captain Caitlin Bowery was a very small woman, Marius thought, as she was escorted into his presence by two hulking Marine guards. Indeed, she looked almost child-like, although that meant nothing in a universe where people could alter themselves to fit any desired form. There was no mistaking the intelligence and determination in her eyes, however, nor the trepidation in her body language. The Marines hadn't cuffed her, but she obviously knew she was a prisoner.

"Welcome aboard," Marius said. He'd invited Vaughn and Tiffany to the meeting, while Williams had insisted on coming along. "I am sorry that we must meet under such circumstances."

"So am I," Caitlin said. She had a rich, warm voice that reminded him, just a little, of his sister. He felt an odd surge of warmth towards her. "Please allow me to congratulate you on your victory."

He heard the bitterness in her tone and nodded.

"I understand from your crew"—of course, Vaughn's Marines had interrogated the superdreadnaught's bridge crew—"that Admiral Justinian made his escape, with a little help from you. You'll be pleased to know that his battlecruiser and a number of other ships made it over the mass limit and vanished."

"I made sure he'd get away," Caitlin said. Her voice hardened. "What—exactly— are you going to do with my crews?"

Marius frowned. It was clear that she believed that her life was already lost to her. Why?

"We won't do anything to the vast majority of your crewmen," he said. He was tempted to point out that they were, in fact, *Admiral Justinian's* crewmen, but decided that would be pointless. "They will be held until the end of the war, then most of them can be discharged from the service. There would be little point in prosecuting them. As Admiral Justinian refrained from war crimes, or acts forbidden by the Articles of War..."

"Apart from mutiny and barratry, of course," Caitlin pointed out sourly.

"I believe that there is little point in holding them for trial by a war crimes tribunal," Marius concluded, ignoring the interruption. "They will be required to give a full account of their service under Admiral Justinian. If we discover that they have lied to us, we may reopen the question of their future standing, but I do not think they will be exiled."

He looked into her quiet brown eyes, wondering what she was thinking. "As for you, I would like you to perform a service for us. If you carry out our request, you will be granted exile or, better yet, a full pardon."

Caitlin made a show of studying his face.

"And what if I believe that you don't have the authority to make such an offer?"

"I have a document from the Senate granting me wide leeway in dealing with prisoners," he said with a smile. "I *can* certainly recommend that they pardon you, but I can certainly offer internal exile as opposed to immediate execution. I can show you the document if you like..."

"No, thank you," Caitlin said. She hesitated. "What do you want me to do?"

Marius keyed his console. A star chart shimmered into existence.

"Admiral Justinian and his remaining ships have fled to Harmony, we believe," he said. He watched her closely, but she had her expression under tight control. Doctor Dunwoody had confirmed that she had security implants that would probably kill her if she was interrogated under truth drugs or torture. She'd probably been given them when she had become Admiral Justinian's flag captain. "We want to put an end to this as quickly as possible..."

"You want me to talk him into surrendering," Caitlin corrected flatly. "What makes you think he will listen to the person who booted him off his own ship?"

"Let me put it like this," Marius said. "The Senate wants this to end quickly. If we can convince Justinian to surrender, the war will be over and normal trade can resume. We could take out Harmony and end the war that way, but that would cause thousands of additional, unnecessary deaths. I am empowered to make Justinian the same offer as I made you; if he surrenders, he will receive exile instead of death—and hundreds of thousands of people will live."

"And you're just going to let me go back to him?" Caitlin stared at him.

"We'll give you your parole," Marius said. "If you swear not to take up arms against us, we will release you when we enter the Harmony System." He frowned. "But should we catch you fighting us in the future, we'll execute you on the spot."

"I can't promise anything," Caitlin said, finally.

Marius nodded, impatiently. He'd expected that.

"But if you wish me to try to convince him to surrender, I will do so," Caitlin finished.

"That suits me," Marius said. He looked up at the guards. "Escort Captain Bowery to her quarters; keep her under guard."

"Aye, sir," the Marine said.

The hatch had barely closed behind the women and her guards when Williams started to froth at the mouth.

"Admiral," he said, so quickly that the words started to blur together, "the Senate will not be happy at the thought of letting the bastard go free."

"Exile is not the same as going free," Vaughn rumbled, his deep voice echoing through the compartment. "He will remain on one world for the rest of his life under permanent supervision by security forces. It may be a comfortable prison, but it will still be a prison. He won't be allowed to leave, ever."

"The fact remains," Williams began, "that you are offering him..."

"Enough," Marius said quietly. "Our objective is to put an end to the war as soon as possible. If offering Justinian exile instead of a bullet in the back of the head succeeds in ending the war, we will accept it and be glad. And besides, this way we take all of Harmony's industrial plants and workers—enough to please your masters, surely?"

Williams flushed. "Admiral..."

"We'll discuss it later," Marius promised. "Now, I have to contact Captain Garibaldi and inform him that he's going to play messenger boy again."

Williams took the hint and stormed out of the compartment.

Marius and Vaughn exchanged a long look, then Vaughn and Tiffany followed the Political Commissioner through the hatch. Marius allowed himself a tired smile, keyed his console and issued orders to *Midway*, and then headed over to check on the reports from the replenishment teams. The fleet train had entered the system after the battle was won and had immediately started reloading ships and arsenals. Marius had warned them that they might be departing for Harmony within a day, so they were now trying to determine how many ships could be repaired on the spot, and how many needed to be sent back to a shipyard.

His intercom buzzed forty minutes later.

"Admiral, Captain Garibaldi is requesting a personal meeting," Raistlin said. There was no hint in his voice that he knew the captain personally, although Marius privately suspected that his young aide was jealous. His father's influence had seen him appointed to a prestigious post that was dangerous, but without the chance to win glory. "He says that it's urgent."

"That doesn't sound good," Marius replied. "Did he say what it was about?"

"No, sir," Raistlin said. "He specified that it was for your ears only."

"Right," Marius said. "Tell him to come aboard. I'll see him in thirty minutes."

∞ લ

Roman had lost his parents before he reached his majority and, like all parentless RockRats, had been sent to live with relatives. His uncle had taken him in and tried to fill the void in Roman's life, although the old man hadn't been in the best of states to take care of a teenager. Despite that, the young Roman had dreaded having to face him when he knew that he was in trouble.

He felt that way now. It was his duty to face the admiral, to tell him how they could approach Admiral Justinian, and yet...it might be the last act of Roman's career.

The hatch opened in front of him and he stepped into the admiral's quarters. A glowing star chart caught his attention at once, but he looked away from it to see the admiral sitting behind his desk. He didn't look forgiving.

Part of Roman quailed, yet he kept walking until he was in front of the desk. He snapped a perfect salute.

"At ease," Admiral Drake growled. "Take a seat. What was so important that you insisted on a personal meeting?"

Roman sat down and pressed his hands tightly together to keep them from shaking. "I saw your orders, sir," he said. "You want us to take Captain Bowery back to Harmony and get her to convince Admiral Justinian to surrender..."

"Yes," Admiral Drake said. It was not a question.

"It may not prove convincing," Roman said. "He may feel that she has been subverted, or threatened, or maybe have even changed her coat. Is he going to be willing to listen to her?"

"I have no one else to send," Admiral Drake said dryly.

"That isn't true, sir," Roman said. "There *is* one other person he'll listen to."

Admiral Drake looked up. "And do you have a secret connection with him that passed unnoticed for five years?"

"No, sir," Roman said. "I have his daughter."

There was a long, uneasy silence.

"I think you'd better start at the beginning," Admiral Drake said, carefully. "And I suggest that you make it extremely good."

Roman outlined the full story, starting with the discovery of the wreck of the *Harmonious Repose* and ending with his decision to keep Henrietta confined on *Midway* rather than hand her over to the tender mercies of the Senate. Admiral Drake listened, his face showing no expression, as Roman explained that Admiral Justinian would be bound to listen to his daughter. The mere fact that she was still alive, without having been executed by the Senate or killed by pirates, would be very convincing. It would be a gesture of good faith.

"You know, captain," Admiral Drake said, when Roman had finished, "I cannot decide if I should promote you, or send you up for court martial."

Roman kept his mouth shut, figuring that anything he said now would only get him in further trouble.

"You disobeyed orders that came directly from the Senate," Admiral Drake said, as if he were building a list of charges. "You kept someone prisoner without reporting her presence to higher authority. You wasted Federation Navy resources on looking after the prisoner...should I go on?"

"No, sir," Roman said.

"On the other hand, you're quite right," Admiral Drake continued.

Roman breathed a sigh of relief.

"His daughter would be a much more effective peace envoy than his flag captain," Drake said. "So...I guess I'll just have to thank you for your foresight and, in the interests of balance, cancel *both* the promotion and the court martial."

"Thank you, sir," Roman said.

"Which doesn't mean," Admiral Drake said in a suspiciously pleasant voice, "that you are to go and do it again. I'm going to have to shield you from the commissioners and come up with some bullshit story about how we captured her. *Do not* put me in a position like that again, do you understand me?"

"Yes, sir," Roman said.

"Return to your ship," Admiral Drake ordered. "Prepare for the mission; brief the admiral's daughter and make sure she knows what's expected of her. And captain?" Roman looked up nervously.

"Good work."

৪০ঞ্ছ

Marius watched the hatch close behind Captain Garibaldi before he broke down in helpless laughter. The sheer *audacity* of capturing the enemy's daughter and keeping her prisoner, without telling *anyone*...he chuckled again while shaking his head. Captain Garibaldi's luck still held strong. Who knows? Perhaps he could end the war without any more fighting.

Still chuckling, he turned back to his console and started to update the operations chart. The fleet needed to move within a day so they'd be in position to support *Midway* if Admiral Justinian turned nasty, and there was too much work to do.

He almost missed Tiffany's entry into the room; only the smell of her perfume alerted him to her presence. He turned to greet her, but she ran into his arms before he'd gotten out a single syllable. Then, she kissed him...his arms went reflexively around her, and for a time, nothing else mattered. Finally they broke for air.

"Do you think Admiral Justinian will surrender?" she wondered. "I mean...he doesn't have any chance of victory, does he?"

"I don't think so," Marius said, answering the second question first. "Actually, the worst thing he could do from my perspective is to flee into interstellar space and head to the Rim. We'd never be sure we'd got him. And if he stumbled across an Outsider world and offered to share technology, he could create a whole new threat to the Federation."

The reports he'd seen from ONI tended to confirm his pessimistic feelings about the Outsiders. *Something* was clearly up beyond the Rim, something that threatened the entire Federation. And here they were, wrapped up in a squalid little civil war.

"Marius, what are you thinking?" his wife asked.

"If he doesn't surrender, we can take out Harmony and then spend a year mopping up," he said slowly. "And if he *does*, the war is over and all we have to do is deal with the minor warlords."

"Yeah," Tiffany said. Her voice sharpened, a legacy of her time in High Society. "Tell me something."

"Sure," Marius replied.

"You're saying that Admiral Justinian has lost the war. But does *he* know that?"

"He should," Marius said. "No professional admiral worth his salt could still believe that he had any chance at ultimate victory in his position."

৪০ঞ্ছ

Admiral Justinian had spent the trip from Lombardi to Harmony considering the virtues of suicide. He'd expected to die in battle, not to have his closest ally stun him and dump him into a shuttle so he could escape, even though it had saved his life. It had taken a day to get rid of the headache that had burned through his skull, and another day to overcome the depression that followed. Afterward, he'd been able to make some plans, although the truth was that he had no idea what to do. Harmony was strongly held, but most of his fleet had been crushed. He doubted the Federation would give him time to rebuild.

With no other choice, he plunged himself into issuing orders as soon as the *Apollo* returned to normal space, just outside the Harmony mass limit. As the battlecruiser plunged farther into the system, he was gratified to see his subordinates working on defense and repairing the damaged ships. Best of all, Harmony operated a large starfighter plant and could turn out new starfighters and gunboats on very short notice. Training up the pilots was harder—especially as the training course would have to be updated to account for the damned antifighter cruisers—but if he had a few weeks, he'd be able to give a good account of himself.

He was still contemplating it when a courier boat transited the Jefferson Asimov Point and transmitted an urgent message for him personally. As soon as he saw the recording, he called a meeting of his subordinates.

৪৩০৪৪

"These recordings were taken by a scout ship I dispatched to Bester," he said before displaying them on the main screen. Some of his subordinates had been quietly muttering about making contact with the Federation—with or without their command—and seeing if they could cut a deal. "The news is not good."

His subordinates watched the dispatch in silence. They saw how the Federation Navy had secured Bester and then departed up the Asimov Chain to Sphinx, followed by the Internal Security operations on the planet's surface. The bloody massacre of the surrendered personnel and the brutal crushing of the early uprisings against Federation control played out in front of them, a mocking reminder that they'd be fools to trust any promise made by the Senate.

He knew Caitlin hadn't known about it when she'd surrendered. She might be dead now.

"Some of you have been considering that it might be best to try to negotiate with the Federation," he said flatly.

No one bothered to dispute it.

"As you can see, the Federation took the surrenders, promised good treatment... and then slaughtered the surrendered personnel in cold blood. That was no accident, my friends; that was cold-blooded murder. The Federation killed men it had promised to spare, along with their families and children!"

He looked around the compartment, his eyes moving from face to face.

"That is the fate that is in store for us when they arrive," he pointed out. "If we surrender, they will kill us and our families once we are helpless. That's why I will *not* surrender to the Federation Navy, not now, not ever. And if any of you want to surrender, you can move to Jefferson and wait for them to capture you."

No one said anything at all.

Admiral Justinian took a deep breath.

"We may not be able to stop them from killing us," he concluded, "but by God, we can make them *hurt!*"

Chapter Forty-Five

An ambush at point-blank range is nearly impossible to survive.
-Observations on Military Tactics, 3500 A.D.

Harmony System, 4097

"Crossing the mass limit now, sir," the helmsman said.

"Transmit our IFF codes and the admiral's message," Roman ordered. "Notify me the moment he replies."

"Aye, aye, sir," the communications officer said.

Roman felt exposed as *Midway* flew deeper into the Harmony System, even though he knew the remainder of the Grand Fleet would be coming in behind him. Still, if Admiral Justinian decided to fight to the last, *Midway* would be almost completely on her own.

Four hours ticked by as they advanced into the system.

Roman ordered the launch of stealth recon drones, which would allow them to develop an outline of the system. What they picked up wasn't encouraging. As the Sector Capital, Harmony had been heavily industrialized before the war, but Admiral Justinian's men had clearly been busy. Harmony's current level of industry now ranked with Kennedy or Roosevelt; given a few more years it might match Earth. Worse yet, the planet itself was heavily defended. That wasn't a surprise, but Roman had still been hoping for a bit less in the way of fortifications.

Roman knew it would be difficult for the Grand Fleet to take the system by force.

"Captain, I am picking up a message," the communications officer said, finally. "They're welcoming us to the system and requesting that we rendezvous with their fleet so the admiral's representatives can be transferred to meet with the admiral."

Roman nodded slowly. There was no hope of a two-way conversation at this distance and no real hope of convincing Admiral Justinian to board his ship instead. He consoled himself by thinking, *At least Admiral Drake's wife isn't in danger this time.*

Besides, even if it was a trap, it would only close around *Midway*. The remainder of the Grand Fleet was too far out of range.

"Transmit back an acknowledgement," he said. The feeling of being exposed was growing stronger. The IFF signal they were pulsing out would allow them to be tracked by passive sensors alone, which meant that anyone lying in wait would be able to target his ship without any betraying emissions. "Inform them that we will rendezvous with their fleet in—" he checked his console "—two hours and thirty minutes."

He felt no calmer when *Midway* finally slowed near Justinian's fleet. It wasn't a particularly large fleet, but it still possessed more than enough firepower to reduce *Midway* to atoms. Nine superdreadnaughts—two of them clearly damaged—five battlecruisers and twenty-seven smaller ships, surrounded by a cloud of starfighters. It wasn't an insignificant force, not on the pre-war scale, but the Grand Fleet would destroy it in short order if it had the chance. Roman was mildly surprised that the

admiral hadn't insisted on meeting on or near Harmony itself—as they had anticipated—and had been preparing to argue that point when it had been rendered moot.
He tried to tell himself that was a good thing.

"Hold us here," he ordered. They were well within shuttle range, but at the absolute edge of missile range. It wasn't a particularly trusting position, but then he wasn't
a particularly trusting man. He keyed his console. "Shuttlebay One, are you ready to
fly?"

"Aye, sir," the shuttlebay operator reported. "Captain—ah, Commodore—Bowery
has been checked out on the shuttle, and is ready to launch."

"Good," Roman said. "Clear her for departure."

He settled back in his command chair as the shuttle departed, heading towards
one of the undamaged superdreadnaughts. One of his crew had suggested rigging
an antimatter bomb in the shuttle and detonating it if negotiations broke down,
but Admiral Drake had vetoed the suggestion, as that would be seen as an attack
on Admiral Justinian under a flag of truce. Roman had accepted the rebuke with ill
grace.

"Captain, she has reached the admiral's ship," the sensor officer reported.

Roman nodded.

"And now, we wait," he said. He looked over at the tactical officer. "Keep us at
condition-one. If they start moving to attack, I want to be out of here before they get
into point-blank range."

ജന്മ

The squad of guards who met them at the shuttlebay were brisk, formal and very
efficient. Caitlin and Henrietta were both strip-searched and scanned using the most
advanced sensor technology, while the shuttle itself was practically dismantled by
shuttle techs. Once their identities had been confirmed and the shuttle itself had
been pronounced clean, they were escorted to the superdreadnaught's flag bridge.
The cry of astonishment from the admiral when he saw his daughter made everything worthwhile.

"I thought you were dead," the admiral said, hugging his daughter tightly. "I
thought..."

Caitlin wasn't too surprised. He'd had years to regret sending his daughter to
marry a stranger, in hopes of binding two warlords together. At least she was alive.

He gave Caitlin a hug as well, and then settled back in his command chair, all
business.

"All right," he said. "Admiral Drake's message said that you were peace envoys.
What do you have to say for yourself?"

Caitlin had known Admiral Justinian for nearly twenty years. There was something in his voice that was odd. Soft...and dangerous.

"Admiral Drake is willing to offer you and your senior personnel, myself included,
internal exile if you surrender without further bloodshed," Caitlin told him. "Junior
personnel will not be persecuted by the Federation."

His face was completely expressionless. That was not a good sign.

"The same offer, in other words, that they made to Bester," Admiral Justinian said. His voice was very cold. "The same offer they wantonly betrayed."

He keyed his console and the report from Bester played. Colonel Scudder must have wanted to send a very clear message to the population, so he'd broadcast the executions live on every news and communications channel. An entire star system had seen the Federation not only go back on its sworn word, but slaughter small children who hadn't committed treason.

Caitlin felt sick. *Had Admiral Drake known about it?* she asked herself. *Had the Senate ordered it, against Drake's wishes?* There was no way for her to know.

"Surrender is not an option," Admiral Justinian said.

Caitlin found it impossible to disagree, even though she'd given her parole. If Admiral Drake had lied to her...where did that leave her? She wrestled with her conscience for a long moment, trying to convince herself that she could rightfully break her sworn word. An oath breaker was owed no consideration by others, she told herself.

"Captain Garibaldi took me in," Henrietta said. "He protected me at risk of his own life—and career ..."

Justinian rounded on his daughter.

"I'm sure he's a perfectly good man," he snapped. "But the Senate ordered the deaths of everyone who surrendered on Bester! Why the hell should we surrender when all we face is certain death?"

He turned and met Caitlin's eyes. "We will lose the coming battle," he said, "but at least we will make them hurt."

There was no time to say a word before the admiral keyed his console.

"All units, this is the admiral," he said. "Open fire!"

ೞೞ

There was very little warning. "Captain, they just locked active sensors onto our hull," the sensor officer reported. "They're..."

"Incoming fire," the tactical officer snapped. "Multiple missile launches; I say again, multiple missile launches!"

"Helm, get us out of here," Roman snapped, as *Midway* spun in space. There was little point in returning fire against the behemoths targeting the tiny cruiser, but they could still launch ECM drones that would confuse the incoming missiles. Or perhaps it wouldn't. They were still broadcasting their IFF right across the system. "Launch countermeasures and cut the IFF!"

The math didn't add up, he realized. They'd been at extreme range when the enemy opened fire, but they weren't able to get away from it before the missiles struck home. Admiral Justinian had fired enough missiles to destroy the ship several times over.

"Bring up the point defense and engage as soon as the enemy missiles enter range," he ordered. "Launch shipkillers as emergency counter-missile defenses."

Midway shivered as she launched the shipkillers towards the enemy missiles. The bean-counters would complain loudly when they saw the cost, but he had a dark suspicion that their concerns were about to be rendered moot. The ship was humming around him as her drive built up power, yet it wasn't going to be enough to escape. The point defense went to rapid fire as the missiles came closer and closer, winnowing their ranks, but too many of them were going to get through the defenses.

"Reroute all power to shields," he ordered grimly. It risked overloading the shield generators and total collapse, but there was no other choice. "Signal Admiral Drake—do a complete dump. He has to know what happened here."

They almost made it, but a handful of missiles entered terminal attack range and went to sprint mode. Four missiles struck *Midway*, one after the other, slamming the ship into an uncontrolled spin through space. A fifth slammed home a moment later and, just for a second, the artificial gravity flickered and reversed. Roman had a moment where he saw the ceiling coming up to meet him, and then the world went black...

⁎⌘

The tactical officer looked up, sharply. "They fired on *Midway!*"

Marius stared, unable to believe his eyes. He'd sent Captain Bowery to Admiral Justinian with a fair offer—more than fair—and the man had opened fire. Why?

What was going through Justinian's head? He had to know he couldn't beat the Grand Fleet; hell, considering Justinian's current position, he couldn't even fall back to Harmony before the Grand Fleet entered missile range. The remains of his fleet were going to be crushed...it wasn't as if Marius could show them mercy, not now.

He shivered. The admiral had even thrown away the life of his daughter.

"All units, accelerate to flank speed," he ordered. He felt as through a stranger was speaking through his mouth, someone hard and cold, willing to do whatever it took to win. "Prepare to engage the enemy."

"Aye, sir," Raistlin said.

Magnificent shivered slightly as her drive pushed her forward, heading right towards the enemy formation. Admiral Justinian wasn't even trying to run! He was coming towards them, as if he hoped he could bull his way into energy range.

"Admiral Mason is requesting permission to launch starfighters, sir," Raistlin told him.

"Granted," Marius said. It was overkill, but he didn't care. The object was to win; he'd worry about the level of force used later. "Status of *Midway?*"

Raistlin checked the readings. "Adrift, total power failure," he said. He sucked in a breath. "But everyone's alive, their communication officer has reported; she's a very lucky ship."

"She has a very lucky captain," Marius countered. "Order a destroyer to be detached for SAR duties; I want everyone pulled off that ship, if possible."

He watched grimly as the two fleets came into missile range. It might not be possible to pull *anyone* off *Midway*, not if the internal compensators had failed. Indeed, the only proof that they had *some* power left was that the ship was still intact. Losing the magnetic containment fields that held the antimatter would have blown the ship into dust. He pushed that thought to the back of his mind and concentrated on the oncoming fleet. Admiral Justinian didn't seem to be launching his own starfighters on strike missions; instead, he seemed to be focusing on antifighter defense and keeping Marius's starfighters off his back.

"It seems he refused to surrender, admiral," Williams said. The Political Commissioner sounded as if he were terrified, but was trying to hide it. "I thought you promised that he would surrender."

Marius bit down the response that came to mind. It wouldn't have helped the situation to swear at the commissioner.

"I know," he said finally. "He can't win. Even if he closes to energy range without getting his ships shot from under him, he still can't win. So why is he throwing his life away?"

He keyed his console as the enemy superdreadnaughts came into range. "Open fire," he ordered.

"Aye, aye, sir," the tactical officer said.

Magnificent shuddered as she flushed her external racks, followed by the slightly heavier sound of the first barrage from her internal tubes. Combined with the other ships in the Grand Fleet, hundreds of thousands of missiles were roaring toward their targets.

Admiral Justinian's barrage—launched at the same moment—was pitiful in comparison. He'd selected a couple of Marius's superdreadnaughts for special attention...which was odd. He was leaving the remainder of Marius's superdreadnaughts unattended.

"Admiral, twelve new ships just lit off their drives," the tactical officer reported.

Marius felt his blood run cold. Had he just led his men into a trap?

"They read out as medium freighters, pulling military-grade acceleration," the tactical officer continued. "They're heading right towards the edge of our formation."

Marius blinked, puzzled. Freighters were not warships, no matter how many weapons and defense systems were crammed into their hulls. They couldn't maneuver worth a damn and a single hit could be devastating. It seemed a pointless exercise, except Admiral Justinian wasn't stupid. Using the freighters suggested that Justinian had more in mind than just distracting Marius from the battle.

"Order the *Longsword* to switch her fire to the lead freighter," Marius said. From the sensor readings, it was evident that someone had also crammed a military-grade shield generator and fusion core into the freighters. No one would waste those resources if they didn't think they could get something out of it. "I want..."

The display flashed white, just for a second.

"Sir, the lead freighter blew up," Raistlin reported. He sounded astonished.

Marius didn't blame him for a second.

"Sir...she was crammed with antimatter. If she'd hit a superdreadnaught, or if the starfighters had engaged her..."

"They would have been blown to dust," Marius concluded. *Kamikazes!* In hindsight, an obvious trick. "Order the destroyer screen to engage the freighters at long range; take them out before they take us out."

There was another benefit from the antimatter-crammed freighters, he realized quickly, feeling numb. As soon as they exploded, they disrupted the datanet that bound his ships together. In the seconds it took to repair the datanet, enemy missiles were able to slip through the point defense. They slammed against his ships.

Two superdreadnaughts vanished in balls of fire, followed by a battlecruiser that had been targeted for some unknown reason. Admiral Justinian's force was being torn apart, and yet he was still continuing the offensive. He was mad.

He had to be mad.

"Switch to rapid fire," Marius ordered, as the enemy ships came closer. They were still fighting savagely, even though Justinian was down to four superdreadnaughts and only a handful of smaller craft. All of his ships had taken heavy damage. "Take them out!"

€SGS

"The freighters have all been destroyed, admiral," the tactical officer reported.

"A shame it wasn't Parkinson in command," Admiral Justinian commented.

Caitlin barely heard him. Her training had been thorough, but she'd never seen such a savage battle in her entire career, even during a direct Asimov Point assault. There was no rhyme or reason any longer, just sheer pointless slaughter. Caitlin looked over at the admiral's daughter and realized that Henrietta was terrified. The poor girl had never been in a real battle.

"Parkinson would have let us get the freighters into ramming position before he opened fire," Justinian concluded amiably, as if there was nothing wrong at all in his corner of the universe.

"Yes, sir," Caitlin agreed automatically. She recalled herself to duty. "Sir, this is madness!"

"I know," Admiral Justinian said. "What other choice do we have?"

The entire superdreadnaught shuddered as a missile slammed against her hull. The damage control teams had effectively given up on repairing the outer compartments, knowing that they would all be blown to atoms before too long. She was still firing, but Caitlin doubted that they would be able to maintain a solid rate of fire for much longer. "What other choice do we have?"

"Surrender to a bunch of murderers?" He waved a hand at the display.

Caitlin opened her mouth, and then closed it again without speaking. The admiral was right. They couldn't surrender, not when it meant their certain deaths. The only thing they could do was keep firing, and pray for a miracle.

"Father," Henrietta said, "they saved my life..."

"Be quiet," Justinian snapped.

Caitlin watched numbly as one of their remaining superdreadnaughts vanished from the display, followed quickly by one of the smaller ships. The enemy switched their fire to other targets and, suddenly, the admiral's ship was targeted heavily. New damage started to mount as enemy missiles slashed into the hull. The shields were failing...

"Admiral..." she began.

And then the hammer of God struck the ship. There was a brief moment of fire and pain, and then nothing.

ဆဦ

"Admiral, the last of the enemy ships is trying to surrender," Raistlin reported. Marius stared at him.

"They've cut weapons and drives, sir," he told him. "They're only maintaining their shields."

"Hold fire," Marius ordered. The darker part of his mind told him to finish the job, to obliterate the madmen who'd fought an impossible battle and lost. But he refused to listen to it. "Toby, launch a Marine Recon unit to secure the damaged ship."

"Aye, sir," Vaughn said.

"And send a message to Harmony," Marius added. "Inform them that we have won the battle and that we require their immediate surrender in order to end further bloodshed."

"Aye, sir," Raistlin said.

It took an hour to receive Harmony's unconditional surrender. Marius spent the time checking on his ships. The savage battle had inflicted far more damage than it should have, leaving too many of his ships out of commission for the time being. At least they'd have access to Harmony's shipyards, once the surrender had been finalized.

He was still mulling over the possibilities when Vaughn called him and informed him that he had sent a file to his private database. Marius opened the file and watched in horror as Bester was purged of unreliable elements, men and women who had surrendered—along with their families. He'd promised them safety—and now they were dead.

Gritting his teeth, he looked over at Williams, who was surveying the reports from the teams that had been dispatched to secure the shipyards, and felt cold rage pouring through his heart. No wonder Admiral Justinian had refused to surrender. He had had good reason not to trust Marius's promises...

Damn you, he thought angrily. He wasn't sure if he was angry at the commissioner, at the Senate, or at himself for not realizing that leaving someone like Scudder in charge was asking for trouble in the first place. *What are you going to do next?*

Chapter Forty-Six

Messages from the Senate have absolute priority on the Interstellar Communications Network. Everyone else has to pay. The advantages this gives the Senate in reacting to events on the Rim cannot be underestimated.
-An Irreverent Guide to the Federation, 4000 A.D.

Earth/Harmony System, 4098
The war had disrupted parts of the ICN. Some sections were delayed because the message had to be conveyed across the interstellar gulf by a starship. But Earth received news of the Battle of Harmony and the death of Admiral Justinian within three weeks of the battle, just in time for New Year's Day.

Grand Senator Rupert McGillivray found himself considering it as the Senate Committee met at his mansion for the seventh time since the war began. President Yang had made a brief speech to the Senate—and Earth's news networks—about the end of the war, but everyone knew that his speech had been little more than platitudes. The *real* decisions would be made in private, well away from the media and the cheering crowds. They did so love a hero, Rupert told himself dryly, yet their cheers wouldn't last. The mob was always fickle and heedless of any long-term concerns. The Senators couldn't allow themselves that luxury.

He poured wine into three glasses, passed one to each of his guests. "Lady and Gentlemen, I give you the New Year," he said, holding his glass high. They echoed him and sipped their wine, the finest champagne from Gaul. "May it be long and peaceful."

"One would hope so," Grand Senator The Honorable Carlton Brockington said. He put his glass down and frowned. "There's no point in dissembling, not here. The war is won. We no longer need Admiral Drake."

"We may need him to deal with the remaining warlords," Rupert pointed out mildly. "None of them pose a threat on the same scale as Admiral Justinian, but they do need to be crushed before their example spreads any further."

"They're small fry," Brockington said disdainfully. "Now that we have assured ourselves of the loyalty of the Federation Navy, we can crush them one by one without his help. Let's face it; he has a fleet that is loyal to him, and a reputation with the mob." He snorted. "He's a threat merely by existing. We need to remove him now."

"We have our contingency plans," Grand Senator Alison Wallisch said, nodding in agreement. "We can activate them now."

Rupert kept his face expressionless.

"There is no need to hurry," he reminded them. "He is going to spend months repairing his ships and securing the remains of Admiral Justinian's little empire. We don't need to order his death now."

"This is *precisely* the time to order his death," Brockington said firmly. "The longer we leave him alive, the greater the chance he will decide to act independently."

"And there was the little matter of his formal complaint," Alison added. "I don't know how that got out into the public sphere, but the mob is up in arms about it. The man is *dangerous.*"

Rupert shrugged. He *did* know how Admiral Drake's formal complaint had reached the media; the Brotherhood had slipped it to one of the better reporters in the system. Admiral Drake had demanded that the people responsible for the Bester Massacre be relieved of command and tried for mass murder, reminding the Senate that they'd given their word that there would be no recriminations or retributions. If they were punished harshly, he'd added, it might put the brakes on the insurgency developing within the sector. The Senators had not appreciated his candor, not least because the people responsible for the slaughter had been appointed by the Senate. It had been, Rupert considered, a brilliant public relations move.

"Very well," he said finally. "May I offer a suggestion?"

They looked at him warily.

"If we send the execution order through the ICN, there is a good chance that the message will be intercepted and decrypted by someone loyal to Admiral Drake," Rupert pointed out. "I suggest sending the message on a courier boat, one of the fast pickets we use to scout new systems. That would maintain security, and there would be no warning to the target."

"We need to move fast," Brockington said. "Besides, the codewords for authorizing the operation are...not likely to arouse suspicion. The ICN will get the message there faster than any starship."

"And besides, we will be able to deny all knowledge of an ICN message," Alison added, nodding. "A starship is far more likely to raise eyebrows."

Rupert wondered, absently, what planet she was actually on, before pushing the matter aside. They'd refused his advice, which meant that he had to act quickly before all hell broke loose.

Once they'd settled in for the night, he accessed his private communications channel and ordered his personal starship prepared for immediate departure. He'd been telling everyone that he intended to take a long vacation once the war was over, so no one would question his departure, at least not quickly enough to do any good. And once he'd left the Solar System, he would run for Harmony. He wouldn't beat the message there unless he was very lucky, but at least he'd be able to make contact with Admiral Drake.

If the admiral survived...

It was a gamble, he knew, but there was no other choice. The Federation was in a state of flux, where everything could be changed and rebuilt. Once the window of opportunity closed, however, the Senate would rule unchecked. The Brotherhood had been planning for this moment for a very long time. Everything rested on him now. Him...and Admiral Drake.

ಬುಡ

Marius was waiting to hear how the Senate had reacted to his demand that they relieve, arrest and hang Colonel Scudder. But so far, they'd sent back nothing of substance.

Since they'd told him nothing, he'd had all the prisoners moved to a deserted island on Harmony on his own personal recognizance, and Vaughn had assigned loyal Marines to guard them—ostensibly from escape, but in actuality, to keep the Internal Security troops from murdering them outright. The Internal Security troops had quite predictably protested, as they were supposed to guard the captured prisoners, but Marius had ignored them.

There wouldn't be another massacre on his watch.

Besides, while he waited, he'd had better things to do.

"I suppose there hasn't been any response from the Senate yet?" Tiffany asked.

Marius, lying back on the bed, thought that she'd never looked more beautiful as she walked around. Her long red hair fell down around her breasts, leaving her nipples winking at him as she moved. He wasn't entirely sure if he loved her—after all, she was a great many years younger than him and certain to outlive him regardless of how long the marriage lasted—but being with her made a quite a few things worthwhile. Besides, she was a lot smarter than he'd expected.

"Just worthless platitudes," he said. "Did your father send you anything in the mail?"

"Nothing," Tiffany said. Her father rarely sent her anything. "He did say that he was proud of me for risking my life and that he thinks I should go back to Earth."

Marius shrugged. "And are you going to go back to Earth?"

"Not if I can avoid it," Tiffany told him. "High Society is rather boring at the best of times...and it won't be very exciting after all this."

"The less exciting, the better," Marius said seriously.

He pulled himself to his feet, kissed her on the forehead, and stepped into the fresher. "I have a staff meeting in forty minutes, love. Are you going to attend?"

Tiffany stepped into the fresher with him, a delightful surprise.

"Of course," she said, as she pressed against him. "You'd only mess it all up without me."

෨෬

The courier drone popped out of the Asimov Point and immediately uploaded its messages to the relay station. There was a brief moment as the relay station's automated computers checked the message headers against its list of authorized senders, and then it started to relay the message across the system to Harmony. Once the message reached the planet, it was inserted into the military datanet and uploaded to *Magnificent*. It appeared inside Blake Raistlin's inbox seven weeks after it was sent from Earth.

The message itself was unlikely to attract attention. It was nothing more than a statement that there was going to be a wedding in the family and the recipient was invited to attend. The reader, however, knew what the message signified. It was time to move.

He swallowed his concern and fear—he'd never wanted to be an assassin—picked up the weapon he'd been given years ago, and checked it carefully. It was still in working order.

Part of him wanted to call off the mission, to retreat from the battlefield, but he knew his duty. He'd been promised a reward for his work, something he desperately wanted. All he had to do was carry out one specific task.

Kill Admiral Drake.

࿇

Roman fought his way to awareness through a dizzying wave of pain and disorientation that threatened to drag him back into the darkness. He could hear voices as he awoke, voices that seemed oddly familiar and yet completely unrecognizable. His memory started to return as he opened his eyes, reminding him that his ship was in desperate danger when he'd blacked out...

"Report," he croaked. His mouth felt impossibly dry. "The ship...?"

"Lie back," another voice said. It was firm and very feminine. "You're on the *Magnificent*..."

His vision stabilized, revealing a young woman wearing a doctor's uniform.

"You took a nasty blow to the head," she said. "Luckily, your helmet cushioned most of the blow and medical crews were able to preserve you long enough for the recovery team to get you into a stasis pod. You should be fine, but lie still."

"My ship," Roman said. His voice felt clearer, even though he could hear a distant roaring in his ears. It seemed to be almost impossible to form a coherent thought. "What's happened to my ship?"

The doctor didn't answer him. "I told you to lie still," she said, firmly.

Her voice didn't sound as though she would brook argument. Besides, a doctor had authority to relieve a captain on medical grounds. And he wasn't even on his ship!

"Your ship is fine," she finally told him.

That was a lie; Roman *knew* it was a lie. His ship had to have been badly damaged, perhaps even destroyed. His survival didn't prove anything. The crew could have pulled him off the ship if their sickbay was overwhelmed. And yet, it was growing harder to think...

"I'm putting you back under," the doctor said urgently.

He opened his mouth to argue, but it was impossible to speak. The words wouldn't come to his lips.

She pressed something against his neck and there was a brief, almost inaudible hiss. "Relax."

There was a brief spark of pain, almost unnoticeable against the pain in his head, and then nothing.

࿇

"The Harmony Shipyard has been most helpful," Commodore Yang concluded. "We have successfully repaired most of the damaged ships without needing to leave the system. A handful of starships will require longer periods of repair work, but I believe they can be towed to Penganga Shipyard or repaired here, as the admiral wishes."

Marius considered it. Using Harmony's shipyards was a two-edged sword. It was quicker than returning to a Federation Navy shipyard and it did give the yard dogs a chance to work for the Federation—and therefore contribute to rebuilding the local economy—but if someone happened to want to sabotage the ship, they'd have a clear shot. The Marines had secured the shipyard, of course, but they weren't experts in repairing starships. They might well miss something, and if they did, the results would be disastrous.

Still, he wanted the entire fleet repaired as quickly as possible. There were other warlords out there...and then there was the ever-present threat of the Outsiders.

"I believe that we can take the risk of repairing the ships here," he said. "Just ensure that the fleet train's repair men work with them. It should make sabotage harder." He smiled and turned to Vaughn. "Toby?"

"There has been little change from my last report," Vaughn said. The Marine looked tired, but confident. "My Marines have occupied the orbitals and various locations on the planet's surface. There has been no sign of overt resistance beyond some grumbling and street protests, which we have ignored as long as they stayed peaceful. The bad news is that we still haven't been able to locate the heavy weapons that vanished from planet-side arsenals prior to our arrival in the system, nor have we been able to locate the Planetary Guard personnel who were wiped from the records. I believe they may be preparing for an insurgency."

"Which is why your orders, admiral, are thoroughly unwise," Williams said. The political commissioner raised the same issue at every status meeting. "Your refusal to allow the Internal Security troopers to land on the planet is contributing to their willingness to defy us, and is placing your men at risk."

Marius kept a tight grip on his temper. After hearing about Bester, he'd unilaterally banned the Internal Security troops from Harmony and ordered them to remain in their transports. Williams had protested, loudly, but the authority Marius had received from the Senate—if looked at in the right way—authorized him to take command of the Internal Security contingent if necessary. Which might have been the only thing that had prevented an immediate explosion.

"That decision is mine to take, and I took it," he said, his tone brooking no argument. He purposefully looked away from the commissioner. "Is there any other business?"

There was none, thankfully. Marius hated status meetings and tried to avoid them where possible, but it was hard to find a workable excuse when they were simply orbiting Harmony and attempting to secure and rebuild an entire sector. At least it would be over soon; once the remainder of Admiral Justinian's little empire had been secured, the Grand Fleet could move on to deal with another warlord. They'd always have work to do.

"Dismissed," he said, as he rose to his feet. "Toby, I need a word..."

Something was wrong. Time seemed to be slowing around him, as if it were pressing against his head. He saw Blake Raistlin pull a tiny weapon from his jacket and point it at him. The weapon fired ...

... And then, Vaughn was covering him, protecting him with his own body.

Marius snapped out of it as Vaughn was blown back into him, knocking him to the floor. And then Raistlin fired again.

A horrific burning sensation flared down his left arm, just before Admiral Mason tackled Raistlin and knocked the weapon to the ground.

Marius tried to pull himself to his feet, but his left arm wasn't working.

"Medic," Admiral Mason shouted.

It was hard to hear him through the haze of pain that burned through his mind. His implants were dulling the pain, yet he could still feel it...and his left arm was completely useless.

"Get a medic here, right now!" Mason yelled urgently.

Someone helped him to his feet. Marius struggled to focus his mind, almost stumbling over something on the deck. It took him minutes to realize that he'd stumbled over his best friend's body. Vaughn's expression made it appear as if he'd died in horrific agony. The treacherous bastard Raistlin must have used a punch disruptor, Marius realized. It was so hard to think properly, but the effects were unmistakable...and Vaughn had taken the full brunt of the blast. Every cell in his body had been ripped open. The shock alone would have killed him, even if the pain hadn't.

Toby, Marius thought drunkenly. *I'll drink to your memory ...*

An injector was pressed against his neck; cold numbness spread through his body. It brought clarity of a sort, a dull realization of what had happened. Blake Raistlin's family hadn't wanted him out of the firing line to keep him safe, he realized. Instead, they'd set him up as an assassin.

That meant that the Senate's response to his demand that Colonel Scudder be punished was clear—they'd ordered his death. And Williams had been in on it. No doubt the Internal Security troops were in on it, too.

"Admiral, stay still," one of the medics said.

Tiffany walked toward him, but was held back by one of the medics. He knew she must be in shock. Tears were running down her lovely face. She looked almost like an angel in that moment, his angel.

"Admiral..." someone said, he didn't care who.

"Admiral Mason," Marius said. His voice felt thick and unwieldy in his ears. "Arrest the commissioners and their troops. Arrest them all and seal them away from everyone else, quickly!"

"You can't," Williams said desperately. The commissioner must have thought he was immune. "You can't..."

One of the Marines hit him with a stun-rod and he collapsed to the deck.

I need to promote that man, Marius thought, before a second injector pressed against his neck.

As he crashed into the painful darkness, he thought desperately. *Most of the Internal Security troopers should be on their transports. If Admiral Mason could hold them there, they couldn't take over his ships. There was still a chance...*

For what?

No matter how far he looked, he could only see one answer.

Chapter Forty-Seven

A council of war can only be convened at the instruction of a fleet commander. Asking for consensus can only mean one thing: a drastic change in orders.
-Observations on the Navy, 3987

Harmony System/In Transit, 4098
  The next time Roman Garibaldi awoke, he felt much better. Elf was at his bedside, reading a datapad and trying to look nonchalant, something that set alarm bells ringing in Roman's head. The doctor checked his vital signs, pressed a sensor to the top of his head, and then grudgingly admitted that Roman could get up.
  "You're cleared for duty, captain," he said crossly. "I'd think that you'd be better off with some more bed rest, but it's all hands on deck here."
  Roman blinked as the doctor stalked off. "Elf," he said urgently, "the ship?"
  "Beyond repair," Elf said. Her gaze was sympathetic.
  Roman flinched.
  "The gravity flickered for a second," she explained, "long enough to cripple most of the crew and inflict severe damage on the ship's internal systems. Then the compensators blew. We're damn lucky that we had already lost speed, or we would all have been killed. Hell, we're even luckier that the containment fields held, or we'd all be playing harps by now."
  Roman swallowed hard. *Midway* had been *his*, in a way that no other ship had been. He'd been her commander, Master under God, and his crew had been his family and friends. Losing her hurt, like losing a first lover.
  He was relieved to hear, as Elf continued to brief him, that most of the crew had survived, but their family was gone. The admiral would reassign them all, even Roman, to other ships, breaking them up. He felt hot tears begin to form at the corner of his eyes and blinked them away angrily. It couldn't be helped, he told himself. Somehow, it failed to be convincing.
  "That's not the worst of it," Elf continued. "Your old friend, Blake Raistlin, tried to assassinate the admiral."
  "He was never my friend," he corrected automatically. Then he stared at her. "He did what?"
  "He tried to assassinate the admiral," Elf repeated. "Raistlin injured him and killed General Vaughn, but no one else was harmed. They even took Raistlin alive. The admiral—ah, Admiral Mason—ordered all the Internal Security troopers locked down, but some of them put up a fight. You're lucky that you were completely out of it."
  She rubbed a new scar on her chin. How had she gotten that?
  "And the political commissioners had to be removed as well," she added. "One of them proved to be surprisingly good with a knife."
  "I have to get up," Roman said. He pushed back the blanket and sat up, swinging his legs over the side of the bunk. His uniform had been neatly folded and left in

the small cabinet beside the medical bed. He couldn't help noticing that someone had removed the golden badge that signified starship command, an ominous sign for the future. If Blake Raistlin had been the assassin, was *Roman*—and everyone else who had graduated with him—a suspect? Even though none of them had truly liked Raistlin?

His legs felt rubbery, but he held himself upright by force of will and started to dress.

"Tell me something," Elf said as he pulled on his jacket. "What do you intend to do?"

"I'm sure the admiral will want me to do something," Roman said. It was a weak answer because he had no idea what his duties were. Maybe there was a starship that needed a new commander. "I can't lie about doing nothing when there's work to be done."

೮ಾೞ

Doctor Yu was, in Marius's opinion, one of the best doctors in the Federation Navy. He'd actually joined late in life, after discovering that private practice didn't really suit him, and he brought over a hundred years worth of experience to the post. The doctor didn't look encouraging, however, as he checked Marius's arm. The disruptor had wreaked havoc on his cells, and the entire arm was dead.

"I'm afraid there's nothing we can do," he said after a thorough check-up. The dead arm had been wrapped in a cast, but he'd warned Marius that the cast was purely a temporary measure. "It's going to have to come off and be replaced, either with a vat-grown arm or a prosthetic."

Marius winced. It was possible to grow lost parts of one's body—as long as there was a single DNA sample to use as a template—in a vat, but it wouldn't feel quite the same as the rest of his body. He'd known men who'd had replacements and then always been uncomfortable with their new organs. And yet, he didn't want to have an artificial arm. It wouldn't suit him, either.

"Right," he said. "How long until I can get a new arm?"

"It'll take a month to grow it, admiral." Yu frowned. "Once it's ready, it will have to be grafted onto the stump—we'll remove the dead arm first, of course—and then it will take you several months to get used to using it again. I could fit you with an artificial arm now, but that would *still* take some getting used to."

Marius nodded slowly. "I don't have the time right now," he said.

The doctor nodded, sombre. News of the attempted assassination had flashed through the entire fleet.

"Start growing the new arm," Marius ordered, "and I'll have it fitted when I have the time."

"As you wish, admiral," the doctor said. "Come back later today for another check-up. I want to be sure that the cellular disruption isn't spreading."

Marius nodded, then stalked out of sickbay. Outside, he met the two Marines who had been assigned to him as a personal guard and Major Papillae, Vaughn's second-in-command. She would have assumed his position at once—the Marine chain of command was designed for rapid shifts—and yet seeing her felt unpleasant, as if he were betraying his oldest friend. Vaughn would have laughed at the thought, but then...Vaughn was dead.

He still couldn't get used to that.

"Admiral," she said formally. Her voice was brisk and efficient. "I completed the ceremonies for General Vaughn. His body has been stored in a stasis tube until it can be returned to his homeworld, and I read his will. He wished you to have this." She passed him a small packet.

Marius opened it, wishing he were anywhere else and that this wasn't really happening. It was impossible to believe that a presence so vital as Toby Vaughn was dead, even though Marius had seen Vaughn die before his eyes. Die to protect him, no less. Inside, there was an old chemical-propelled projectile weapon and a handful of clips.

Marius pulled it out in surprise and saw the golden globe and anchor that decorated the weapon. Traditionally, every Marine who made it to command rank was presented with such a weapon—a reminder of the different national services that had been blended into the Federation Marines—and was expected to keep it with him at all times. Vaughn had once joked that any Marine officer who had to fire the weapon in action was in serious danger, because projectile weapons didn't have anything like the range and firepower of modern plasma cannons. But he wouldn't have given up the weapon willingly, not until he died.

Having it passed on to him, Marius knew, was a great honor. And he would have given it up in an instant if it brought his friend back to him.

Papillae allowed him a moment to contemplate the weapon, and then cleared her throat. "The remainder of the Internal Security shitheads"—the news of the massacre at Bester had also spread through the fleet—"are in their transports, apart from a handful who were killed resisting arrest. The transports themselves are in lockdown, and I have a company of Marines on each of them, ensuring that the bastards cannot escape. We had to separate some of the political commissioners because they were in danger from the troopers."

"Good," Marius said. He strapped the weapon to his belt and looked up at her. "And the interrogation?"

"Raistlin spilled his guts," Papillae said. "That was lucky, admiral, as we discovered—just in time—that he'd been given suicide implants. He shouldn't have had them at all until he was promoted to captain, but luckily someone thought to check before we injected him with truth drugs. He received his orders directly from the Senate itself. His father put him in place just after the Battle of Boskone, waiting until he received orders to assassinate you."

Marius nodded numbly. If Blake Raistlin had been just a little smarter, he could have assassinated Marius—and Tiffany too, perhaps—in his quarters and made his escape; instead, he'd tried to assassinate him in public. And now, Marius knew who to blame.

"The worrying news is that you weren't the only target," Papillae continued. "Raistlin had orders to purge your entire command staff, whereupon the political commissioners would assume command and allow Internal Security troopers to secure the remaining ships. My guess is that he intended to slaughter everyone at the briefing, and chose his weapon accordingly."

"So we were *all* meant to die," Marius said. He looked up at her. "Do you know what this means, Major?"

Papillae said nothing.

"It means that I have no choice but to follow the path Admiral Justinian blazed, and declare war against the Senate. That, major, is what it means!"

She simply looked at him gravely, but made no attempt to stop him from doing anything. After a beat, he nodded at her in silent thanks.

He keyed his wristcom.

"All staff, this is the admiral," he said. "Report to Briefing Compartment Two in thirty minutes. We have a lot of work to do."

ৎড়৩

Tiffany gave him a hug as soon as he entered the compartment, while the other officers rose to their feet in a gesture of respect. Part of Marius wondered if *Tiffany* had been given orders to assassinate him as well, before he pushed that thought aside. Tiffany was too independent-minded to follow orders from Earth. Even so, Marius hated the paranoia. He'd pulled together an excellent command team, fought beside them...and now it was impossible to know who to trust. He silently damned Blake Raistlin under his breath, remembering the excellent report he'd planned to submit, one that recommended Raistlin for promotion and command of his own ship. Who could he trust?

The irony wasn't lost on him. Admiral Justinian had spent ten years preparing for his rebellion, and he'd still failed. Marius had had bare hours since he'd been attacked and Vaughn had been killed. His plans, such as they were, remained unformed. All he could do was to focus on one issue at a time.

"Gentlemen and ladies, please be seated," he ordered. "For those of you who haven't seen the recordings of Raistlin's interrogation, the Senate ordered the assassination—the assassination of me *and* my entire command staff. You were *all* targets. You were all marked for death."

He felt, rather than heard, a dull rumble of anger spreading through the room. Good; if they were angry, they weren't scared or hesitant.

"This leaves us with a choice," he continued. "Returning to the Federation is not an option, nor is staying here. We can head to the Rim and beyond, hoping that we will remain undiscovered when the Senate sets its dogs upon our trail, or we can head to Earth and...remove the Senate."

There was a long pause. No one said anything; they appeared to be holding their breath.

"Let's be honest, shall we? The Senate has become a threat to the entire Federation. Their corruption helped fuel this rebellion, just as it fuels countless hopeless rebellions right across the galaxy. Their mishandling of Admiral Justinian led to the disaster at First Jefferson and made it almost inevitable that others would rebel against the Federation, too. Their willingness to slaughter their enemies—and the families of their enemies—led to bloody slaughter, for no one dared surrender. And you have all seen the report from Bester. The Senate ordered the slaughter of all of the senior staff, including innocent women and children.

"And they tried to kill us all," he added. "I won't pretend that I don't take that personally."

He paused, gauging their reactions. Some looked personally affronted, others—including Captain Garibaldi—were shocked. They'd believed the Senate would keep its promises. How wrong they'd been, Marius noted. They deserved better leaders.

"I swore an oath to the Federation. I swore that I would uphold the fundamental unity of the human race, the unity that has made us masters of half the galaxy. The Senators swear a similar oath when they are sworn into power—and look what they've done. They have forced people into a position where they can either fight or die—why shouldn't they fight? The unity of the human race, so expensively restored in the Inheritance Wars, is coming apart at the seams. And the Senate is the driving force behind the collapse.

"We all know how they rape the colonies for raw materials and taxes they desperately need to pay for their social programs. We all know how they back some industrialists at the expense of others, ensuring that their companies are favored while their competitors are ruthlessly crushed. I think we have all seen the effect this has on our ships, and our operational readiness. We all know how they planned to appoint Federation Governors to the worlds we captured and strip them bare of everything they have, turning the people into corporate slaves. We all know what their refusal to challenge pirates and the Outsiders has meant—along the Rim, millions die while the Senate does nothing. I submit to you that the Senate must be removed."

There was no disagreement. Part of him found that terrifying.

"Admiral Justinian wanted supreme power for himself. I don't. I want to remove the Senate and put something better in its place, something more representative of humanity as a whole, something that will be harder to corrupt and turn into a reactionary force for rebellion. If this be treason, let us make the most of it!"

He took a long breath. "And yes, they *will* call it treason, particularly if we fail."

There were some chuckles.

"I believe that my duty must be to remove the Senate," he said finally. "If any of you do not wish to join me, I will understand. You can wait on Harmony for news of the result. I won't be a vindictive bastard about it, but I do need to know your answers now."

"Respectfully suggest, sir," Admiral Mason said, "that you stop insulting us and start preparing for the march on Earth."

Marius allowed himself to relax as chuckles ran around the room. His command staff were all pragmatists and, more importantly, they all knew that they were already on a death list. They could run to the Rim, but even that wouldn't guarantee their safety. If the Senate won, they'd never be able to return home.

"I will make the same offer to the crewmen," he said firmly. "You can do the same to your subordinates. There is to be no recrimination if someone chooses to sit this out, understand? Have them transfer themselves to the shuttlebays and send them down to the planet."

"Aye, sir," Admiral Mason said.

"I want the Grand Fleet ready to depart in twelve hours," Marius ordered. "Make sure the fleet train is loaded with supplies from Harmony"—one other advantage of a civil war was that both sides used the same weapons—"and is ready to support us as we advance. If we are lucky, we won't have to fight our way into Boskone and the other worlds we set up as nodal defense points..."

"One point," Papillae said. "We have been unable to confirm that there isn't a message already winging its way back to Earth with a warning. The Senate may not know that we're coming, or they might suspect the worst."

"You can't pick out an encrypted message?" Admiral Mason snorted.

"The message might be something innocuous," Papillae said. "Something that would pass unremarked. The message that activated Raistlin didn't say anything directly."

"We'll assume that we're heading into hostile space," Marius said with a nod. "We leave in twelve hours. Until then...dismissed!"

৪১ ඟ

Roman had asked to see the admiral as soon as possible. He was surprised when he was called in only an hour after he sent the message, and even more surprised to see the two Marines guarding the admiral's hatch. It was a break with tradition and, worse, it suggested that the Admiral no longer trusted his crew. The Marines searched him thoroughly but gently, and then allowed him to enter. The admiral himself was seated on the sofa, his left arm wrapped in a cast.

"Admiral," he began. Words abruptly failed him. "I'm glad to see that you're all right..."

"Save it," Admiral Drake said. He looked up. Roman was surprised to see a new intensity burning in the admiral's eyes. "I assume you want a new ship?"

"Yes, sir," Roman said. He'd checked on *Midway* and had to admit that the report had been accurate. It would be cheaper to build a new assault cruiser than to repair a badly damaged one. She'd be sent to the breakers and her hull metal would be used to produce new ships. "Why did he open fire?"

"The Senate decided, in their infinite wisdom, to massacre all the prisoners we took on Bester," Admiral Drake explained. His bitter voice shocked Roman to the core. "Admiral Justinian decided to go out in a blaze of glory."

He frowned. "I don't have a ship that needs a commander at the moment," he added.

Roman couldn't keep the disappointment off his face.

"I do need an aide, however. If you take the post now, I'll give you a ship as soon as possible."

"Yes, sir," Roman said. He was surprised that the admiral wanted him—he'd graduated with Raistlin years ago, not that they'd ever been friends—but he knew better than to refuse. "When do I take up my duties?"

"Now," Admiral Drake said. "We're leaving in twelve hours and I want every ship that can fly and energize a beam going with us."

ଚ୍ଚେ୪

Twelve hours later, Marius stood on the command deck and watched as the Grand Fleet slid into motion, heading towards the Jefferson Asimov Point. He would have found it hard to describe his feelings at the moment, knowing that he was rebelling against the Senate, crossing his own personal Rubicon.

One way or another, the die had been cast.

Chapter Forty-Eight

The shortest route between two points isn't always a straight line when considering Asimov Points. A spacer knows that doubling back on his course can sometimes get him to his destination quicker.
-Observations on the Navy, 3987

In Transit/Earth, 4098

The *Prince George*-class space yacht had originally been designed for ten passengers and a crew of five. After the Brotherhood had the ship quietly refurbished in a military shipyard, the yacht had the speed of a destroyer and could be operated, if necessary, by a single person. Rupert had kept three of his most trusted retainers on the ship, but he'd dismissed the rest of the crew, even the woman who ran the galley. He'd had to eat packaged meals for the entire trip. After four weeks, even the pleasures of watching entertainment dramas he'd always meant to watch had worn off, and he was cursing his own mistake at not bringing along someone to share his bed.

But there hadn't been much choice, or much time to arrange the desperate flight to Harmony. He'd hoped that there would be more time, either to send a warning message ahead of the assassination order, or for the Brotherhood to make other preparations on Earth, but they'd underestimated the Senate's determination to act quickly. The assassination order was now winging its way to Harmony—no, it would have got there by now. And if Admiral Drake had been assassinated, the Brotherhood's long-term plan would have fallen apart.

Silently, he cursed the two Factions under his breath. Who would have dreamed that Conservatives and Socialists could ever find themselves in agreement, if for radically different reasons? Perhaps the threat of being overthrown had made them panic and react quickly, even though there was no immediate threat.

He brooded on it as the ship went through another Asimov Point—using his Senator's codes to gain immediate access—and wondered, again, what he would find when he reached Harmony.

They were midway through the Java System when the alert sounded.

"Senator," Captain Windsor reported, "we are picking up military starships transiting the Asimov Point ahead of us."

For a long moment, Rupert felt a flash of panic. His worst nightmare was discovering that the Senate had realized that he wasn't going off on vacation and sent another message ahead of him, ordering his arrest or execution. The Senate would not, normally, have issued a kill-order for a Senator, but these were far from normal times.

His second thought was that Admiral Drake was ahead of him, and was bringing his fleet to Earth. As far as he knew—and he had had access to all of the Federation Navy's reports—there wasn't any other large fleet ahead of him. Admiral Drake's force should have been the only one in the area.

"Hail them," he ordered. "Transmit my Senate codes, and request permission to dock."

There was a long pause.

"They're declining permission," Windsor reported. "They're ordering us to vacate this space, or they will open fire."

Rupert's lips twitched. After everything, after his escape from Earth, dying at the hands of Admiral Drake would be the final irony.

"Send back another message," he said. "One word: Arunika."

There was a second pause.

"They are sending a Marine shuttle to dock with us and pick you up," Windsor said. "I'm afraid that we cannot evade them, or escape either."

Rupert bowed his head. At his age, there was no longer any point in fearing death.

"I understand, captain," he said, "Follow their orders. I suspect that our lives are no longer in our hands."

ℝ℞

The transit from Harmony to Jefferson had been smooth. Marius had had Admiral Justinian's forts secured by his Marines prior to the assassination attempt, so no one had tried to bar the fleet's passage through the system. Admiral Justinian hadn't built any further fortifications until the Asimov Point leading to Boskone, but they had been secured as well. The real danger had come when they'd passed into the Boskone System, yet the Senate hadn't thought to issue orders barring the Grand Fleet's passage. Besides, Marius had selected the system's defenders personally and they had been horrified to learn about the assassination attempt.

He'd continued onward until they reached the Java System. The commander of the system's defenses had balked until Marius had offered him the flat choice between surrender and being blasted out of the way. With only two fortresses, the commander had swallowed his pride and allowed his fortresses to be secured and occupied. Marius's fleet hadn't waited for the operation to be complete before they'd started heading towards the next Asimov Point. And then his sensors had picked up the yacht.

"Order the Senator brought onboard," he ordered as soon as the cryptic second message had arrived. "Once he is aboard, resume course for Earth."

He'd plotted out the course while preparing to leave Harmony. The shortest way to Earth led to the Gateway, but the Gateway defenders would definitely balk at allowing the fleet into the system without a fight, and the Grand Fleet would be bled white if it tried to break in by force. Admiral Justinian had had the right idea in crossing interstellar space to reach Earth. The key to the Solar System wasn't Earth itself, but Home Fleet. Admiral Justinian had believed that he could take Earth before Home Fleet could intervene. Marius knew better.

He looked up as the Marines escorted Grand Senator Rupert McGillivray into his quarters. Marius hoped they hadn't been too rough, although he couldn't blame them for feeling paranoid due to the assassination attempt. The silver ring on the Senator's hand caught his attention at once, informing him that the Senator was a member of the Brotherhood. A dark suspicion flared through his mind, which he pushed aside and waved the Senator to a chair.

"Welcome onboard," he said tartly. "What happened?"

McGillivray made no pretense at being puzzled by the question. "The Senate decided that you were surplus to requirements," he said flatly. "I came to warn you."

Marius snorted. "You're a month too late," he pointed out. "You should have sent a message."

"The Senate had locked out all communications to the Grand Fleet," McGillivray explained. "I had hoped that I would be able to send you a message from Terra Nova, but they'd locked it out by then. I could only hope that you survived the assassination attempt."

"Right," Marius said. The Senator's story was reasonably plausible. "And now that you know that I am still alive—and driving towards Earth—why are you here?"

McGillivray took a breath.

"Can I ask, first, what your intentions are towards Earth?"

Marius studied him for a long moment, reminding himself not to underestimate the Senator. McGillivray was older than Marius, older than Professor Kratman; the last survivor of the Imperialist Faction in the Senate. No one lived so long without gaining a vast amount of experience...and no one would remain in the Senate without knowing precisely where the bodies were buried. Old he might be, but McGillivray had lost none of his intelligence or knowledge.

"I intend to remove the Senate and create a new representative government," Marius said flatly. There was no harm in the Senator knowing that. "Why are *you* here?"

"You need to do more than that," McGillivray said. "You need to declare yourself Emperor."

"Are you insane?" Marius stared at him.

"No," McGillivray said. "Are you?"

"I don't want to be Emperor," Marius said after a long pause. "Why do you, a Senator, want me to become Emperor?"

"I shall explain," McGillivray said. "The bonds of loyalty that held the Federation together have been fraying for a long time. The Inheritance Wars inflicted a colossal level of trauma on us, because the Colonial Alliance wanted to be independent of the Federation and that could not be allowed. The Blue Star War damaged the Federation's sense of unity. And now Admiral Justinian and the other warlords formed their own little kingdoms."

He shook his head. "Very few people have any loyalty to the Senate. They certainly don't want to go out and die for the Senate. And who can blame them when it is increasingly obvious that the Senate is a closed world, dominated by a political elite that not only doesn't care about the people, but is willing to actively harm even those who have worked for them to get what it wants? There is no longer any connection between the ruled and the rulers. We need, somehow, to reawaken the bonds of loyalty."

"We need someone who can serve as the focus of that loyalty. Someone who is respected and—more importantly—trusted by the population. Someone who is canny enough to know what needs to be done, and is willing to cut through the knots that prevent it from being done. How many people do you think have that kind of base to work on? You—just you."

"You—the Brotherhood—promoted me on Earth," Marius pointed out dispassionately. "Did you have this outcome in mind from the start?"

"And throughout the Core Worlds," McGillivray agreed. "We hoped that the rebellious warlords would force the Federation Senate to change or die. They refused to change and, partly because of your heroic efforts, survived the war. If they don't leave power, soon, they will try to lock down the entire Federation. All the fault lines running through our society will shatter, and the Federation will come apart. The result will be chaos on a galactic scale."

"And with the Outsiders moving in, the Federation will be vulnerable," Marius said. He couldn't deny the Senator's logic, yet...he didn't want to be emperor. Perhaps he could hold the position for ten years, and then put it down. "I think..."

"Consider Earth," McGillivray said, interrupting him. "Why is the population so high? Answer: the Senate feeds the population, allowing Earth to survive with a much greater population than any other planet. What can we do about this? Answer: we can put contraceptives in the state-supplied foods, cutting the birth rate. Why aren't we doing this? Because the program is blocked in the Senate every time it is suggested."

Marius had been listening patiently. Now he leaned forward.

"How do they benefit from keeping the birth rate high?"

"They can skim money off the programs to take care of the kids," McGillivray explained.

He took a breath. "The Conservative Faction wants things to remain exactly as they are," he said. "They won't support change for that reason alone. The Socialists believe that they have a duty to help and support people—whether the people actually want it or not—and insist on providing free food and other social programs to the poor. Both factions will block any attempt to actually deal with the problem—and both factions are unwilling to admit that the problem is likely to explode, sooner rather than later.

"We need an emperor to cut through the Gordian knot before the entire Federation comes apart," he concluded. "Whatever support we can give you—or I, as a Grand Senator, can give you—is yours. All you have to do is declare yourself emperor and take Earth. The Federation will give you a chance."

"And what if my decision to declare myself emperor isn't accepted?" Marius frowned.

"Then we're no worse off than before," McGillivray pointed out. "The political lassitude that allows the Senate to rule without challenge—to push through useless or actively harmful programs—will work in your favor. You will have a chance, admiral, and I believe that you will succeed."

"If we win," Marius pointed out. "We're not going to challenge the Gateway, Senator, but we will have to face Home Fleet. Or has the Brotherhood subverted the fleet?"

"No," McGillivray admitted. "We have some people with the fleet, but not enough to subvert it."

Marius wasn't surprised. If the Brotherhood *had* managed to subvert Home Fleet, they wouldn't have needed Marius and the Grand Fleet. It wasn't good news, however; Home Fleet didn't have the experience of the Grand Fleet, but it possessed nearly as much firepower and, if combined with Earth's orbital defenses, would be a very tough customer.

Marius nodded.

"I understand," he said. He looked into the Senator's eyes. "I have to consult with my wife and...advisors. The Marines will escort you to a cabin; I suggest you stay there, at least for the time. Feelings are running high at the moment."

ဆဂ

"I think it's a good idea," Tiffany said, once Marius had outlined the gist of McGillivray's explanation. "You'd make a good emperor."

"I don't want the job," Marius protested. His dead arm felt heavy as he sat down on the sofa beside his wife. Doctor Yu had told him that his vat-grown arm wasn't ready for grafting yet and he had no choice but to endure. "It's a trap."

"I think that not wanting the job is the first qualification for the job," Tiffany countered. "And for that matter, I don't want to be an empress, either. But what does that have to do with anything?" She turned to look up at him. "High Society would accept an emperor, even though they wouldn't accept an admiral. It also neatly separates your rule from military rule, as an emperor wouldn't be a *direct* military ruler. He'd be commander-in-chief, yet a civilian..."

Marius scowled. "Only for ten years," he said firmly. "We take power, fix the problems on Earth and the Core Worlds, make sure that all worlds are represented in the Senate, and then we resign."

"You'd have a hell of a time as an ex-Emperor," Tiffany pointed out. "Where would you go?"

"I'd have the Survey Service reactivated," Marius said. "I'd write myself a commission as my last official act and go beyond the Rim."

"I hope it's that easy," Tiffany said. She smiled sadly.

Marius smiled back.

"We have to win the coming battle," he reminded her. "Let's not count our crowns until they're on our heads, shall we?"

ဆဂ

Grand Admiral Featherstone's voice was very calm. Too calm.

"He's on his way here."

Grand Senator The Honorable Carlton Brockington prided himself on remaining calm and collected under pressure, even during Admiral Justinian's attack on Earth. It was, he felt, the very essence of the Conservative Faction. If they refused to panic and considered everything carefully, they could decide how to act—or if they should act at all. Even so, he felt a tremor of panic run through his mind.

"Who's on his way here?" Grand Senator Alison Wallisch asked Featherstone impatiently. He had been a bipartisan appointment, a man who had never commanded a starship, let alone an entire battle fleet; he'd been appointed because he didn't have a single disloyal bone in his body. "Who?"

"Admiral Drake, My Lady," Featherstone said. His hands nervously rubbed together as he spoke. "I received a transmission from the fortresses covering Gotham. Starships positively identified as belonging to the Grand Fleet transited into the system and boarded the fortresses. The last transmission stated that Marine boarding parties were securing the fortresses and that resistance was futile. Admiral Drake forced them to surrender without firing a shot."

Calm, Carlton told himself. "They didn't even try to engage him?"

"The Grand Fleet possesses enough firepower to punch through anywhere short of the Gateway," Featherstone explained. "The fortress commander decided not to sacrifice his men in a futile attempt to delay him."

"But...but this is disastrous," Alison said. Her eyes were wide with panic. "What does he *want?*"

"We tried to kill him," Carlton reminded her dryly. "What do you *think* he wants?"

Featherstone looked blank. "I believe that he will be here within two weeks, perhaps less," he said. "It depends on the course he takes to reach Earth and if he intends to try to punch through the Gateway. I think..."

"You have to stop him," Alison snarled. Her voice was breaking in fear. "The entire Federation is at stake, admiral! We have to stop him!"

"We could try to negotiate," Featherstone said seriously. "Or..."

"There's no point in trying to talk to the bastard," Alison hissed. "He's going to kill us all unless we kill him first!"

Carlton tapped the table and Alison, wonder of wonders, fell silent.

"Admiral, can Home Fleet stop the Grand Fleet?"

Featherstone might not have been a military expert, but he knew the right answer. "Absolutely, sir," he said. "Combined with the defenses around the Gateway, there will be more than enough firepower to stop him dead in his tracks."

"Excellent," Carlton said. He looked over at Alison. "We can stop one last rebellious admiral, and then we will have won the war."

"And what if he wins the battle?" Alison didn't look convinced.

"We'll have to try to bargain with him." Carlton shrugged. "Admiral Drake is an honorable man. It should be possible to come to some...arrangement with him."

⊰⊱

Two hours later, Carlton started to wonder if he'd been wrong. Somehow—and there was no way to know how—the news had leaked to the media despite his order of a complete media blackout. The news was spreading fast; the Senate had ordered the murder of the admiral—a popular hero—and the admiral was on his way for revenge.

The rumors were spreading even faster, ranging from the believable to the absurd. The admiral was dead and his wife was leading the fleet for revenge. The admiral had somehow come back to life and was a zombie, out for revenge. Aliens had invaded the Federation after the admiral's death and the Senate was fleeing...there was no rhyme or reason to the rumors, but they were spreading right over the planet.

The riots started soon afterward.

The Senate Hall was heavily defended, of course, but the same couldn't be said for most of Earth's infrastructure. It wasn't easy to maintain at the best of times; with an endless series of riots tearing it apart, entire city blocks lost light and heat and power. The police—backed up by the Federation Army and Internal Security troopers—found themselves under siege in their own bases.

When the riots were only a few hours old, the death toll had already passed two million people. How long would it be, Carlton asked himself, before the mob marched on the mansions that housed the political elite?

If we can only beat the admiral, he thought, *we could still win...*

Chapter Forty-Nine

A fleet, backed up by armed fortresses, is a powerful foe. Military doctrine, therefore, calls for isolating the fleet from the fortresses, by any means necessary.
-Observations on the Navy, 3987

Earth (Sol) System, 4098

Admiral Featherstone knew himself to be a coward. Deep inside, he was ashamed of his weakness, the weakness that had prevented him from graduating from Luna Academy and serving as a proper officer should. His well-connected family and his willingness to sell himself to the highest bidder had ensured a rapid rise to the top of the hierarchy, but he'd always remained in the background. He'd never commanded a fleet in combat and would never have had the chance if Admiral Justinian hadn't destroyed Navy HQ. It had been sheer luck that Featherstone hadn't been in the building at the time, and his promotion upward—filling a dead man's shoes—had seemed wonderful at first. Everyone knew that Home Fleet never saw combat...well, it *had* seen combat during the first attack on Earth, but what were the chances of that happening again?

He fought hard to keep his expression blank as he sweated inside. Admiral Drake was on his way, with enough ships and experienced crews to take on Home Fleet and win. Featherstone had ordered reinforcements to be summoned as quickly as possible, but his most optimistic estimate was that any reinforcements would arrive in the system after Admiral Drake. Matters weren't helped by Senators sending him messages at all hours of the day and night, demanding that he use his new position to further their interests. Home Fleet's current position near the Gateway defenses was a result of one such instruction. Apparently, a number of highly-placed Senators had interests in the Gateway that needed to be guarded.

"Admiral," a voice said. He turned to look at Commander Farrell, who had been assigned to him as an aide and general assistant. Featherstone knew that the younger man held him in contempt, but—so far—he had refrained from destroying the man's career. "The survey satellites just picked up a large footprint at the edge of the mass limit."

Featherstone cursed under his breath, silently damning all Senators to hell. Home Fleet was normally positioned at Titan Base, or near Earth itself, but instead they were caught near the Gateway forts. Featherstone was no tactical genius, yet even *he* knew that only an insane commander would tangle with those forts if there was any other choice. And the Senate had refused to allow him to position his ships near Earth, where they could fall back on the orbital defenses and boost their firepower by a factor of ten.

"Show me," he ordered, looking up at the holographic tank. "I suppose there's no chance that this could be a diversion?"

"Not unless they have a second fleet as large as the Grand Fleet," the younger man said. His voice was calm and professional, yet Featherstone was sure he heard amusement lurking behind his tone. "They're not even trying to hide."

Featherstone took a breath. It had been years since he'd studied a display, and most of his lessons had been forgotten. There was no real-time data on the enemy fleet, but it was clearly heading right toward Earth, unless their commander decided to change course for some reason of his own. Featherstone doubted it. Earth was the key to the Solar System.

"Bring up our drives and plot an intercept course," Featherstone ordered. At least he could now claim a military emergency as an excuse to avoid reading messages from irate Senators. Even *they* couldn't argue with the Grand Fleet bearing down on them. "I want us underway as soon as possible."

Even as he spoke, he knew it was going to be a tight shave.

୫୦୧୫

"Launch probes," Marius ordered. He was the only calm person in the compartment. The remainder of the crew knew they'd crossed a line when they'd followed him back to Earth. "I want a location on Home Fleet, now!"

He'd assumed all along that their journey would be detected and that warnings would be flashed to Earth. If he'd been commanding the defenses, he would have positioned Home Fleet roughly three or four light minutes from the mass limit and gone doggo, stepping down his emissions as much as possible. He knew that anyone who wanted to reach Earth in the shortest possible space of time would *have* to arrive from a certain direction, and there was no reason why someone else couldn't draw the same conclusion. Marius had planned on encountering Home Fleet at once and he was mildly surprised, as the probes sped further and further away from the fleet, to find that Home Fleet appeared to be missing.

Earth's Solar System was the most heavily industrialized in the Federation. Over a period of nearly two thousand years, asteroids had been converted into factories to supply a growing population with whatever it might need. Others had been melted down and turned into starships at the Jupiter Shipyards, or developed into habitats that held huge populations. The gas giants were surrounded by cloudscoop platforms that sucked up gas and converted it into fuel for fusion reactors. And thousands of civilian spacecraft thronged through the Solar System, transporting goods from all over the Federation to Earth. It was an awe-inspiring sight.

There was a chime from the tactical console. "I have a lock on Home Fleet," the tactical officer reported. "The fleet is positioned near the Gateway."

"Interesting," Marius commented. "But I imagine they will change position fairly rapidly once they see us."

It was an odd choice of location. The Gateway was the one place in the Solar System that *didn't* need Home Fleet to back up the defenses. Marius himself had supervised the enhancement of the defenses after the first attack on Earth, and any rational admiral would have quailed at the thought of punching through them. The cost would be staggering.

The Sol System was surrounded by a chain of watchful automated platforms, which—by now—would have picked up the Grand Fleet and flashed an urgent warning to Earth. Marius knew that the fleet could probably have slipped in unde-tected, but he'd deliberately chosen to arrive in style. It was important, McGillivray had assured him, to show that he wasn't afraid to confront the Senate in their den. Marius had reluctantly accepted the Senator's advice.

"Admiral, Home Fleet is on the move," the tactical officer said. A new set of icons appeared on the display. "They're advancing to meet us at Point Alpha."

Marius nodded as the icon glittered on the display.

"Continue our present course," he ordered. "We don't want to be late for our appointment with Home Fleet."

80C8

Admiral Featherstone rubbed his tired eyes and then looked around, hoping that no one had seen the brief moment of weakness. If any of the crew had seen, they kept it to themselves.

Home Fleet was blazing across the system at flank speed, hoping to intercept the Grand Fleet before it reached Earth, yet all he could think of was how *slow* it was, even on an interplanetary scale. At least the Senate's demands that he immediately engage the enemy had trailed off, once someone on the planet got the facts of basic space combat through a few thick heads. This deep within the mass limit, no star-ship could pull more than 0.5C. They had to hope that the enemy would be obliging and not pile on extra speed before Home Fleet reached a position that could be used to block the intruders from Earth.

It made no sense. Admiral Drake could have piled on the speed and reached Earth well before Home Fleet could intercept him. Instead...he was deliberately keeping his speed low, daring Home Fleet to intercept his fleet. Featherstone couldn't under-stand it, unless Admiral Drake was supremely confident.

And if Admiral Drake was that confident, Featherstone asked himself, what did Drake know that Featherstone didn't know?

He rubbed his eyes again, fighting down a yawn. They'd crawled across the Solar System for hours, and he hadn't dared to leave the bridge. At least they were coming into interception range within the next ten minutes. Once the battle started, he was sure he would feel better...

80C8

"Admiral," Garibaldi said, "you asked to be notified when Home Fleet was ten minutes to engagement range."

"So I did," Marius agreed.

He studied the display, allowing himself a brief moment of amusement. Home Fleet hadn't been drilled properly, and it showed, as their gunners hadn't even tried to intercept the drones Marius had ordered launched. The Grand Fleet, on the other hand, had been drilling since before launching the operation that had beaten Admiral Justinian and his rebels. Marius had no doubt of the outcome if the two fleets col-lided, but it might just be avoidable.

"Communications, open a channel," Drake said. He knew that the officer would understand what he was talking about, as they'd discussed the details during the long voyage to Earth several times already.

"Aye, sir," the communications officer said. "Channel open."

Marius keyed his console.

"My name is Marius Drake, Commanding Officer of the Grand Fleet," he said. His words would be heard all over the Solar System. "You probably have been told that I am a rebel, that I followed in the footsteps of Admiral Justinian, Governor Hartkopf and the many other warlords. You probably have also been told that I have come to take over Earth and the Federation for myself. None of those things are true.

"I swore an oath that I would defend the Federation against all enemies, foreign and domestic. I meant every word of that oath. I come now to remove one of the greatest threats to the Federation, the corrupt and decayed Senate. The Senate issued orders to slaughter—in cold blood—people it deemed to be a threat to their interests, so it could claim their land and property for itself. The Senate, in doing so, triggered an insurgency that will claim the lives of millions of soldiers as well as civilians in the coming months. The Senate even tried to have me killed by one of my own crew.

"We all know the truth. The Senate has become a monstrous entity tearing at the heart of the Federation. We all know that the Senate passes laws intended to allow interstellar corporations to ravish the colonies and exploit them for their own ends. We all know that the Senate's interference in military affairs has led to stunning defeats. Is there anyone who can deny that the Senate has become the domestic enemy of the entire human race? Is there anyone who doubts that the Senate has been fuelling the tensions that force worlds to consider seceding from the Federation? Is there anyone who feels, as I do, that the Senate has gone too far?

"My fleet and I are here to remove the Senate. We will replace it with a fairer system that cannot be exploited so easily. My government will not last longer than ten years, perhaps less; but that will be long enough for us to push through real and lasting reforms. I swear that upon my name and the honor of the Federation Navy.

"I speak now to the men and women of Home Fleet, and Earth's defenses," he concluded. "If you want to join us, please do; we will welcome you. If you are uneasy with removing the government and choose to stand aside, we will not treat you as enemies. But if you choose to fight, consider carefully. You may be fighting on the wrong side. The choice is yours."

He released the console and took a breath. If they were lucky...

⅓∓

Admiral Featherstone felt every one of Drake's words slam into his tired mind. He couldn't deny the truth of what he said, yet Featherstone had gone too far to simply change sides. His patrons had boosted his career and ensured that he reached the very highest levels, yet he'd always known that there would be a price.

He would have been happy to stand aside, but he had no choice. The Senate had to be defended. It was the legitimate government of human space and changing it by force, for whatever reason, was wrong. The population could vote out the Senate if they chose.

"Prepare to engage," he ordered.

It all happened very quickly. The sensor officer drew a weapon from under his console and opened fire, gunning down the four Internal Security troopers on the bridge. Featherstone froze, feeling hot liquid trickling down his legs, as two other officers opened fire. A stray blast hit one of the consoles, which exploded in a shower of sparks, just before a plasma bolt slammed into his head.

He was dead before he hit the deck.

&oCg

"Admiral...Home Fleet seems to have gone mad!"

Marius nodded slowly. Home Fleet had fallen right out of formation. A handful of starships were still continuing towards the Grand Fleet, but the remainder seemed to be drifting or had simply come to a stop. Several smaller ships had turned and were accelerating away as hard as they could, while one superdreadnaught had opened fire on its neighbour. Three other superdreadnaughts fired on the offender and blew the ship into flaming plasma.

His gamble had worked, he realized. He'd known that discontent had been spreading through the Federation Navy, but he hadn't realized just how bad it was, or how many crewmen had been making preparations for mutiny. Part of his mind wondered, grimly, if future historians would claim that this was the moment when the Federation died; the remainder concentrated on the here and now. There would be time to consider the implications later.

"Admiral, a number of ships have surrendered," the communications officer said. "Several more are gripped by heavy fighting and are urgently requesting help..."

"Send the Marines," Marius ordered. There was no time to waste. "I want at least a platoon of Marines on each ship, with a scuttling charge. We will establish their *bona fides* before we trust too much."

He looked up and, for a moment, his eyes met Garibaldi's. The younger officer looked stunned, but then he'd never had the displeasure of serving in Home Fleet, where there was no action to trim out the worthless incompetents who infested the fleet. Home Fleet had never been expected to see serious action, at least until Admiral Justinian had reminded the Senate that they could be threatened.

"Helm, take the fleet to Earth," he ordered. There was no point in dawdling any longer. "Best possible speed."

"Aye, sir," the helmsman said.

Marius looked up at the display. Earth was surrounded by civilian starships, each one trying to flee before the warships arrived at Earth. Marius shrugged, ignoring them. They didn't matter. All that mattered was capturing the Senate and ending the struggle before it could begin.

&oCg

"Home Fleet is in a state of mutiny," the dispatcher reported. He sounded hysterical. "Admiral Featherstone is dead!"

"What do we do?" Alison demanded. "What do we do?"

Carlton was having similar thoughts. If Home Fleet could be subverted, so could

Earth's defenses. Even if they remained loyal—and that couldn't be guaranteed, even with the presence of Internal Security troopers on each platform—the Grand Fleet could break through the defenses and bombard Earth into submission. Hastily, he reviewed his emergency plans and realized that there wasn't time to activate them before the Grand Fleet reached orbit. They had placed far too much faith in Admiral Featherstone...

"I need to think," he snapped, with a glare that cut Alison off before she could continue to bleat like a scared lamb. "I think we need to surrender now, while we still have something to bargain with."

Alison stared at him, her eyes going wide. "But he'll kill us!"

"He's a man of honor," Carlton said sharply. "The point is, we have something to bargain with now, our control over Earth's defenses. That allows us to ask for better terms than we might expect if he breaks through the defenses, or if they go over to him."

"We could run," Alison protested.

Carlton snorted.

"Where would we go? We can't get to the spacecraft in time to get off-planet, while anywhere we would want to live on Earth would be easy for him to find. Do you want to flee into the slums and pretend that we were never Senators...?"

"No," Alison hissed. "Very well; you talk to the bastard. Tell him that we will surrender on terms."

৪০৫৪

Marius kept his expression blank as Grand Senator Brockington made his plea for terms. He'd anticipated that the Senate would fold, once they saw what happened to Home Fleet, and he'd had time to consider what he'd offer them. He'd come up with some very generous terms, but he doubted that the Senate would see it that way.

"Here are my terms," he said. "You will order the defenses of Earth to stand down and prepare to be boarded. You will order the ground-side police force to remain at their posts until they are relieved. You will surrender yourselves to my Marines— every Senator on Earth, your families and anyone who wants to go with you—and prepare to be transported to exile. If you refuse these terms, there will be no further negotiation."

There was a long pause as the message winged its way to Earth.

Eventually, a reply came flying back. As he'd expected, the Senate had accepted his terms. Marius figured they intended to return one day and resume their positions of power, but it wasn't going to happen. They'd be sent to a comfortable world— Manchu or Paradise, perhaps—where they would live out the rest of their lives without contact with the Federation. That would put an end to them and their meddling.

He leaned back in his command chair. "Well," he said to no one in particular. "We just took over the Federation. What do we do now?"

No one, not even Garibaldi, tried to frame a reply.

Chapter Fifty

In war, winning is only half the battle. You have to capitalize on your victory.
-Observations on the Navy, 3987

Earth (Sol) System, 4098

"I'm going to give you *Valiant*," Admiral Drake said a day after the Grand Fleet had captured Earth. Roman had been half-convinced that the admiral had forgotten him in the whirlwind of securing Earth's vital locations and transporting the Senators and their families to temporary accommodation. "Technically, you're too young to serve as a commodore, but I think I'm going to have to give you a temporary promotion anyway."

Admiral Drake tapped the display, which focused in on the Rim. "There are too many worrying reports coming from this Sector," he said. "You'll see the intelligence reports; if they're accurate, we might have at least two hostile races in the Beyond. Your task would be to defeat the pirates in the sector and survey the stars beyond the Rim."

"Yes, sir," Roman said. He didn't want to be promoted out of a command chair, even for a short while, but he suspected he didn't have very much choice in the matter. If nothing else, there would definitely be room for independent action. The Rim was just too large to be patrolled by a task force operating as a single unit. "I won't let you down."

"I'm promoting your girlfriend to Major and assigning her command of a Marine Regiment," Admiral Drake added. "I dare say you'll find something to talk about on the trip to the Rim."

"Thank you, sir," Roman said, blushing. He hadn't wanted to admit that he was worried about losing her comforting presence on his ship—and in his bed, of course. "I think she'll enjoy the chance to stretch herself a little farther."

"Just remember, you're not out there to invade a whole alien empire by yourself," Admiral Drake cautioned. "We may have to extend the Rim out to enclose their space—and bring them under our control—but we need to put our own house in order first. The remaining warlords need to be mopped up and crushed; the Survey Service needs to be restarted...there's too many things we need to do. And we need to secure the space lines so that regular shipping can restart. There are too many pirate ships operating out there because of the war."

He shook his head. "Be careful out there, Roman," he said, clapping Roman on the shoulder. "I don't want to lose any more good people out along the Rim."

"Thank you, sir," Roman said. "I won't let you down."

ഇൽ

"Tell me something," Marius said, once they were in a secure compartment. "Was this what the Brotherhood had in mind all along?"

Professor Kratman shrugged.

"Not in particular," he said. "We believed that something would have to happen in order to force the Senate to reform before the entire Federation shattered. You becoming emperor..."

Marius scowled. It hadn't taken more than a few hours before High Society— what was left of it—had started clamoring to recognize the emperor. He'd promised himself that there would be a brief and formal coronation, but High Society seemed to think that it needed a grand event with a golden crown. It was galling, in a way; he'd taken supreme power, and he was as much a prisoner as most of the Senate.

"Still, you have to be careful," his former commander warned. "If you move too quickly, you run the risk of causing an economic disaster. The industrialist strangle-holds will have to be broken carefully, or they might destroy the economy out of spite."

"And even threats won't deter them," Marius sighed. He looked up. "I'm appointing you to my cabinet, by the way."

Professor Kratman blinked. "Why?"

"I want you where I can see you," Marius said firmly. "I think the Brotherhood has spent too long in the shadows. It's time to come out into the light."

"And besides," he added, "I trust you."

"I don't think..."

"We'll discuss it later," Marius said. He tapped the pistol he wore at his belt. Vaughn's old pistol, as ready for use as it had been the day it was produced. "I have one piece of unfinished business left to complete."

ଛଡ଼

The Marines had been fairly gentle with the Senators and their families, although the Senators had complained loudly and bitterly before being ordered to shut up. Most of their families—including some very young children and a handful of trusted retainers—had been transported to a bulk carrier for the journey to Paradise—a resort world that would suffice as a place of exile—but a number had been kept on Earth. Marius had issued specific instructions for the twelve most senior Senators— including the leaders of both factions—to remain behind, and those orders had been obeyed.

He wrinkled his nose as he stepped into the prison. It was normally used to house involuntary emigrants—men and women who had been arrested on Earth and sen-tenced to exile—and it was clear that the Senators hadn't adjusted well to their cap-tivity. Each of them had one hand firmly cuffed to the wall, restricting their mobility and ensuring that they posed no threat to the warder and his men. The room itself stank of piss and shit and human sweat, the feelings of the arrested people who would never see Earth again.

"Admiral," a voice gasped. "You have to get us out of here!"

It was Alison, formerly the leader of the Socialist Faction. Now, her face had been washed clean by the wardens and her fine clothes had been replaced by a shape-less prison garment. A bruise on her face marked the spot where she'd run into a wall while the Marines were trying to arrest her. Marius had read the report on the incident and it was clear that one of the Marines, an exile from a world under Socialist control, had done it deliberately.

Marius deliberately allowed his eyes to wander away.

"And why," he said in a tone of feigned unconcern, "should I do anything to help you?"

"But...but...you gave your word of honor," Alison protested.

The other Senators murmured in agreement. "You promised us..."

"I did, didn't I?" Marius allowed himself a tight smirk.

He allowed the moment to drag itself out.

"Let me tell you a little story, to help us all pass the time," he said. "Once upon a time, there was a great chaos in a planetary sector and no one knew which way to jump. And in this sector, there were men and women who had lives and families and friends of their own—just people, ordinary people. And some of these people jumped to the right side, and others jumped to the wrong side. And, as so often happens in human history, the right side won and the wrong side lost. After all, we *know* the right side won because the winners write the history books and they were the winners. Of course they were the right side."

They were all listening to him, perhaps wondering if he'd gone mad.

"And the people who had sided with the wrong side panicked," he continued, wondering if any of them had drawn the correct conclusion. It wouldn't be long before they all understood. "They thought that they were all doomed, because the winners had threatened to kill all the losers. And some of them fled and others tried to do their duty as best as they could, hoping that they could scare the winners or at least hurt them enough to make them back down. But they couldn't, you see; they couldn't stop the inevitable wave of fate rolling over them. They were trapped, helpless—and doomed.

"And then the winners came to them and offered them a chance to live. The losers were relieved and delighted. They might have lost, but it wouldn't cost them their lives; their families and friends would be safe. They accepted the offer gratefully and everyone was happy—well, everyone apart from some of the winners. Once the losers were helpless, they went back on the offer. I'm sure you can imagine the results."

His voice darkened. "The losers were all slaughtered," he said. "And the winners went on to win."

Alison's voice, when it finally came, was weak and feeble. "But you promised!"

"Just imagine it," Marius said. "Being told that the sentence of death—for you and your family and your friends—had been passed, and there was nothing you could do to avert it. Just imagine the hopelessness and despair. And then the joy and relief when you discover that you're going to live after all. Your friends and family will be safe!"

He smiled darkly, daring them to speak.

"And then you get orders to board an old freighter," he added. "And perhaps you wonder...but you convince yourself that all is fine; you know you're going to have to leave your home, so maybe you're leaving quicker than you expected. And then you realize that you're sealed in and there's no way out, yet perhaps that too makes sense...

"And then you realize that the air is being let out of the hold," he said. His hand grasped Vaughn's pistol as he drew it from his holster. "And you realize that you've been betrayed, and you're going to die, and there is nothing you can do about it. You watch as your children struggle to breathe, their faces turning purple with the lack of oxygen, the life draining out of their eyes as they run out of air. And then you choke to death yourself, knowing that you were betrayed..."

He lifted the pistol and pointed it at Alison's head. "Imagine how that feels..."

The former Senator stared wildly at him.

"But you gave your word," she gasped. "You swore..."

"I did," Marius agreed.

He pulled the trigger. The pistol jerked in his hand—he was more used to plasma pistols than projectile weapons—and splattered her brains over the bulkhead. He turned as the Senators started to scream for help and mercy, knowing that neither would ever come. The pistol barked again, then again and again, until all of the Senators were dead.

Automatically, he returned the pistol to its holster, refusing to look away from what he had wrought. He'd executed twelve people in cold blood. In the end, the men and women who had ruled half the galaxy had died by his hand, yet he didn't feel anything but cold satisfaction.

The innocent dead had been avenged.

Shaking his head, he walked out the compartment and sealed the hatch behind him.

"Clear up the mess and dump the bodies in the incinerator," he ordered the warden, who had enough sense not to ask the questions that were clearly running through his mind. Cuffs or no cuffs, enough unwilling colonists had managed to kill their fellows while in the holding pens to make disposing of their bodies a regular occurrence. "Once that's done, forget everything that happened today."

Not waiting for an acknowledgement, he strode away, back to the shuttle that had brought him to the prison. His mind was elsewhere, considering the future. For humanity to survive the coming storm from beyond the Rim, hard decisions would have to be made about the future. He had never wanted power, certainly not on this scale, but he wouldn't shrink from using it. Humanity would be safe, whatever the cost.

Once he was back in the shuttle and heading back to orbit, he keyed his communicator. "Tiffany, contact my Cabinet and inform them that we will be meeting in one hour," he told her. "We have a lot of work to do."

End of Book One

The story will continue in:
The Shadow of Cincinnatus
Coming 2015

Afterword

There is a line I remember from a science fiction book I read (unfortunately, I have forgotten which one) that ran "*if the Empire knew what sort of lessons could be learned by studying history, they'd ban it.*" It may be a coincidence, but I never had a proper history class at school. What little I did have was boring.

Anyone who knew anything about young men—boys—would have known that they would be interested in wars and great heroes of the past. It goes without saying that most of the history lessons I received did *not* cover areas of history I considered to be interesting. We spent six months studying Lancashire Cotton Weaving—boring—and relatively little time studying World War One. I probably don't need to add that the version of World War One we learned about was the stereotypical one, where conscripted infantry were made to stand up and walk very slowly towards the enemy, where they would be mown down by machine guns, while their officers remained behind and enjoyed themselves.

And that doesn't include the political bias that was woven into the material. In my later years, one of my teachers was a Scottish Nationalist who painted a very unpleasant picture of Margaret Thatcher. Another refused to acknowledge that Britain had ever had an empire. A lecturer on the American Civil War called it "The War of Northern Aggression." In short, what little formal history I was taught was unsatisfying.

I was lucky enough to be able to read from a young age and that gave me access to a vast selection of history books and sources that my teachers pretended didn't exist, or didn't matter. I read stories of wars, of men who built empires and men who broke them, of entire areas of history that my teachers had declared *verboten.* In my youthful imagination, I saw myself flying with the RAF in 1940, invading France with Eisenhower and Monty in 1944; waging war beside Clive and watching as Caesar crossed the Rubicon. As I grew older, I delved deeper into the underlying reasons behind wars and their outcomes, for even dull economics could be made interesting.

I do not claim to be a historian. I have certainly had no formal training in researching history. But then, I have never felt the lack.

Those who do not learn from history, as the saying goes, are condemned to repeat it. This lesson, echoing down the ages, still applies today. Let us consider, for example, the events that led up to the insurgency in Iraq. The Coalition merrily assumed that the Shia—who had suffered horribly under Saddam—would rise up in support of the invasion. This was, as a cursory look at the history of the region would have shown, a naive assumption. In 1991, the Shia rebelled against Saddam, under the impression that the West would come to their aid. The West did nothing to stop the slaughter. It was easy to predict, even without hindsight, that the Shia wouldn't risk rebelling again. Why should they trust the Coalition to protect them?

I cannot claim, either, to be a specialist in any given area of history. My interests have always been wide-ranging and, if I cannot give you precise details on the Court of the Sun King, I can tell you why the French Empire never matched the British

Empire. (Think economics and relative power projection capabilities.) However, in studying different societies and how they interact (internally and externally) I have come to two conclusions about human societies.

-First, any system of government is affected by entropy. It can and it will decay. There will be a massive growth in governmental responsibilities, bureaucracy and quite probably a separation of the rulers (the political class, however defined) from the ruled. If you imagine the government as a human body, imagine its arteries slowly being jammed with fat.

-Second, the entropy process can be slowed or even reversed through two agents; the active participation of the ruled in ruling and the presence of a hostile competitor. If the government is accountable to the population, the political class is pushed into remaining honest or risk losing power. If there is a nearby enemy eyeing the state with covetous eyes, the state is forced into competition, which keeps it honest.

Let us consider, for a moment, Imperial China. At the risk of generalising, the Chinese Government decayed to the point where the entire country stagnated. The Chinese system simply could not adapt when new and very unwelcome people made their appearance in China. The Chinese rapidly found themselves helpless before the modern technology of Britain, France, Russia and even Japan. Had China's government been flexible enough to realise that change—and reform—were desperately needed (even as late as 1900), the history of China would have been very different. Instead, China endured a long period of misery and now groans under Communist rule.

A second example might be Imperial Japan. The Japanese adapted fairly well when they were confronted by hostile nations; they managed to remain independent and mastered modern technology. Their political system, however, remained insulated from the population (and reality) and the Japanese deliberately started a war with a far stronger nation. The result was Japan's burning in 1945 and a long period of occupation.

A third example might be the Union of Soviet Socialist Republics, the USSR. The average member of the USSR's government (effectively Russia's government, with the other nations as satellite states) had very little connection to the general population and, therefore, was capable of inflicting untold misery on them without either knowing or caring what was going on. The forced collectivization of Soviet agriculture stole the incentive for actual production from the farmers, so the USSR was never able to feed itself; the absence of incentives for actual work from industrial workers crippled the Russian industry, the ever-present supervision of the KGB destroyed political discourse and the crushing weight of Marxist doctrine prevented a rational attempt to cope with Russia's colossal problems. The USSR literally rotted away from within and left behind a traumatised continent.

A fourth example might be Saddam's Iraq. At one time, Iraq appeared to be on the route to dominant power in the Middle East. Unfortunately, all of the power rested in Saddam's hands (a typical problem in dictatorships) and disagreeing with Saddam rarely led to a long life. Saddam's failure to understand that invading Kuwait would bring Iraq into conflict with the West meant that war was inevitable; his failure to abandon Kuwait before the Coalition attacked meant that Iraq was going to be hammered; his refusal to abandon his WMD programs meant that there would never be peace; his failure to learn the lessons of Gulf War One meant that Gulf War Two was a quick defeat for Iraq. Iraq's core problem was that Saddam was insulated from both reality and his own population. He didn't care about their suffering, although it did allow him to cynically blame it on America.

What, therefore, does history teach us about the future? First, tyrannical states (however defined) cannot be expected to care about the suffering of their own population. Second, tyrannical states will act in ways we consider irrational because the well-being of their own people isn't on their list of concerns. Third, an unquestioned doctrine (Marxism-Leninism or Fundamentalist Islam) can push its high priests into doing stupid or irrational acts in the name of the doctrine. Fourth—and most importantly—no amount of concessions will change their behaviour. It has to be made clear that the leadership *will* be targeted if rogue states decide to cause trouble.

History, I'm afraid, also teaches us that far too many people will refuse to grasp those points.

But what does this all mean for the West?

The West (by which I mean Europe, America, Australia and New Zealand), on the face of it, doesn't have those problems. We have not birthed a tyrant who took the reins of power and wreaked havoc. I am perfectly aware that people threw mud at President Bush and are throwing mud at President Obama. Even so, the worst of the West's recent rulers (Jimmy Carter? Richard Nixon? William (Bill) Clinton? Tony Blair? Jacques Chirac?) was never a tyrant.

The West is not perfect. Far from it. But the West is still paradise compared to even a "benevolent tyranny," if such a state can be deemed to exist outside theory.

Even so, the West has problems. One of them is that there is an increasing separation of rulers and ruled. It doesn't take much investigation to see political leaders acting in ways that—if done by anyone else—would have resulted in the most serious of consequences. Sometimes—as in the UK Parliamentary Expenses Scandal—they become a farce. If that wasn't bad enough, there is a growing trend among politicians to assume that if they hang on long enough, the world might forget the scandals and they might be able to continue in power.

Our politics are rapidly becoming poisonous. Just consider the amount of mud thrown around about President Obama's birth certificate. Or Bush's supposed lack of intelligence. Or Brown's rather dubious grasp of national and international banking. Or Blair's honesty and integrity. No one can enter politics without being smeared or insulted by his opponents—one example of epic fail is the old lie "if you oppose immigration, you're a racist"—and accusations of past failings and unfortunate remarks.

The politician (or should it be *pollution*) who wins the prize for sheer bare-faced arrogance and unsuitability for office is, in my opinion at least, Shahid Malik of the British Labour Party. Having been caught red-handed (he was hardly the first politician to be caught during 2009) fiddling his expenses, Malik counterattacked by accusing his critics of racism. Later, when he lost his seat in 2010, he claimed that an independent candidate had been brought in specifically to make sure he lost. It did not seem to occur to him that his own conduct might have been the cause of his downfall.

But then, what else can you expect from the political class?

This has had a disastrous effect on the West. Where long-term planning is required, short-term planning (plans to run up to the next election and no further) has been used instead. The governments have created an increasing number of bureaucrats and bureaucratic regulations that strangle small business, along with writing laws that border on the absurd or are never properly scrutinised or discussed. The vital pillars of society—police, fire brigades and even the military—have become political footballs. Political correctness has damaged freedom of speech. And, perhaps worst of all, faith in governments and public institutions is declining sharply. The public no longer trusts their government.

And there are barbarians at the gates. Like it or not, we are at war.

Clemenceau said, back during the First World War, that war is too important to be left to the generals. Like most quotes, it is often taken out of context. I believe that he meant that war and politics had become tangled and battles couldn't just be fought for purely military objectives. Levelling an entire town in Iraq for harbouring a sniper would work perfectly, from the military point of view of suppressing enemies, but it is the kind of act that tends to make enemies.

Just as war is too important to leave to the generals, politics is too important to be left to the politicians. Whatever you (and they) may feel, democratic politicians work for the public, not themselves. Who pays the piper calls the tune. If you want real change, change people can actually believe in, get out there and get involved in politics. Remember, if there is one thing that politicians fear, it is becoming unpopular. They will bend over backwards to avoid it. Find out what you need to do and get out there. Keep the bastards honest. As to why you should do it, Heinlein put it very well:

"Because you are needed. Because the task is not hopeless. Democracy is normally in perpetual crisis. It requires the same constant, alert attention to keep it from going to pot that an automobile does when driven through downtown traffic. If you do not yourself pay attention to the driving, year in and year out, the crooks, or scoundrels, or nincompoops will take over the wheel and drive it in a direction you don't fancy, or wreck it completely.

When you pick yourself up out of the wreckage, you and your wife and your kids, don't talk about what "They" did to you. You did it, compatriot, because you preferred to sit in the back seat and snooze. Because you thought your taxes bought you a bus ticket and a guaranteed safe arrival, when all your taxes bought you was a part ownership in a joint enterprise, on a share-the-cost and share-the-driving plan."

And why is this important? Consider the chaos that followed Saddam's removal from power, or the collapse of the USSR. Why did it occur? One possible answer is that there weren't enough people who knew (from experience and/or theory) how to make a democratic society work. I worry that we're running out of them over here. We need competent and serious men.

Where are they?

Read some history. Then get out and make it.

Christopher G. Nuttall

2014

Federation of Humanity Timeline

2030: Establishment of Armstrong Base on Luna. First shipment of lunar HE3 to Earth.

2031-35: Establishment of Japanese, Russian, European and Chinese mining bases on the moon. Launch of first asteroid capture missions.

2037: Launch of first Mars mission.

2038: Effective collapse of the Middle East owing to the replacement of oil by HE3

2040: First large-scale colony ship launched to Mars. First military bases established on the moon.

2045-50: Third World War pits Americans and Europeans against Russians and Chinese, fighting it out for control of NEO and access to space-based resources. War ends in orbital bombardment of China and Russia, followed by unconditional surrender.

2051: Terran Federation established by victorious powers as a replacement for the discredited United Nations. Mars population booms as seven new colony ships are launched towards Mars.

2051-2100: First Expansion Era. Settlements on all planetary bodies and thousands of asteroids. New political units form, including the Kingdom of Titan and the RockRat Association. Most of Earth's industrial base is steadily being moved into space as a response to increasing security problems on Earth.

2070: Free Mars movement formed in pursuit of an independent Mars-based state.

2090: Hundreds of generational arks—mainly formed from asteroids and crewed by RockRats—start heading out, seeking freedom from an increasingly repressive national security state.

2097: Doctor Irene Asimov deduces the presence of "gravimetric points" within Sol's gravity field.

2103: Discovery of the first Asimov Point, leading to a nearby Sol-type star.

2104: Discovery of Sol's second Asimov Point. This one leads to a system that includes an Earth-like world, which is named Terra Nova.

2105-07: Settlement begins on Terra Nova. The process is an uncomfortable one as the Federation finds itself compelled to include an even mix of Earth's nationalities and religions.

2107-30: Second Expansion Era. Fourteen Earth-like worlds are discovered. Settlement of Kennedy, Novaya Rodina, Britannia and others. Earth-based governments start offering settlement incentives, hoping to push as many people into emigrating as possible. First orbital tower completed.

2132: Discovery of Graveyard, a world that was apparently destroyed in a nuclear war.

2134: Zion, a solely Jewish world, is colonised over the objections of various parties in the Federation. The State of Israel—which has constructed three frigates as part of its contribution to the Federation Navy—announces that it will defend their right to a homeworld.

2140-60: The First Interstellar War. The Snakes emerge from an undiscovered Asimov Point in the Zion System and attack the Jewish world. Planetary bombardment is followed by invasion, forcing the settlers to resort to insurgent warfare to remain alive. The Snakes follow up their advantage by pushing through the other Asimov Point, but fail to detect the Type-3 Asimov Point in the Marianne System that would allow them to punch through to Earth. The Federation mobilises for war, military forces are united and political differences are forgotten. Zion is liberated in 2052, followed by a military campaign that takes humanity into the heart of the Snake Empire. When the Snakes refuse to surrender, planetary bombardment is used to depopulate their worlds. The sole remaining Snakes are transferred to a marginal world at the end of a chain of Asimov Points and barred from developing any form of space travel or indeed high technology ever again.

2161: The Federation is reconfigured under the leadership of President Vane. The Federation Protocols are signed, creating the united Federation Navy and Federation Marines.

The Brotherhood of Humanity is founded by the survivors of Zion. In the following centuries, the Brotherhood provides a disproportionate percentage of recruits for the Federation Navy, before becoming a quasi-underground secret society.

2161-3005: Third Expansion Era. Humanity settles over five hundred worlds by moving through Asimov Points. Several new alien races are discovered, not all of them friendly. Owing to prevailing xenophobia after the First Interstellar War, aliens—even those living within the Federation—are not enfranchised or regarded as equals. At least two alien races are exterminated by human settlers.

Unluckily for the Federation, the Protocols did not envisage such massive expansion and tensions within the Federation started threatening to tear it apart. Foremost among them is a growing secessionist crisis among the border colonies, led by the Colonial Alliance.

2610: Professor Bainbridge produces his theory of collapsing gravity points. The Federation launches the Bainbridge Initiative in response. Eventually, the research leads to a way of travelling FTL without Asimov Points.

3006: The Inheritance Wars begins with the Colonial Alliance's declaration of independence.

3007: The Battle of Spider (later renamed Spider Bite). The first use of Compressed Antimatter in combat sends the Federation Navy reeling back.

3008-3109: The Inheritance Wars effectively stalemate with neither side being able to gain a significant advantage. War rages as both sides try to break out of the stalemate. As time goes on, both sides start resorting to atrocities and terror tactics.

3110: Development of the Continuous Displacement Drive by the Federation.

3112: Battle of Athens. Use of CDD by Federation Navy (bypassing the Asimov Point network) allows the Federation to score a decisive victory.

3114: Colonial Alliance surrenders, ending the Inheritance Wars. Thousands of unrepentant Colonists take starships and head out into the great unknown; others try to make what peace they can with the Federation.

3115: The Conference of Earth settles the question of the restructured Federation and future expansion. The defeated worlds are treated relatively well, but the question of representation in the Senate—which the Colonial Alliance fought the war over in the first place—is not up for discussion.

3116-4024: Fourth Expansion Era. Conservative, Socialist and Imperialist factions develop within the Senate. The position of the President is reduced to a mere figurehead, while real power rests with the Prime Minister and his Cabinet—subject to the Senate's approval. Political dynasties come into open existence.

4001: Marius Drake born on Mars.

4017: Marius Drake reports to Luna Academy.

4021: Marius Drake commissioned as a Lieutenant and assigned to Frontier Fleet.

4025-29: The Blue Star War. The Imperialist Faction provokes a war with a newly discovered alien race in order to seize control of Sapphire, a blue giant with an unprecedented number of Asimov Points associated with it. Expecting an easy victory, the Federation Navy commits a blunder and divides its forces in the face of the enemy, resulting in two disastrous defeats. The overpowering might of the Federation eventually prevails, by which time the Imperialist Faction has been badly discredited and effectively absorbed by the other two. Marius Drake sees action in the war.

4070: Marius Drake is promoted to Commodore and given command of a battle squadron.

4072: Roman Garibaldi is born on Isogloss, a RockRat asteroid habitat.

4073: "Outsiders"—a ragtag bunch of pirates, rebels and aliens—start raiding along the Rim, the outermost edge of Federation territory.

4077: Marius Drake is promoted to Vice Admiral and sent to wage war on the Outsiders.

4087: Roman Garibaldi wins a prize scholarship to Luna Academy.

4091: Marius Drake is recalled to Earth for "consultations."

4092: Admiral Justinian launches his coup.

About the author

Christopher G. Nuttall is thirty-two years old and has been reading science fiction since he was five, when someone introduced him to children's SF. Born in Scotland, Chris attended schools in Edinburgh, Fife and University in Manchester before moving to Malaysia to live with his wife Aisha.

Chris has been involved in the online Alternate History community since 1998; in particular, he was the original founder of Changing The Times, an online alternate history website that brought in submissions from all over the community. Later, Chris took up writing and eventually became a full-time writer.

Current and forthcoming titles published by Twilight Times Books:

The Decline and Fall of the Galactic Empire SF series
> *Barbarians at the Gates* book 1
> *The Shadow of Cincinnatus* book 2

The Schooled in Magic YA fantasy series
> *Schooled in Magic* book 1
> *Lessons in Etiquette* book 2
> *Study in Slaughter* book 3
> *Work Experience* book 4
> *The School of Hard Knocks* book 5

Chris has also produced *The Empire's Corps* series, the *Outside Context Problem* series and many others. He is also responsible for two fan-made Posleen novels, both set in John Ringo's famous Posleen universe. They can both be downloaded from his site.

Website: http://www.chrishanger.net/
Blog: http://chrishanger.wordpress.com/
Facebook: https://www.facebook.com/ChristopherGNuttall

If you enjoyed this book, please post a review
at your favorite online bookstore.

Twilight Times Books
P O Box 3340
Kingsport, TN 37664
Phone/Fax: 423-323-0183
www.twilighttimesbooks.com/

CPSIA information can be obtained at www.ICGtesting.com
Printed in the USA
BVOW08s0859221115

428052BV00003B/185/P